THE

A TALE OF TRIALS

BEST

AND ERRORS

PEOPLE

MARC GROSSBERG

GREENLEAF
BOOK GROUP PRESS

Published by Greenleaf Book Group Press
Austin, Texas
www.gbgpress.com

Distributed by Greenleaf Book Group

For ordering information or special discounts for bulk purchases, please contact Greenleaf Book Group at PO Box 91869, Austin, TX 78709, 512.891.6100.

Design and composition by Greenleaf Book Group
Cover design by Greenleaf Book Group
Cover images: Dwight Smight, 2019. Used under license from Shutterstock.com and ©iStockphoto.com/Chris Boswell

Publisher's Cataloging-in-Publication data is available.

Print ISBN: 978-1-62634-655-0

eBook ISBN: 978-1-62634-656-7

Part of the Tree Neutral® program, which offsets the number of trees consumed in the production and printing of this book by taking proactive steps, such as planting trees in direct proportion to the number of trees used: www.treeneutral.com

TreeNeutral

Printed in the United States of America on acid-free paper

19 20 21 22 23 24   10 9 8 7 6 5 4 3 2 1

First Edition

THIS BOOK IS DEDICATED TO
Lee Ann, Toni, Nicole, Cyvia, Sandhya, Nikhila,
Keshav, Carly, Naveen, Jaya, Max, and Sadie.

"My mind was cloudy, and my good judgment was influenced by my need to prove something."

—NELSON DEMILLE, *THE GOLD COAST*

"You think if only you can acquire enough worldly goods, enough recognition, enough eminence, you will be free, there'll be nothing more to worry about, and instead you become a bigger and bigger slave to how you think others are judging you."

—TOM WOLFE, *A MAN IN FULL*

CONTENTS

PART
ONE

GETTING STARTED

PADDY MORAN WAS SO PUMPED he ran the five blocks from the Harris County Civil District Courthouse to his office. After watching one of Houston's most successful and audacious trial lawyers woo a jury panel into the palm of his hand, every positive juice in Paddy's body flowed as he barreled onto Congress Street past the concentration of county buildings. "The sumbitch won the fucking case before the opening statement," he said out loud to no one as he reached his building. "Hot damn!" He bounded up the stairs two at a time to the third floor.

"I wanna be as good as he is. I want people crowding the courtroom to watch me when it's show time. I want people to think if they don't hire me, they've left their best chance on the table. I want other lawyers to offer bigger settlements because they don't want me to whip their ass. I'm gonna . . ." Visions of a boundless future exploded in his mind—packed courtrooms, being a regular on CNN prime time panels of legal experts, articles in the paper.

Reaching his desk, he loosened his tie, settled into his chair, and let the air conditioning cool him. He imagined himself commanding the rapt attention and admiration of judge and jury and awing and humbling opposing lawyers.

His office was on the top floor of an early 1930s Art Deco building, just east of Main Street. The district that once housed premier business locations had gone to seed, but additions of new courthouses, Minute Maid Park, the George R. Brown Convention Center, and Discovery Green helped revive the area. Modern apartment buildings catering to millennials had sprung up where just a few years before people had feared walking after dark. He shared offices and Bernice, the secretary/receptionist/bookkeeper/office manager/paralegal/gofer, with George Accurso, a fellow former Houston Police Department policeman turned lawyer. The rent was cheap because both the landlord and the historical society had neglected the building for years.

His view to the west and south was magnificent—shimmering skins of the skyscrapers dominating the dramatic Houston skyline. His favorite was the Bank of America building, fifty-six stories with spires and gables that made him think of Batman's Gotham City, where, in his childhood fantasies, Paddy took turns being superhero and super villain.

Two weeks earlier, thirty-six-year-old Paddy had been sworn in to the Texas bar. He had gotten a late start, but if he was going to let that bother him, he wouldn't have headed down this road to begin with. He spent most of his days roaming from courtroom to courtroom hoping to catch the city's best lawyers in action. He had yet to have his first client and he knew he had to get clients if he was going to be the baddest lawyer in a city of great lawyers. It would happen. With four million people in Harris County, about half of them in Houston, some forty thousand civil cases were filed every year. He was sure that sooner or later he would get his share of the good ones.

"You have a call, Mr. Moran," Bernice said, interrupting his reverie. "He says his name's Jed."

Jed was Paddy's best friend from his days at the HPD. Paddy grabbed the phone, smiling. "Hey, pal. What's up?"

"I'll tell you when I get there," Jed said in a cold monotone.

"Sure. Come on," he replied, puzzled.

While he waited, without much to do other than pulling up his tie, he read yet again the framed certificate on the wall across the room. Each time he read it, his thoughts wandered to great victories that he, a six-foot-five, red-haired Irishman, super-sized Cousin Vinny would achieve.

This is to certify that Patrick Xavier Moran, having fulfilled all requirements and having subscribed to the official oath, is, upon motion of the Board of Law Examiners, hereby duly admitted and licensed as an attorney and counselor at law to practice in all Courts of the State of Texas.

May 16, 2007

Hearing Bernice greet Jed, Paddy spun around, eager to see his good friend, then shrank back, his toothy smile fading as he saw Jed sporting several days' beard and dark circles under his eyes. Instead of his uniform, Jed was wearing Levi's, scuffed boots, and a T-shirt so faded that one could barely read its message: "Keep Houston Un-Weird." His shoulders slumped. He clasped his hands at belt level as if they were cuffed. Paddy figured Jed would not be receptive to one of his bear hugs.

"You look like shit."

"Thanks," Jed said, as he dropped into a chair opposite the desk. "Jessie kicked me out. It's done. She found out I was doing Darlene."

"Darlene? Again?"

Jed's gaze fell, and he nodded. "Yeah . . . again. This time Jessie filed."

It dawned on Paddy that he was looking at his very first client. He resisted replying as he would have if they were still fellow cops, "Schmuck, what did you expect?" Jed didn't need to hear what others had doubtlessly already told him. Catching his own reflection in the window—a man in a suit, groomed, and looking professional—he decided this conversation should be devoid of the "fucks" and "shits" that were a part of their normal banter. Intending to communicate his care and confidence, he said, "How can I help?"

Jed's brow furrowed. "You're a lawyer, aren't you?"

"Yes, but I'm still your friend."

"Yeah, well, how about just being a lawyer?" Jed snapped. "What're you gonna charge?"

Determined not to let Jed's frustration stir his own temper, Paddy said, "I dunno. Tell me a few things first. What assets do you and Jessie have?"

"My pension. The house with a mortgage that might be more than what we could sell it for. A rental property. It has about ten in equity. I got my truck. She's got a Yukon. I make both payments."

"We both know I don't have a lot of experience," Paddy said, "but I'm pretty sure how this will play out unless there's something big you haven't told me. With those assets, Jessie will get the house and from half to fifty-five percent of your pension. She gets her car. You get yours. Everything else will go fifty-five percent to her and forty-five percent to you."

"Why does she get more than fifty percent?"

"Theoretically, under the community property laws, that's all she's entitled to, but you're working, she's not. You cheated on her. Yada yada yada. The extra five percent isn't worth fighting about. How old are the kids?"

"Valerie's twelve and Jed Junior's eleven."

"How much was your last W-2?"

"I'm not sure, but if you throw in moonlighting security jobs, say a hundred thou."

He quickly looked online for the Family Law Code schedule of child support payments based on income.

After Paddy told him the amount, Jed breathed deeply, shook his head, and said, "I really fucked up."

"First time was a fuckup. I don't know what to call this one."

"Just tell me what you'll cost," Jed growled.

He should have spent more time thinking about fees. They don't teach that stuff in law school. He could say a flat seven fifty. He could make it hourly. But Jed was a buddy, and he was busted. Whatever he charged would be more than Jed could afford, though he would somehow pay it. He'd probably end up unhappy no matter what, even if he thought Paddy had done a good job, because he was unhappy with the situation he'd gotten himself into.

Then synapses exploded in Paddy's brain. His savings would keep him afloat for at least six months. Jed was highly respected, with many years on the force. Soon he would make captain. Jed promoting him could be the best kind of advertising. And Jed really was his best friend.

He walked around the desk. Putting his massive hand on Jed's shoulder, he said, "If you promise, I mean promise"—Paddy squeezed tightly—"not to tell anyone, and if the facts are no more complicated than you've told me, I won't charge you a thing. You pay out-of-pockets, like court costs."

The tension left Jed's face. He sat straighter. "Buddy, you don't know what that means to me. Not just the money."

"Look, you're my pal. You came to me at one of the lowest points in your life." Lowering his voice to a gravelly pitch, assuming what he intended to be a wise counselor's expression, he said, "That means a lot to me." In fact, his guess was Jed had come to him because he assumed Paddy would be cheaper than more experienced lawyers. After all, it wasn't going to be a complicated divorce. Nevertheless, Jed was overcome with emotion.

Feeling a tiny bit emotional himself, Paddy added, "If I can't help a buddy out when he needs me, then what kinda guy am I? Just don't go telling people I didn't charge you. I can't afford to become a fuckin' legal aid society for cops who get busted by their wives."

Jed pushed his chair back, stretched out his legs, and said, "When you first joined the force, I thought you were a lifer. I was hoping you would be. I never saw anyone better at making the right decision in a critical situation. I knew that when my ass was on the line, I wanted you to have my back."

"You guys really took me in," Paddy said. "Even let me join the weekly poker game. The only reason you still let me play is because I lose most of the time."

Paddy's thoughts went back to the now distant universe that had once been his Brooklyn, where a cop's life would have given him all the respect he could have wanted. Walking, sometimes strutting, neighborhood streets, he saw shopkeepers smiling appreciatively and punks avoiding eye contact. He felt in complete command, entirely comfortable with his environs. It was good. Then a new captain took command. He and Paddy had a serious run-in because Paddy hadn't been tough enough on some young black kids suspected of a purse snatching. Paddy knew the teenagers and their parents. The captain did not. But Paddy also knew this guy could make his life miserable for a long time.

The next day Paddy opened an email posting a job with the HPD. "Saints be praised," his grandmother might have said. On a whim, he responded.

Basically a loner with no family he wanted to be around, he would miss no one in Brooklyn. The pay was decent and the cost of living way less, and his pension seniority would transfer. A week later, he was in Houston. Instead of walking the streets during shifts, he cruised in a Ford Crown Victoria.

It didn't take him long to see that all kinds of people could make it big in Houston, people who came to the city with nothing and became big shots. He wanted that, but he doubted he'd reach great heights as a policeman. He began taking night classes at South Texas College of Law. Tired of dealing with perps, he wanted no part of criminal law. He focused on family law and plaintiffs' personal injury, two areas that weren't dominated by the large law firms.

"Hey," Jed said, damming Paddy's stream of consciousness. "Speaking of poker, you doing anything else at least once a week?" Jed winked.

"Nah. Like they say, the law's a jealous mistress. I just go to the gym and my place, watch TV, read lawyer novels. Ya know, chill. That's enough." He didn't mention the hookers.

CHAPTER 2

SOMETHING NEW

JED KEPT HIS WORD. He told no one Paddy hadn't charged him. He did say he was doing a great job and his fees were reasonable. After Jed's first meeting in Paddy's office, at least three police divorce cases a month came in. All routine. All uncontested. All done at a fixed fee. It wasn't much, but it was a start. He was also working the phone at the bar association's free legal line. It was win-win. Poor folks have some of the same questions rich folks do. The more situations he had to contemplate, the better prepared he would be for whatever was coming. Besides, he began to understand that sometimes the best thing lawyers can do for people is to let them know they aren't alone when faced with navigating the slippery slopes of the legal system. Even a rocket scientist couldn't do it alone.

Into month six, around 9:30 on a Monday morning, a cop in his mid-forties strutted into the office. Paddy assumed the guy wanted a divorce.

"I got rear-ended," the cop said. "By a Porsche."

Pushing his lower lip out and arching his eyebrows, Paddy whistled and said, "Sweet car. What happened?"

"Attorney-client privilege?"

"Of course," Paddy said.

"This hotshot is right on me, you know? I can't even see his front bumper in the mirror. The light turns yellow, and it's raining like it is now. He thinks I'm gonna keep going. I'm thinking that, too. I start to push it, and then it occurs to me I'm driving this shit car, behind in child support, bills up the ass. I mean, all this goes through my head in less than a second. So I hit the brakes. He plows into me. I move slowly. I'm, you know, groggy, holding my neck. He's really pissed, about to say something. I let him know I'm a cop. Shuts him up. His eyes get narrow, he gives me this smile like he already knows the game and how it's going to play. To make sure, I call one of my buddies who comes and tickets the guy."

"Did you exchange insurance?"

"Yeah, but I don't think Mr. Hotshot wants to file a claim. Rich bastards usually don't unless it's something major."

"Were you really hurt?"

"What do you want me to say?"

He studied the man. This sure sounded like a scam. It was new to Paddy, but clearly it wasn't new to the cop. As Paddy wondered if it was ethical to take the representation, the cop said, "Moran, I'm putting something in your green-ass lap. Word is you're a good guy, and I want to help you get started. If you think you're too good for this—" He stared at Paddy, reading him. "Jed told me you're inexperienced but smart. He didn't say you were a by-the-book guy."

Paddy shot him a cold look. "Before I start picking and choosing which parts of the book I'm gonna follow, I need to know the book backwards and forwards. My job is to represent clients in lawsuits, but their claims have to be for real."

Abruptly the cop switched gears. "It wasn't intentional, Moran. I had an irresistible impulse to slam on my brakes."

"Irresistible impulse." He remembered the defense from a showing of *Anatomy of a Murder* at law school. A sane person momentarily snaps and does something he can't control. Paddy nods. "If you say you had an irresistible impulse, I'll take your word for it. If you didn't cause the accident intentionally, in my book, that would make it legit." He pulled out a legal pad, picked up a pen, and asked, "When did this happen?"

"Yesterday."

Smiling broadly, he said, "What the fuck took you so long to get here?"

The man chuckled.

"Seen a doctor?"

"Do you know which doctor I'm supposed to go to?"

Leaning forward, Paddy said, "This isn't just attorney-client privilege. This is dead man's talk. What you say goes no further than this room. Okay?"

The cop nodded, smiling like a Cheshire cat. He tilted his chair back, making a cracking sound. Paddy winced, but a passing feeling told him he could afford a new chair if this played out the way he thought it might.

The cop nodded. "Jed said he liked riding with you."

"I appreciate Jed saying that. If you want to hear my quick take, it's that you know more about what needs to be done here than I do—*this time.* Take me through it, what doctor and so forth."

Paddy scribbled. The cop—now his client—even told him what his share of the recovery would be.

When the letter of the rules says it's okay to do something, but your gut tells you it's wrong, what do you do? If by the book it's okay, then it's okay.

He was just getting started. Cops were his only natural referral source. He better aim to please if he wanted to get out of the chute. It would be a learning experience. Paddy shrugged his shoulders and then accessed an online form book and contingency fee agreement. He let the cop tell him how to fill in the blanks.

"Maybe this go-by will help." The cop handed him a demand letter to be sent to the driver of the Porsche.

"You came prepared," Paddy said, impressed with the bald ruthlessness of the plan. "It'll be done on my letterhead and sent today."

"Certified and regular mail," the cop said.

"Got it!"

<hr>

A FEW DAYS LATER, the judge entered Jed and Jessie's final decree of divorce. After the proceedings, Paddy gathered them outside. He put a hand on Jessie's shoulder and one on Jed's and said, "Okay, Jessie, Jed fucked up. You got even. You did what you had to. And, by gawd, it was what you should've done. But I can tell you, he's been miserable. And you don't look like someone who's ready to celebrate. Are you?"

Jessie raised her head. "No, I'm not."

"Then for your own sake and for your kids' sake, get your asses back together."

"C'mon, honey," Jed said. "Can we give it a try?"

She shook her head, wheeled around, and headed for the exit. Jed followed her. She turned and said, "No!"

Jed looked at Paddy, who shrugged his shoulders.

ON HIS WAY BACK TO THE OFFICE, his phone vibrated. "Moran," he answered. The caller identified himself as the attorney for the Porsche owner. He offered five thousand dollars to settle. A thrill ran through Paddy. Tamping his excitement, he said, "Sounds low, but I'm obligated to take any offer to my client."

"Five thousand!" his client said. "That's a crock. Tell him I won't settle for less than a hundred thou."

"Are you fucking kidding me?"

"Tell him I said that."

"What'll we really settle for?"

"We can't go so high that he figures it's better to turn it over to insurance. Fifteen?"

"Sounds reasonable."

He called the lawyer back and told him a hundred thousand, but he thought he could make seventy fly if they moved quickly. The lawyer seemed to choke. Clearly angry, he said, "That's outrageous, but I too have to present the offer to my client."

Not an hour passed before the call came. "My client is really steamed, but he wants this done. He'll pay twenty-five for a complete release. The offer's good for two hours. Understand, Moran. It's not going any higher."

Twenty-five grand and a quarter of it was his just for sending a letter? Sweet!

"Hey, good job, man," the cop said when Paddy called him with the news. "But, if they'll go for twenty-five, then maybe—"

"No. Trust me, pal. I listened carefully. They're pissed. They're at their limit. Don't push it. You wanted fifteen. I got you twenty-five." He lowered his voice. "Take it."

"Okay. Nice work. You're a quick learner."

That was exactly what he wanted to hear. He did a little jig when he rang off.

PILAR

PILAR QUINTANILLA GALT SAT at Gaucho's Margaritas waiting for her friend Sunny. It was the new Thursday meet-up place, close to downtown office buildings, in the center of Midtown, Houston's hottest area for under-thirty-fives. She tried to act interested in the kitschy Dia de los Muertos decor as she gave icy responses to the guys in the happy hour crowd who hit on her, one after the other. She kept her eyes on the entrance as she sipped her frozen margarita.

"Another," she said to the bartender, just as Sunny arrived.

"Sorry," Sunny said. "Last minute rush for the boss."

"No prob."

Sunny appraised Pilar. "You look fabulous, girl."

"It's from intense workouts every day and Spanx. Order up."

"You ladies want a photo?" the bartender asked as he set a frozen margarita in front of Sunny. "There's a lot of hot women here tonight, but you two win the prize."

"You're sweet," she said, then she turned to Pilar. "What's goin' on, girlfriend? Let me see the latest of that baby."

"She's a love." Pilar handed over her phone.

"I hear that in your voice," Sunny said as she scrolled through photos of Pilar's daughter, all dimples, toothless smiles, and wisps of fine black hair. "I'm happy for you."

"My aunt is staying with her tonight," Pilar said. "She thought I needed a girls' night out." She straightened her back. "I signed on with a temp agency today."

"Wait a minute. You're not going back with Innoveismic?"

"Probably, when maternity leave's over. I'll temp on weekends and nights so I don't have to be around Ronnie. Let me be clear: I want to be gone when he's at home and not sleeping."

"It's that bad already? How long's it been?"

Pilar winced and nodded. "Today is our six-month anniversary."

Pilar expected her usually unfiltered friend to make a joke. Instead, Sunny held Pilar's hands and said nothing.

"The baby annoys him. He didn't want her. He doesn't understand why he can't have sex on demand like he used to. I'm trying to see what I saw in him."

Sunny looked as if she was going to respond. Pilar sat stiff against the back of the bar stool, bracing herself for a sharp retort from Sunny. Pilar saw that Sunny recognized now was not the time to be flip.

"Have you seen the lineup for this year's rodeo?" Sunny asked. Pilar shook her head, smiling, happy to change the subject to the inane.

"I have to be up and alert super early tomorrow." Sunny noisily slurped the last drops of her margarita. "It's past eight. I'm outta here."

Pilar shook her head. "I think I'll finish mine before I go."

"You sure? Maybe you've had enough?"

"I'm fine."

Pilar gave Sunny a warm hug and watched her leave. The alcohol had already blunted the raw edge of her anger at Ronnie, but she wasn't quite where she wanted to be yet. A man quickly slid into Sunny's seat. Pilar glanced at him. He was nice looking, but his cologne was so strongly loaded with patchouli oil she nearly gagged. She turned away to avoid the sickly-sweet smell. She could feel his eyes flicking over her, then away, trying to play it cool. Without speaking to her, he called out to the bartender, "Bring the lady another one."

She still couldn't quite bring herself to look at him directly, but she felt relief that someone else had made the decision for her to have another drink. She took a big swallow as soon as the bartender served the cocktail.

"You're a thirsty filly, beautiful señorita."

She rolled her eyes and took another swallow. "Thanks," she said, looking forward. Normally, she wouldn't have accepted the drink. Normally, she would have left with Sunny, but her anger at Ronnie combined with the alcohol were playing her. She was desperate for a reason not to go home yet. She sipped. The smell of his cologne mellowed, then dissipated altogether. He put his hand on her thigh. She gave him a plus for his confidence. She sipped again. His fingers slid under the hem of her skirt.

She opened her legs slightly, invitingly. As he began to slide higher, she leaned toward him, and softly said, "Don't freak out when you reach my balls."

He jerked his hand back. She threw her head back, laughing. Finally, she looked at him fully. Shock still framed his face, which was quite handsome. His build was buff. He looked kind. She took his hand, held it to her, so that it pressed into the side of her breast. "Gotcha," she said.

Now he laughed, too.

"Jesus," he said.

"No, sweetie. It's Pilar."

She drained her drink. He offered to buy her another. Her head was spinning. A little horrified at herself, she shook her head.

"I need to go outside." She got up, pushed through the crowd, and weaved to the door.

He hurriedly tossed more than enough cash onto the bar to cover the tab and rushed after her. She felt his hand on her back when he caught up with her.

Her thoughts pulsed quickly back and forth in binary fashion, the 1s and 0s slightly *desfinado*, from the high of guilty delight from spiting her husband and entrancing the horny, bewildered man she had in tow to the low of shame she already felt. Outside, she led him to her car in a dark corner of the lot.

"Get in," she said, unlocking and opening the passenger door.

He seemed confused but definitely willing and delighted. She reached down, unzipped his fly, and took him out. In spite of the drinks he'd had—not many yet, she guessed—he was already erect. Wanting it over quickly, she reached under her skirt. *Oh, God, the Spanx,* she cursed to herself, struggling to get them down far enough to allow her to slide into the car and over him.

Inside the car, looking down at him, she thought, *oh my God, a complete stranger. What the hell am I doing?*

"You don't have to do this," he said.

If she had any doubts before, they were gone now. She grabbed his head and pulled his lips to hers. Ronnie would never have spoken to her with such tenderness.

She leaned back, smiling, imagining herself a vamp goddess in complete control. "You've probably been fantasizing all your life about something like this. Well, you can tell your buddies tomorrow you hit the jackpot."

His expression was a mix of disbelief and wonder.

She began to move on him.

"Oh, yes," he said.

At least, she thought, *it wouldn't be long.*

He reached his hands down to her butt to pull her deeper. She threw her head back.

A bright light cut abruptly into the car, blinding her, as a fist banged on the roof.

"Oh, shit," she said.

The guy jumped beneath her, knocking her sideways. "What the hell?"

"Police," a voice yelled. "Out of the car. You're engaged in an act of public lewdness."

Pilar's head throbbed. She tucked her chin to her neck and covered her face.

"You gotta get off first. I can't move unless you do, and this guy sounds serious."

"You get out first," she said, sliding off his now limp self as she fell awkwardly on her side into the driver's seat. She struggled to get the Spanx back in place.

Stunned and stumbling, he steadied himself against the car's roof.

The cop said, "You, too, lady."

"Give me a minute, please," she said, fighting with the Spanx.

Eyes focused on her feet, Pilar managed to exit the car. The light hit her in the face again. She held her hand up to block it as she heard, "Holy crap! Pilar?"

The light dropped. When she could focus she saw who it was. "Jed," she whispered. "Oh, no!"

"Christ," he said, shaking his head. "What are you—?"

Pilar felt dizzy and hot and very near to throwing up. The last time she had seen Jed was in her own backyard. He had offered Ronnie advice about how hot the coals should be, and Ronnie responded as if to say if you know so much, how come I make so much more money than you. Jed looked at her now as if he'd never seen her before. He must be disgusted. But it wasn't just that. She saw more in his face. A flash of understanding—or perhaps pity.

"If I'm looking at you in five seconds," Jed said to the man, who now had his pants firmly reattached beneath his belly, "you're spending the night in the tank. Get me?"

The man didn't have to be told twice. He took off across the parking lot.

"Jed," she said again, pleading this time.

"Pilar, I can't believe this."

She staggered to him, crying.

"Don't tell Ronnie. He gets so mad. So, so mad you wouldn't believe it." She grabbed his hands, squeezed them and looked down.

"I don't know—what are you saying, Pilar? What's this about? Do you do this all the time?"

"No, never. I met my friend for a drink. I stayed to finish mine after she left. This guy bought me another one. One too many. I was feeling sorry for myself and very angry at Ronnie. He made a move, and I just . . . I don't know. I didn't care anymore. I wanted to hurt Ronnie more than anything. Please don't tell anyone."

"I don't know whether to believe you or not. Can you drive?"

Pilar stepped back carefully, straightened her clothes, put her hands through her hair as she moved it back into place, and breathed in deeply. The nausea had passed. Her head had cleared somewhat. On the entire police force, she didn't know anyone nicer than Jed.

"I'm fine."

"I can drive you home," Jed said. "You can say your battery died."

"I'm fine."

"Then get out of here."

Humiliated and totally defeated, she moved to open her car door.

"Wait!" Jed said. "I can't let you leave without saying a few things. First, you can't do this again. And if you do, for Christ's sake, not in a public place. You hear me?"

She nodded.

"All right," he said. "Listen, if it's really that bad with him, and, knowing Ronnie, I can believe it is, you need to do something. Not this. Something real. Leave him. He's not going to change."

"He beat me."

Jed shook his head. "This is not the way to fight back."

"He only did it once."

He narrowed his eyes and rocked back and forth from his heels to the soles of his feet, nodding as he reflected: He had certainly seen a few women who were more beautiful than Pilar, but even after having a baby and being messy drunk, her sensuous presence left him nearly breathless. She was beyond gorgeous. And damaged as hell. Why did those two always seem to go together? His mind went to what he had lost when he and Jessie split. He wished he could call her right then.

"It'll happen again, Pilar. Get your ass out of there."

"I don't know—"

Jed held his hand up.

"There's a guy I know. He does work for a lot of cops. He's a good guy. He won't take advantage of you. He'll steer you right."

Jed's warm demeanor made her feel safe. She nodded. "Let me think about it."

He took his wallet from his rear pocket, fished out a card, and handed it to her. "Call him."

CHAPTER 4

PILAR SEEKS HELP

PILAR SAT AGAINST THE FAR WALL, staring at the back side of the black letters on the opaque, wire-mesh glass pane of the door: Law Offices of George Accurso and Patrick A. Moran. She said a small prayer that baby Grace, sleeping in a carrier on the floor, would stay asleep when the man arrived.

She'd come without an appointment and expected to be turned away, but the receptionist said she could work her into the schedule. "Mr. Moran's just finishing up at the courthouse. I'm going to lunch. Mr. Accurso's out," the receptionist said. "If you don't mind being here by yourself, it's fine for you to wait. I'm sure it won't be long."

Each time she had started to call, an inexplicable dread came over her. Having finally acted, she would wait. Since her encounter with Jed nearly three weeks ago, when she was alone, sometimes she screamed out loud, mortified, when the memory of her drunken indiscretion came back to her.

Things had not gotten better with Ronnie. Last night, she acknowledged they never would. This morning, before leaving to take a stroll with the baby, she told herself she was just looking for a quiet place to walk, but she had dressed carefully. Before she knew it, as if her car had driven itself, she'd pulled into a parking space near the address on the lawyer's card Jed had given her. She took finding a parking place on a street near the courthouses as a good sign.

She put her phone camera on selfie mode and checked her makeup three times. Forty minutes passed, and she calculated how much time she had left on the parking meter. She texted Sunny. She checked her email and Facebook account. She wished she had downloaded something to read. She shifted her weight, trying to find a comfortable position on the unforgiving wooden chair. *This must be how one feels waiting for a root canal*, she thought.

Boot heels made an abrasive sound as they slid to a stop on the cracked white-and-black hallway tiles. She could see the blurred outline of a large man through the opaque glass. He opened the door and held it open with his body so he could pick up the briefcase he'd set down. He held another in his other hand.

Totally focused on preparing a motion for summary judgment in a pro bono case, Paddy looked up to see not frumpy, black-rimmed glasses Bernice, but a striking woman. She was dressed simply yet stylishly in a navy gabardine skirt and a cream silk blouse, a thin strand of gold around her neck. A baby carrier sat on the floor next to her. He looked at the briefcases as if they had appeared from nowhere.

She noticed that her looks had registered with him. Could be good. Could be bad.

He glanced around the reception area, took a deep breath, set the briefcases down, and approached her, extending his hand.

"Paddy Moran," he said.

His conservative suit and tie indicated to Pilar that he wanted to be viewed as a professional. He also looked like he had ten things on his mind.

"Pilar Galt," she replied. "The secretary told me I could wait for you." His eyes opened a bit wider, but he didn't respond. "It's not a good time, is it?"

"Actually," he said, pulling a chair over to sit in front of her, "I need a break from the case I'm working on, so it's a great time. How'd you end up here?"

"Jed sent me. He said you were the person I had to see."

"You said the magic word, 'Jed.' Let's talk."

She looked carefully to see if anything in his facial expression or body language indicated that Jed had disclosed to him her disgraceful encounter. She saw no sign. "I really just stopped by to make an appointment. I can come back." She started to rise.

Paddy held his hand up as a stop signal. "You almost got it covered up. But not quite."

"Oh," she said, touching below her eye lightly. "I'm sorry."

"Why are *you* sorry? Husband do that?"

She nodded.

"The no-good mother—. Is that why you're here?"

Finally, he let go of everything else he had carried in his head when he entered the office. He focused on her. "You look familiar."

"I'm Ronnie Galt's wife, Pilar."

Paddy seemed to groan inwardly.

"What?" she said.

"I once held a steak to the eye of one of Ronnie Galt's girlfriends. At a barbecue a long time ago—a lot of cops, a lot of beer, and a lot of food. A neighbor must have heard what she thought was too much yelling and called 911. A bunch of cops arrived, took in the scene and, of course, all they did was grab some beers and ribs and pretend to take a report. But this girl was in the bathroom by then, sobbing and swelling."

"That sounds like Ronnie." She felt a small door had opened.

"He's still at it, I see."

"Yes. Last night." She felt her face darken.

"I'm not surprised. What an asshole." He looked away from her.

The ghost of a smile flickered across Pilar's face. "Good. I hope that means you'll do a good job for me."

He turned back to her and took a deep breath. Who could hit that face? She's smart, too. He already sensed she was the whole package, the real deal. Something in her reminded Paddy of himself. From a poor place, undoubtedly, a barrio in some Texas city or Mexico, but with her looks and snap, she'd been able to move up, educate herself at least a little. And now, she was ready to stop bully Ronnie from knocking her around.

He took her graceful, manicured hands into his own massive paws and said, "Listen, Pilar, honey, I'd like to help you. I really, really would. Seeing that asshole squirm would be sweet and squeezing whatever we could out of him for you and that beautiful baby would be a good thing. But I can't."

She brought her hands to her stomach, as if she'd taken a hard shot to the solar plexus. "Why not?" she said, clearly disappointed. "You called Ronnie an asshole. You know he is."

"It's got nothing to do with Ronnie. I'm just starting out. I take whatever comes in the door. For the time being, what comes in the door is cops, mostly cops getting a divorce. For now, that's the bread and buttah." He paused, realizing Brooklyn had slipped out and that she'd noticed.

He made an effort to speak more deliberately. "Representing a cop's spouse could affect my business relationship with the law enforcement community. I'm seen, for better or worse, as a cop's lawyer. And I'm afraid that if I took on a cop's spouse, that'd mark me as somehow having gone over to the other side—the dark side, they'd say."

"That shouldn't make a difference. Ronnie's not a cop anymore. He's got a fancy title as director of security with an energy services company."

Paddy nodded. "He still goes on ride-alongs with them. He gets some of them moonlighting jobs. He goes to the cookouts, the bars. I know because they still invite me, too. I guess that's how I recognized you. He may not be a cop any more, but in that crowd, he still is."

"And so are you."

"Look, it's a state of mind. For me, I can assure you, it's not a life sentence. I plan on moving up in the world. But I gotta get there first. For now, getting there means keeping them happy, making it seem like I'm still one of them."

"And if you take me on, you won't be anymore."

Pilar bit her lip, and her eyes darted. Panicking, she felt short of breath. She was on the verge of crying, but she would not let it happen. She lifted her head and kept her jaw straight. "Then tell me what to do," she said evenly.

He admired how she had held back her tears and met his gaze. "You're a fighter," he said. "I can see that. You fight like I fight. Houston, in its own way, is a small town. My guess is we'll meet again, hopefully when we're both a lot better off. One thing I know, in just a very short minute, a New York minute, if you will, I can tell that I like you and I respect you and, even though it may not seem that way now, I believe you have good things in store for you."

"That's great. I like you, too. But, just as you have to do what you have to do, I have to focus on what I need to do. The problem is I don't know what the hell to do." The baby started to move. Soon the crying would come.

"I know how to fight for cops," he said. "You need someone who fights for wives and kids—who's done it before. There's a woman in town named Margaret Walden. I took her pro bono divorce clinic when I was in law school."

Pilar liked that he had helped people through pro bono work. It fit the image Jed had given her.

"Since then we've butted heads," Paddy said. "Truth is, I don't like her. I think she's a mean-spirited, self-righteous . . . I've seen her leave good cops sobbing like babies. On the plus side, she's smart as hell, aggressive, and nothing makes her angrier or better in court than a woman who's been kicked around by her husband. I'll give you her info. Go see her."

"Thank you."

"Let her know I sent you. She'll get a big kick out of that. Tell her I hope she scalps Ronnie."

She stood up in one fluid motion and smoothed down her skirt. She bent and picked up the baby carrier. She held her other hand out to him. He really was huge. He towered over her.

"You sure are . . ." he began. "Goodbye, for now," he said.

She put on her sunglasses and went for the door. He said something else as she left, but she didn't make it out. It didn't matter anyway. She was already crossing off "Hire Paddy Moran" from her to-do list and adding "Talk to Margaret Walden," both under the heading "Leave my abuser, sack-of-shit husband."

A faint scent of jasmine lingered after Pilar left. Paddy closed his eyes for a moment, taking it in, smiling. He looked at his watch to force the scent and her out of his mind. It was almost time for his appointment with Constable Ernest Grissett.

CHAPTER 5

KNOW YOUR CLIENT

ONE OF THE REQUIREMENTS for successfully playing the game with the big boys was developing connections with folks involved in the justice system in Harris County. Paddy had been told that if he made friends with constables' deputies, the people who serve defendants with lawsuits, those friends could get his cases served more quickly. Therefore, when Ernest Grissett, a prospective new client, called, announcing he was a deputy for a Harris County constable before asking for an appointment, Paddy was excited. However, when he first saw Grissett in person, he had to force himself to give a welcoming smile. At about five feet five inches tall, Grissett was corpulent and red-faced, with a web of blood vessels converging at the end of his bulbous nose. His stomach pooched out over his belt, nearly obscuring a large, jeweled, gold Lone Star of Texas buckle.

"Howdy, son," Grissett said. "I'm here to help you have a big payday."

Feeling that the deputy thought he was looking at a six-foot-five, red-haired, freckle-faced idiot, Paddy said, "Howdy," in exaggerated fashion and shook Grissett's fleshy hand. He released immediately, then stuffed his right hand into his pocket, wiping it on the lining while motioning with his other hand for Grissett to sit down.

Paddy sat behind his desk and nodded while Deputy Grissett told his story. No surprise, a guy in a brand-new Escalade had rear-ended him. Paddy advised Grissett to see the usual friendly doctor and receive the usual soft tissue injury report. Then he wrote the driver, making a demand.

Two days later he called Grissett. "You won't believe the response I got from the guy who hit you. The fuckhead wrote, 'Sue me!' Can you believe that?"

The constable said, "I knew that guy was a hothead. Let's grant him his wish."

"You mean file suit?" Paddy said, lowering his voice.

"You bet."

"Come to my office."

When Grissett arrived, Paddy grabbed him by the arm, pulled him close, tilted the deputy's chin up so that he had to look Paddy in the eye, and with a barely audible yet menacing tone, said, "What about this case do you know that I don't know?"

His client hesitated. "Like what?"

"Like why the SOB might say, 'Sue me.'"

"Nothing."

"I never had a response to a demand like that before."

"Well," Grissett drawled, "you're still pretty new. I'm sure lots of things hadn't happened to you yet."

He recalled a moment from a Trial Practice seminar taught by a wizened, old trial lawyer. On the first day of class, the professor said, "I never saw a case get better than the first time my client told me the facts."

After the Porsche case, Paddy represented several more cops involved in wrecks. The cases didn't make him rich, but his name was getting around. He was getting experience dealing with other lawyers, knowing when to push, when to retreat, and how to manage a client's expectations. He didn't feel that great about being part of a scam, but the rich fucks who were getting scammed wouldn't miss a meal because of the hit.

He never asked a question that would confirm the collision was intentional, and he held up his hand to shush a client who he sensed was about to tell him too much. That satisfied his obligations under the letter of the Code of Professional Conduct, though maybe not the intent and certainly not his conscience. Until now, each time he had sent a demand letter a quick settlement was reached. His only court experiences were routine appearances in the Family Law Court and some dispositive motions for pro bono clients. Even those were instructive because he watched lawyers interact with each other, and he watched judges while he waited for a case to be called. Some of the lawyers and judges even recognized him and called him by name.

After practicing nearly a year, he was anxious to actually try a case. However, his instincts told him this was not the one. He didn't need whatever money he was going to make from Grissett, but he did need a good relationship with the constable's office. On the other hand, he sure didn't like Grissett or trust him. But how bad could it be?

He looked at form books and personal injury suit petitions at the courthouse filed by some of the best-known plaintiff's lawyers before he drafted the plaintiff's original petition. He edited and re-edited. He got Accurso, his office mate, to look at it. When he thought it was as good as he could make it, he had his client read it. Once again, he asked if there were any missing facts that could result in an unpleasant surprise.

Grissett grunted, "No."

He didn't file the suit for a week, trying to assess all the different aspects that bothered him. He felt the same anxiety he had felt as a policeman approaching an apartment in response to a domestic violence call. It wasn't because this was the first non-divorce petition he had filed. He had a gnawing feeling he'd missed something, and he was certain his client was holding back. One day after the case was filed, Grissett saw to it that the defendant was served.

That night was poker night. He asked Jed if he knew Grissett. "No. There's lots of deputies. I don't know many," Jed said. "I will tell you I've got dinner with Jessie Saturday night."

"Well, that the best news I've heard in a while."

"It's just dinner. I'm not getting my hopes up too much."

"And Darlene?"

"History."

Paddy knew defendants rarely answered early, yet the answer came just a week after the suit was filed. When he read the title, "Defendant's First Original Answer and First Original Counterclaim and Cross-Petition," he felt as if a million claws were clenching his innards. He flipped to the end to see which lawyer had signed the pleadings. He didn't recognize the name, Marlin Seaborn, but he sure recognized his firm, Walker & Travis.

Paddy had won the Walker & Travis Moot Court Award at South Texas. In a law school known for its trial advocacy program, the award was a big deal. He treated himself to a weekend in Vegas with the prize money. He appreciated the award and especially the recognition that came with it. What he didn't appreciate was those Walker & Travis assholes refusing his request to be put on the list of law students they would interview for jobs. He looked up Marlin Seaborn. Stanford undergraduate, UT Law School, law review, Order of the Coif, clerk for a judge on the U.S. Court of Appeals for the Fifth Circuit, a young partner at Walker & Travis, board-certified in personal injury, insurance defense. They were the same age.

He read Seaborn's pleadings. The answer portion was typical, a general denial. When he read the counterclaim, he slammed his fist on his desk.

Accurso and Bernice burst into his office. "What happened?" they asked in unison.

"Nutten," he snapped, his eyes blazing.

The counterclaim alleged Grissett intentionally caused the accident, choosing to slam on his brakes even though there was no reason for him to stop suddenly, resulting in Seaborn's client, Mr. Hunter, colliding with the rear end of Grissett's vehicle. After the collision, both men got out of their vehicles. Grissett showed Hunter he was a peace officer and, demanding an outrageous amount, said that if he knew what was good for him, he would settle up immediately. When Hunter refused, Grissett made a telephone call, and moments later a police officer arrived and gave Hunter a ticket, explaining they always ticket the party who rear-ends the other vehicle.

In the portion of the counterclaim where money damages are pled, not unfittingly called the "prayer", Seaborn asked for twenty-five thousand in actual damages to the Escalade, more than fifty thousand in actual damages to Hunter, and a million in exemplary damages.

Feeling a lack of oxygen, Paddy called his client. "Come over here. I want you to read the answer to your lawsuit," he gasped.

"*My* lawsuit?"

"Yeah, *your* lawsuit. They are countersuing, saying you intentionally caused the accident, and they want money from *you*."

Grissett arrived in minutes. "Lemme see it."

Moran handed him the answer and counterclaim. His client scanned the pages quickly. "That's bullshit."

"It sure as hell better be, sir. If not, you're in a heap of trouble."

"How would they even prove something like that?" his client asked.

"Why would you ask me that question? Do you have something to hide?"

Grissett stood, put his hands on the front of Paddy's desk and leaned the top part of his body backward. "Of course not," he said in the most formal tone Paddy had heard him use. "I was just curious."

"Well, I think you're holding back on me. Surprises aren't good for either of us."

"Don't worry, counselor. No problemo."

Seaborn's only settlement offer was that Grissett pay seventy-five thousand. He would not join in a motion to continue. A hearing was held, and the judge denied the motion, saying, "Mr. Moran, if you filed the suit, you ought to be ready to try it."

This left him with two weeks to get ready for his first trial, one for which he was quite sure he did not know all the facts. His adversary was a seasoned trial lawyer from a big firm with a rich client. He was going to be very busy preparing right up to the moment of the opening bell.

"Showtime!" he repeated to himself as he pored over his condensed versions of the rules of evidence and procedure. "Showtime!"

CHAPTER 6

PADDY'S FIRST TRIAL

"ALL RISE," the bailiff said as the judge entered.

Sweat ran beneath Paddy's overly starched shirt and best suit coat. He knew it was not just the damn Houston humidity causing him to overheat.

"Be seated," the judge said. He read the case number. "Are both parties ready?"

Paddy rose, cleared his throat and said with perhaps too much volume, "Plaintiff is ready, Your Honor."

His opponent, a well-manicured specimen of the Houston bar dressed in a gray tailored suit and red club tie, stood. "Marlin Seaborn of Walker & Travis for defendant and counter-plaintiff. We are ready."

Paddy winced as he heard "counter-plaintiff." That phrase had haunted him from the moment he received Seaborn's response to his original petition.

"Your Honor, are you going to bring the jury panel in now?" Paddy said. Success, he knew, began with the right jury, though he had actually never picked one. All week he'd found himself mumbling, "Voir dire, voir dire," at odd moments, except the Texas pronunciation was "vore dyer." He liked how the phrase, which felt unsuited to his natural Brooklyn accent, slipped off his tongue. He had learned how to memorize names and faces of members of a jury panel. Now he could put that skill to use.

"There will be no jury, Mr. Moran."

Standing to the full measure of his six feet, five inches, in a tone he hoped was full of both indignation *and* respect, he said, "Why not, Your Honor? My client has a constitutional right to a trial by a jury of his peers."

"You are absolutely correct, Mr. Moran. Since I've been on the bench, I've marveled at juries' wisdom in ascertaining witnesses' credibility. But, unfortunately, neither you nor Mr. Seaborn demanded a jury and paid a jury fee."

Paddy glanced sideways. Seaborn placed his hand firmly on his client's shoulder. It took every ounce of his inner strength to not pick up a chair and smash it. He could do it, too. Had done it several times in the past, but he wasn't in a Brooklyn barroom now and the release he felt then wasn't going to happen in this courtroom.

Feeling the heat of Grissett's stare, he said, "I am familiar with the Texas Rules of Civil Procedure, but there's an interpretation of the rule in the case of a counterclaim—" He stopped midsentence, hoping his pause seemed natural. "Your Honor," he said, "notwithstanding your modesty, my client and I are quite confident that you have the wisdom, clarity, and impartiality to make a fair determination in this dispute."

The judge nodded, perhaps relieved that he did not have to further embarrass the inexperienced lawyer any more than he already had.

"Opening statements?" the judge asked.

As Paddy thought how to adapt his opening statement intended for a jury to a presentation to the judge, Seaborn quickly said, "Defendant and counter-plaintiff waive opening statement."

"Mr. Moran," the judge said, "I assure you I have read all the pleadings. I believe I'm familiar with the issues, but I'll be happy to hear from you."

Paddy had practiced a short, but he hoped persuasive, opening statement: "This is a simple case of a hard-working public servant, a peace officer who risks his life every day for the people of our community, whose body was injured and whose property was damaged and whose flow of life was interrupted by a rich man's negligent act. A rich man, who, refusing to direct his anger at himself and accept responsibility for his actions, is using his considerable resources to abuse the system of justice and punish Deputy Grissett." Should he make his statement to the judge?

"Mr. Moran?" the judge interrupted while Paddy ran through the lines he was certain would have persuaded a jury.

Mustering as much nonchalance as he could, Paddy said, "Plaintiff waives opening statement also." He would save it for his closing.

The judge nodded. With a kind smile and a firm tone, he said, "Mr. Moran, call your first witness."

He called Officer Mark Hadley, who'd arrived at the scene of the collision. After establishing Hadley's experience in accident investigation, Paddy questioned him about the facts. Hadley said, "When I got there, the parties had already moved their vehicles away from the busy intersection. There were no skid marks from the Escalade, indicating the driver did not apply his brakes before impact. There were skid marks from Officer Grissett's truck." Hadley testified he had no reason to distrust Officer Grissett when the officer said he was in pain. He testified he had issued a ticket to Mr. Hunter, the driver of the Escalade, because it appeared to him that the accident was avoidable, and Mr. Hunter was at fault.

Paddy passed the witness.

Seaborn lounged back in his chair, clasping his hands behind his head. "Officer Hadley, were you acquainted with Mr. Grissett before the accident?"

"I had seen *Officer* Grissett at law enforcement gatherings, but we aren't close friends."

"I thought police officers didn't go to the scene of automobile accidents if no one was injured."

"We go if we're called. And he was injured."

Seaborn inspected his nails as he asked, "Did Mr. Grissett leave in an ambulance?"

"I didn't see him leave."

Seaborn stood. He walked toward the witness stand. Hands in pockets, he planted his feet in front of Hadley. "Have you talked to Mr. Moran before today?"

"Yes sir."

"Did he ever suggest that you state these facts in a way that was more favorable to *Mr.* Grissett?"

Paddy seethed. Again he thought about breaking a chair, this time over Seaborn's head.

"No, sir," said Hadley.

"Did he tell you what to say?"

He had at least anticipated that one and prepared Hadley for his response. Hadley said, "He told me to tell the truth."

"That's always good advice," Seaborn sighed. "As Mr. Grissett is also an officer of the law, you would expect him to tell the truth as well, am I right?"

"Yes."

"Did he tell you how the accident happened?"

Hadley's voice leveled. Clearly, they were reaching safe ground again. "He said he was making a left turn and saw a pedestrian step off the curb. He thought the pedestrian might walk in front of his vehicle, so he jammed on his brakes."

"Were there any other witnesses around when you arrived?"

"There were people standing around."

"Did anyone who was around when you arrived corroborate the story about the pedestrian?"

Hadley glanced at Paddy. "I didn't talk to any of those people."

"Why not?" Seaborn said.

Hadley paused, again looking to Paddy. For Christ's sake. He'd told Hadley not to look at him. How hard could it be?

"Let's try this," Seaborn said. "Could Officer Grissett have stopped because he saw a new Escalade behind him, because he saw a way to make some fast money by causing a rear-end collision?"

Paddy jumped up. "Objection!" he shouted. "Officer Hadley is not a mind reader. The answer would be pure speculation."

"Sustained."

Seaborn continued. "Officer Hadley, may I ask you a hypothetical question?"

"Yes sir." A smirk grew on Hadley's face.

"Imagine with me that you arrive at a collision scene," Seaborn said in a friendly tone. "A person comes up to you saying, 'Officer, I not only saw the whole thing, but I recorded it on my digital camera. When I viewed it, I didn't see anybody step off the curb to cross the street.' So you look at the video, and sure enough, no pedestrian was stepping off the curb. What do you do then?"

Aw, shit, thought Paddy, as the judge, who'd been leaning back a little, suddenly sat up straight.

"Well," said Hadley, a serious look on his face as he moistened his lips with his tongue. "I'd certainly ask more questions."

"I see," Seaborn said. "Mr. Hadley, is there anything in your experience, either in your capacity as an officer investigating accidents or personally, where the driver in front intentionally caused the accident by jamming on his brakes for no apparent reason, and the person driving behind him in a new and expensive vehicle rear-ends him?"

Up to that point, Grissett had not been particularly attentive to Hadley's testimony, perhaps entertaining himself with the thought of being at the wheel of a new Dodge Ram Charger. He abruptly sat forward and gripped the table so tightly that his knuckles paled.

Paddy jumped to his feet again. "Objection."

The judge looked at him. "On what grounds, Mr. Moran?"

"Uh, on the grounds that it is speculative and highly inflammatory."

The judge cracked a slight smile. "Well, Mr. Moran, unless I'm mistaken, *you* established that Officer Hadley is an expert, so he can respond to a hypothetical in the area of his expertise. As to being highly inflammatory, we don't have a jury here, and I have a pretty high threshold of being inflamed. Objection denied."

Hadley loosened his collar. "Not that I recall."

"Have you ever been in a collision where you were the car in front, and you jammed on your brakes, and the person driving behind you, in a new and expensive vehicle, rear-ended you?"

"Some years ago I was rear-ended."

"Who was your lawyer?"

"George Accurso."

"George Accurso, isn't he in the same office suite as Mr. Moran?"

"Yes."

"Mr. Hadley, did you talk to Attorney Accurso regarding your being a witness in this case?"

Paddy jumped up. "Objection."

"State your grounds, Mr. Moran," the judge said.

"On the grounds that Mr. Seaborn is asking . . . uh . . . Officer Hadley about attorney-client privilege matters."

The judge sighed. "That privilege is not for you to assert, Mr. Moran. Only Officer Hadley may assert his attorney-client privilege."

Paddy looked at Hadley, trying not to appear too obvious.

"I assert my attorney-client privilege on any discussions with my attorney George Accurso."

"That's fine," the judge said. "You don't have to answer questions regarding your discussions with your attorney."

"All right, Officer Hadley," Seaborn said. "Were you aware of anyone who might have made a recording of the accident?"

Turning to his client, sweat beading at his temples, Paddy mouthed, "What the hell is going on?" Grissett held his gaze for a moment and then closed his eyes, turned his head, and shrugged.

Officer Hadley answered, "No, sir."

"Were you aware that Mr. Grissett threatened my client with his authority as a law enforcement officer and tried to get him to make a payment immediately?"

"Objection, Your Honor," Paddy shouted, simultaneously kicking his client under the table.

"Please remember to state your grounds," the judge said, using a mildly reproving tone.

Paddy hesitated. Think. Think. Think. He rifled again through his handbook of objections. He felt all eyes on him. Finding the right page, he said, "Because it assumes facts not in evidence."

"Very good, Mr. Moran. I will sustain your objection."

Seaborn was soon finished with Hadley.

"Mr. Moran?"

"No redirect, Your Honor."

Paddy's next witness was the doctor who saw Grissett for evaluation. The doctor described Grissett's injuries as soft-tissue damage, saying they would not show up on an X-ray or an MRI but nevertheless were painfully and temporarily disabling.

On cross-examination, Seaborn worked at discrediting the doctor by grilling him about testifying for the plaintiffs in numerous rear-end collision cases.

After the doctor's testimony concluded, Paddy announced, "I now call Deputy Constable Ernest Grissett."

Grissett pushed his chair back with a noisy squeak and waddled toward the witness stand. Turning to smile at the judge, he wiped sweat from his face with his uniform sleeve.

The judge, expressionless, nodded back.

He took Grissett through the collision that led to his injuries, his pain and suffering, and the money damages he incurred. He asked, "Did you ever try to 'shake down' Mr. Hunter?"

Grissett said he had not.

"No further questions, Your Honor."

Grissett looked as if he wanted more questions, but Paddy had his head down, intentionally not meeting Grissett's look. Grissett shrugged, put his hands on the wooden railing, and started to rise.

Hunter tried to whisper something to his lawyer, but Seaborn tipped his chair back away from his client. Buttoning the top button of his suit coat, he said, "Oh, please stay where you are, Mr. Grissett. I get to ask you questions now."

Although the heat on a day like today would have bested the HVAC system in the old Harris County Courthouse building built in 1910, the new courthouse's air conditioning was working just fine. Nevertheless, sweat dripped off Paddy's face.

"May I approach the witness?" Seaborn asked.

"You may."

Seaborn's initial questions were innocuous, regarding Grissett's tenure and duties as a deputy, yet his tone was insinuating, at times even threatening. Grissett kept looking toward Paddy. Seaborn followed his gaze and moved to stand between them. Seaborn never gave Paddy the least opening to make objections. At one point Seaborn leaned toward Grissett and, staring into his eyes, nearly touched his nose to Grissett's forehead.

At long last Paddy yelled out, "Objection! For whatever reason Your Honor allowed Mr. Seaborn to approach the witness, it wasn't to get so close that Mr. Seaborn's breath could fog Officer Grissett's eyeglasses."

The judge gave a stern look to Seaborn.

"Keep your distance, Mr. Seaborn, or return to your seat."

Seaborn nodded as he backed up a step. Then, hands clasped behind him, neck turning so his eyes never left Grissett's, he managed to pace and block any eye contact between Paddy and his client. "Miss-ter Grissett," he said. Seaborn's pronunciation made Paddy think he'd been studying Charles Laughton in *Mutiny on the Bounty*.

"Is it your testimony that you did not intentionally slam on your brakes to cause Mr. Hunter's vehicle to collide with your vehicle?"

"It darn sure is," Grissett replied, turning to look at the judge for approval.

"And do you swear under oath you did not attempt to extract a great deal of money from Mr. Hunter at the scene of the incident?"

Grissett tried to look at Paddy. Again, Seaborn blocked him. Grissett reached under the folds of his neck skin, pulled at his collar, and said, "I do."

Seaborn pivoted. "Call your next witness, Mr. Moran," he said. He'd taken the judge's prerogative so firmly and naturally that it went unchallenged. Despite himself, Paddy was impressed, but also anxious. He looked at his legal pad. All the testimony and evidence he'd needed to establish liability on the part of Mr. Hunter and damages suffered by Officer Grissett had been admitted.

"Anything else, Mr. Moran?"

"Attorney's fees, Your Honor."

Before the judge responded, Seaborn rose and said, "Your Honor, if I may?"

"Mr. Seaborn," the judge replied.

"To save everyone's time, we will stipulate that reasonable attorney's fees would be an amount equal to one third the amount of damages, if any, awarded Mr. Grissett, net of any damages awarded to Mr. Hunter. Would that be satisfactory Mr. Moran?"

Paddy paused. That's what he'd wanted. Was it a trick? He didn't want the judge to think he was wasting the court's time, so he responded, "Yes, Mr. Seaborn."

"Well, then," the judge said, "we have agreed on that."

"Thank you," Paddy said. "The plaintiff rests."

"That's it for today. We will reconvene at 8 a.m. Monday to proceed with your case, Mr. Seaborn."

"All rise," the bailiff said in a loud voice. The judge exited to his chambers.

Seaborn slapped a document on Paddy's table. "A settlement agreement. Call me between four and six tomorrow to accept it."

"On Saturday?"

"You don't look like an Orthodox Jew, Mr. Moran."

"How about a Seventh-day Adventist," Paddy responded.

"My guess is you're not that either."

"Why precisely between four and six?"

Seaborn brushed an imaginary speck from his suit coat. He replied in a bored voice, "I have a ten o'clock tee time with my regular foursome at the club. We'll finish and play bridge. My wife's meeting me at the club for dinner at six. It's a simple agreement."

Paddy resisted calling Seaborn a pompous asshole. Instead he said, "Oh, dear. You have such a schedule. How, oh how, will I reach you?"

"I'll have my office number forwarded to my cell phone between four and six. If I don't get your call, I'll spend some time working on the file Sunday."

"On Sunday?" Paddy asked.

"After church, of course."

"Of course. For what it's worth, I didn't figure you for an Orthodox Jew either."

Grissett ignored the not-so-good-natured banter between the lawyers as he reached for the settlement agreement, as Seaborn walked away. "How much?" he asked as he looked. "Ten thousand! Let's take it."

"You fucking, lying shithead. When you brought this case to me, you said you wouldn't settle for less than fifty. Now you're so excited to get ten."

"Well, maybe they got a better lawyer, Yank."

Paddy controlled his anger. "Maybe he's got a better client, dipshit. Something's going on I don't know about. What the fuck is it, Grissett?"

"Damned if I know," Grissett said. He took a container the size and shape of a hockey puck from his back pocket. He put a chaw of Red Man in his cheek. The faint smell of tobacco reminded Paddy of the aroma that had greeted him some mornings as he took possession of an HPD Crown Vic from a guy who had just finished the night shift.

"I think you do know. Let me ask this. Did you try to get him to pay you on the spot?"

Grissett spit into a Styrofoam cup. "Well, you know, people get excited when they're in an accident like that. I don't know for sure what I said."

"Have you and Hadley ever been involved in the same 'accident' before?"

"Hey, buddy. You're supposed to be my lawyer."

"And you're supposed to tell me everything so I won't be surprised."

"Surprised like you were when you didn't do what you were supposed to do to get a jury?"

Paddy clenched his jaw just as the court reporter, a tiny man who made more noise fingering his keyboard than he did talking, re-entered. "Left my keys," he mumbled apologetically.

"No need to whisper," Grissett bellowed. "School's out for the day." The reporter scooped up his keys and scurried out, gently closing the door behind him.

"I'm glad we don't have a jury," Paddy said. "The problem here is possible *per*-jury. The problem here is that instead of a recovery for you, there could be a judgment against you. The problem is that you could lose your fucking job."

"Rest easy, counselor. Everybody does this," said Grissett, spitting more saliva and tobacco juice into his cup. "You oughta know. This ain't your first rear-end rodeo."

True. Paddy realized Grissett probably didn't know this was his first trial. "Yeah, well, not everybody who puts his hand in the cookie jar does it while he's on *Candid Camera*, and if I get the drift of Seaborn's cross-examination, maybe you had an Allen Funt encounter. Seaborn seems pretty darn sure he's got something on you, Miss-ter Grissett. If he has the evidence he acts like he has, we are fucked. But I made a discovery request."

"Then what are you worried about?"

"You tell me," he said firmly, realizing at that moment the stench of sweat wasn't just coming from Grissett. His own shirt and suit coat were drenched. "I've got to review this more closely."

"Why don't we get something to eat? I'm runt-of-the-litter starved," Grissett whined. "Is there any place around here has decent chicken-fried steak?"

"You're on the fucking *Titanic*, and you want to go down with a full stomach?"

"I'm hungry. You coming with me?"

"No!" Paddy yelled.

"Okey dokey," Grissett nodded, spat in his cup again. He began to leave, hesitated, turned toward Paddy, and said, "When do we get the ten thousand?"

Paddy put Seaborn's settlement agreement in one of his briefcases. He knew now, at least, how he was going to be spending his weekend. He looked down at Grissett, his brow furrowed, his expression serious, and said, "I don't trust that white-shoes prick Seaborn. I need to read this fucker carefully."

CHAPTER 7

A VIP

THE WEATHER FORECAST PROMISED comfortable temperatures and low humidity, perfect for Pilar to spend an afternoon outside in the sunshine with Grace. Last Saturday she had pushed the stroller through the lush, shady paths of Sam Houston Park, by its water and ducks, venturing across the street for her first close look at the Art Deco city hall on downtown's western edge. The east side barrio's Moody Park of her childhood was on her punch list for this Saturday.

Marie from Workforce called just as Pilar was packing sunscreen and diapers for the excursion the next day. "I need you to work Saturday."

Pilar resisted, but Marie really leaned on her. "This is not just any job, and I know you're way overqualified for secretarial work, but I need you to do this. Hear me loud; you want to do this. In addition to premium pay, I'll throw in the cost of a babysitter."

"Wow! What's the assignment?"

"Our client is VJ Simon."

"Shut up!" Pilar replied, suppressing a gasp. VJ Simon, the legend. Stories of his success in business were beyond what Pilar could imagine. She didn't know how many buildings in the Medical Center and Museum District bore his name, but there were quite a few. She figured her chances of seeing the great man himself were remote, but just to get inside his company would be very cool.

〰

VJ SIMON DRESSED CASUALLY most days at the office and especially on Saturdays. His laid-back appearance didn't fool his employees, who knew he was all about work and focus. They also knew he was a tad superstitious. When the stakes were high, he did things in a certain way, in a certain order. On major projects, after preparation was deemed complete, VJ always demanded time before a deadline to "sleep on it," a phrase everyone in his organization heard him say all too frequently. What they did not know was that after a key document had been finalized, VJ went to a private place, usually his personal, soundproof restroom, stood in front of a mirror, and read the document out loud from beginning to end. It was part ritual, part simple good sense. In his experience, flaws could almost always be uncovered by reading a document out loud. The English language was one of his joys, and he knew that a bad sentence could sink a great project, especially one that was new and visionary like the one they were working on today, the Downtown-UH corridor venture.

He and his staff were in the early secretive stages of planning a huge, mixed-use development in the Third Ward between downtown and the University of Houston central campus. Two key tracts had become available. It was time to make a presentation to investors who could be relied upon not to reveal the project's existence for as many as five years while the rest of nearly two hundred contiguous acres of land, comprised mostly of small tracts with old, single-family houses, many of which were shuttered and in disrepair, could be acquired for redevelopment. The end result would be a green corridor like nothing the city of Houston had ever seen.

George Mitchell's vision created The Woodlands, a planned township north of Houston, out of a forest. Eventually, The Woodlands became the home to major corporations, small businesses, and the entire spectrum of life for its nearly one hundred thousand residents. But an overnight success it was not.

The Green Corridor wouldn't be either. The investors had to have confidence and staying power for at least two decades before significant returns came, and they had to buy into affordable housing and community facilities for the mostly black, low-income people who would be displaced from the old Third Ward shotgun houses. It would take plenty of political muscle and persuasion to make it happen. Real estate development was not primary in VJ's many successes, but he invited a small group to attend his presentation, people and institutions who had richly enjoyed the fruits of his past visions and who had a shared sense of socially responsible capitalism. He was putting up ten percent of the initial cash. He was expecting commitments for the balance.

Another superstition of VJ's was to hire an outside secretary to work with his regular staff for final preparation of a presentation document for a major project. His explanation was that it was always good to have a fresh pair of eyes. Workforce, Houston's best temp agency, knew that when VJ Simon called they better be sure to send the most qualified person they had.

※

AS INSTRUCTED, Pilar arrived at 9:00 a.m. sharp. Mr. Simon's office manager, Bea McDonough, met her at the door. Smiling and welcoming, she led Pilar to a kitchen and made her a cappuccino using a De'Longhi machine. She then led her to a glossy cubicle made of molded blond wood and told her to sit and wait.

"Mr. Simon and the members of his VIP team are here. Usually, staff has weekends off, but today there's something important and time-sensitive."

"VIP team?"

"Very important project," she said, smiling as if she had said something cute. It was the same smile she'd had while making Pilar a cappuccino. Her tone changed: "On that note, assume everything we do here is confidential. What you will see today is especially top secret, a VIP. Now if I could ask you to sign this confidentiality agreement?"

"Of course," Pilar said. She signed the document without reading it. Handing it back, she asked, "Is it okay to say I worked here?"

"That's okay, but nothing else."

Pilar doubted she would learn anything she would want to drop into a conversation with her friends anyway. What really mattered was that she would be working for VJ Simon, not what she worked on.

Bea showed her the location of the supply room and the printer. She told her to help herself to more coffee anytime and showed her how to operate the elaborate machine. The office was both functional and ultra-modern, yet somehow timeless. Strange lamps and leather and chrome chairs looked like something she had seen in magazines. She felt as if she were in a museum. Carefully hung paintings occupied nearly all the wall space. One in particular caught her eye. It was an oil painting of a woman, surrounded by shapes in blue tones, staring off into the distance. The signature was Picasso, a name she recognized. She wished she knew more so she could fully appreciate seeing such an amazing private collection, one that must have cost a fortune.

After a long, slow hour, during which Pilar checked with the babysitter, read nearly all her unread emails, sent many unsubscribe replies, deleted photos, and practiced using the features of her new mobile phone, Bea popped up again, perky as before. "Now we'll meet Mr. Simon."

Bea bustled. Pilar hurried to keep up. To check herself out, she glanced at her reflection in a mirror that was aligned exactly opposite an identical mirror so that she saw an infinite number of images of herself. They approached a glass-enclosed conference room. Inside, an older man and two young people were sitting at a round table.

"He's got a thing about round tables," Bea said. "Like the knights of King Arthur, you know?" Bea chuckled. "He says it's less intimidating if no one sits at the head."

"That's very chill," Pilar said as she peered through the glass at the back of his head, waiting for him to turn around so she could see his face.

"Let me assure you, no matter what he says or where he sits," Bea said, "he's always at the head of the table. Now go tell him you're here."

Pilar entered the conference room, but VJ Simon was focused on a document and did not see her. Two young people at the table looked anxious. MBAs, Pilar remembered Bea mentioning. One was a bespectacled Asian man wearing a Polo shirt and neatly pressed designer jeans. The other was a woman with intentionally disheveled blond hair and a dark, long-sleeved T-shirt over a slightly longer white one. She wasn't wearing makeup, and her jeans were faded and had worn threadbare spots, which Pilar knew had cost extra. The young woman turned quietly to Pilar and held her finger to her lips. Pilar nodded and stood motionless.

Simon read and made marks, he seemed to be having a conversation with himself. He moved back and forth from his waist. It was almost as if he were praying.

Pilar studied him. His face was tanned and lean, his eyes dark. He was handsome. He had a strong jaw. He didn't look as imposing as she had expected.

He began to speak before he lifted his head. "Okay, guys. Good job. I think this is it. Let's—" At which point he saw Pilar. She noticed that his eyes had widened. Maybe his face had reddened as well. Was it because from his sitting position he couldn't help staring right at her chest? She blushed, backing away slightly, crossing her arms, grasping her biceps.

"Hello," he said, friendly but cautious.

"Hello, I'm Pilar Galt . . . the temp?" She tried to speak in her most professional, businesslike tone. "Ms. McDonough, Bea, told me to let you know I was here to do typing, take dictation, do revisions, whatever needs to be done. Sorry. I'm afraid I interrupted."

VJ self-consciously diverted his line of sight, but she was unnerved from that unguarded moment of his first look. She had grown used to men being dazzled by her, but she couldn't remember ever feeling so awkward about it. Was she reacting this way because of who he was? She hoped not. She liked to think of herself as more badass than that.

"Bea has shown me around, and I'm ready to work," she said firmly.

He rolled his chair back and stood up. "Good, good," he said hurriedly. He introduced himself and Ross and Charlotte, the two MBAs.

Simon was wearing khaki cargo shorts. Pilar noted that he had great legs, especially for an older man—she guessed he was in his fifties. He was fit, but he had a slight paunch.

"Actually," he continued, "your timing was impeccable. We've just finished marking up what we hope will be the last draft. It's ready for you. Do you know how to find it in our document management system?"

"Ms. McDonough showed me, and I've used that system before."

"I'm sure she mentioned that everything is confidential. I cannot stress that enough."

"Yes, sir. Of course."

"Good. If you have any questions, I'll be in my office. It's right next door. Otherwise, just bring it to me when you're finished."

Pilar returned to her desk and pulled the document up on the computer. Bea came in and stood beside her. Pilar asked Bea, "What's he like to work for—Mr. Simon?" She wanted to ask, "Does he hit on all the girls?" but she knew that wouldn't be appropriate.

"He's just wonderful," Bea said almost reverently. Pilar listened as Bea told how he never forgot the children's birthdays, how he was kind and understanding, a good husband—though here Bea's tone shifted. Pilar picked up a vibe that perhaps Bea was not a big fan of Mrs. Simon. "He's just a good man, sometimes a little shy and awkward in unfamiliar situations but with a steel-sharp mind and a big heart. And he *is* a gentleman," she said, as if she had read Pilar's mind.

No question that woman is Team Simon all the way, thought Pilar. She began typing as Bea walked away. Within a few sentences, she saw the need for confidentiality. This was a big project, a very big project. She frowned, determined to get every little detail right. By the time she'd reached the halfway point in the document, Bea was back, standing beside her. "I'll be going now," she said. "If you run into a problem, here's my cell number."

"Thanks, Bea. You're so nice. This is a wonderful place to work."

Bea smiled. "Thank you. I hope we see you again."

"Me too," Pilar said. She hunched forward as she focused on each word, parsed each sentence, and absorbed each concept.

Ross and Charlotte passed in front of her desk, and Charlotte said, "The great man has dismissed us for the weekend. Nice to have met you."

Pilar smiled, appreciative of being acknowledged.

When she finished the document, she carried it to his office, where she paused to study a small decorative case attached to the doorjamb.

"It's a mezuzah," VJ said.

"Actually, I knew that. I was just wondering—"

"I'm half Jewish. I'm not observant but I do continue that tradition. I have a few Vishnu and Sai Baba objects, too."

She smiled, closing the door behind her. As she did, she realized they were probably the only ones left in the office, unless there had been others she hadn't seen.

He was at his desk. In front of him were several stacks with Post-its sticking out. It appeared to her he had been going through mail.

"You have no idea how many pleas for money I get," he said. "From charities, political campaigns. 'Be a sponsor.' 'Buy a table.' Every time I make a contribution, it comes back with a thank-you letter requesting more money."

"Here's the document, Mr. Simon."

VJ was strangely dizzy. He made small talk to disguise his total intoxication with her. He leaned closer to take the paper, fighting the unfamiliar feeling of nearly total distraction. Her beauty. Her carriage. Her figure. Her skin. Her smile. She was wearing a short khaki skirt that displayed her perfect legs and ankles and her exquisite dusky olive skin.

"Thank you," he said.

"Yes, Mr. Simon," she said, sounding business-proper.

"VJ is fine."

"Do you want me to wait while you look it over?"

"You don't need to. I'll call you when I'm done."

"Actually, if you don't mind, I'll wait while you read it. I want to be sure I've got it right."

"Uh," he said. "Well, sure. Sit down, please."

She chose an armchair in front of his desk.

He reviewed the document, feeling her eyes on him. He realized that she had asked to be evaluated, which amused him, but the truth was he respected the impulse. Good workers wanted their efforts to be acknowledged. He noted approvingly that she had clipped the previous draft and a redline to the new one, and he separated them, laying one beside the other. As he scanned from draft to new, checking the changes, he nodded and smiled because each had been correctly made. He came to a page that had a Post-it stuck to it.

"That page," she started. "I hope it's okay to say this. I thought the language was a little awkward. It may just be that I'm not familiar with the subject matter."

He looked at his mark-up. Then he looked at what she had written.

"Hmm. You're right. What you wrote would be much better," he said. He smiled. She smiled back. Earlier her smiles had been perfunctory. This one was real. It lit up the room. She wanted very much not to just be a body and face, especially to someone like him. She wanted to be considered smart. Analytical. Confident.

As he read, she looked around his office. She couldn't quite believe she was sitting here, at the very heart of such a hugely successful operation. A simple space yet terribly tasteful, of course. Elegant and understated. It fit him in the best way.

Photographs lined a coffee table in front of a tan leather couch that looked so soft she thought she might sink into it if she were to sit there. She focused on a photo of a woman, who she guessed was his wife. The woman was not glamorous, but she had a strong sense of presence. The next picture was of an older woman, darker, possibly his mother. In spite of herself, she gasped slightly but audibly when she came to a photo of VJ with the president. It was inscribed by the man himself.

VJ looked up at the noise she made. She felt stupid now, like a school girl. "I'm sorry," she said, straightening.

"No worries. I'm really pleased. You made all the changes correctly. You did a very fine job, Ms. Galt."

She caught his hesitation over the indefinite "Ms.," wondering perhaps if she was married or not.

"Pilar's fine," she said, smiling again.

"I want to go over it one more time. Do you have the time?"

"I'm here as long you need me."

"You don't have to sit here. I'll call you when I'm through."

She knew he was watching her leave the room. She suspected that he knew that she knew. Anxious and happy, she closed the door behind her.

She googled him. Wikipedia reported he was fifty-five and had been born in India. Before she could read further the phone rang.

"This is Pilar Galt," she answered. She heard a chuckle. "I guess you knew that," she said to VJ. "Sorry. That's me at the office."

"No problem. I made a few more changes. Make those, and you'll be done."

"I'll be right there."

When she came back with the new document and a redline, she closed the door again.

He stood when she came in. "Thanks. You can go now. I very much appreciate your work."

"No, please," she said. "Check it over. I want to be absolutely sure I've got it."

He nodded and smiled and sat. After his review, he said, "Perfect. I do appreciate good work. Do you have a regular job?"

"Not now. I was an assistant office manager for a division at Innoveismic. I took a—uh—maternity leave. I've decided not to go back. I'm doing temporary work now." She felt her voice wobbling slightly. "I don't usually take secretarial assignments, but my agency said it was important. I'm glad I did. Believe it or not, temp work is interesting. You learn about different businesses. You meet people." Taking what she knew was a chance, she handed him a Post-it. "These are my cell and home numbers. Call if you need me."

VJ took in her words—"assistant office manager," "Innoveismic," "maternity leave." They were stored but not yet heard, or he would have asked her to fill in the blanks. Instead, he felt overwhelmed again by her presence. The air conditioning had gone off automatically an hour before. He had neglected to call to have it turned back on. She had unbuttoned the blue button-down shirt after she had left his office the last time. What was revealed was a white cotton T-shirt that seemed molded to her breasts and midriff. The bottom flared ever so slightly and somehow was spaced exactly a quarter inch from the top of her skirt, teasingly revealing a band of belly.

"Well, I guess I'll be going," she said.

VJ rose from his chair and moved toward her as if some force compelled him. He imagined holding her close to him, smelling her hair, feeling her skin, kissing her. She had a puzzled look on her face. He stopped as if jarred into a reality he didn't wish to re-enter.

"Ms. . . . uh . . . Pilar, I hope we meet again."

"I better get going Mr. Simon."

"Look, I—I—."

She was in control. It was so odd, this mover and shaker, this world-changer. She carefully exhaled so as not to let him know she was also recovering from the moment.

He straightened his posture, relaxed his shoulders. In a soft yet firm tone, he said, "Look, I don't know anything about you other than you seem to be very special. If you think I can be helpful to you in some way, it would make me happy to be able to do so."

"I really appreciate that," Pilar said, reverting back to a business-like formality. "I may take you up on your offer. It was nice working for you and meeting you."

"Same here. Same here. Let me walk you to the elevator."

"Stay where you are," she said. "I'll be fine on my own."

She knew he wanted her to say something more, but she didn't say a word. She turned on her heel and walked out, not stopping until she was alone in the elevator. Then she allowed herself to exhale heavily. She realized she was shaking.

It wasn't new for a man to be attracted to her, but *this* man?! Her heart pounded as she realized she was as attracted to him as he clearly was to her. He was nice looking. She liked the tone and texture of his not-quite dark skin, his fit body, his presence. She wondered if she was intoxicated by his fame and wealth and power. There *was* that, but there was also something else, a secret sauce, a connection, and a heat, things that all combined resulted in an attraction she had never experienced before.

Maybe he was the most polished and clever sleaze she had ever encountered, but she couldn't believe that. The famous VJ Simon. They weren't done with each other. There was something between them; she was absolutely certain. But what?

CHAPTER 8

CAVEAT EMPTOR

PADDY PLANNED TO WORK as much as he could after court, but exhaustion came over him like a fog. It was all he could do to get home and pass out. By Saturday morning, he woke energized enough to wade into the Ernest Grissett miasma. It wasn't good, but he could face it.

Seaborn's document basically said Hunter would pay Grissett ten thousand dollars, and Grissett would release Hunter from any claims he might have. It said the case would be dismissed. It largely resembled the settlement agreements in his other cases, yet he knew something wasn't right. He couldn't identify the issue. He wondered if his earlier agreements had the same, thus far unidentified, flaw. What was it, though? He turned on the TV and flipped through channels with the volume muted. It was political stuff, mostly, and none of it caught his attention. His mind was on Seaborn's document.

After stewing for an hour, it occurred to him to call his law school Contracts professor, Alexander Porter, a man students called Professor Bingo. Grissett was a tort case, but he knew his Torts professor wasn't the man.

It took him a while to find Bingo's number, but soon his old professor's familiar scratchy voice bellowed.

He gave Bingo a rough outline of the case. Then he sent Seaborn's agreement by email. A few minutes later, Bingo called. "You know, when you were a student, I told you your instincts were good. Well, they still are. First of all, what kind of case is this?"

"Tort."

Bingo was chewing on something crunchy. Probably Cheetos. The man had always loved them. Paddy realized then it was almost noon and all he had eaten was a small yogurt hours ago. He was hungry.

"And you called me because?" Without waiting for an answer, Professor Bingo continued, talking with his mouth full, "Who's the opposing counsel?"

Paddy wondered why he asked the question since the answer was on the signature line of the agreement. "Marlin Seaborn of Walker & Travis."

"I seem to recall you won the Walker & Travis Moot Court Award."

"Yeah, and I seem to recall those . . . they wouldn't give me an interview."

"I also have that recollection." After more crunching, the professor asked, "If you missed something, what would happen?"

Now on the speakerphone, standing at attention, as students were required to do when called on in law school, he said, "My client could sue me because of something in the agreement or not in the agreement."

"And in what area of law would the agreement be?"

"The settlement is a contract, so I guess Contracts."

An empty snack-food bag crinkled. "Bingo! That's why you called me."

The professor could not see him nodding.

"Let's assume your client and the other party sign the settlement agreement, and the other party pays your client the money. Suppose then that your client learns he was actually much more seriously injured than he thought and needs a hundred thousand for medical treatment. Could he go back to the other party for more money?"

"I guess not. The release is pretty explicit. It says 'claims, known and unknown.'"

"Right. Now, if the other party sues your client, claiming your client was at fault and seeking damages against your client—"

"They made that claim here. The agreement says the suit is dismissed."

"Read it carefully again, please, Mr. Moran. What's not there?"

Paddy looked at the agreement again. "It says 'dismissed.'"

"What's not there, Mr. Moran?"

Paddy remembered those moments in law school. "It doesn't say 'dismissed with prejudice.'"

"Very good. You've filled in a number on your card, but it's not bingo yet."

Paddy flexed his toes like a diver waiting to spring off the high board. "There's also a provision that says entering into the agreement is not an admission of liability."

"Another number filled. Keep going," Professor Bingo said. "What else is not there?"

Hunter had lots of money and didn't like being scammed. He was angry and Seaborn liked toying with Paddy. Whoa! He stopped rocking. "I get it. You mean because we released them, but they didn't release us, even though the suit is dismissed, they could refile, and come back against us?"

"Very good. You just need one more number on your card. How would you fix that?"

His heart beat quickly. "I would get them to release us also and have the suit dismissed with prejudice."

"Bingo! We have a winner."

"And if they won't, I have to tell my client what the risk is."

"Which is?"

"What could happen to him if the other party doesn't release him?"

"Ding! Ding! Ding! And how would you tell your client?"

"In writing."

"Okay, Mr. Moran. Good luck. I liked hearing from you."

The call ended.

What Paddy loved about the professor was that he never actually answered a question. He kept asking questions until bing, bang, bingo! Paddy called Grissett, who answered with a throng of loud voices behind his.

"Where are you?"

"I was celebrating the settlement."

"Yeah, well, not so fast. I'm going to email you two documents. I want to discuss them with you before I call Seaborn."

"Why two?"

"Because if you sign the agreement that pretentious asshole gave us, he will pay you ten thousand dollars and then, almost as surely as day follows night, turn around and sue your fat ass for a lot more, and I won't be your lawyer in that suit. If you want to take what he offered, one document is for you to release me from any claims you might have when he sues you again. The other is a revised document that I would be comfortable for you to sign."

"You got my attention," Grissett said. "I get it. Wait a second."

Paddy heard Grissett yell, "Separate checks!" Then, "Okay, Moran. Just take care of it however you want."

He sent a confirming email to Grissett. Then he emailed an amended settlement to Seaborn just after noon. For the next four hours, he worked out at the gym. At precisely four o'clock, he called Seaborn's direct dial number. The phone stopped ringing, there were some clicks, and then he heard Seaborn's voice say, "This is Marlin Seaborn," like that was a big deal.

"This is Patrick Moran," he responded, aping Seaborn.

"What's this I'm reading, Moran?" he said.

"We'll only settle with mutual release and dismissal with prejudice."

"I can read. I meant why would you insist on that?"

Big-firm jerk. "Well, you're the one who brought up religion. It would be against a basic tenet of my religion to do it otherwise."

"How interesting. And what is that tenet, Mr. Moran."

"Always cover my ass."

"I have to confess, Mr. Moran, I find it hard to disagree with that sentiment. However, the deal was take it or leave it, just as I presented it."

"We leave it."

Seaborn hung up.

He braced himself for another call with Grissett.

"It was just as I suspected. That fuckhead was trying to trap us. He wouldn't agree to mutual releases. Be back in court Monday morning. And once again—I mean it—is there something you haven't told me?"

After a long pause, he replied, "Nada, counselor." Grissett sounded like his mouth was full of something.

Saturday night and all day Sunday Paddy got up to speed on the rules of evidence for electronic video and audio recordings. Seaborn had something, and it had to be bad. Paddy kept a muted TV on because he liked the slight distraction. Sunday evening, as he was about to leave to pick up Chinese takeout, an image on the screen caught his eye. He unmuted. It was old footage of Lyndon Johnson, that great Texan, glad-handing some senator in the Oval Office. Paddy could almost feel the strength of LBJ's grip, the heat of his breath as he pulled the senator close and leaned down into his face, smiling as you knew he was threatening him. That was how LBJ worked close up—physical intimidation, a steel fist in a velvet glove.

Paddy reached forward, pretending to take Seaborn's hand. He squeezed so tightly his fingers ached. Leaning forward and down, he smiled and said, "We'll work this out, Mr. Seaborn. I'm sure of it."

CHAPTER 9

A TRIAL SEMINAR

AT 7:56 A.M. MONDAY MORNING, Grissett entered the courtroom, toothpick in mouth. "How you holdin' up, boy?"

"How am *I* holding up?" Paddy said through clenched teeth. He wondered how Grissett could be up at all. Grissett's breath smelled worse than a sticky bar floor on a Sunday morning, a smell Paddy recalled from his twenties.

Hunter, on the other hand, was dressed elegantly and conservatively: Hickey Freeman suit, shirt, and tie and Gucci loafers.

At precisely 8 a.m., the bailiff entered the court and said, "All rise." The judge sat in his bench and motioned for everyone to sit down. "Mr. Seaborn."

Seaborn rose and announced, "Your Honor, I call to the stand Nolan Kerbow."

Paddy whispered to Grissett, "Who is Nolan Kerbow?"

"Beats the shit outta me," Grissett said quietly. "Shouldn't you know who his witnesses are going to be?"

Paddy flinched. "Objection. Mr. Kerbow wasn't on the witness list."

"That's true," a smug Seaborn said. "How were we to know Mr. Grissett wasn't going to tell the truth, requiring us to call impeachment witnesses, Mr. Kerbow being the first? The rules do not require us to give notice of impeachment witnesses."

The judge nodded and waved his hand for Seaborn to continue.

Nolan Kerbow, as it turned out, was an architect. Doing site research for a major development, he'd been recording video at the southwest corner of Buffalo Speedway and Westheimer when the collision occurred.

"And what did the video show?" Seaborn asked.

Paddy jumped up. "Objection. Because—"

"Because it is hearsay," the judge interrupted, "and it is not the best evidence? Because the video would be the best evidence?"

"Yes, Your Honor, that's right."

"Well, thank you, Mr. Moran. I think I'll sustain your objection. Or was it mine?"

"Not a problem, Your Honor," Seaborn said. "We would like to introduce the video and show it to the court."

"Objection," Paddy said, grasping.

"Because it hasn't been authenticated, Mr. Moran?" the judge asked. "Let *me* ask a few questions of Mr. Kerbow." He turned to Kerbow who looked suddenly nervous. "Mr. Kerbow, tell the court how the camera came into Mr. Hunter's possession."

"I stayed around because I had work to finish. I decided to approach Mr. Hunter when the policeman and the driver left."

"You mean you didn't tell the policeman you had a video of the accident?" the judge asked.

Kerbow tucked his chin down and shook his head.

"Is that a no, Mr. Kerbow?" the judge snapped.

"It is a no, Your Honor."

"How much did Mr. Hunter pay you?"

"Two thousand dollars."

The judge whistled through his teeth. "What kind of camera?"

"It was a PowerShot."

"What did you pay for it?"

"With the memory card, it cost about four hundred dollars. Mr. Hunter said he wanted to make up for any inconvenience the loss of my camera caused me."

"Was two thousand dollars the only amount discussed?"

Kerbow hesitated. "No, Your Honor."

"Tell the court, Mr. Kerbow."

"Actually, I asked him to pay me three thousand dollars." Kerbow fixed his eyes on his lap.

"You didn't give the video to the police because you thought it would be worth something to Mr. Hunter?"

Kerbow blushed. "That is correct, Your Honor."

Paddy rose. With the greatest tone of righteous indignation he could muster, he said, "Your Honor, I object to the introduction of the evidence because Mr. Kerbow withheld evidence from a police investigation for his own personal profit. It would be against public policy to admit the evidence."

"That's interesting, Mr. Moran," the judge said, "and very perspicacious of you. Very. In fact, I admire the high-mindedness of your objection and on general legal principles I would be inclined to sustain it. But I sense some relevant truth may be forthcoming that may reveal some less lofty action on the part of your client. I will rule on the objection later. If I sustain I will disregard anything that comes in relating to the video."

Over the next hour, Paddy watched Seaborn establish the credibility of a forensic digital photographer who authenticated the video. It was like watching a boat sink from inside the cabin. All that was left was to drown. Paddy knew he'd been had. Grissett let Paddy know he knew it too by grinding the heel of his boot onto Paddy's toe, using his ample but seldom exercised core for strength. Paddy nearly yelped but ground his teeth instead. What worried him was the Wheeler boots he'd splurged on. The idea was that they'd persuade prospective clients he was successful. He pushed his chair back a little to glance at them and was relieved to see Grissett hadn't done any visible damage.

"Let it roll," the judge said.

The video showed the corner where Grissett had said a pedestrian stepped off the curb to cross the street. Two people were about four feet from the corner, standing well away from the curb at a bus stop. The corner was then obscured as Grissett's truck made the turn off Westheimer. Hunter's shiny, new Escalade followed close behind. Grissett slammed on his brakes. The video then zoomed in. Although grainy, one could actually see Grissett's and Hunter's faces. When it was replayed, slowly, Grissett appeared to be looking in his rearview mirror just before he jammed on his brakes. Hunter, at that same moment, appeared to be looking west on Westheimer. The Escalade slammed into Grissett's pickup. The two people who had been standing at the bus stop reappeared and rushed forward to get a closer look, shielding their eyes from the sun. One of them stepped close to the curb.

Afterwards, Paddy asked for a copy and a recess. "Your Honor, it would only be fair for me to at least take a careful look at this video. I mean, how many times have people looked at the Zapruder film and still disagree on what they see?"

"Mr. Moran, that's a reasonable request and nicely argued. Since it's nearly lunchtime, I'll give you an hour and a half. I'll tell you what. Make it two hours." The judge banged his gavel and rose from his chair.

Following the bailiff's "All rise," no one spoke. Hunter had a smug smile on his face. Grissett was glowering. Seaborn's assistant put his materials on a dolly and wheeled them out. Paddy remained in his seat until the courtroom was again empty except for him and his client.

Grissett shouted, "Hey, Mr. Patrick Moron! You fucked up big by not knowing about the dang video in advance!"

Paddy grabbed Grissett by the back of his neck, squeezing the loose flesh with his massive hand so that for the first time in years, if ever, the skin at the front of Grissett's neck was pulled so tight his Adam's apple appeared. It was a move Paddy hadn't made since leaving the force. Ten inches separated his face from Grissett's, who put a hand between them. Without loosening his grip or redirecting his gaze, Paddy said, "If you ever tell me again I did something wrong because I didn't find out in advance that you fucking lied to me, you will find out what I learned from the Brooklyn Mafia about dealing with double-crossers, but you won't know it for long."

Grissett trembled, nodding.

"Now I'm going to run to my office and try to figure out how to repair the damage. I know you can't run. You walk to my office, sit in the reception area, and wait until I call you to come into *my* office. Don't even think about stopping for lunch first."

Grissett dropped back in his chair. "Take it easy. You worry too much."

"You want to know what I'm worried about? I'll tell you, you sorry sack of shit. I'm worried that somehow they'll nail my ass because they'll not believe me when I say that you weren't square with me, and I'll lose my ticket to practice law. My career as a lawyer will be over."

Grissett cocked his head, suddenly energized. "Are you saying that your duty to me isn't as important as you takin' care of yourself?"

"I'm saying that in a heartbeat, you worthless motherfucker."

"Well, Brother Moran, you're right. If I get fucked, your ticket, as you call it, will be worth as much to you as a roadkill raccoon. Don't think I won't have them laughin' at your ass for fucking up over not having a jury, not knowing who their witnesses were gonna be, and not even seein' their video evidence. There's lots you can overcome, but you can't overcome people thinking you're a dumb ass. Yeah, they'll call you Paddy Moron, the clown of the courtroom. I like it. Paddy Moron has a nice catch to it, Yank. I think it'll stick."

Grissett knew he had flashed a card he would never play. For a moment both men were quiet. In that moment they both sensed that whatever happened from this point on, they were as one.

"What do you want me to do?" Grissett asked.

Paddy responded unguarded, his body slumped. "I don't know. I would almost approach the judge and tell him . . . Shit, I don't know." He paused. "Goin' in, I wanted to win. I was going to show that stuck-up prick Seaborn what a street-smart guy like me could do with him. Now, it isn't about losing. That seems to be the least of my—" Paddy started to say "fears," but he wouldn't let the word out of his mouth. Grissett shifted in his chair.

They packed up Paddy's cart. As Grissett held the door for him, Paddy said, "And about Paddy Moron, I sure hope I don't have to push that fat belly of yours into a puddle of maple syrup, pour corn flakes on you, and roll you into a pile of army ants."

This time Grissett smiled. He gave a salute. Paddy gave him a "we're-in-this-together" smile, for the first time actually feeling close to Grissett. Then he headed briskly to his office. Grissett followed as quickly as he could.

〰〰

WHEN THE TRIAL RESUMED, Seaborn called Hunter as a witness. Hunter testified that when he got out of his Escalade, Grissett flashed his badge and asked him, "Do you want to take care of this the easy way or the hard way?"

Paddy turned to his client, but Grissett didn't meet Paddy's eye contact.

Hunter testified Grissett said, "Pay me twenty-five thousand, and we can go our merry ways." Hunter said his response was "I won't put up with blackmail." To that he said Grissett replied, "Have it your way, pilgrim."

Hunter testified Officer Hadley was playing on Mr. Grissett's Team. Paddy's objection was sustained. Hunter testified that Officer Hadley said Grissett was a very well-respected law enforcement officer, which to Hunter meant, "Buddy, play ball or you'll have serious trouble."

Paddy objected. The judge sustained.

When Seaborn finished, Paddy rose to cross-examine. "May I approach the witness, Your Honor? He isn't wearing glasses, so I won't be fogging anything up."

The judge laughed. "Just keep a proper distance, Mr. Moran."

"Would you consider yourself a careful driver?"

"Yes, very careful."

Paddy positioned himself to block Hunter from being able to see Seaborn. "Does a careful driver exceed the speed limit?"

Hunter responded without hesitation, "One can be a careful driver and exceed the speed limit depending on the traffic and weather."

"People of your station in life, do they get to choose when the rules are applicable to them?"

Hunter craned his neck, trying to find Seaborn as Seaborn stood, saying, "Objection."

"Sustained."

"Have you ever received a citation for speeding?" Paddy asked.

"I've been driving more than thirty years. I've received a citation for speeding."

Paddy held up a piece of paper. "Mr. Hunter, haven't you received three citations for speeding *since* the collision with Officer Grissett?"

"I believe Mr. Grissett had his police friends looking out for me."

"Objection," Paddy said. "Not responsive."

"Answer, Mr. Hunter," the judge ordered.

Hunter gritted his teeth, squirmed in the witness chair, and said, "Yes, I have received three citations since the incident."

"And they're all set for trial. Is that not right, Mr. Hunter?"

"Yes."

"Did you set them for trial because you did not want to be found guilty of speeding before *this* trial?"

Seaborn rose and said, "Ob-jection."

Paddy did not wait for the ruling; he pressed on with his next question. "Please assume, for the sake of argument, that Officer Grissett did have a reason to apply his brakes suddenly. You still would have hit him, wouldn't you?"

"I think I would have seen whatever he saw and braked also."

"You think so, but you don't know. How new was your Escalade?"

"I had it about a week."

"I'll bet you were pretty steamed that a brand new, expensive vehicle like that had been damaged."

"Yes, I was."

"You would have been angry whether it was your fault or someone else's fault. Isn't that right?"

"I suppose."

"Are you a wealthy man, Mr. Hunter?"

Seaborn rose. "I object, Your Honor. Relevance."

The judge looked at Paddy.

"Your Honor, the relevance is this: If Mr. Hunter is wealthy, then a wealthy man can spend the fight out of a poor man like Officer Grissett if he is angry enough."

"I'll allow."

"Mr. Hunter, is your net worth more than ten million dollars?"

"Yes."

"No further questions." Paddy returned to his chair. Grissett gave him a pat on his shoulder.

After Hunter's testimony, Seaborn rested his case. The judge asked Paddy if he had anything to present in rebuttal. Paddy had gone over the video more than twenty times during the recess. He'd made Grissett watch the video alongside him to prep him on a new line of questioning. "Yes, Your Honor," Paddy said, rising to his feet. "I would like to recall my client, Deputy Grissett."

"Deputy Grissett," the judge said. Paddy hoped it was a good omen that the judge called him "Deputy" and not "Mister."

Grissett sat in the witness stand.

"Remember, Deputy Grissett, you're still under oath," Paddy said.

"Yes sir."

"Now, you stated you slammed on your brakes because a pedestrian was about to step off the curb. Is that correct?"

"Yes sir, that's what I said." Grissett's tone had much less bravado than when he'd testified before.

"But the video clearly shows there was no pedestrian stepping off the curb. Were you lying before?"

"No sir."

"Then how do you explain it?"

"Darned if I know." Grissett rubbed the back of his neck. "I thought I saw someone about to step off the corner. Maybe I thought one of those people standing for the bus was going to crost the street. All I can tell you is I saw or felt something that made me slam on the brakes."

"The video shows you looking in your rearview mirror before you put on your brakes. Why did you do that?"

"Well, you got to understand everything happened quickly. Somethin' made me think I had to hit the brakes. I knew someone was behind me. I was hoping he wasn't so close that he couldn't stop if I did."

"Officer Grissett, how did you know how close Mr. Hunter's car was behind yours?"

"I looked in the rearview mirror."

"No further questions."

Seaborn rose. "Mr. Grissett, Friday you swore under oath a pedestrian was stepping off the corner to cross in front of you and that was why you slammed on the brakes. This morning you are saying you thought someone was about to cross the street—make that 'crost' the street. What is the difference between last Friday afternoon and this morning, other than watching the video that caught you lying?"

Grissett turned red. He took three deep breaths. Then he answered just as Paddy had instructed him to should that question be asked. "Mr. Seaborn, I can see how you'd want the judge to think that, but my eyes must have played tricks on me. I looked at that video some, and I don't know. I'm just sayin' I hit the brakes because I was afraid I was gonna hit a pedestrian."

"'You're just sayin,'" Seaborn mimicked. "And you never told Mr. Hunter that if he didn't pay you twenty-five thousand right away, he was going to have a problem."

"I told him that I wouldn't have transportation to get to work and that since he was clearly at fault, if he would settle with me right away it might be cheaper for him, and I could get a loaner while my pickup was getting fixed. He must have misunderstood me. And if you think twenty-five thousand is so much money, why did you demand seventy-five thousand for me to pay to settle your counterclaim?"

"Objection," Seaborn yelled.

The judge waited as he fought back a smile. "The court will disregard Officer Grissett's last comment as being unresponsive."

With disdain, Seaborn said, "No further questions."

Both parties waived closing arguments. The judge ordered a one-hour recess.

Seaborn shoved his files into his briefcase and locked it. Then he and Hunter strode from the courtroom. Grissett got up slowly. He walked heavily to the door.

Paddy said, "Good job, Ernest Grissett."

He could see that Grissett was grateful for his approval. His client pursed his lips, nodded, and said, "You're no moron, Moran."

Paddy stayed in the courtroom alone. He tried not to think. He paced. He looked at oil portraits of former judges who had served in the same court hanging on the walls. He packed everything he had brought.

Grissett returned a few minutes before Seaborn and Hunter.

Precisely one hour after the judge had left the courtroom, the bailiff ordered everyone to rise. After they had taken their seats, the judge said, "Mr. Seaborn, you did a fine job of not just defending against a rear-end collision case, but also advocating an affirmative recovery for your client."

"And Mr. Moran, I was thinking that you probably learned more today than you did in any ten classes in law school. I was even wondering, if I were you, how I would muster enough courage to come back to this court-room. I truly admire how you picked yourself up and probably worked with your client so that when he took the stand this afternoon his testimony was pretty credible. In any event it was a lot closer to what happened and how it happened than I expected to hear. Today won't be your finest day, but, and you'll probably be unhappy to hear this, it's also not likely to be your worst. My guess is all that is yet to come."

Paddy looked at his feet, his hands clasped behind him.

"I will also tell you to recognize that this case should be a pivotal moment in your career. You have the industry, the intelligence, and the resourcefulness to be a very fine lawyer, but learn from this experience that lawyers have to make choices." He looked down and said sternly, "Make good choices, Mr. Moran."

Looking at the judge, Paddy nodded and said, "With the deepest respect, thank you, Your Honor. I will remember your words." Paddy told himself he *would* remember the judge's words. He reflected how he had taken a matter he knew was wrong, for a client he didn't like or respect. He vowed to himself not to make those mistakes again.

The judge said, "Mr. Hunter, I do feel badly for you. You will probably ask yourself time and again how you happened to be at the wrong place at so much the wrong time and, without me saying whether I believe you were or were not wronged, you had a very radicalizing experience."

To Grissett, he said, "Let me say I would expect more from an officer of the law."

The judge paused. "Gentlemen, I've given this careful thought. Officer Grissett, as to your case against Mr. Hunter, I find that you did not sustain your burden of proving that Mr. Hunter was at fault. You'll take nothing, and you won't be awarded attorneys' fees."

Grissett nodded.

"This is not the first instance my colleagues and I have observed a law enforcement officer being in the front car of a questionable rear-end collision. Any degree of frequency of claims of this nature is disturbing. My fellow judges and I will henceforth be wary of cases like this and, at least from this point forward," he turned his head to look at Paddy, "be wary of the lawyers who take those cases."

The judge paused. In a hushed voice, he said, "Gentlemen, I'm instructing the court reporter not to record what I am about to say. Do I have your agreement that what I am about to say is not only off the record, but was never said?"

Paddy nodded, completely in fear of vomiting right there.

Grissett shifted from one leg to the other, his huge belly straining not to burst the two buttons of his khaki shirt just above his belt. Seeing Paddy nod, he nodded too.

Hunter, for the first time in the entire proceedings, lost his carriage of arrogance and looked up to the judge as if he were waiting for a communion wafer from a priest at St. John's Episcopal Church.

Seaborn maintained his posture. Only he knew his heart was pounding. From the moment the judge complimented him, he understood that whatever was coming wasn't going to satisfy him.

The judge spoke in a hushed tone. "Now, let me tell you that if either side appeals this case or there is a retrial, you better hope I have been struck by lightning, because whoever asks for the new trial is going to have his ass handed to him on a platter. Do we understand each other?"

Everyone nodded in unison.

"Back on the record. I find in favor of the cross-plaintiff, Mr. Hunter."

Paddy's heart stopped. His stomach went into a clinch.

Seaborn smiled confidently and smugly.

"I award Mr. Hunter the sum of three dollars in actual damages, three dollars in punitive damages, and two dollars in attorneys' fees." Then he banged his gavel and said in a loud voice, "Next case."

Turning to walk out with his client, Seaborn clasped Hunter's shoulder, pulling him close. "Great victory." Hunter, who had spent more than fifty thousand with Seaborn and his firm, did not express agreement.

Grissett said to Paddy, "Thank you, counselor." Paddy nodded several times. He said nothing. Lesson learned.

PART

TWO

CHAPTER 10

MARGOT SHEAR

PADDY PULLED ON SHORTS, a worn HPD T-shirt, and running shoes and stepped out into a muggy, eighty-degree, mid-November morning. His hangover had delayed his starting time, but Crystal, or whatever her real name was, had been great last night. Groggy, he laughed, remembering lines from an old Fats Domino song:

> *Sunday mornin' my head is bad*
>
> *Though, it worth it*
>
> *For good times that I've had*
>
> *But I've got to get my rest*
>
> *'Cause Monday is a mess*

Docket call wasn't until 8:30 a.m. Monday. He could handle that. However, getting to Carl's Tavern today in time to meet Jed for the Texans' noontime kickoff was going to be a struggle.

When he arrived, Jed pulled him aside. "Expect a call from Margot Shear," Jed said. "She's a Highland Park girl from Dallas, a cut above your usual clients. So mind your manners, you crude asshole, because I think her case will be great for both of you."

Highland Park didn't mean much to Paddy. An image of Brooklyn's Borough Park popped into his mind. He guessed Highland Park didn't have a lot of Hasidic Jews walking around wearing black hats and long coats.

What caught his attention was "a cut above your usual clients." Paddy was more than ready for that. He'd vowed to himself that he wouldn't work with any more lowlifes. No more Deputy Grissetts. No more scams. For months after the Grissett trial, he had beaten himself up. When the cop who sent him the original rear-end case called to say he was going to refer someone to him who had been badly hurt in a real accident and that he would expect twenty percent of his fee, Paddy responded, "You ain't a lawyer, buddy. I can't split my fees with you." The referral never came, and Paddy was fine with that.

He was coming on two years of practicing, and he'd begun focusing on upgrading his clientele. He met respected lawyers with good practices by getting involved in bar activities. Toastmasters gave him experience speaking as well as meeting white-collar people. Greater Houston Partnership breakfasts gave him an opportunity to hobnob with movers and shakers. He hadn't gotten a break yet, but he was confident networking would produce. Maybe Jed's Margot Shear would be a chance to break through.

"She's lived pretty well," Jed said. "My guess, though, is she's been through tough times. She teaches at a private school, but recently she opened a Saturdays-by-appointment-only jewelry store in an office building. That's how I met her. She said she needed security because she was selling estate pieces. When people she didn't know came in, I could tell she was selling her own stuff. I don't know the details of her case. I do know she could use some money."

"Who couldn't?" Paddy said. "Thanks. I'll take good care of her." He paused, then asked, "How're things going with Jessie?"

"I'll let you judge for yourself. How about coming over for dinner Tuesday?"

"You bet. That's the best invitation I've had in a long time. When did you move back?"

"Last week. I was going to tell you today. For us to stay together and be happy, our relationship will always be a work in progress. I'm committed to being a much better husband."

"What kind of lawyer am I? I can't even make an uncontested divorce stick."

"You're a good lawyer," Jed replied. "The best."

When he returned to his apartment, Paddy typed "Highland Park" into the search bar. He learned it was the most exclusive residential area in Dallas, much like River Oaks in Houston, maybe even more so. Eagerly anticipating her call, he frequently looked at his new iPhone to see if he had missed any. Finally, Tuesday mid-morning she called and made an appointment.

Wednesday was one of those unseasonably, incredibly humid Houston days, with air outside so heavy it felt like an added dose of gravity dragging everything down—clothes, hairdos, attitudes—even if one's encounter with it was as brief as a one-block walk from an air-conditioned car to an air-conditioned building. No matter how brief the encounter, nothing could prevent the immediate condensation that coated lenses on glasses as one exited one's car.

Margot Shear, however, looked like she was in early autumn in New York. Her short, feathered, brown hair perfectly framed her high cheekbones and smooth forehead. She wore a knee-length, pale cotton skirt and white clogs with three-inch cork heels. Her bare legs were tan, athletic. Remarkably, no sweat glistened anywhere her skin showed. A peasant blouse revealed, without calling too much attention, her shapely modest breasts. A classy broad.

She sat across from Paddy, tossed her sunglasses into a large purse, and began relating the facts of the case. Six months before, she'd gone to the emergency room of one of Houston's most prestigious not-for-profit hospitals in the Texas Medical Center with severe chest pains that could have been symptomatic of a heart attack. She presented to admissions a printed list of all her medications, names of her physicians, and her medical history. Written in all caps across the cover page, was the phrase ALLERGIC TO CODEINE.

After she was admitted, the ER doctor ordered the nurse to give her a codeine-based drug for pain. "My body reacted violently, Mr. Moran. I could have died." She recovered with no lasting effects, but she was angry. "Now, I'd like a different sort of violent reaction," she said. "I want to sue." Her nostrils flared. Her eyes flashed.

"Well, ma'am, it sounds like the doctor would definitely be liable. That's the good news. The bad news, real wins have two parts. One is liability, which looks easy to prove. The other is damages. From what you're saying, it doesn't sound like I can make it add up to much. How much were you expecting?"

She leaned forward, her eyes now slits. "Let me get this right. You're telling me that because I didn't die or become brain damaged, I can't get much from them? They should pay *something*. Would fifty thousand dollars be enough to teach them a lesson?"

His heart was pumping. His chest was tight. "Ma'am, on the one hand, it's not likely we'll get anything. On the other hand, what the hell, let's go for it. But remember, I can't promise you anything other than I'll bust my ass trying."

Margot smiled. "Why, Mr. Moran, you have such a way with words. I believe you will, as you say, 'bust your ass trying.' Jed told me you were smart and hungry." With her elbows on the desk, she rested her chin on the smooth backs of her hands. Fluttering her eyelids, perfectly imitating Vivien Leigh as Scarlett O'Hara, she said, tone high and sweet, "Besides, I'm counting on that money for my Christmas shopping at Van Cleef & Arpels."

Paddy was eager for a real challenge, a chance to ramp up his practice into a high-dollar arena. A search of the defendant index of suits filed in Harris County revealed Margot's ER doctor had been sued multiple times for malpractice, with egregious medical errors claimed. Paddy noticed each alleged malpractice took place at a different hospital. Paddy figured the doc would get canned when an incident happened and move on. Lucky for the doc, Houston had so many hospitals. Not so lucky for the patients.

Paddy hired a private investigator, who was able to quickly gather information. "Your ER doctor is a cokehead and a drunk. Twice he's been to the fancy dry-out center in Atlanta that specializes in addicted MDs. Always checked out early. He's had complaints, but his license has never been taken away or even suspended. According to his credit card charges, your guy *always* stopped at the same bar before he went on duty, including, you would be interested to know, the day of the incident."

Paddy cracked his knuckles and whistled. "Good work, buddy. Thanks for the gift basket, packed full of delicious evidence."

After the giddiness of knowing he had the doctor nailed for liability purposes—a drunk and drug addict who repeatedly committed malpractice—Paddy's stomach clenched. The fucker had to be broke.

A successful plaintiff's case had three elements, not just two. Paddy would first have to prove liability. Margot would then be awarded damages. Finally, she would collect—if there was anything available to collect. His research revealed that collecting judgments against doctors rarely yielded a big payday. Many docs have mechanisms in place so that a judgment creditor can't reach their assets. Plus, they generally have only enough medical malpractice insurance to satisfy hospital requirements for staff privileges and their legal fees come out of that. There's usually little or nothing for the victim of malpractice.

Paddy slammed his fist on his desk. He stormed out of his office and went to Carl's. Jed met him there.

"Your lady, Margot," Paddy said. "She has a great case, but the doctor who nearly killed her is probably judgment proof." He related the facts to Jed.

"Shouldn't the hospital be liable? They have plenty of money."

"Good question. You just got a free beer. I'll work on that angle."

Jed had a good idea. Go after the deep pockets, the hospital. Paddy sorted the facts in his mind. The doctor had only been on staff for a week when he treated Margot. The hospital's defense would be that they didn't know his history. That's true. Unless there had been another incident with the doc before Margot's, they would have no knowledge of his issues. But wasn't it their job to know his history? Wasn't it negligent not to look into his background before putting a doctor to work in the ER?

He figured a punitive damages award would be easier, but the law required a relationship of the "punies" to the actual damages. Translating Margot's pain and suffering into significant dollar damages was a biggie. But how, he kept asking himself, could he make his beautiful, well-connected client happy?

He prepared a thorough presentation of the facts, emphasizing the doctor's history and the hospital's failure to make a due diligence investigation before taking him on. He'd figure out how to see the hospital's CEO and apply pressure and go from there.

Paddy wrangled an appointment by sweet talking the assistant to the hospital's CEO. He stood before the CEO feeling like an unwanted salesman. He presented her with his memorandum with copies of public records attached, and said, "The hospital has a choice. Settle now on my terms or have a *very* public lawsuit that is certain to get the attention of others who have been treated at your hospital by the same doctor. Or," he paused, "by their survivors."

The CEO waved the back of her hand as if shooing away a mosquito. "You'll hear from our attorney."

A week later, Paddy received a call from the hospital's in-house counsel, who began the conversation by saying, "Mr. Moran, the hospital has discharged the doctor and reported him to the state board. Thanks for calling his problems to our attention. We're glad your client didn't suffer any harm."

"You're quite welcome and nice try. The problem is, the hospital never should have put Doctor Guzzle Snort in the ER in the first place. And my client most certainly did suffer harm. It just wasn't permanent. Don't think canning the doctor is going to make us stop here."

The counsel sighed. "Okay, Mr. Moran. Come to my office. We'll talk."

The counsel's sigh told Paddy his pressure had been effective. He could only guess what skeletons the hospital feared might be coming out of the closet, or maybe, more precisely, the morgue.

Elated, Paddy called Margot to update her. "I feel good about the chances to recover something."

"How much?"

He laughed. "I don't know. Something. Don't go to Van Cleef & Arpels any time soon." Maybe he shouldn't have said anything. Managing her expectations might turn out to be a job. He had to manage his own expectations as well. Nothing was certain.

Paddy didn't tell Margot the amount of his "demand," the quaint term Texas trial lawyers used for a plaintiff's settlement offer. Though his gut said he made the right choice, he also knew making such a high demand came with risks, the biggest of which was it could piss them off, enough so that they would refuse to settle for any amount and fight the case. But he had to reach high, didn't he? Reach high and hope for a decent fraction of what he demanded.

Before hanging up, he said, "Wish me luck."

"Win or lose," she said, "I'll tell my friends how good you are. Getting your foot in the door was huge."

〰〰

AT THE MEETING, Paddy demanded a million and a half dollars.

The in-house counsel looked as if he was about to go into cardiac arrest. "That's preposterous," he sputtered. "I'm turning this over to outside counsel."

"When you do that, be sure to tell them I plan to file suit in two weeks if we haven't settled by then."

Paddy paused as he turned to leave. "Your call," he said, willing himself to look cool.

CHAPTER 11

PILAR MAKES A CALL

"RONNIE WENT BERSERK," Pilar told Sunny, cradling the phone to her ear as she eyed Grace, who was on the verge of falling asleep. "He screamed, 'How do I even know she's mine? I should have a paternity test! I bet you'll be knocked up by your boss within a week of getting hired at your next job.'"

"All because you told him the child support was late?"

"Yep. I could hear him breaking things, so I hung up. My attorney filed a restraining order. She's a ball buster, but she's my ball buster."

Pilar remembered Paddy Moran's description of her attorney, Margaret Walden. It had worked out as well as those things can.

"I can't believe I was ever with him."

"I can't believe you married him. You could have had an abortion."

Pilar suddenly went cold. "Goodbye," she said, throwing her phone down. She looked over at Grace, and her face softened. Pilar closed her eyes, took a deep breath, opened them, and focused on her sleeping child. It was a pity Ronnie was the father, but Grace was the best thing that had ever happened to her. To hell with Sunny and her big mouth. But she knew she couldn't stay mad at Sunny, totally unfiltered, dear, dear Sunny, who said what came to her. The truth is she did have a choice. She didn't make that choice, but the choice was hers to make. And it wasn't like Pilar had any other true friends. Who else was always there to catch her? No one.

They'd both had it tough coming up—Pilar from the barrios and Sunny from a series of white-trash apartment complexes in the near north side. Pilar realized that people seeing them together probably couldn't imagine what they had in common. They certainly gave off different vibes. As soon as the fashion magazines hit the stands, Pilar began quests for knock-offs of the best designs. She knew she looked exactly right wherever she went. Sunny's look was usually over the top, like she was an extra in *Sordid Lives*. Her skirts dangerously short, her eye shadow a little too blue. Didn't the girl ever read *Elle*? Inside, where it mattered most, no one was sweeter, more genuine, and more savvy than Sunny when it came to Pilar's dilemmas.

Pilar stared her phone, willing Sunny to call. Finally, she sucked it up. "Hey, Sun. Sorry I hung up."

"And I'm sorry for what I said."

"Hey! Fuhgettaboutit."

Sunny laughed.

"I'm just so . . . fed up with my life," Pilar said softly.

"That would be me, too," Sunny declared. "That's why we're treating ourselves right tonight. Get that cute little Gracie a babysitter. We're heading for the best bars in town."

"I'm sort of tired," Pilar replied glumly.

"Nope. Not listening. I'm on my way. If you're not dressed by the time I get there, I'm picking your outfit." Sunny giggled.

"Where are we going?"

"Wherever the richest guys in this town go to have a drink after work. I predict two rich Mr. Rights are going to buy us drinks and dinner."

"And that is where?"

"How do I know? That's your department, unless you want to go to a kicker place."

Pilar always knew the hottest bars. Before Ronnie, Thursdays were meet-up nights. Sunny would come to Pilar's apartment after work. Pilar would look at Sunny, wag her finger, say, "Another fashion catastrophe," and pick something from her closet for Sunny to change into. A couple of drinks before they took off enabled them to get a buzz going. That way if some guy didn't pick up the tab they'd be fine nursing one drink so as not to run up a huge tab. Even the happy hour drinks were pricey at the bars Pilar chose.

Pilar and Sunny did not go for the same kind of men. Normal everyday guys—cops, military, mechanics, oil field workers—were for Sunny. Pilar looked for someone who was, in her words, "going somewhere," or as Sunny put it, guys who were "hot on themselves." It was a big difference between them: Sunny was only comfortable with what she knew, and Pilar dreamed big. Somehow that helped make their friendship perfect—they didn't want the same things, and especially not the same men, but they both cared about each other.

Pilar believed she knew way more about how the world worked than Sunny did, but she loved her friend's ability to live in the moment and the clarity of her insights. When Pilar met Ronnie, Sunny saw the coming catastrophe long before Pilar did.

It had started out well enough. On the day she had been promoted to assistant office manager at Innoveismic, she tripped in the elevator and fell right into Ronnie. She apologized, and he said, "No problem." Noticing his mustache and the muscles under his suit, Pilar smiled up at him. "Thanks for catching me," she said. After that, they frequently saw each other in the elevator. Pilar flirted a little. It didn't take much. As assistant vice president of security, Ronnie easily learned where her office was. He asked her for coffee, then lunch, then dinner.

The first time Sunny met him, however, she took Pilar aside and asked, "What about that guy is right for you?"

"Are you kidding? He has a title with one of the world's hottest companies."

"You're getting there, too," Sunny said.

"Maybe." Pilar sighed. "But there's just so far I can go. If Ronnie and I were together, with two salaries, we could get a house, I could have a good car. We could have a nice life."

"Listen, girl. Something about him isn't right, not right for my friend Pilar."

Pilar wished she had paid attention. After the divorce papers had been signed, bad memories of Ronnie's hair-trigger temper still made her shiver. She was relieved he didn't exercise his visitation rights although she would have enjoyed bursts of freedom from time to time.

〰〰

WHEN SUNNY ARRIVED THAT EVENING, Pilar poured them each a drink.

"I thought you'd be dressed already," Sunny said.

Pilar shrugged. "It's more fun getting dressed up together."

They went through Pilar's closet.

"I have an idea," Pilar said. "The new hotel by the Galleria."

"Oh, perfect," Sunny said.

Not. As soon as she and Sunny entered, Pilar knew it was a mistake. The bar was mostly empty. A few businessmen leered at them as if they were hookers. They sat at the bar. A particularly unctuous man put his hand on Pilar's. "Hey, baby, want to par-tay?" he said. "No thank you," Pilar said, using her frostiest professional voice. Their drinks took a long time to arrive.

"I never understand why service is worse when a place isn't busy," Pilar said.

Sunny was trying to look like she was having a good time. "C'mon. We're supposed to be having fun." Pilar gave her a look. She so didn't want to be there. Suddenly, she knew what she wanted to do—what she had to do. "I'll be right back."

In the lobby, she found a private phone room. She pressed the numbers. The phone rang and rang. Pilar was about to hang up when she heard a click. She took a breath. Her palms felt sweaty. Hearing his voice made her feel both happy and nervous.

"Hello, it's Pilar Galt."

After a moment, she heard, "Well, hello. What a nice surprise."

"Thanks. I wasn't sure you'd remember me," she said, half taunting, half fearing it was true.

"How could I possibly . . . I mean."

She swore she heard him blushing.

"To what do I owe," he said, then stopped. That made her smile.

She felt relieved, too. He sounded as nervous as she felt, which was a good thing. She remembered how his dark eyes slanted up when he smiled.

"I wasn't sure I'd ever hear from you again. Why are you calling, Pilar?"

She wanted to say, "I was in a room full of horny, rich old jerks, and I realized what a special person you are, and I didn't want to lose the opportunity to get to know you." Instead, she simply said, "To be honest, I just felt like calling you. I'm not even sure I know why."

"Well, also to be honest, I'm really glad you did. Are you okay? Is there something I can do for you?"

"No. No, I don't know. Nothing really."

"How's the baby?"

"Thank you for asking. She's a delight."

"Good. Are you working?"

"I didn't go back when my maternity leave was over. My ex-husband works at the same company, and I didn't want to be around him. I'm still temping but . . ." Now she felt what little confidence she'd mustered slipping away. Not a good idea to let a man know you were struggling. It was dumb to call him. He was married, a big shot. He was so far out of her league. She felt like she was shrinking.

"I'm glad you mentioned that. I wondered if you were married."

"We were in the process of getting a divorce the day I worked at your office. Married, motherhood, and divorced, all within one year."

"Are you doing okay?" He seemed genuinely interested.

"Fine," she said though she didn't feel fine. She was struggling financially. She wanted a challenging job that paid well. She loved Grace, but she wished she had someone who could relieve her. She didn't expect to have someone to share her life, but it would be nice to have a man she trusted and could feel close to just being with. Going to bars for happy hour wasn't really very happy.

She cleared her throat, and in a "this conversation is over tone," said, "I guess I just wanted to let you know I'm glad I know you. I mean that I met you." She hoped she sounded a little mysterious instead of merely lame.

"I'm glad you did. May I call you sometime?"

She was surprised. Her heart pounded. He sounded like he really meant it. "I'd like that," she said. She whispered "Bye," and quickly pressed the "end call" icon.

Back in the lobby, she noticed a number of young women wearing stiletto heels, very short, tight skirts, revealing tops, and almost—but only almost—too much makeup. Each was pacing just outside the bar, talking on a cell phone.

That explained why all those horny barflies looked at her and Sunny like they were hookers.

The bar was more crowded with creepy-looking men, a few almost equally creepy-looking women, and hookers. Many of them.

Sliding onto her seat at the bar, she found Sunny in a foul mood.

"I don't believe it," Sunny moaned. "This guy buys me a drink. He seemed all happy and good to go—and then this woman joins us, and—you're not going to believe this, Pilar—this woman? She was his wife! And they wanted me to go up to a room with the both of them. Yuck! Thank God you're back. Let's get out of here, okay?" Sunny flung her arms around

Pilar. She was very tipsy. "Pilar, tell me the honest truth," she drawled, looking serious. "We aren't going to end up old and alone, are we?"

"No way," Pilar replied, recalling with a lilted feeling her conversation with VJ. "But right now, House of Pies on Kirby—strong coffee for you *and* pie for both of us! After that, I'll follow you home."

CHAPTER 12

PADDY GOES TO ELEGANTÉ

"... I CAN MAKE IT ANYWHERE," Paddy sang out to the tune of *New York, New York*. He was driving toward Eleganté, which nearly everyone agreed was Houston's finest restaurant. He'd seen pictures in *PaperCity* magazine of Houston's rich and famous throwing parties in private rooms of Eleganté. Its extravagant entrance, with two life-sized topiary lions guarding the front walkway, came into view. He reflexively straightened his tie. Approaching the valet station, he realized he didn't want to pull up in his shitty, dirty Dodge Ram truck that had more than a hundred thousand miles on it.

That morning, six months of negotiations had concluded at a heated meeting. With the hospital's in-house counsel, outside trial counsel, vice president, and general counsel of the hospital's parent holding company seated on one side of a large conference table, and Paddy on the other side, a settlement had finally been reached.

Paddy's hand trembled as he held his phone. He started to give Margot the good news, but she insisted they meet at Eleganté so he could tell her in person. "Honey, you're a Texan now," she'd said theatrically. "Don't you know it's all about staging?"

Paddy couldn't believe what a day he was having. Hugely successful settlement. Lunch with a beautiful woman. Swankiest restaurant in town. Could it get any better?

He parked a block away. Enduring the ninety-eight-degree temperature, he was drenched with perspiration by the time he reached his destination. Valet parkers greeted him as he approached. He looked for a condescending sneer as in, "You cheap bastard, you didn't want to pay us," but what he saw were friendly, welcoming smiles from nice-looking Hispanic men who didn't seem wilted by the heat. He made a mental note to remember how pleasant they were.

Inside was fancy—nicer than any place he'd been. A lovely hostess stood behind a podium. Before he could speak, a man in a tuxedo appeared at his side. "Mr. Moran, allow me to take you to Ms. Shear's table."

Paddy followed closely, the air-conditioning quickly cooling him. At a center table sat Margot. He thought she looked like a queen as she rose, extending her hand. Her gesture merged with a memory he had from a movie in which the leading man takes the leading lady's hand, bows, and brushes the back of her hand with his lips. Not fully realizing what he was doing, Paddy did the same.

"Oh, Mr. Moran," she tittered. "How gallant."

"Guh-lahnt" is what he heard. He looked around quickly. Not knowing another soul in the place was a good thing if he'd just embarrassed himself.

Margot, however, it seemed, knew everyone. Each time he began telling her about his meeting, someone new approached her to say hi and request an introduction. Most were women who were tan, with sparkling white teeth, and wearing crisp, beautiful designer clothes. On any other day, he would have been thrilled to meet these people. Not now. He was nearly bursting with his news.

Sensing his frustration, Margot whispered, "They're just curious about this new giant hunk of a man. It'll quiet down in a few minutes. Besides—" she briefly touched his thigh, "most of the fun is in the anticipation."

Before he could reply, a woman approached. "Oh, Margot, who *is* this gorgeous man with you?"

Paddy blushed. Margot looked faintly discomfited. "Hello, Norma," she said. Her tone was not friendly.

Norma was maybe five feet five inches tall, counting six-inch patent leather stiletto heels liberally speckled with gold studs. She wore a cream-colored suit that was accented by loads of diamonds. Her white-blond hair did not naturally partner with her olive complexion. Paddy was astounded that he was clueless as to how old Norma was. The best he could do was narrow it down to somewhere between mid-thirties and mid-fifties.

He rose, looking down a foot into her eyes. "I'm Paddy Moran."

"He's my lawyer," Margot said. "And a good one. Paddy, this is Norma Nambé."

"Well, what kind of law do you practice, Mr. Moran?" Norma's voice sounded as smooth as syrup pouring from a jar.

"Mostly personal injury and divorce."

"If you're any good at that divorce work," Norma smiled, "and you can crack into the club, you could make a whole lot of money."

"The club?"

"Yes, Mr. Moran. The club is an elite group of divorce lawyers. They get nearly all the big-dollar divorces in town." She ran fingers through her hair. "I haven't heard of you, but if Margot says you're terrific, I'm sure I'll think so, too. You might even get to join T.B.P." She turned her attention to Margot. "You know you have an open invitation, darling."

Norma put her hand on Paddy's shoulder and quickly withdrew it. Paddy realized her reaction was an involuntary reflex signifying she didn't approve of his suit material—a gray, cotton-rayon blend. Glancing at people seated at tables around them, he thought, *My best suit is a shit suit*. Norma recovered quickly. "Always nice to see you, Margot," she said. "Especially nice to meet you Mr. Moran. I'm sure I'll hear more about you."

Once Norma was out of earshot, Margot said, "What a wannabe. She appeared a few years ago. She claims to be a financial advisor. She also claims to be a full-blooded Indian—Native American, I should say. She makes what she can of that."

Paddy felt startled. Until this moment he had not thought Margot could sound so harshly judgmental about anyone.

"Of course, I realize that all of us, in our own way, are wannabes," she said. "Maybe my problem with Norma—I'll just say it—is that she's a social climber, and she's *so* obvious. She tries to buy her way in by paying for expensive tables at charity balls. Things like that. She spends a fortune on her appearance. She tries for the best-dressed list every year. She camps out here nearly every day at lunch. My guess is she's hustling customers. I have yet to feel any part of her is genuine."

Norma's strategy seemed pretty good to Paddy, but he knew not to share that opinion.

"Anyway," Margot said, "as a Native American woman, she gets contracts with businesses she couldn't get otherwise. She milks her heritage to the max."

"You don't like her." Paddy said, each word delivered in successively lowered terms.

Margot smiled ruefully. "That obvious, huh? Something about her rubs me the wrong way. I don't even believe she's Native American."

"Is she any good at what she does—investing money for people?"

"Who knows? I've heard she is, but then again, who wants to admit they hired a loser to handle their money? Anyway, never mind Norma. If you want to see someone who I *know* is successful at making money for other people, look at that fellow over there."

She nodded toward a dark-complexioned man with a deep complexion and black hair that was graying at the temples. He wore a midnight blue pin-striped suit, a very white shirt, and a muted red tie. Even to Paddy's untrained eye, the suit's shape and the fold of its lapels suggested power. The prime minister of England might wear that suit.

"His name is VJ Simon. He has made fortunes for himself and others."

"How?" Paddy asked.

"VJ seems to know what's coming before others do and what's going to be around for the long haul. He isn't afraid to take smart risks. He doesn't buy stocks. He says he invests in people. He has had amazing success putting money into companies just starting up. His most recent home run was Partumeeze, a drug that somehow manages a woman's body chemistry after childbirth so that it entirely eliminates even a hint of postpartum depression."

"Is there a big market for that?"

Margot gave him a level stare. "Every woman who has a baby is at risk for postpartum depression. The market for Partumeeze is enormous."

"Have you had any babies?" Paddy immediately felt red all over, beating himself up on the inside. "I'm sorry if that's—"

"No, Mr. Moran," Margot said, smiling. "No babies. Also, I've never married."

He started to say, "A good-looking woman like you." Instead, he said, "Maybe I should use VJ Simon myself."

"I hear he doesn't take new accounts with less than fifty million. He makes an exception for me because I got to know him when I gave his wife's godchildren piano lessons."

"Well, since I can't teach piano, I guess I'm not quite ready for him," Paddy said.

"No, but he may be ready for *your* services, some day," Margot said. "Let's just say there are rumors."

Paddy leaned in closer to Margot. "Tell me more."

"No. I shouldn't have said that. He's my friend. I want happiness for him. Anyway, forget that. Forget everything else except what's most important—my Christmas shopping. Tell me about my case."

"Oh, that?" Fascinated as he was with Margot Shear's world, he had been bursting to tell her about his great victory. He toyed now, making her wait longer as punishment for doing the same to him. "Oh, yes. There is that."

"Well, I've agreed to a settlement without filing suit. I did it without consulting you because you had already told me you'd be okay if we got fifty thousand, right?"

"Yes, I did. Now, just tell me, Mr. Moran." For all her talk about anticipation being fun, she was now tapping her feet.

He got a big grin on his face, opened his eyes wide and made his eyeballs go up and down. "I figured if you would settle for fifty thousand you'd be happy with ten times that amount."

"You're saying you settled for five hundred thousand?"

"That's what I'm sayin', and I'm stickin' to it," he said.

Margot jumped up, clapping. She immediately sat back down with a quick glance around the room. She took his hand. In a hushed voice, she said, "I can't believe it! I can't believe it!"

"I hate to admit it," he said, "but if you'd asked me at the outset what the odds were, I would have said a million to one. As it turned out, I guess the odds were exactly half that. I could see pure hate coming from their fancy-assed, big firm lawyer. He didn't want to settle, but I guess his client did." He squeezed her hand. "I didn't want to get your hopes up, but once we started having meetings with the outside counsel, I knew we were going to get something well north of fifty thousand."

He realized he'd pronounced it "nawth" and wondered if she'd noticed. But what the fuck did it matter? He'd proved himself.

While they ate, he explained that the settlement agreement had a standard confidentiality provision as well as a provision in which Paddy agreed not to represent any other clients against the hospital in claims involving that doctor. Margot nodded, beaming.

A lull came as both food and victory were digesting. Margot, her contented eyes half-closed, asked, "Why'd you become a lawyer?"

Pursing his lips, he took a deep breath. Despite unfamiliar surroundings, despite their disparate backgrounds, despite her awing presence, he felt safe being unguarded with her. He couldn't remember if he'd ever had that sort of comfort. He said, "I can tell you. I love Jed like a brother, but I could never have told him this."

"In my neighborhood in Brooklyn, a lot of us aspired to be policemen. They made more money than my old man. I guess everybody did. Cops had respect. About ten years in, I was having a difficult relationship with my new captain. I learned HPD was recruiting officers from the Northeast. I heard Houston was a great town, and I wanted to see if I could make it somewhere besides New York. My New York. It wasn't long after I got here that I realized, more than I liked to admit, Houston cops are here to serve the rich and the powerful. Hell, maybe it's like that everywhere. Maybe I just finally noticed. They're here to make those people feel secure in their homes, where they work, when they go out to play. After all, isn't that how you got to know Jed? He worked security to protect you and your rich customers."

Margot raised her eyebrows. Paddy, clueless to her reaction, went on. "You may not like what I'm saying, but the cops and these people have sort of a code. So long as the rich and powerful don't go overboard, cops give them slack that people who live in the barrios or Third Ward or the trailer parks don't get."

Margot's head pulled back involuntarily.

"Surprised to hear that, huh? I was invisible to those people, but they weren't invisible to me. The funny thing was that many of them weren't that different from me. Some of them were even cruder. Imagine that," he said with a self-deprecating laugh. "The difference was they had money. I studied them. I wanted that life. It wasn't the money. It was the respect the money brought. I began to read the glossy magazines that covered Houston's rich and famous, and I listened to people. I watched the news. You wanna know who got the most publicity?"

"Tell me," she said.

"Heart surgeons, oil business people, or should I say 'awl biniss', and lawyers. I knew for damn sure heart surgery was not for me. I didn't have a clue how to get into the oil business. But a lawyer—I could be a lawyer. There were no limits. I'll never forget the *New York Post* headline when that Joe Jamail got a four-hundred-million-dollar fee on one case alone. It takes a lot for somebody west of Broadway to make the top fold of the *Post*."

"Pennzoil!"

"Right. I scheduled work around the classes the best professors were teaching. Getting the best the school had to offer was worth taking longer to finish, but not one law firm that interviewed at the law school offered me a job. Most didn't even let me, an older guy who worked his way through law school as a cop, on their interview list. Even though I won a moot court award named after one of those firms, they had no use for me. Let me tell you, sweet Margot, I've got no use for any of those big outfits now."

"I picked up on that when you told me how you settled my case," she said.

"You think?"

After a pause he said, "A part of me wanted to be a lawyer because maybe, every once in a while, I could level the playing field when the little guy is fighting the big guy. That part of what I did for you was as satisfying as the big payday. As soon as I passed the bar, I quit HPD and hung out my shingle. I had no debt and enough put away to give me a cushion. I met you. I had my first big case. End of story."

They sat in silence, each taking quiet spoonfuls of their crème brûlée. Finally, Margot said, "Well, you've been very candid, Mr. Moran. I see some compassion. I see a glee in fighting the establishment, which you, in a sense, did for me. You're ambitious, very ambitious. Your ambition and creativity worked very well for me. You're going to have to make your own judgments about your path, but if you need me, you call me. I'll respond." After a brief pause, she continued with a little less conviction. "I won't judge you. Something else, you're lucky you chose Houston. It's a true meritocracy here. I'm from Dallas, which is much more closed. Houston is wide open. Here, you work hard, you succeed. It doesn't matter who your parents or grandparents were. Nearly all doors are open. If one isn't, you build your own door and march right through it. That's what makes Houston, Houston!"

"It's a terrific place," Paddy said.

Leaning toward him, Margot added in a low voice, "But let me tell you one more thing, Paddy Moran. This comes from hard experience. Be careful. This may be the fourth-largest city in the United States, but everyone knows everyone here. It's a bad place to fall."

It occurred to him how disastrous Grissett's case could have been.

"Another question?" he asked.

"Sure."

Her tone eased into reassuring, less maternal than mentor-like.

"What is 'T.B.P.?'"

"The Best People. To me, it's Norma's pathetic attempt to elevate herself. She gets together with some people, mostly . . . mostly people who have recently made some pretty good money and who, for the most part, are pretty unpolished."

Paddy's expression changed.

She quickly changed gears. "To be perfectly honest, some of 'The Best People' are really good folks who are nice. They generously support important work and institutions in Houston. It's just that the ringleader is Norma, and the name is so embarrassingly pretentious."

As they left, Margot introduced Paddy to Luigi Ganté, Eleganté's owner. "What a nice man," Paddy said.

"About five percent business nice, ninety-five percent nice-nice. He is a genuine sweetheart."

They passed a table with five women. Margot waved but didn't stop to chat.

"They look alike. Are they sisters?"

"No, they just go to the same plastic surgeon," she deadpanned.

Paddy smiled.

She also introduced him to Mal Malowitz, a colorful, well-known real estate developer. "Nice to meet you here," Paddy said.

After they were past earshot of Malowitz, Margot said, "I picked up on that 'here.' What was that about?"

"Remember I told you I was invisible to rich people?"

"Yes."

"Well, I worked security for Malowitz several times when he had parties at his Memorial swankienda. He used to chat with me like he cared about me. Gave me big tips. Today it was as if he had never seen me before. I'm not saying he isn't a nice guy. I'm just sayin.'"

※

WITHIN A WEEK of his lunch with Margot, Paddy received the hospital's settlement check made payable to him and his client.

He looked at it.

He kissed it.

He pressed it to his heart.

He had a color copy made.

He took the copy to a framer.

Then he deposited it in his IOLTA bank account, as required by State Bar rules. He wrote Margot a check for $333,333.33. He wrote a check to himself for $166,666.67. At that moment, he felt a rush.

Deposit slip in pocket, Paddy went to a Mercedes dealership where he leased a C300 sedan. From its leather interior to its glossy red paint, nothing had ever made him so happy. Still, he decided to keep his truck. He wasn't going to drive a Mercedes around his policeman buddies, but he was planning a return to Eleganté soon. When he did, he wanted to drive up in style. He wanted to look like he belonged.

His next stop was Saks Fifth Avenue. He'd never been inside the place, but being from New York, Saks was sure to have what he needed. He guessed someone snooty would help him decide what that was. He was greeted by a tall, very elegant, polished black man. Paddy said he wanted to get a new business suit.

The salesman gave Paddy a skeptical look. With raised eyebrows, he said, "Perhaps, sir, you might find what you want at a big-and-tall shop."

Paddy gave him a cold, Brooklyn stare. "Look, buddy, let me put it this way. I am about to go places where some people think I don't belong. Truth is, I probably don't. One thing I can do is dress like I belong. I need some help in that department."

Paddy firmly placed his hand on the salesman's shoulder, applying a bit more than friendly pressure. In a tone that was almost threatening, looking slightly down into his face, Paddy said, "My guess is you understand what I'm talking about."

His eyes flashed up into Paddy's face.

"Besides," Paddy said, "I'm sure you're on commission. I might spend a lot of money in this place. I can do that with you if you take care of me."

The salesman relaxed, easing out of his acquired persona. He smiled, putting out his hand. After introducing himself, he said, "You know, brotha, you got me."

The salesman selected a solid navy Armani suit made of Super 100, a perfect weight for Houston, together with a white Gucci shirt, two

Armani ties, a pair of black Ferragamo lace-up shoes, navy calf-high cashmere socks, and a Cartier reversible leather belt with a silver buckle. When the bill exceeded Paddy's credit card limit, he pulled out his checkbook.

"You're going to need more than one outfit, Mr. Moran. Give me your business card. We have a sale coming up. I'll put some things aside in your size. We'll help you fill in your wardrobe."

⁓

PADDY MOVED TO A LARGE Midtown apartment complex. It had a workout room with weights and cardio machines. More important, it was dog friendly. Paddy found a registered Irish Setter online. It was love at first sight. He named him Mick.

At last, Paddy could see good things were going to happen. He hoped his first real success was the beginning of a streak that would propel him to be one of Houston's legendary trial lawyers.

CHAPTER 13

VJ MUSES ON HIS MARRIAGE

PILAR'S CALL INTRIGUED VJ, preoccupied him even. Taking meetings, going through his usual business routine, making his short drive home, he kept returning to his problem: Pilar Galt. Not that she was a problem—not being able to stop thinking about her was the problem. Images of her came into his mind relentlessly. Even so, for a few days he resisted calling her. But one night in his home study, door shut, he dialed her number.

His heart beat faster hearing her voice. The conversation was innocent enough, but when it was over, he was smiling. He turned off the lights and began what was a nightly habit with him—to sit in a darkened room and repeat at least ninety times "molahs," a mantra his grandfather, Zaide, had given him. If his thoughts strayed, he would start over. Occasionally it was a productive strategy, his own version of mindfulness. Even if no great ideas came of it, he usually felt better afterwards, but not today. Today his thoughts immediately were of his wife.

Fifteen years earlier, he had first set eyes on Georgette Carver at a fund-raising gala for the Houston Grand Opera at the Wortham Center. She was exchanging an empty champagne glass for a fresh one. She smiled at VJ. He bowed.

"Oh, how gallant," she said. "You must be the maharaja of Tel Aviv I've been told about. I'm Georgie."

He laughed out loud at the nickname she'd bestowed on him. "I guess I do sort of stick out in this crowd."

"It's talent and initiative that make you distinctive. Your reputation precedes you."

He looked at her more closely. She was lean, tall, and energetic looking. Her gray eyes met his in a direct stare. She wasn't flirting, which he appreciated. "Tell me something funny," she said. VJ smiled. They were both bored, hoping to find someone with whom to have an interesting conversation.

He knew her name. Her late father was a legendary rags-to-riches success, a behind-the-scenes powerbroker. VJ had seen him in action. While VJ always felt he was an outsider, Georgie's father had been a chief among the belongers. Now meeting his daughter, VJ saw a mystique that he found attractive. He would not have called her beautiful in any conventional sense. Her face held the scarring of severe acne when she was younger, and she had probably always been reed thin. Yet her carriage and confidence gave her a commanding, almost intimidating presence, and he admired her strong sense of style. She wore a long, elegant dress made of soft forest green gabardine, but it was the unaffected flair of her accessories that dazzled him. He recognized that her bangle bracelets were from Mumbai, but he suspected the scarf she used as a sash and the squash blossom necklace were picked up from local artisans at street markets in various places she had traveled. He appreciated the way she mixed and matched— Navajo silver and Bengalese earrings.

"Let's go outside for a smoke," she said in a husky voice. VJ eagerly followed. In their whispered conversation outside the entrance to the Wortham Center, he learned that she was very well read, up-to-date on current events, and a skilled mimic of certain state and local politicians.

"There's something I like about you," she said.

"Maybe I'm just different from the men you usually see at these affairs, Georgie." Georgie—it felt good to call her that.

She laughed, "Oh, I'm sure you're right about that. Tell me how you ended up in Houston, Texas? Miss Marple here deduced you aren't a native."

"Can't fool you," he said smiling. "My father's family escaped to India from Eastern Europe in the late thirties. After the war, my father met my mother when they were both teaching in an English prep school. His family was fine with the marriage, but her Brahmin parents were not. In the mid-fifties, my parents left India and moved to Israel. Although my father was not observant, my mother converted to Judaism, without giving up her origins. I was born there. I'm a Sabra. When I was about fourteen, my father was offered a position at a prep school outside of Boston, so they immigrated to the US. Looking back, I realize how lonely my mother must have been in the remote, unfriendly, xenophobic town when father and I were at the school. I went to the school for free. Nearly all the other students were WASPs. They made it clear I wasn't one of them."

"You don't say," she said with a smirk on her face.

VJ looked at his shoes. His face flushed as he recalled indignities he suffered at the hands and mouths of his prep school classmates. Then he grinned as he basked in the pleasure of having bested them in one of the two things that was most important to them—if Forbes was right, he made more money than any one of them had or even inherited. "I went to Columbia for undergraduate school. Then I went to business school at MIT."

"I'm impressed."

He smiled. "When your parents are Indian and Jewish, they aren't expecting you to play football or even be president of the United States. It's education, education, education."

She laughed. "But that doesn't get you to Houston, Texas."

"A venture capital company sent me to Houston to work with people who were developing medical devices and pharmaceuticals in the Texas Medical Center. For a long time, my life was nothing more than wake up, go to an office, digest complex engineering and chemistry proposals, crunch numbers, then crash back at my apartment. While making a good bit of money for the company, I also made a name for myself among the board members of the medical center institutions. Your father was on several of the boards. He impressed me very much."

She nodded, remembering her father mentioning a "brilliant Jew-Indian." "And you impressed him."

"Really? He never let me know."

"Did he listen when you talked?"

"Yes, he did."

"Then he let you know. Believe me, I know about that."

"He told me something once. We had been in a board executive session. It was a tense meeting. Some key people were terminated. Afterward, he put his arm around me, saying, 'There's a lesson for you, son. If you don't have a seat at the table, you're on the menu.' It was powerful."

"You generally have a seat at the table these days, don't you?"

VJ chuckled. "Anyway, to make a long story longer, I decided to start my own shop. Some of those rich and powerful people I met risked a few dollars with me. They only risked money. They didn't risk their social status. We never met at one of their clubs. We had lunch at Maxim's in the beginning. Later at Eleganté. I thought of it as the five o'clock curtain.

When my first deal turned out to be a quick home run, my name became a buzzword. To my surprise, there have only been a few overt snubs here in Houston."

"You're smart. You're charming. You're handsome. You made them money. What's not to like?"

"Now you're playing with me," he said.

～～

AN ONLY CHILD of a loveless marriage, named for her father, George, who had wanted a son, Georgie had inherited considerable wealth. Since she was a few years older than VJ when they started seeing each other, many assumed his real attraction was to her money. Her money was not important to him, although he did question himself as to whether her family name was part of her appeal. He wondered if part of besting his prep school tormentors was marrying into one of the "best" families.

Although their romance wasn't heated, the sex was comfortable and good. He had a serious love interest in graduate school, but since then, he had gone through a series of meaningless relationships. More than a few times he declined advances by wives of his WASP investors. With Georgie, there was certainly a level of ease and intellectual stimulation, so six months after he began seeing her he asked her to marry him. Georgie said, "I suppose it's about time I got married. I never let anyone else hang around long enough for them to ask." With a trace of unconcealed reverie, staring off, she added, "The ones I wanted to hang around never came around to begin with." Returning her focus to him, she said, "You're more like them, except you came around." Not missing a beat, without giving him a moment to reflect, with rapid fire, she continued, "By the way, I don't know if you're interested in having children. I'm not. Probably too old. I wouldn't anyway. My parents didn't do a great job of parenting. I doubt I would either. If that's a problem, tell me now."

He was overwhelmed by the changes in trajectory and weight of all she had said in such a few moments. Realizing he had to respond, he shook his head. Having children wasn't anything he'd really thought about. In fact, there wasn't much about his personal life he had thought about since graduate school.

VJ and Georgie's wedding was simple. It was performed by a federal judge whose husband VJ had made wealthy enough for him to be able to make substantial contributions to presidential and senatorial campaigns that resulted in his wife's judicial nomination and confirmation. Other than the judge's husband, only Georgie's two godchildren attended. Georgie wore a white silk pantsuit and no veil. VJ stomped a glass at the end of the ceremony, and that was it.

He moved into her home, a John Staub-designed mansion on Lazy Lane with large, magnificently gnarled oaks she had climbed as a child. She had lived in the house all her life.

VJ gave up smoking shortly after they married. Georgie did not. Her smoking, not his long work hours, created the initial friction in their relationship. In time, she developed a hacking cough. When VJ, the reformed smoker, insisted that she rid the house of the accumulation of generations of stale smoke, she took the opportunity to redo the house and furnishings less grandly but more elegantly than her mother had. The house was finally free of the stench, but he made clear to her she was not.

She suggested separate rooms. He didn't object.

After that, she never appeared interested in sex. Nonetheless, she willingly and enthusiastically accommodated VJ's needs whenever he made them known.

Georgie had accepted invitations to serve as godmother to the children of two of her friends since childhood, a relationship taken very seriously in Southern WASP society. She was generous to her godchildren and was delighted when they came to the house for piano lessons on her Steinway grand piano. Although VJ usually wasn't there, he did meet and strike up a friendship with their teacher, Margot Shear.

Georgie traveled extensively with her friends—any destination was fair game. She sent him postcards from each stop—a line or two written with a fountain pen, with only her initial as a signature: 'Love, G.' As for VJ, he worked long hours when he was in town and traveled a great deal on business. He never had affairs, but sometimes he thought perhaps he should know the thrill and abandon of having one. A lot of his investors did. He had not intended to have a marriage without physical passion; he just assumed it would be there. Unlike most of his business assumptions, his assumption about his personal life was wrong.

Many evenings they had to be one of the grand couples who politely and insincerely kissed airy mwahs at balls and first nights. On other nights—on the rare times when they were both in Houston at the same time with nothing on the social calendar—he frequently felt disappointed to find her there when he came home.

The engaging mystery he once felt emanating from Georgie was replaced by his loathing of the lingering smell of cigarettes when he was near her and, increasingly, her slurred speech. She no longer displayed much enthusiasm for him. If, in fact, she acknowledged him when he got home, she had little to say. "Working hard?" she would ask in a mocking tone. "Why don't you go to the study? I'll have a tray sent."

That's just what he did. Soon it became routine.

Having repeated the mantra ninety times, then having sat in the dark letting his mind wander, his thoughts migrated from Georgie. He had been living half a life for too long. It was time to focus on what he had left on the table. Surely there was more than what life with Georgie offered.

The thought of Pilar Galt suddenly coursed through him, exciting him. He turned on the nearest lamp. A pool of light flooded the study. He looked at his watch. It was nearly midnight.

The very next evening, before leaving work to head home, VJ dialed Pilar's number. After that, his talks with her became an exhilarating habit. When he knew Georgie was home, he called Pilar from work. When Georgie was travelling or out with her women friends, he called from his study. His heart always raced as he dialed her number. Often Pilar sounded soft and happy to hear from him. Sometimes she sounded frustrated when her day had gone badly. She shared pieces of good news. Grace had a brilliant insight into the deeper meaning of *The Giving Tree* or made friends with a neighbor girl her age whose mother seemed like someone Pilar might become friends with. She had gotten a temp job as a manager, and if they liked her she might be taken on permanently. He found himself sharing her moods—commiserating when she sounded fed up, elated when things were going well for her. He was surprised to find himself enjoying sharing her life as much as he did.

One night there was no answer. His first feeling was disappointment. Then he wondered if there was another guy. His heart raced. He paced the length of his study. He tried distracting himself by catching up on business news. Unable to stop himself, he dialed her number again.

"Hello." She was home.

He felt a surge of relief. "What's up?" This had become his normal greeting to her.

"I'm fine," Pilar said. "I'm happy to hear from you."

He wanted to believe they were drawing closer, and that lifted his heart. Even making money on a clever investment didn't feel nearly as good. He was intrigued by her, but also puzzled about why she had such an impact on him. She was pretty, but he'd known lots of pretty women, some of whom had been obvious in offering themselves to him. It wasn't that. Pilar was something different.

The song *Bewitched, Bothered, and Bewildered* came to his mind

"You beguile me," he said to her.

"Oh, my," she said, clearly flattered. "Tell me what you mean."

He didn't answer. He had to think about what it did mean.

"Are you there?" she asked.

"Yes. Yes, I am. It means you enchant me, and I don't know what to make of it."

CHAPTER 14

ESTELLE COOK

THE CALLER INTRODUCED HERSELF as Estelle Cook. As they talked, Paddy ran her name through an online database. She was fifty-five years old, had a River Oaks address, good credit, no criminal record, and hadn't been a party in a Harris County lawsuit. He was intrigued. He was elated. Someone from River Oaks was coming to see him.

Estelle Cook told him Margot had sung his praises "like a nightingale over a glen of divorce lawyers, pointing me in the right direction." That sounded weird, over-the-top affected. He didn't even know what the hell it meant other than it was a compliment.

The database reported someone else living at the same address. His name was James Allen Cook. A further inquiry reported that James Allen Cook was a partner at Walker & Travis. Now Paddy was totally intrigued.

BERNICE ANNOUNCED Mrs. Cook's arrival. As he greeted her, he noticed she was appraising the offices. Through her eyes, he realized he had only the bare necessities: an old desk, mismatched chairs, and his framed law school diploma and law license hanging on the wall. It was functional, sure, but until that moment it had never occurred to him his office should impress a client. Maybe his Saks outfit would impress her.

"Hello, Mrs. Cook. Our offices aren't very fancy, but we're close to the courthouse."

She appeared embarrassed for having been caught judging.

Though attractive, Estelle Cook did not look as young as a fifty-five-year-old woman with her means could look. However, her appearance had been carefully crafted, accentuating her assets and diverting attention from her liabilities, those being extra pounds. Her clothes were elegantly simple:

a black, unrevealing shift, white pearls, and pearl earrings. Her makeup drew attention to her pretty face.

As if she were conferring a gift, she said, "Mr. Moran, I will tell you my story."

"Please do," Paddy said, in a formal tone.

Once seated, she was composed, almost matter-of-fact. "My husband, James Cook, is a senior partner in Walker & Travis. He is head of its trial section and a management committee member."

More out of curiosity than anything else, Paddy asked, "And what does that entail?"

"Being on the management committee, as you would guess, takes a lot of time."

Actually, Paddy didn't know law firms had management committees.

"Being Trial Section head is more tribute than duty. His real power, glory, and money come from all the toxic tort cases in James's domain."

Paddy nodded, but his naiveté must have shown through. Mrs. Cook sighed. "Toxic tort cases are the gifts that keep on giving to the defense bar."

"The plaintiffs' lawyers file class action cases," she continued. "It's a big risk for them. They front all the expenses and wait a long time for a settlement or a final judgment. The defense bar, however, is paid on an hourly basis every month. They attack cases with a vengeance, assigning large teams of lawyers whose hours are rarely checked. They file motion after motion, in hopes, their clients think, of wearing the opposition down. Although some prominent defense attorneys may publicly clamor for tort reform to please their clients, let me assure you that to a one they want to keep things just as they are. It's so hypocritical. It's downright—"

"What you say," Paddy interrupted, "reminds me of an old law school joke about a guy who was the only lawyer in a small town. He was starving until another lawyer moved to town. Then they both got rich."

She had a steely look as she tilted her head downward. "My point is, James is a major profit center for the firm."

Paddy sat back. He decided to contain his interruptions.

"I met James when he was a 3-L. I was an undergraduate at the University of Texas. In those days young women from good families went to college to find suitable husbands. James's family was of modest means from a small town in Oklahoma, but when he accepted an offer from Walker & Travis,

James Cook became very suitable in my mother's eyes. In turn, my family's standing in the community may have fit in with his plans to succeed at Walker & Travis. I was very attracted to him, and, I believe, he was attracted to me. We married. Of course, my family paid for the rehearsal dinner."

"James has done very well at Walker & Travis. However, when James turned fifty-five, he bought a new Porsche Carrera, got a face lift, and, as I now know, began an affair with his twenty-seven-year-old personal trainer who also happened to be married to Gary Martin, a young lawyer who worked directly for James. I knew Gary and his wife, Monica, socially—they were guests in my house often." Her voice shook. She struggled to gain composure. "She . . . well, *he's* a fine young man."

He suspected Estelle Cook would never call Brooklyn Paddy a "fine young man."

"He's from a good family. He went to the best schools. As for Monica, I don't want to sound uncharitable, Mr. Moran, but she's a personal trainer without a brain in her head. However, she is young, pretty, and, I have to admit, she does have a terrific body, though I don't think her breasts were God-given."

Paddy worked hard at not changing his facial expression.

"When James began using Monica as a trainer—dumb me—I thought it was a good idea. He needed exercise for his health. My guess is her attraction to him was his power in the one universe in Houston she and Gary knew: Walker & Travis. When she went after my husband, he fell for her hook, line, and sinker." She pursed her lips, shook her head, and then said, in a sweet, unguarded tone Paddy hadn't heard from her, "I am so angry. I am so angry I could spit!"

Every word until "spit" had a tone of sad desperation. "Spit" was delivered with defiance. It made him think how royalty might express righteous indignation.

Paddy nodded. "With good reason, I might add. If I may ask, how do you know this story in such great detail, Mrs. Cook?"

"I'm sure I don't know it all. Most of what I know was in Gary's divorce petition, which some anonymous well-wisher sent me in the mail."

Paddy grimaced. "Ouch!"

"Exactly. Here it is. I don't think you can get a copy any more. I'm told the petition is sealed. In any event, after Gary filed for divorce, I'm also told he confronted Tom Frost, Walker & Travis's managing partner, with details of the affair. Gary expected James to be booted out of the firm. He was wrong. Soon thereafter, Gary quietly departed, taking a position with a prestigious New York firm."

"So how are things with you and Mr. Cook?"

"Not warm. What's worse is I don't have a clue what my husband has in mind, whether he wants a divorce, or he wants to keep up his current arrangement."

Paddy straightened his posture. In the most righteously indignant way he could manufacture, he said, "It's shocking and outrageous that a person in your husband's position would be so disloyal and arrogant," thinking that was what she wanted to hear. Tilting his head, he said, "I understand you want a divorce. What I don't understand is why Estelle Cook, of the highest echelon of Houston society who has been exposed to only the white shoes of the Houston bar, is coming to see the likes of Paddy Moran?"

Estelle Cook cocked her head to one side. "Isn't it strange, Mr. Moran," she said a little sadly, "when we're talking about a life, it just comes down to money? I came to you because I bet I'll get more money with you."

His experience in big, contested divorce cases was nonexistent. He'd had a few hotly contested divorces, nearly all with discovery battles, numerous motions, child custody, and visitation issues, the sorts of dramas angry spouses create and too many lawyers encourage to ratchet up their fees. He vowed to resist being part of that ugly spiral, even though it would boost his cash flow. Nevertheless, he was the beneficiary when his opponents became unnecessarily aggressive because he had to respond. None of his cases was anywhere close to the league Mrs. Cook's case would be. Paddy wanted to scale that platform. He especially wanted to put Walker & Travis on notice that he was no longer someone to fuck with.

He was about to speak, but she waved his attempt away. "The reason is simple, Mr. Moran. You have no connections to Walker & Travis or, for that matter, to any of the large firms. You'll have no reason to hold back for fear you'll lose future referrals. Margot tells me you have connections to the police. That could also be helpful. Most importantly, however, she says you are ambitious, clever, smart, and hungry. You have nothing to lose. You can only gain by using whatever you can think of to help me get the settlement I deserve."

Paddy liked what he heard, but then she said, "On the other hand, you have no connections to the judges. If that becomes a problem, we will add another lawyer to our team, someone who's well-connected." Paddy turned red.

Mrs. Cook noticed. In a voice that reminded him of his third-grade teacher who never needed an excuse to cut Paddy down, she continued, "Mr. Moran, this is not and will *never* be about you. It's about me. I won't let you trade my chance for a great victory for your pride. Rest assured, even if we bring in one of those prima donnas, when we win, everyone will know it was you who pulled it off."

"Okay, Mrs. Cook, you made your point." Smiling broadly, he said, "So, a personal trainer, a very personal trainer."

Estelle Cook stood up, straightened her back, and brought herself to her fullest measure. Her eyes pierced him. "A gym rat. A *fucking* gym rat, Mr. Moran."

Paddy blinked. "Yes, ma'am, Mrs. Cook. You do have a way of letting your true feelings be known."

"Call me Estelle, please."

He nodded. There was a short silence.

"You should know, too, that my husband's law firm—hell, all the establishment law firms in Houston—will do anything to protect their prestige, including buying you off."

Paddy smiled. This is one tough, smart cookie.

"They won't be able to buy me off."

"Most of your cases are contingent fee, aren't they?"

"Personal injury cases," he said.

"What's your hourly rate?"

He had to think about answering. No one with her resources had paid him by the hour before. "Three fifty an hour," he said, trying not to sound tentative.

"I'll pay you one seventy-five an hour plus twenty-five percent of what you get over a 55-45 split."

"I usually get a third."

"You usually don't get paid by the hour plus a contingency," she shot back. "I don't want anything to be more important to you than this case. No other client. No wife. No girlfriend."

"Don't worry about that," Paddy interrupted. "No wife or girlfriend here."

"Or boyfriend."

"I don't have one of those either," Paddy snapped.

"Great, but whatever else you do, no to that as well."

"Mrs. Cook—I mean, Estelle, I have a dog. His name is Mick. An Irish Setter. I promise Mick will be your only competition."

"Fair enough." She shook his hand.

As she picked up her purse to leave, she said, "I'm used to seeing time reports by lawyers. I've been a lawyer's wife for a long time, Mr. Moran. I know what's real, so no *pad*ding, *Pad*dy."

"Cute," he said. "Not to worry. There will be expenses, though. For sure, I'll need to hire a private detective. You may not really want a report on everything."

"Agreed," she said, lips still pursed.

He escorted her to the door. She turned as if remembering something vital. Her eyes were full of heartache, but she only said, "There won't be any failure of communication on my part."

"I'm sure of that." He put his arm around her as he walked her to the elevator.

This could be it. A check coming in every month, a client he could trust, a big-time divorce, a shot at one of those Walker & Travis cocksuckers. This *could* be it.

CHAPTER 15

AFTERNOON DELIGHT

PILAR HAD VJ SIMON'S PHONE NUMBER on speed dial. She didn't use it often, because most evenings around seven he called her. Sunny joked that Pilar really had him trained. In spite of his money and power—both of which intimidated her and drew her to him in equal measure—she felt herself growing closer to him. She was happy when they talked, when he sounded genuinely interested in her life. And that *the* VJ Simon was attracted to her made her want to strut.

But she began to feel restless. "I don't mind how things are," she told Sunny, "but I can't help feeling like one of us has to make a move, and that scares me. What if we ruin everything?"

Sunny looked confused. "What are you talking about? You've never even had lunch with the guy. What's to ruin? You got nothing."

"We have something. We really do. I don't know how to explain it, but I know I have to kick start it to another level."

"You got nothing," kept piercing Pilar's thoughts at odd times the following week. The next Saturday afternoon, as she was flipping through her magazines—*Elle, Vogue,* and *Harper's Bazaar*—she noticed that every issue had an article about younger women and older men—younger women who thought their married older lovers were going to leave their wives but, after way too long, never did, and the younger women were left no longer so young and on their own, alone. "You got nothing," Pilar murmured. She walked over to her bureau and looked in the mirror.

"Shut up! You're hot," she said to her reflection.

Pilar replayed her conversation with Sunny yet again. She narrowed her eyes, like a tigress with her sights set on her quarry. Not giving herself time to reconsider, she dialed VJ's direct line at the office.

"Hi, there," she said, in a tone much more flirty than usual. "How are you doing?"

She could tell he recognized the difference in her voice and was trying not to sound too excited. He said, "I'm great now."

"Are you busy with anyone?" she asked.

"No, I'm the only one here."

She had hoped for that. "May I stop by for a minute?" Her heart was pounding. She imagined his was as well.

Twenty minutes later, she stood, restlessly moving from one cork clog to the other outside the glass and steel entry to the lobby of the Simon building. "Hurry up," she whispered, listening to his phone ring.

"Hey, it's me. How do I get in?"

"Oh, I'm sorry. I forgot. Access on Saturday afternoons is limited. I'll come right down."

She imagined this world-famous rich guy racing to meet her, and, sure enough, she saw him hurrying to the entrance. He pushed the red button to let her in.

She had on jean cutoffs as short as any he had ever seen. Her cropped T-shirt revealed toned abs. Her white teeth shined, and her eyes sparkled. She seemed delighted by his reaction to her.

"Hey, you," she said.

"Hey back," he said, his face burning.

Once, when VJ was a sophomore in high school, walking in the hall with friends between classes, the most beautiful girl in the school, a senior, said, "Hello." He couldn't believe such a goddess knew he existed. Looking at Pilar, he felt that way again.

He used his electronic key to summon the elevator. They got in. The atmosphere was charged.

"You said no one else is here?" Pilar asked.

"Yes, that's right," VJ said as they reached his office and went inside.

Pilar smiled, closed the door behind her, and approached him. He looked down at her. She pulled him close, looked up, and they kissed. Their mouths opened as they explored each other with their tongues.

She pulled back. "There's something I want to give you."

He was disappointed because she had pulled away. He didn't want to stop kissing. Skeptically, he asked, "What?"

"This." She dropped to her knees and then enthusiastically used every trick she knew to pleasure him. And he was pleasured.

"Oh, my God! Oh, my God!" He roared with pleasure.

He put his hands under her chin and raised her face so he could look at her. Then she stood up. He leaned down to kiss her. She took his hands and moved them across her body as she eagerly received his kiss.

He felt he was supposed to say something but felt awkward. "I ... uh ... you're wonderful!" he said. "You're wonderful! You're wonderful!"

She smiled.

He took her in. She was so beautiful. She was so sensuous.

"You liked it, huh?"

He twisted his head to the left and, to tease her, he responded in kind. "No. Not at all."

"Any time, VJ, any time."

"What was in it for you?"

"To give you pleasure is for me," she said simply.

He believed her.

Pilar believed herself.

She knew that no wife could compete with a great blow job. She had done it on an impulse and, leaving him, she was very pleased with herself. She had accomplished her mission even if she wasn't entirely sure what her mission had been. Of greater importance, she felt closer to him. They were bonding, growing together.

She loved that.

CHAPTER 16

WORKING UP THE CASE

FOR WORK ON ESTELLE COOK'S CASE, Paddy hired a private investigator recommended by Accurso, a guy named Codwell Pennyworth, known
as Cod. He reported that even before everything blew up, it was common
knowledge at Walker & Travis that James Cook was sending Gary on out-
of-town assignments just so Cook and Monica could have their trysts.
Rumor was they'd even had sex in the massage room at the Houston Country Club—on a Monday, when the golf course was closed.

Paddy absorbed what Cod had told him, but he didn't process it immediately. That night he couldn't sleep. He channel-surfed and paced, Mick,
the Irish Setter, following two steps behind him. After a while, the two
of them drove downtown, past the building where James Cook worked
and past the Family Law Center. Paddy drove back down Allen Parkway,
through River Oaks, down the street where the Cooks lived, down River
Oaks Boulevard to the country club and then made a U-turn and headed
for his Midtown apartment.

Estelle Cook had a problem, and any problem she had was his problem. The real value of James Cook's interest in the law firm was the Walker
& Travis brand. The precedent was clear. If James Cook owned part of a
company that made widgets, Estelle would get the fair market value of her
community half. But when it comes to an interest in a law firm, judges—all
lawyers—take care of their own. Estelle Cook would have no claim to his
or Walker & Travis's future earning power. She would get a share of his capital account, which was only a small fraction of the real value of his partnership interest. *Bupkis*. Estelle's lifestyle came from James's income, and she
wasn't going to get that anymore. In Texas, alimony is limited. Estelle had
no earning power. Her separate property was not significant. She would
need a lot of money up front from a settlement to maintain her standard
of living. She had no skills marketable enough to replace what she got from
James's income. The Cooks' other assets were fine for a comfortable living

if they stayed together. But a 55-45 split wouldn't cut it. She would get the house, now valued at well north of two million. It had no mortgage, but she would have to maintain it. His retirement plan was good, but not available for a while. No, no matter how he looked at it, Paddy had to find an angle that would increase the stakes.

He called her. "Estelle," he said, charging full blast. "You told me about having to entertain associates and their wives. What else did you do?"

She yawned. "I'll admit when I told you I wanted your full attention, I didn't have two in the morning in mind."

He looked at the time on his cable box. "Sorry. I'll call back."

"You know my husband *is* home."

"I called on your mobile. Can he hear you?"

"No. He's been sleeping in the guesthouse."

"Are you sure?"

"Mr. Moran, I can see the guest house from our bed. The light is on. I fall asleep watching it every night. Just give me a second to collect my thoughts."

He heard a cat purring and imagined it resting on Estelle's breasts as she took the call in bed, searching the guesthouse windows for movement. Finally, she said, "Well, I raised the children without much help from James, but really, I did what was expected of the wife of a Walker & Travis senior partner, which in and of itself is a full-time job."

"Like what?"

"Like being active in charities and country club affairs and entertaining, entertaining, entertaining. There was something nearly every day of the week."

After the call, he lay with his arms behind his head and his eyes open. After a while he jerked straight up and said to the night, "I have it."

Startled, Mick barked.

Up at sunrise, he waited until he was confident James Cook had left the house and then called Estelle. He told her his plan.

"I like it," she said. "I like it because it's right. It's brilliant, Mr. Moran. Go for it!"

"Do you have a joint checking account with James?"

"Of course."

"Do you have a separate property account?"

"Actually, I do. It's a brokerage account."

"You might want to transfer funds from the joint account to your separate account. James may not take too kindly to our filing the petition, but be careful to keep good records of what goes in and out. Fine with me if you take your credit cards and shop 'til you drop."

"Won't this all appear to be an act of war?"

"I'm just sayin'. You know James better than I do. Do what you're comfortable with, but my guess is he isn't going to complain if the bump in spending isn't too extreme. He probably will feel too guilty to complain. You may want to wait until we ring the opening bell for the main event."

"I think that would be wisest," she said. "He's very competitive. I don't want him making counterattacks yet. On the other hand, I probably do need to do some shopping."

That day Paddy filed a plain, vanilla petition for divorce.

When James Cook was served the petition, the attorney who signed as Estelle's attorney was not a name he recognized.

Upon arriving home later that evening, James said—in the same tone he used to comment on new flowers in the house—"I got your petition today."

"I don't want to talk about it now," Estelle said.

"I looked up your attorney. He hasn't been practicing very long. Went to South Texas. Used to be a policeman. For God's sake, Estelle, he's from Brooklyn."

"I'm hoping it won't be necessary to have someone better known, James." Estelle looked at him. She made sure to bat her eyelids, hoping that old trick still worked, even though she felt more like kicking him in the shins. "To be honest, well—I don't even know if I want to go through with it, bu—"

James smiled to himself smugly. Estelle noted the smile in her internal list of reasons she would nail him to the wall.

The next day James engaged Terry Lyons, one of the "club" of divorce lawyers who knew their way around the Family Law Center, and more particularly, its judges. Since James had only disdain for family law practitioners and he wanted to be in control, he also enlisted the aid of a trusted associate, Will Marshall.

Will Marshall was the senior associate on James's litigation team at Walker & Travis. Will not only had the necessary intellect, thoroughness, and skills to do the job, but he was also so desperate to make partner he would do anything to please James. Will was waiting with James when Lyons entered Cook's office. "Will Marshall will be second chair to you, Terry, at the courthouse," James said, "but first chair on research, fact gathering, and pleadings. Review Will's work. If you and he disagree on anything, I'll be the final arbiter. In any event, I will read all pleadings before they are filed. I expect to have them in time to make a careful review."

Terry bristled but kept his mouth shut.

"Ever had anything with her lawyer, Patrick Moran?" James asked, peering at both men over his half-lens reading glasses.

"Never," Terry said. "In fact, I've never even heard of him."

"But rest assured," Will added, earning a nasty glance from Terry, "he will soon know he's playing in the big leagues."

"Good man." James cuffed him on the shoulder. "I know I can count on you, Will."

Will Marshall was used to being counted on. With his Tobey Maguire looks and impeccable manners, Will was the kind of person who could always be counted on to hold down the fort—whether it was chatting to a boring executive or making a good show at the annual golf charity tournament. He was third-generation River Oaks, so to the extent that there was society in Houston, he had the pedigree. He went to the Hill School and was on track to go to Yale, however, in Will's last year at the Hill School, his father lost all his money and all Will's mother's money as well. There was just enough money left in a college trust fund to get Will through the University of Texas in Austin.

"Will Rusk Marshall," his mother had said, emphasizing his middle name—her maiden name—as she was driving him to Austin for fraternity rush, "I know it will be difficult, but I am counting on you. Remember, you have a name."

Will wasn't sure what she meant or what she was demanding of him, but he felt the weight of it—a weight that had crushed his father and had led him to take the foolish risk that turned out to be the financial disaster from which he never recovered.

One night in his dorm room, Will had an epiphany while watching Elaine May's film, *A New Leaf*, on a cable channel. Rapt, pizza box resting on his knee, he watched a broken-spirited, once wealthy Walter Matthau walking down the street of his former opulence, acknowledging his new reality: "Poor. I'm poor."

Will committed to himself on the spot to keep the same from happening to him. Tipping the pizza box to the floor in his enthusiasm, he vowed to do whatever it took to develop the right game plan to have enough money to live very comfortably—not showy rich, but enough to never worry about being poor. He would not end up like his father.

His lineage got him into the right fraternity. He started dating Muffy, a girl he'd known since childhood. He wasn't actually physically attracted to her, but he cared for her a lot, though perhaps not as much as someone should for a long-term relationship. The summer after he finished undergraduate school, at dinner at the Bayou Club, the most exclusive club in the city of Houston, Will asked Muffy to marry him. He had arranged through Muffy's mother for the ring to be presented on a red velvet cupcake as he sank down on one knee to pop the question. Her family gave them a monthly allowance while Will attended The University of Texas School of Law. He did well there, but not spectacularly. He didn't make law review, but he excelled at moot court. Though law review was usually a prerequisite for Walker & Travis, Will's and Muffy's combined family backgrounds was enough boost to get him an offer.

Will was assigned to the trial section. His work quickly made a favorable impression on James Cook, who took an instant personal liking to him. Most important, Cook was confident he could rely on Will's work product. He took young Will under his powerful wing. Working on Cook's divorce seemed the perfect opportunity to gain further favor, even if the work didn't count in Will's billable hours. Cook's unmitigated support was essential to Will's career because becoming a partner at Walker & Travis required not only excellence and substantial numbers of billable hours, but also sponsorship by a partner who had muscle. Cook, not surprisingly, had a one hundred percent track record of making his "boys" partners. Will couldn't have picked a better mentor. Now his mentor was counting on him.

As Will dove in, he became privy to important information. He learned that Cook had made over two million dollars the previous year. It was a handsome sum for most people. Will, who was making just under two hundred thousand, figured he was, at best, two years away from making partner. He had no idea how many years he was away from earning any-thing close to what Cook was paid.

Will began to spend part of his day—sometimes his entire work day—at Terry Lyons's office, reviewing documents and working on pleadings, requests, and motions. Lyons wanted to bury this Patrick Moran with paperwork. It was a task Will was up to. He employed skills he learned in the toxic tort litigation world.

Lyons said Estelle Cook was a fool not to have hired one of the big names. "James will have to pay for her lawyer anyway," he said. "Why not go first class?"

Will raised his eyebrows. He observed that Lyons and the other "first class" lawyers who practiced in the family law courts were quite broad-brush and frequently unprepared. It was all very clubby, and the judges went along with it. They were much more patient than the judges in the state civil district courts and federal courts where Will's practice had taken him. The friendly judges tolerated discovery produced late, poorly drafted motions, and, in particular, endless hearings on innocuous items. Many family court judges understood that members of the club had to make a living—a good one. How else could the lawyers make hefty contributions to their re-election campaigns and entertain them so lavishly?

Lyons's plan was to mount early pressure on Moran, a solo practitioner, hoping to force a settlement quickly. Cook expected a solution fitting of their station—quiet and without rancor. Before the judge entered the court, the lawyers introduced themselves to each other. Lyons was five feet seven inches tall, very slim, wore rimless glasses, and sported a pencil-thin mustache. He extended his hand to Paddy, who in contrast appeared to be a giant. Paddy grasped Lyons's hand in the Lyndon Johnson squeeze he'd practiced, pulling him close. He leaned his head down, smiling. Looking straight into Lyons's eyes, he said, "It is a pleasure to meet you, Mr. Lyons." A clearly rattled Lyons nodded.

Will instantly recognized the maneuver. He smiled both with admi-ration and enjoyment. When Lyons nervously introduced Will to Paddy, Will stepped in close, grasped Paddy's hand tightly, held his floor posi-tion, and looked straight up into their opponent's menacing face. Smiling, showing not the least bit of intimidation, Will said, "It is nice to meet you, Mr. Moran." Paddy nodded with a grudging respect.

The bailiff stepped into the courtroom. "All rise."

The judge entered the courtroom. Everyone rose.

"Thank you," he said. "Please be seated. Well, hello, Mr. Lyons." The judge smiled as if Lyons was his best friend. "What do we have here today?"

Paddy flinched. The judge's opening was not a good sign. Paddy had checked the online report of contributions to Judge Babson's campaigns. Lyons was a major contributor. Walker & Travis, whose practice did not include domestic relations matters, also contributed. Paddy was not surprised that he felt like an outsider in the court. If he had any doubts before, he now knew the judge wasn't going to do him any favors.

"Good morning, Your Honor," Lyons said. "Judge Babson, may I approach the bench to introduce you to Will Marshall?"

"Of course," the judge said.

They stepped forward. Paddy sensed he should as well, and he did.

"Mr. Marshall," Lyons said, beaming, "is a brilliant young man, an associate at Walker & Travis. He will be assisting me in representing James Cook."

"That's wonderful," said the judge in a kindly tone. "You can learn a great deal from this man, Mr. Marshall."

Then, looking at Moran, he said, "And you, sir?"

"My name is Patrick Moran, Your Honor. I represent Estelle Cook."

Although Paddy had represented numerous policemen in divorces, he had never been before this judge. All his police divorces had been assigned to associate judges, who were appointed by elected judges to handle cases, usually smaller cases.

"I don't think you've been before me, Mr. Moran."

Paddy straightened up to his full height, towering over his opposing counsel, eye-to-eye with the judge, who was sitting on the raised bench. "No, sir, Your Honor, I have nawt." Leaning forward, Paddy stared right into the judge's eyes. In a respectful though stern tone, he said, "But Your Honor has a reputation for being fair, objective, learned, and just, so I'm sure my client is pleased her case was assigned to your court."

The judge took a deep breath, glancing awkwardly at Lyons. "Thank you, Mr. Moran."

That signaled the end of the hearing. Lyons left the courtroom with no spring in his step, motioning for Will to gather documents on the counsel table. Will put their papers in his briefcase. After Paddy finished loading his briefcase, Will extended his hand.

"Mr. Moran. I just wanted to say I thought you were very effective. That was a nice display. You took control from the judge. I think if I were the judge, I'd be very careful in this case."

Paddy's gut told him Marshall was being genuine. "Well, thank you. You can call me Paddy."

"You're welcome. I'm sure we'll see each other again soon." Will hesitated, looking up at Moran. "Hey, it's about lunchtime. Do you have time to grab a bite with me?"

Now Paddy was really taken aback. "Yeah, that's just fine," he said. "Where do you want to go?"

They walked to a nearby Vietnamese place. Paddy called Estelle outside while Will got them a table. "We had our first hearing in Judge Babson's court," he told her. "Would you believe I was not as welcome as your husband's team?"

"Surprise, surprise," she said. "I warned you."

"Will Marshall is working with Lyons on the case. At his suggestion we're having lunch. What can you tell me about him?"

"Birds of a feather."

"You're kidding," Paddy said. "He's preppy and polished. I *ain't*." He waved to Will through the restaurant's window.

"Will is very comfortable among the rich and powerful," Mrs. Cook said. "But he's just as hungry as you are, and, be warned, he works as hard as I expect you to work."

"He's the first person I've met in any of the large firms who has ever been friendly to me."

"That doesn't surprise me, but remember, his success in life is tied to my husband."

Paddy laughed. "So is mine."

CHAPTER 17

GETTING TO KNOW YOU

AFTER THEIR AFTERNOON ENCOUNTER, VJ was unable to stop thinking about Pilar. He couldn't shake his physical hunger for her. He feared he was obsessed. Yet he also felt happier and more energized than he had in a long time—unhappier, too, when he was with Georgie.

One night as he entered the house, Georgie was in the hallway, pulling on a simple, casual, lightweight leather jacket. It passed through his mind that the credit card statement showed that jacket cost more than six thousand dollars.

"Girls' night out," she said, with a look that was both impish and smug, breezing past him. After twelve years, he believed he knew her less well than he had when they married.

When she was gone, his feeling of loneliness turned abruptly to anger. "I'm on top of the business world," he said to himself, "but my personal life is a bloody sham." Feeling surprisingly aggressive and suddenly bold, he called Pilar.

"What are you doing?"

"Laundry. Reading *The Cat in the Hat* to Gracie. What are you doing?"

"I'm on my way to come get you and take you out."

"What about Gracie?"

"She'll come, too. It's Thursday. The Children's Museum is open late, and it's free."

"What if you see someone you know?"

"It's possible but not likely. People I know are not likely to go to the Children's Museum on the free night."

"But if you do?"

"I'll introduce you as my daughter from a previous marriage and Grace as my granddaughter," he joked. "While I'm driving over, work on your Indian accent. If you do it well enough, you can pass. Up and down. Up and down."

"But you're from Israel."

"That accent is harder to mimic," he said, laughing.

They had a grand time. After they left the museum, Gracie fell asleep in the car. VJ drove, pointing out the many institutions in Houston's Museum District.

"I'd like to go to all of them," Pilar said dreamily.

"And so you shall. We shall," he added, as if correcting himself.

Soon VJ was living for his times with Pilar; he wished he could see her more than once a week, but Pilar always said no. Even though she was divorced, she was not as available to him as he wanted. She gave him lots of excuses, mostly to do with Gracie. He could respect that and wanted to believe it, but sometimes he wondered if she was playing him, or if she was seeing someone else. He knew he had no right to object. He didn't own her. They had no agreement. She never asked him for anything. But somehow she had become the most important thing in his life.

When they weren't going out to a museum or a film, they usually met at her house. It was a small, 1970s ranch house in a dull neighborhood in southwest Houston that was not quite close in enough for developers to buy as a teardown and build a mansion in its place, though that might happen in time. Pilar seemed content there, but VJ wanted more for her and Gracie.

One evening after dinner, he helped put Gracie to bed. Then he and Pilar held each other and kissed and touched, losing themselves in their passion for the other, but she drew the line at having intercourse.

"I'm not ready to go there until we've made a commitment to each other."

"I *am* committed to you."

"I think I believe you, but you're married," she said. "I want you to be fully committed to me."

He always felt disappointed when she refused him, though he convinced himself he understood. He didn't see her as a challenge. He felt instead that she had become part of his fabric. He could no longer imagine his life without her. At the same time, he wondered ceaselessly what she was really thinking.

<hr />

PILAR CALLED SUNNY on a Saturday morning and suggested they meet at the Menil. Sunny was nonplussed. "The Me-what?" When Pilar explained that the Menil Collection was an art museum in a beautiful building and on lovely grounds, Sunny was unimpressed. "Pilar, you're getting weird," she said. "Who even goes to places like that?"

"People like us," Pilar said brightly.

It was a beautiful day. There was a festival with food trucks in the parking lot and face painters and clowns on the lawn. "This is so fine out here," Sunny said, "why ruin a great time and go inside the joint?"

As they stopped at a shaved ice truck, Pilar said, "I don't know what to do about VJ. He is really into me. Like no one else has ever been, and I think I'm really into him, too."

"So what's the problem?"

"He's married."

"Is that really a problem?"

"Of course, it's a problem. He likes me and respects me. He's great with Gracie. But those things with married men, they never work out."

"It's like *Cosmopolitan* always says," Sunny agreed sagely, "if a guy cheats on his wife with you, he'll cheat on you too."

"I know that's usually how it is, but he's not like that. I can feel it. His wife is older. She drinks. He doesn't love her. They just go through the motions."

"That's what every woman thinks when she's involved with a married guy. You knew he was married from day one."

"I did, and at first I was intrigued that a rich and powerful man was attracted to me. But I never imagined it would—" she searched for a word other than "evolve"—"turn into something really serious. But this time, it's the right thing to think. The problem is, I don't believe he'll ever leave her either. He's too nice, you know?"

"I don't think it's a problem. You can get him to buy you a condo with a pool!"

Pilar bit her lip. "I would never do that."

"And that's because?"

"I have a child. It's not just my future. It's hers, too. I don't want to be some guy's mistress, Sunny. It would feel wrong because—well, because I really like him. I guess I love him. But then there's the age difference—I don't even know what kind of love it is."

Sunny laughed. "Pilar, you are loono-tuno. One of the richest guys in town, maybe the world, is sniffing, sniffing, sniffing around you, and you don't know what to do about it? How is he in bed?"

"I don't know. We haven't gone to bed."

"That's radical."

"Well, I know this is different. He could be my friend for life, and I don't want to screw it up over sex."

"And this is okay with him? Is he gay?"

Pilar threw her head back, laughing. "Not. But he's also not a player."

"All men, at some point, are players. Is he weird or something? I mean does he want to have sex?"

"Most def he does. No doubt about it. He tries every time."

"And you say no?"

Pilar nodded.

"Girl, all the time I've known you, I've never seen you . . . going through a process like this. Don't get mad, but you've jumped in the sack with guys you didn't care about. What is it about this guy?" Sunny glanced at her friend. "Never mind, I don't want to hear you moon about him. But you're asking me what you should do to keep him, am I right?"

Pilar nodded again.

"Keep him dangling. It's not knowing if he's going to get laid that makes a man want you more. I hate to say it, but it's true." She raised her eyebrows and put her index finger on her chin. "Here's a thought—I am so channeling *Cosmo* today!—do what he's interested in and show him you have interests in common. What does he like to do?"

"Go to museums and poetry readings and concerts and stuff," Pilar mumbled.

"Concerts sound like fun. Do that."

"Not those kind of concerts. Classical music."

"Oh, wow. Bummer. Well, tell him you *love* that stuff. Start going with him. That way he'll think you're the whole package." Sunny punched Pilar lightly in the arm. "Okay, Miss All-About-You, why don't you ask about Sal and me?"

CHAPTER 18

PADDY VISITS GARY MARTIN

THE INVESTIGATOR DISCOVERED that Gary Martin, the husband of Estelle's husband's gym rat lover, now practiced at a prestigious Wall Street firm. Paddy hadn't been back to New York since he'd left. He found himself looking forward to seeing the old city with new eyes and better clothes.

During his flight, Paddy thought about his move to Houston. He had researched what the vehicle of choice was among his soon-to-be new buddies in blue, purchased a used Ram Charger, and drove the sixteen hundred miles. He preferred the view from above. The first-class cocktails were nice, too.

"I doubt I can tell you anything that will be helpful," Martin said in his office, clearly shaken by Paddy's sudden arrival. "In fact, I know I can't. I don't know why you would bother to come all the way to New York to meet with me."

If Martin was going to let down his guard, Paddy felt Martin needed to be in charge of the meeting. "I'm not sure myself," he said. "But if I don't meet with you, Mrs. Cook will think I wasn't doing a good job representing her. I'm sure she would take it as a personal slight by you."

Martin's tone changed to one of reflection. "I can see how she would feel that way. She was always nice to me. I think it was beyond her duty to be nice to one of her husband's associates. I think she genuinely liked me."

"That's what she told me. She said you were a fine young man."

Martin suggested they go to the bar in The Pierre hotel. There was nothing like The Pierre in Brooklyn. It was old but nice. Paddy searched for the right word and settled on "refined." Martin led him to a table in the back. On the way, Paddy noticed most of the customers were men. Their ages varied, as did their height, their weight, their ethnicity, but it seemed to Paddy each had the same confident, self-assured mien. His new navy, pin-striped suit fit the dress code. He wondered how he would look if he too had longer hair slicked back with a moist look. Even though it was early evening, everyone looked as fresh as they probably had when they started their day.

Martin was six feet two, maybe a hundred and eighty pounds. His looks were the kind that improved with age if one had the confidence that came with success but became blander if one did not. His blondish-brown hairline was, Moran guessed, a good two inches farther back than it had been when he was a kid, and his hair looked a little windblown. Paddy wondered if that was because Martin hadn't had a chance to spiff up in the men's room when he arrived or if it was a contrived, I'm-busier-than-you look. Whichever, Martin had a bit of confidence about him.

Martin ordered a Chopin dirty martini straight up with blue cheese-stuffed olives.

"Not Tito's?"

Martin didn't smile. "Not much of Texas I wanted to take with me."

"While we're here, you're my co-counsel," Paddy said. "Everything I tell you is privileged unless I say it isn't. Anything you tell me that you don't want repeated will be dead man's talk."

Martin shrugged.

"How do you like New York?"

"I get paid more, but it costs a lot more to live here. I thought I worked long hours at Walker & Travis. Those hours wouldn't cut it here. On the other hand, that's not exactly a bad thing for me now. I really don't want too much time to myself."

"So, this firm is working out for you?"

"Yes. In fact, I am more advanced than my peers because of my Walker & Travis experience. Not a single one of them had ever taken a deposition by himself," he paused, "or herself, or attended a client meeting."

"You're kidding."

"The big firms here take brilliant people and give them plenty of work—research, reading depositions, examining documents, lots of hours, but hardly any contact with anyone outside the firm, except when strength in numbers is an image to be portrayed or to justify an invoice. I've leap-frogged them in a sense. It makes me more certain that I am on partnership track."

"Are you divorced?" Paddy asked.

"It's final," Martin answered.

"Got a girlfriend?"

Martin gave Paddy a wry grin, "Not quite yet ready for that."

"How did you get your job?"

"Walker & Travis got me the job."

"You're with a great firm, making lots of money. You must really appreciate that."

Martin gave Paddy a gimme-a-break look.

"I know some parts of what happened. I'm thinking that Mrs. Cook—Estelle—she has a cause of action against Walker & Travis."

Martin took a deep swallow from his martini. Paddy nursed his Irish whiskey.

"That might almost be novel and surely not without merit," Martin said, his posture suddenly relaxed.

"I know you've been betrayed," Paddy said, "your life turned upside down." He paused to see Martin's response, but he couldn't read it. "I don't want to cause you any more hurt than you've already experienced, but—" He took a full swig and felt the heat as the whiskey went down. Martin shifted away from him. Paddy had somehow lost some credibility. He had to get it back. He motioned to the bartender to bring him another.

"You think I'm bullshitting you," Paddy said. "You think because I just met you twenty minutes ago, I don't care about you. Mr. Martin, I have known you since Mrs. Cook first interviewed me. I have felt for you. You got kicked in the nuts, betrayed by the two most important people in your life. Yet you pulled yourself off the mat—you didn't creep off—and now you're well on the way to becoming a success on a grander platform than Walker & Travis." Paddy sensed he was getting him back. "You're young, Mr. Martin. What are you, twenty-nine? You'll get past it. You left a town you were barely ever in. Now you're with a great firm in the world's greatest city."

Paddy took a gulp of his second whiskey. "Estelle Cook is fifty-five. Her life and her world as she has known them have been demolished. Many of her so-called friends shy away from her. Houston's the only place she's ever lived. She needs to maintain not only her lifestyle, but more important, her dignity, her self-esteem. I'm not in any way trivializing your devastation. I'm saying you have what it takes to get past it. You're on the way up. Estelle Cook is not."

He let his locker-room speech sink in. He'd rehearsed it twelve times. "Trivializing." He worked hard to find that word and to make it seem natural for him to say. Now he felt the meeting with Martin was going as well as he hoped, perhaps better. "She didn't pick me because I am the best," Paddy added. "She picked me because I don't have to worry if I piss off the powers that be at Walker & Travis."

Martin nodded. "What's your theory, Mr. Moran, the one that can establish liability on the part of Walker & Travis?"

"I'll get there. First, a few questions, please."

Martin nodded.

"To begin, before you found out what was going on with Cook and your wife, do you think other people in the firm knew what was going on, including people on the management committee?"

"That would be my suspicion."

"How would they have known?"

"Large firms are interesting places, Mr. Moran. They are their own universe, and the masters of that universe are all-knowing, even when the information is about one of their own."

Paddy studied Martin, the way he swished his martini in its glass, how he half-closed his eyes as he talked. Martin had spent a lot of time thinking about this. Without Martin noticing, Paddy motioned to the bartender to bring another round. Paddy asked, "Where do you live?"

"I bought an apartment near the UN building."

"You bought it?" Paddy said, but he knew already. The investigator had been very thorough. "Wow! What kind of mortgage do you have?" Paddy knew Martin didn't have one.

"I don't have a mortgage."

"Did you inherit a lot of money?" Paddy knew Martin had not.

"Maybe I need to quit talking," Martin said. "It's a very small apartment, and the New York housing market was at a low."

"Did you and Mr. Cook enter into an agreement?"

"No."

"Did you and Walker & Travis enter into an agreement?"

"I can't answer that one."

Bingo! He laughed at himself for appropriating his professor's line. He said, "What would you do if I deposed you or called you as a witness?"

"I wouldn't lie under oath."

"I don't think we will ever get that far." Pretending the meeting was over, Paddy extended his hand. "Thank you so much."

Martin kept his right hand on his martini glass and said, "Your theory, Mr. Moran. What is it?"

"You want to hear it? It may be painful."

"Haven't you determined I'm past that?" Martin snapped.

Paddy leaned over, allowing the pace of his words to accelerate. "One, the law firm conspired with Cook to destroy his relationship with Mrs. Cook. Two, it facilitated that destruction by allowing him to send you on out-of-town assignments, so he could be with your wife. Three, there was an unwritten contract between the law firm and Mrs. Cook and, I suppose, all the wives, but her for sure, that part of the price for her husband's success was her participation in firm events, firm recruiting, and enhancing the firm's image by her participating in such things as charitable events, country club events, maintaining a home on the Azalea Trail, you name it."

Martin held up his third martini and twirled the glass in his hand, staring at the swirling remaining liquid. He nodded to Paddy and held out his glass until Paddy raised his and the glasses clinked.

"You are dead on there, Mr. Moran."

"By facilitating, or, at best, knowingly standing by, while he destroyed their marriage—"

Martin stared at him.

Meeting Martin's gaze, Paddy said, in a strong, firm voice, "Yours, too, of course, but my case is for Mrs. Cook, how the firm, as I said, facilitated, or, at best, knowingly stood by, while her marriage was destroyed. They breached the contract they had with her. She's entitled to actual and punitive damages." He relaxed his arm on the back of his chair. "I'm still tinkering with it. My plan is to put all this in pleadings, hand it to them before I file, and see if they want to settle first."

Martin, his eyes darting above Paddy's head as if following a fly, said, "Don't give them too much time to decide. They'll figure out a way to keep you from filing those pleadings or, failing that, keep them sealed."

That was a surprise. Suddenly, Paddy felt vulnerable, a feeling he hated perhaps more than anything. "What are you saying?"

"They're powerful. They can be ruthless, and they know how to protect themselves."

Paddy leaned forward again. "Interesting. How do you suggest I deal with that?"

"What do you think, Mr. Moran?"

Paddy smiled, "You remind me of my Contracts professor. That's a good thing. Let me think." He looked up. He moved his hand from side to side. "How's this? I demand that they make a quick decision. I let 'em know I've got someone at the courthouse ready to file if they don't meet my deadline."

"You may not think they can act that quickly. Let me assure you, they can."

"I really appreciate this, Mr. Martin."

"Okay, Mr. Moran," Martin said, smiling broadly, his words flowing more loosely. "To my great surprise, the pleasure's all mine. Something tells me Mrs. Cook may be . . . no, she *is* in good hands. She may not have picked you because you were the best, but she might have gotten the best anyway."

Paddy felt warmth in his cheeks. They shook hands, and as they were about to part, Paddy asked, "What is your opinion of Will Marshall?"

"Setting aside the fact that he has kissed Cook's ass since he joined the firm, intent on being his heir apparent, there's more to him than he lets on," Martin said. "He likes to make people think he is a River Oaks version of a good ol' boy, but because he had and lost all the trappings growing up, he has a hunger. Why do you ask?"

"Well," Paddy said, "his name is on the pleadings after Cook's divorce lawyer. I have gotten to know him a little. I hate to admit it, but I like him."

"I can understand that. A lot of people might not, but I can. Even so, don't let your guard down. Will's future at Walker & Travis is very much tied to Cook. He can't afford to lose this case."

Although confident he hadn't slipped up, Paddy still winced a little, thinking back to his lunch with Will.

"Thanks for that, too."

"You're going to do just fine, Mr. Moran, so long as you're careful."

As Paddy made his way to his hotel room, warm and just a little wobbly, he nodded to himself, more with relief than exhilaration. His mission had been accomplished.

CHAPTER 19

PILAR DOES POETRY

VJ WAS SURPRISED when Pilar said she wanted them to do more literary and arts activities together. "Like what?" he asked.

"I was thinking maybe we could form a book club or something," Pilar said quickly, "or you could take me around to all those places you like to go—you know the poetry readings and stuff, those museum openings? I want to be prepared when Gracie gets older."

"I guess we could form a book club for two people," he said. "Why not?"

"Well, we are unusual." Pilar was pleased with her response, though she was thinking that she never should have followed Sunny's ridiculous advice. But it was too late, because now VJ was getting into the idea. "I know," he said. "We'll read *Pride and Prejudice*. Every woman I know loves that novel."

"Really? How many women have you known?" There was no humor in her voice.

Embarrassed, he said, "To be honest, I've never read it. My wife said it was the book she read in college that she liked most."

Pilar felt sulky. She had come up with the whole book club idea to make him *not* think about his wife. She opened her mouth to say something sharp, but she stopped herself.

When they next met, he handed her a copy of the book. Pilar stared at the cover joylessly. "Great title," she said. She opened it and read a few lines: "It is a truth universally acknowledged that a man in possession . . ." Immediately, she began to feel herself having a panic attack. It sounded like the Declaration of Independence. How was she ever going to get through it, never mind discuss it with VJ? "I better buy a dictionary," she said out loud. VJ reached into the bag at his feet. "I bought you one," he said. Pilar eyed it grimly. A hardcover *Merriam-Webster's Collegiate Dictionary*.

"Well, I loved the movie," she said, trying to muster some enthusiasm and change the direction of the conversation. "Maybe we should read a different book—"

"Seeing the movie usually doesn't spoil a good book for me."

"My *abuela* used to say her favorite movie was *The Ten Commandments*, and I know she read the book," Pilar said, throwing her head back in that laugh he loved. "All right. Let's go for it."

⁂

ONE NIGHT HE BROUGHT DINNER from Eleganté to her house—Greenberg salad, lump crab meat, and short ribs. After dinner, but before dessert, they finished the last chapter of *Pride and Prejudice*.

"I think this is now my favorite book," Pilar announced.

"Really? Why?"

She frowned, her fork hovering for a moment over the tiramisu in front of her. He realized he was holding his breath and released it as she said, "Well, it's not *just* because we read it together, but that's definitely part of it." She reached for his hand. "Actually, a big part, but it's also because just one truly good deed can bring salvation. A person can be self-centered and snobby toward everyone, a real jerk, but if they do just one heroic thing, one truly selfless act, it's all made okay. They are forgiven and loved. Besides that, for such a famous classic, it sure is funny."

Pilar caught him looking at her and turned away. It was true that she had only begun to read the book to impress him, but something truly surprising had happened. She had grown to love the characters. Even the crazy difficult words didn't bother her that much. Though she had to look up a few of them, most of the time she could figure out what they meant—and she enjoyed the stimulation of having to do that. Mostly, though, she loved Elizabeth Bennett—now her pal Lizzie—so much more than she could possibly have anticipated. Of course, her real heroine was Jane, or Miss Austen as she would probably rather be called. No pretentious assholes could get away with being pretentious assholes around Miss Austen without her calling them on it. "You go girl," Pilar longed to tell her, except, of course, she was dead. "I'll never forget this story, these people," she said to VJ.

They began to frequent bookstores together. Pilar remained hesitant at first, in spite of the success of *Pride and Prejudice*. But soon enough she found herself enjoying book reviews in the paper and, from their references to other books, chatting with him about books she wanted to read and books he suggested. It was kind of crazy; she just had to sound interested in a book and there it was. *The Great Gatsby*, Anne Frank's *The Diary of a Young Girl*, *The Color Purple*, *How the García Girls Lost Their Accents*, *The House on Mango Street*. VJ bought them for her, and she devoured them. One book Pilar read, *Is That You God? It's Me Margaret*, struck her as important to share with Gracie when she was older, and she looked forward to the time when they could read it together. Pilar was pleased. "We are going to be such a reading family, Gracie and I," she said.

"I'm not in your family?" he said, sounding genuinely hurt.

"No, but you do bring the books," Pilar replied. "That gives you a seat at our table."

Then one afternoon VJ suggested they meet at a poetry reading. The thought of it filled Pilar with dread. Books were one thing. Stories were fun, but poetry? Plus, taking into account who the usual attendees were, they shouldn't be seen seated together. As planned, VJ entered before her and took a seat in the reserved section, saving one for her. Just as the lights went down she came in and took the seat beside him.

The first poet was a handsome young man with long blond hair, wearing blue jeans and an untucked plaid shirt. Seeing him, Pilar wondered if the event would turn out interesting after all. Women were sitting in the front rows, obviously hoping for the handsome poet to notice them and see how enthralled they were with his work. From the moment he opened his mouth, Pilar was the opposite of enthralled. Listening to his poetry was challenging, worse than she'd feared. Words like "lacunae" and "sensorium" labored out of a ridiculously solemn voice. Worse, she couldn't even tell what a single one of his poems was supposed to be about. "Canary breath on my shoulder/ where am I going in this nest of giant straws." Really? Did his pauses make the words more important? They surely made his poems longer. Fighting to keep her eyes open, Pilar glanced at VJ. He sat silently, not indicating his like or dislike. Could he actually want to be here listening to this? Thirty minutes later handsome poet stepped off the stage to polite but less enthusiastic applause than when he took the podium. She felt she had paid her dues, and she signaled to VJ that it was time to go, but he ignored her. When she started to leave, he gently but firmly pressed her forearm. She stayed.

The second poet was attractive and cheerful and seemed grateful for the audience. Who knew what would happen when she opened her mouth? Her first poem was about a twelve-year-old girl being tormented by boys in a garage, and how she stopped them by being brave. Pilar gasped when the last line was read and, without thinking, grabbed VJ's hand. Then she quickly took it away and secretly glanced to either side of her. As the poet read on, Pilar found herself transported to a place where everything in the world seemed vivid and clear. It was a place of pain, but also joy, a place Pilar had never really explored emotionally or intellectually. Every line was crisp, like a perfectly focused photograph, and gave her a shivery feeling inside. She knew exactly what this woman was talking about, and for the first time ever, her remembrance didn't make her shudder. She was struck by how a poem could condense important concepts with just a few words. When the reading was over, the enthusiastic applause of the audience jarred her back into the here and now.

As the audience filed out, Pilar took a different path than VJ. In the lobby, the poet was sitting at a table signing books. Pilar stood in the line, holding the book VJ had given her. When it was her turn, surprised and embarrassed to find herself struggling to maintain her composure, she said, "That poem you read, 'Sixth Grade'—I knew that place. You got it perfectly."

The poet grabbed her hand and squeezed it. "What's your name, honey?" she asked.

The poet smiled and nodded and busily wrote, then handed the book back. Pilar opened it to the page where she had signed. Her heart swelled as she read, "To Pilar, my soul sister, you will always be brave when you have to be. Marie Howe."

She wanted to tell Marie that she hadn't been so brave and strong when she was confronted with a similar situation, but she couldn't bring herself to say it.

After that evening, Pilar checked out the poets and told VJ which readings she wanted to attend. Mostly she was pleased. VJ was happy to oblige though it was a little awkward. He and Georgie had season tickets to The Inprint Margarett Root Brown Reading Series, where the world's most famous and accomplished writers and poets came to Houston to read their latest works. Although Georgie enjoyed the readings, she was embarrassed by her uncontrollable hacking cough, so she rarely went anymore. VJ and

Pilar continued attending separately but together because a lot of Georgie's friends did attend. At first, the charade added some excitement to the events. Then, even though it was his idea, VJ began to find it annoying that he had to pretend not to know Pilar.

"You're the person I most care about, and I can't figure out why I should care who knows it," VJ said as she took her seat one evening.

Pilar could hardly believe her ears. Later, in an embrace, he asked if he could stay the night. She remembered the promises she'd made to herself. Her ambivalence was revealed in the gentleness with which she pushed him away. She saw he was unsure of whether or not to persist. She touched him and said, "Now that I've been to a bunch of poetry readings, I'd like to start learning more about art."

"I've created a monster," he exclaimed with great exaggeration. "You've read too much Jane Austen. Long courtships with no sex." But, of course, VJ was happy to oblige her desire. Separately but together, they made the rounds of stunning exhibitions. He avoided opening nights. They discussed the artists in hushed voices. He bought her a patron's membership to the Museum of Fine Arts, Houston. Sometimes, Pilar, alone, went to exhibitions he told her were important. Pilar especially liked Frida Kahlo. "It's as if she's working to see herself as clearly as she possibly can," Pilar gushed. "As if from outside, but with everything laid out for everyone to see, like she's holding a mirror up to her heart, and I am peering into the mirror from behind her, but I also see my heart in her heart." Pilar's cheeks turned red. "That's ridiculous isn't it?"

"No," VJ said. "It's beautiful."

CHAPTER 20

TAKING ON THE BIG FIRM

EVEN BEFORE PADDY FILED the original petition he had drafted amended pleadings, adding the law firm as a defendant because it facilitated the affair, claiming a breach of the firm's unwritten contract with Estelle. Fully, carefully, he recited the facts in chronological order, followed by claims for damage, a technique that worked for Margot's claim against the hospital. There'd be no thrill of the courtroom, but he'd have a happy client and a handsome payday. Having been forewarned by Mrs. Cook and Gary Martin, he was also playing beat the clock. This time there would be no rounds of negotiations over months. His pleadings and his personal presentation to Walker & Travis would have to be flawless. Without a quick resolution he would drown in discovery, have to fight motions upon motions, and respond to every tactic an adversary with unlimited resources could use.

There was also a looming unknown. He would have to make new law for Estelle to recover against the firm. There was that. His own assessment of the limitations of his experience and resources were preying on him. Estelle was right. If he didn't settle in his first shot, he would need to assemble a team just to get him to daylight. Could he maneuver Walker & Travis into doing the right thing immediately and, not so incidentally, protect their precious brand?

He needed a settlement agreement that anticipated the protections Walker & Travis would want so a signed document could come quickly.

He called Professor Bingo and agreed to meet at the professor's office.

In Bingo's office, they drafted a settlement agreement that contained everything Paddy wanted for Mrs. Cook and everything the professor thought Walker & Travis would want for themselves.

"You have balls, Mr. Moran," Bingo said, munching on Funyuns. Always mindful of Bingo's fondness for the junkiest of junk food, Paddy had brought an ample supply of his favorites. "Make sure they don't know I helped you. They might destroy the law school."

Paddy smiled. "I think you're kidding on the square, as my Uncle Séamus used to say." The professor raised his eyebrows. He nodded with a rueful expression on his face.

"Don't worry, sir. They'll never know."

〰〰

PADDY WENT THROUGH TEN MORE drafts of the pleading. He rehearsed his presentation. He practiced his responses to questions and comments he anticipated would come. He paced his living room, Mick following two steps behind. He imagined exchanges as he stared in the bathroom mirror, sat on the commode, walked Mick, and drove to the supermarket. For his dress rehearsal, he met with Mrs. Cook. They went over the pleadings and his presentation line by line by line.

"And if they don't make a deal with you," Mrs. Cook said, "then what?"

"That would be your choice. We could file and do our best, or you can live unhappily ever after with your husband. You never know. Bill and Hillary seem to be doing okay."

"I don't have a lot in common with Hillary Clinton."

Paddy shrugged.

〰〰

PADDY ARRIVED AT WALKER & TRAVIS at precisely the appointment time, amended pleadings and settlement agreement in hand. Prepared for a wait to let him know he was not important, he had barely settled in his chair when an attractive woman in her mid-forties called his name. He followed her through a door and then along a path past secretarial cubicles on the interior side and solid oak doors with lawyers' names on brass plaques on the exterior side. One plaque he passed read "Marlin Seaborn." His mind danced with possibilities, including chewing a major chunk out of the hide of Walker & Travis so that prick Seaborn and his other partners would have to put money in instead of take it out. However, he knew not to count his chickens before they hatched. They reached a corner office with a brass plaque that announced, "Tom Frost, Managing Partner." She led him in.

Tom Frost barely glanced up when Paddy entered the room.

Paddy had never seen an office so well appointed. Gilt-framed portraits hung high on the walls. Past managing partners, no doubt, some smiling, some stern, but each looking down. Two chairs faced the managing partner at his desk. Tom Frost appeared young—young in Paddy's mind to be a managing partner anyway. His closely cropped hair had a little gray.

"Mr. Morgan, please have a seat." Frost gestured to the two seats in front of his desk.

"It is Moran, not Morgan. I'm guessing you knew that."

Frost's eyes opened wide. "I didn't mean to say your name wrong. I apologize. No slight was intended."

Paddy was thrown off a bit by his openness.

"Sir, you know I represent Estelle Cook in her divorce proceedings with your partner?"

"Yes, I do. Estelle Cook is a lovely person. I'm very sorry about all this."

"I believe you mean that. You're probably wondering why I've come to see you."

"Yes, I am."

"Well, I'm handing you something. I request that you read it while I am sitting here."

"What is it, Mr. Moran?"

"It speaks for itself, sir."

Paddy watched as Tom Frost read the pleading, lightly tapping a very large Montblanc fountain pen on his desk as he did. Finally, he raised his head. His eyes were slits, his eyebrows lowered. "Have you filed this? Are you asking me to accept service?" No trace of his earlier, friendly tone remained.

Paddy had rehearsed this next part to sound professional, yet firm, not gloating or arrogant or like an extortionist.

"I haven't filed it yet, sir. It occurred to me before I did you might appreciate the opportunity to settle before it becomes public record."

"Mr. Moran, this is outrageous," Frost snapped.

Paddy saw Frost could be a formidable adversary. He returned his steely gaze. Using a tone of righteous indignation, he said, "If you're talking about Mr. Cook's conduct and this law firm's conduct, I agree. It *is* outrageous."

There was silence. Frost looked into Paddy's eyes. His face hardened. "If I'm supposed to be frightened, Mr. Moran, I'm not."

"I didn't expect you to be. Originally, I was going to file it and wait to hear from you." It was this moment he had practiced over and over. His final shot. If this didn't work, there were too many variables. He had to play this perfectly from here.

"I guess you're telling me I should have filed. Okay, I'm done." Paddy closed his brief case. Rising, he locked his eyes with Frost's. "How is this going to affect your recruiting?"

Unguarded, Frost said, "Our recruiting?"

Paddy sat back down. In a faux drawl, he said, "Well, I know you—that is, the law firm—has the judge in its pocket. If you don't settle, I reckon he's going to throw out my suit against the law firm. I'm gonna appeal. I think I'll win. But the reality is, I might not. That's the stuff nobody can control. But one thing I do know. This is going to be a case of first impression, a very high-profile one. For me, high profile is great. Win or lose, my name gets around. And this is a pretty juicy case to have my name attached to."

The moxie fighter from Brooklyn sprang from the corner, fists flying. "I'm a winner no matter what. That's not true for you, Tom Frost. The allegations about the way your firm treated this poor woman will probably make the *Chronicle*, *The New York Times*, and *The Wall Street Journal*. And you can bet, the appellate decision on the novel issue of a law firm being liable for permitting a partner to trifle with a subordinate's wife will be a reported case, and the *Texas Law Review*, the *Houston Law Review*, and, yes, maybe even the *Harvard Law Review*, will publish notes on the case. Who woulda thought the likes of Paddy Moran would make the *Harvard Law Review*? And, along the way, Walker & Travis becomes a bathroom joke, and it will have happened on your watch, Tom Frost."

He took a long pause to let that sink in. "I'll tell you something. My client, Mrs. Cook—who gave as much of her life to this firm as her husband has—actually, I'm not sure what she would want most: enough money to live the way she's supposed to live for the rest of her life or the satisfaction of exposing the firm that treated her shabbily and turned her life into a tawdry tale for the local rumor mongers."

"We don't yield to threats, Mr. Moran."

"Do you think this is a threat? Gimme a break. If you were representing my client, you'd be delighted to come up with a novel theory to increase her chances for justice."

"We don't sue other law firms."

"Well, aren't you special? Let me assure you, *we* do. And, despite your self-righteous protestations, sir, if the right client asked you, you'd sue another law firm in a heartbeat."

Silence.

"Mr. Frost, Estelle Cook can't be just another plaintiff to this law firm."

Frost's posture changed. "You're right about Estelle."

For the first time, Paddy felt a favorable shift.

"Okay, sir, here's the deal. Your partner, Mr. Cook, agrees to her getting the River Oaks home, the River Oaks Country Club membership, and a 70-30 split of the rest of the community property. And," he said deliberately, "the law firm pays her five million and seventy-five thousand dollars. I have drafted a settlement document. If I don't have signed copies by three o'clock today, my amended petition will be filed."

"You expect us to hand over five million dollars and get Cook to agree to a 70-30 split and do all that in less than six hours?"

"I know you can do it. And it's five million and seventy-five thousand. The seventy-five thousand is for attorneys' fees." Paddy had added that just for fun. "Frankly, I can't really say I am expecting settlement. That's Plan A—we settle by three this afternoon. Plan B is filing amended pleadings naming Walker & Travis as a codefendant at one minute after three. I have someone waiting at the courthouse, so even if I get hit by a truck before then, it's filed. Just in case you choose Plan A, I thought I would speed up the process by preparing a settlement agreement."

"Why are you in such a hurry?"

Paddy stood. "Let's just say I have tremendous respect for the power of this law firm. If I give you overnight to respond, you will have a hundred lawyers staying up all night to figure out how to silence me. I can't give you much time. In fact, six hours may be too much."

"I have a duty to discuss this with my management committee."

Paddy assumed that would include James Cook, but he didn't mention it. Instead he said, "You can reach me on my cell."

"Mr. Moran," Frost called out, "I doubt that we will accept your offer. However, on the off chance we do, it might be best that you remain at our offices."

"Are you telling me I can't leave?" Paddy was genuinely alarmed. He thought about Gary Martin's warning. Sweat began to bead at his hairline.

Frost held up his hand, clearly embarrassed. "No. No, of course not. You're free to leave. However, you're the one who's given us such a short deadline. It's in everyone's interest that you be immediately accessible until three."

"Point well taken." He started to say he would have to rearrange some things, but it wouldn't have had any credibility.

〰

THE CONFERENCE ROOM had a southern view, and Paddy could see all the way to the Texas Medical Center. At two o'clock, he began to get fidgety. He started pacing. Then he stopped. What if they're watching? At two thirty-three, he heard a knock on the door.

"Come in," Paddy called.

Tom Frost entered. Paddy's heart raced.

"Mr. Moran, the firm and James Cook accept your terms. We have some wording differences on the document, but I don't think they will trouble you."

Paddy tried to hide his giddiness. The proposed changes didn't bother him. Walker & Travis's most important concern was the confidentiality provisions. He and Professor Bingo had anticipated that provision in the draft, but Walker & Travis wanted belt *and* suspenders. Fine with Paddy.

"Understand we do not accept the validity of your legal theory, nor do we fear any consequences to the pleadings being a public document."

"Bullshit," Paddy resisted saying.

"What we do accept is that Estelle Cook has been a great asset to this law firm."

"Double bullshit," also suppressed.

Frost made his posture even more erect.

"Each member of the management committee expressed his admiration for Estelle." His posture relaxed. "The truth is we care about her. I, for one, was—am—a particular admirer. When I joined this firm, I was really still a boy, a boy from a small, poor town in East Texas who somehow did really well in law school. She took me under her wing."

The East Texas had been entirely exorcised from this polished, carefully spoken man.

"Let me say," Frost looked past Paddy, "she was the most beautiful, the most sophisticated, the most enchanting woman I had ever seen, much less known. I think she knew . . . how taken I was with her. She took great care not to make me feel a fool."

Frost took a long pause before returning to the moment. "Mr. Moran, I'm sure you think there's more to this story than what I'm saying. You're thinking large law firms don't pay out five million dollars because someone is nice and was faithful and devoted to the firm."

You got that right, buddy, Paddy thought, but what Frost saw was a man nodding his head in a knowing and sympathetic way. Paddy had learned the trick from a funeral parlor director in Brooklyn.

"For Estelle Cook, this law firm does. Here are four copies of the agreement with our changes. Return two copies signed by Mrs. Cook and by you, and we'll wire the money."

Paddy rose to shake Frost's hand, but he had already turned to head to the door.

Paddy looked at the document again and quickly did the math. A rough calculation of his fee came to about a million and a half dollars. He could barely suppress his euphoria. Then he noticed the date beside the signature. It was the third anniversary of his passing the bar. "Getthefukouttaheah! I'm a goddam millionaire."

On his way out, he again passed Marlin Seaborn's office. This time, Paddy stopped at the open door. He motioned to catch Seaborn's attention. Seaborn looked up. Paddy gave him a broad smile, a big wink, and an exaggerated wave. Seaborn responded with a puzzled look. He'd find out soon enough why Paddy had a shit-eating grin on his face.

Paddy asked the receptionist if she stamped parking tickets. She smiled and handed him some vouchers to put in the parking garage exit machine.

〰️

PADDY DIDN'T HAVE TO CALL off the person poised to file the pleadings. There was no such person. He did call Estelle Cook. She was ecstatic. "I'll keep my promise, Mr. Moran. The settlement agreement may be confidential, but the fact that you cleaned their plow is not. I'll sing your praises in all the right places." She asked him to meet her at Eleganté to sign. He agreed, but he felt somehow wronged. Exiting the garage, he realized what bothered him. For the first time, he felt going to Eleganté was a consolation prize. Why hadn't Mrs. Cook invited him to her country club?

What the fuck did he care? He was a goddam millionaire, and he was about to be hot!

CHAPTER 21

A TURN FOR THE WORSE

PILAR ACCEPTED SMALL GIFTS FROM VJ, but she refused anything with a high price tag and any offers of money, no matter how broke she was. On one hand he admired her integrity but on the other hand he was frustrated at not being able to experience the joy of giving to her. Her birthday was drawing close, and he wanted to do something special. She would just have to deal with it. He went to a jeweler and told him a business associate was caught out of town and hadn't gotten his wife a birthday present, and VJ had offered to select one for him. The jeweler, knowing VJ pretty well, bought the story. VJ selected some tastefully simple but stunning diamond earrings. The night of Pilar's birthday he gave them to her.

Pilar gasped and cried. "I can't take these. Oh, my God. I've never had anything so exquisite in my life."

"I insist. It makes me very happy. Please put them on."

She put the posts through her ears, fastened the backs, and went to the mirror. "They are *so* gorgeous."

"They look as if they were made to set off the exquisite beauty that comes between them," VJ said. He didn't care if that sounded corny. He came up behind her and took her in his arms, relishing her softness.

"People will wonder how I could have something so . . . so expensive."

"If someone is crass enough to ask, tell them they're zircon."

Tears formed, and she held him tightly. She wondered if this was the time she should give in to what she knew he wanted, what she wanted, too. He resolved the dilemma. "I'm going now. You said Sunny was having a birthday party for you. I don't want to make you late."

He kissed her and was out the door. She wanted to chase after him. Instead, she hung her head down as she watched him walk away.

"WOO-HOO! I'M BLINDED." Sunny lifted her arm as if to shield her eyes from a bright light.

"Oh, Sunny. He makes me so happy."

"And he's still married," Sunny said.

"Which is why I can't invest any more in him than I have already," Pilar sniffed. "That's why I can't have sex with him and—"

Sunny rolled her eyes. Pilar could tell by her friend's expression that she thought their relationship was just plain screwy.

~~~

THAT FRIDAY, VJ invited her to see a rerun of *Like Water for Chocolate*. It was a sensual yet very funny film, but she identified Tita's and Pedro's plight with her own situation with VJ. They went back to her house and, as usual, were soon kissing and holding and touching.

Pulling him down on top of her, she said, "I want you now."

Afterwards, as he left, he said, "I'm telling my wife I'm leaving her and getting a divorce." Pilar could barely contain her joy. "For real?" she asked, her eyes glistening.

~~~

THE NEXT EVENING VJ arrived home early. He called Georgie's name as he walked in the door and said he had something he needed to discuss with her. She sat down beside him on their long leather couch.

"Georgie, I like you. I admire you. But I need something more, and I can't imagine that you don't. I think it's time we end it."

Georgie shrieked, "No!" She covered her face with her hands. "I can't get a divorce. I won't. It'll ruin my life. It will ruin me." She began to sob as if her heart would break. She turned to him, her eyes wild, her hands poised as if to strike. She hissed, "If you do this to me, I'll break you." Then, sobbing again, "Everyone has left me. I won't let you leave me, too."

"What do you mean break me?" VJ's tone was cold.

"Divorces can be very expensive."

"Georgie, I've thought this over carefully. Let me tell you something: on my worst day, you couldn't break me."

"Is there someone else?" she asked, both threatened and threateningly.

"No. Of course not," he said, his lie undetectable.

"I want you to listen carefully," she said, her face drained of color. "If you leave me, I'll kill myself."

Her life as he knew it played through his mind like a silent home movie. Tended by nannies as a child, shipped off to boarding school as soon as she was old enough, always feeling unwanted. He had thought perhaps her friends were enough for her—her old college chums, the artsy, smart women she took trips with—but now he realized in a flash that from her perspective, she had never let them get close to her either. She was their rich, witty, entitled friend. It made them feel important to say they were with her. She knew that.

"Georgie—" he said helplessly.

"I mean it," she said.

He believed her. He had no doubt she would attempt suicide and perhaps succeed. He nodded, got up, went to the bar, and poured himself a whiskey, even though he rarely drank hard liquor. The amber liquid burned his throat.

He looked over at his wife, sitting on the couch, still as a stone. "I understand," he said, though he felt devastated. He had failed Pilar more than he had failed himself. He downed the whiskey and set the glass on the bar.

꩜

THE NEXT FEW DAYS were a waking nightmare. VJ knew Pilar wanted to hear from him. He could picture her, sitting in her little house, waiting for his call, and he felt an immense sadness. What had he done? What could he do to fix this? Finally, he dialed her number.

"Georgie threatened to kill herself," he told her. "And I believe she would, Pilar. I absolutely believe her."

"What does this mean?"

"It means I can't get a divorce."

Pilar felt as if a heavyweight boxer had hit her in the stomach. She gasped for air. Once composed, she said, "I never asked you to leave your wife. Why did you say you would if you didn't plan to go through with it? I feel totally betrayed." She hung up. She allowed herself to heave with crying.

THE NEXT DAY HE CALLED and asked to see her. "This isn't going to work for me," she said. "The other night was wonderful, but I was fooling myself. If you loved your wife, I would never have let it get this far. But you don't, and I really believed you loved me enough to marry me. You've been a wonderful friend. You've enriched my life in so many ways, but whatever we have has to stop."

"I love you," he said. "I love you so much it makes me ache."

"That's how I feel about you too, and that's the problem. No more, VJ. *No más.*"

In the following days, VJ could not eat or sleep. He felt guilty for not having the courage to leave Georgie. He knew he had no right to call Pilar, to ask her anything, but he called regardless, and he called more than he should have. But she almost never picked up, and when she did she refused to talk. He had never wanted anyone as much as he wanted her. The wound was overpowering.

Weeks passed. Then months. Georgie became even thinner and began smoking inside again. VJ didn't have the courage to object. One night he called Pilar, and as usual, there was no answer. Unable to help himself, he drove to her house. Though it was after nine o'clock, the house was dark, and her car was not there.

His hands were shaking so much he could barely hold his phone. He called her landline. No answer. He called her mobile phone. She didn't answer. He called it three more times. Finally, she answered.

"You're not home," he said.

"Are you checking up on me?" Pilar said. "How dare you? You don't own me. You don't even have the right to call me."

There was silence for a moment. Then VJ said, "You're right. I don't, but you know how much I care for you."

Pilar ended the call. VJ was hurt and confused. He felt abandoned, but knew he was getting exactly what he deserved. He vowed he would not call her again. His body felt as if he was a heroin addict quitting cold turkey.

VJ WAS AFRAID his business would suffer, but he seemed able to work no matter how miserable he was. Yet every day was torture. He didn't want to stay at the office, and he didn't want to go home. He began stopping by Eleganté in the evenings and having a drink with Luigi, a specially crafted cocktail the bartender had made for him, a HinJew martini—half Bombay Sapphire, half slivovitz, straight up, with four olives stuffed with nut chutney. The drink was always on the house, but VJ's tips far exceeded the cost.

The friendship with Luigi began as VJ became a frequent and valued customer. Eleganté had been in the midst of elaborate renovations when Houston's economy hit one of its down cycles. VJ volunteered to provide what was needed. To Luigi, loyalty begat loyalty. They became closer friends. Now, for the first time, it was VJ who was the friend in need.

Luigi had a pretty good idea what was bothering VJ, but he wasn't about to bring it up. He would sit with his friend and either say nothing or chat about safe subjects like the Astros or the investment climate or who was doing whom in Houston's biggest companies or how much hotter or muggier it could possibly get.

〰️

ON A WHIM, VJ TOOK Georgie to London for the theater and to visit her favorite galleries. He thought getting away would help, but he couldn't get Pilar out of his mind—or his heart.

In the National Portrait Gallery, Georgie caught him staring at a blank wall. "Waiting for the next exhibit to be hung, darling?" she said crisply. He mumbled something apologetically. "I have no earthly idea why we made this trip together," she said. "I hardly see you in Houston anymore, and we certainly aren't enjoying each other's company here. Are you so angry about my not giving you the divorce that you hauled me across the ocean to punish me?"

He did not respond.

"Call the pilot and tell him we're ready to go back to Houston. On second thought, have him drop me off at Teterboro and then you go to Houston." On the plane ride, he caught Georgie staring at him with a look of pity. He wondered if she had any idea how dead he was inside. *No más.* He heard it over and over again.

IT'S A DEAL

FOR PADDY, ESTELLE COOK'S CASE was a bonanza. Almost overnight, his name had jumped onto the list for the suers and the suees to choose from. Spouses caught being unfaithful, coming out of the closet, suddenly rich or suddenly poor or feeling stuck after the nest had emptied were among the many reasons people chose to sue for divorce. He was suddenly inundated with work. He still found time to take care of the good cops and he was doing quite well financially with the new clients that came to him, but it wasn't enough. He needed some kind of a shtick to kick things into really high gear. And he had an idea of exactly who to call.

SOON AFTER PADDY MORAN'S visit to Walker & Travis, James Cook was no longer a management committee member. He was no longer one of the Brahmins. Cook's fall from grace substantially diminished—if not completely ended—Will Marshall's chances for making partner. Tom Frost, the managing partner, still seemed to like him well enough, but without Cook in play, Will was where he had promised himself he would never be again—on the outside looking in. Competing with the Houston offices of New York firms, Walker & Travis paid its associates well, but not enough to satisfy Will. The big payday was making partner.

He'd just hung up from a conversation with an opposing lawyer at one of the plaintiff's firms out of New York when Paddy called and invited him to lunch. Will was pleased, looking forward to visiting with his brash, friendly former adversary. He accepted, wondering why Eleganté. It was a bit of a drive from downtown and rather upscale for Paddy to choose for lunch.

Arriving at the restaurant, Will watched from his car as the parking valet opened the door of a Mercedes in front of him. Paddy stepped out of the Mercedes and shook hands with the valet, then headed toward the entrance as his car was moved close to the valet station.

Will pulled his car forward and the valet handed him a claim check and drove his car to a lot on the side of the building. He hurried to catch up with Paddy.

As they entered the restaurant, the hostess smiled and said, "Hello, Mr. Moran. Let me take you and your guest to your table." Paddy beamed and followed her with the confident, cocky, proprietary strut of a successful trial lawyer. He greeted people at nearly every table they passed. As the hostess patiently waited, he leaned over toward a seated woman blocked from Will's view. He kissed her cheek. "Margot, it's so good to see you. I would like for you to meet Will Marshall."

"Actually, Paddy, I've known Will for a long time. You're both in good company."

While most of the women diners looked studiously put together, Margot, as usual, looked effortlessly exquisite in a cream-colored silk shift with a simple strand of amber beads. Will gave her hand a squeeze. He was truly impressed. Moran must be a decent enough guy to have Margot in his corner.

Once seated, Paddy said, sounding completely sincere, "How you holdin' up?"

"You did a great job," Will said, "but, to be honest, I feel like the victim of a drive-by shooting."

"It wasn't your fault," Paddy said.

"You don't know how big firms work."

Paddy interrupted. "Actually, a former associate of Walker & Travis gave me a pretty good idea."

Will laughed. "I could guess who that might be. I'm laughing, but I could be crying. When Cook crashed and burned, my chances for making partner went from sure thing to long odds, very long odds."

"Then you can't be too happy with me, I'm guessing?"

"Why? You got a great result for a deserving client. You certainly didn't make it personal as far as I was concerned."

Paddy put his hand on Will's forearm. The gesture struck Will as brotherly. "You got that right. In fact, you have no idea how much I appreciated you asking to join me for lunch that day. We connected from day one. In spite of myself, I couldn't help liking you, feeling comfortable around you, and . . . and I trusted you."

"Same here." Will realized it was true as he said it.

"What are your options?"

"I've been thinking. I could stay at the firm and hope for the best. They wouldn't fire me, but I could be a permanent associate. That would be humiliating. There are a few around the firm. God knows how they can show up at the office. In summary, no money, no respect, no self-esteem, and no money. And, oh, did I mention, no money?"

Paddy nodded. "I guess it's worse not having it if you grew up with it. Me, I like having it. I like what it's brought so far. What I really like is now people take note of me. Sure, I dig the fancy car and fancy digs, but I feel like I could go back to being busted if I had to, you know? Did you ever see the movie *Fritz the Cat*?"

"I think I missed it," Will said.

"I wasn't supposed to see it. It was X-rated. My old man let me go because it was an animated movie. He must have thought it was Felix the Cat. This rich crow is offered some peanut butter. He says, snooty-like, 'Peanut buttah. I don't eat peanut buttah anymore.' Then he says under his breath, 'But I keeps a jar.' I'm like that crow. It could happen. I still have my beat-up Ram Charger."

"I could make a lateral move to another firm," Will said, as if he hadn't heard Paddy, "but since I don't have portable business even if I made a move, it would merely be sideways."

Paddy shifted his body. "What are your assets?"

"My assets?"

"Whadduhya bring to the table?"

Will pursed his lips and arched his eyebrows. "I've got good trial experience. I'm really expert on pleadings and procedure."

"For Chrissakes," Paddy said. "I'll tell you what your assets are, because apparently you haven't fucking figured it out."

"Please do," Will said, sitting up.

"I asked about you after we had lunch. Gary Martin said you were smart and capable, a good guy even if you were Cook's . . . *boy*. So did Estelle. She said you were well connected, well known, and well respected for having handled adversity so well. She said people admired you."

"That's lovely. I'm flattered. But what will that get me in the law practice?"

"Clients," Paddy said.

"Clients," Will repeated. Inching closer to Paddy, he said, "How do I get clients? The toxic tort targets want an army of lawyers. Tell me more."

"You're right. You are not likely to get Fortune 500 companies. They will continue to go to big firms and premier litigation boutiques."

"What would they come to me for?"

"Estelle said you and I were two peas in a pod. I didn't get it at first, but I do now. You know exactly the life you want to lead. Unless you have a rich wife, you'll have to make it yourself. You're on the make. Just like me."

"Actually, one day Muffy may inherit some money. But who knows when?"

"Right and who knows if you'll be married to her when she does."

Will flinched.

Paddy nodded. "Maybe that was out of line. I hope you stay married forever. My point is this: lots of people you know will not stay married. You know nearly every rich person inside the Sam Houston Tollway."

"How does that translate into clients?"

"If there's something I've learned it's that people don't really like their divorce lawyers. If they could turn to someone they already liked and trusted, they would sooner go to that person than someone in the 'club' who might take advantage of them."

"You didn't know anybody. You're going great guns."

"I am walkin' the walk. After representing Margot and then Estelle Cook, I got some buzz and bounce. I started hanging around here and at the Houstonian. I've met a few who made their money later and a few rich trust-baby outcasts. I'm getting calls. Most of the clients like my results, although sometimes I have to convince them what a great job I did. There are big opportunities out there."

Will nodded. "You know my story. What's yours?"

"Let's just say I didn't grow up privileged. I think my family would be called underclass. My father was injured on the job when I was young. The union sold him out. He never worked again. He was angry and mean. My mother . . . I'm not gonna go there. We were poor. I got through college by working, scholarships, and student loans. No one else in my family finished high school. My joining the NYPD was a very big deal."

"But you left that."

"I took a chance."

"Looks like it is working out."

"So far, so good, but I'm just making a dent. There's so much more out there. Maybe it's time for you to take a chance," Paddy said.

Will tilted his chin up. "Are you asking me to the dance, Paddy?"

Paddy grinned. "Like they say in college basketball, 'The Big Dance.' You'd have to take what they call an entrepreneurial leap, but you've seen Lyons's crowd. Lazy lightweights. We can kill 'em."

Will smiled. "I think we would be a winning combination, and I think that's an obvious niche."

Paddy recoiled at hearing "neesh."

They talked about the possibilities of forming a boutique firm. Paddy could dream up ways to put the other side to a disadvantage. Will could provide a more academic perspective when needed. Will had a great deal more experience actually trying cases, although not sitting in the first chair. They would both work hard. The rewards could be great. Will could make a lot more than he was making at Walker & Travis, maybe even more than he would make if he became a partner. Which would be the greater shame— being a permanent associate at Walker & Travis or having his name on the door of a two-man firm that never made the top tier?

They would share equally in expenses and income. Their practice would be limited to family law. The firm name would be Marshall & Moran. Although Paddy didn't like it, he agreed that Marshall went first because of his Houston roots and large-firm patina, the price he had to pay to transfer some of Will's respect to him.

A substantial front-end investment would be necessary to get them off to the right start. Paddy had a big cushion from his Cook fee. Will had some money available from a modest inheritance from an aunt. They needed to do more than merely contribute to family court judges' campaigns. They had to host fundraisers and make the judges personal friends.

It occurred to Will he needed to tell Muffy, really discuss the decision with her. As he was thinking about how to do it, Paddy grabbed his arm.

"Okay, buddy, it's a deal." Paddy said.

Caught off guard, with his eyes suddenly wide open and his hair tingling, in a voice almost resembling a shriek, Will said, "Yes. It's a deal!" They shook hands again.

In a complete tonal change, Will said, "Paddy, you sowed the seeds of my destruction. May you also sow the seeds of my resurrection."

Paddy turned his head, so Will couldn't see him roll his eyes. *I'm going to have to put up with that shit*, he thought.

CHAPTER 23

PILAR DECIDES TO PLAY IT SAFE

IT WAS THE END OF THE SUMMER. Houston was hot and sticky. It felt like too much work to go anywhere or do anything. Even so, Pilar invited Sunny to have a drink after work.

"That'd be great. It's been too long, but it better be in a place with a gooood AC. And goooood drinks," Sunny said.

They met at Manhattan Margarita, which fit both bills.

After Pilar quickly sucked down her drink, she said, "I've been seeing someone, Sunny. He's one of the young executives where I had my last temporary assignment."

"You seem to find perks at work that I don't. Why have you kept this from moi?"

"Maybe I didn't want to jinx myself. Tell me about Sal first."

"Oh, you actually asked."

"C'mon. I care."

Sunny shifted her position. "Sal's not so bad. Actually, he's a really sweet guy. I like him. He likes me. Only he's gone a lot. His job takes him to New York state too often. When he's here, he needs to spend time with his kids. You know that whole divorce thing. It's like super complicated. I have to be very flexible to even see him."

"Is he a loser?"

"No, he's not. Mos def he's not. In fact, I think he's a winner. But he's not Mr. Man of My Dreams either. It's real though, I have to say that. It's not like he's proposed or anything. I'm trying to manage my expectations."

"Oh, Sunny," Pilar said holding her hands.

"I don't want to talk about it. Tell me about your new guy."

"His name is Bob. He's never been married. Kind of—well, square. He's good with Grace though. And he's nice looking but has no fashion sense."

"And? . . ."

Pilar laughed. "And nothing. What can I tell you? I'm taking it slow. Whenever I feel like rushing I have this mantra I use: Ronnie. Ronnie. VJ. VJ. It totally works. We've seen each for a while. We're starting to get physical," Pilar grinned. "And I'm using protection." A shadow crossed her face. "It's all fine."

"You don't exactly sound thrilled about it. Are the two of you serious?"

"*I* am, and I think he is. We've talked about getting married. His family is wonderful. Like the family I never had."

"You would be marrying him, not his family. Do you love him?"

Pilar took a deep swallow of her drink. Fiddling with the straw, she said, "I don't know. He's pretty nice. We've been going to church with his folks nearly every Sunday."

"Church?" Sunny said with a touch of sarcasm. "That sounds serious."

"Uh-huh, kinda," Pilar said. "I don't like the church. It seems mean-spirited." She glanced around the room. "But it's important to Bob, or it's important to his family." She shrugged.

"What about the older guy?"

"VJ?" Pilar sighed.

"You're bizarro. He was crazy about you."

"Maybe he was, maybe he wasn't. It doesn't matter. He'll never divorce her. I don't want to be the other woman even if he would set me up for life—not that he ever said he would."

"He would have. You wouldn't let him."

"I didn't want to be that person."

"Must have been hard to turn him away," Sunny sighed. "Condo. Pool. Credit line at Saks. Nei-man Mar-cus for-ever. Unlimited spa days." Sunny couldn't seem to stop herself.

Pilar held up her hand. "Not funny. I liked him—a lot. You know that. I never asked him to leave his wife. When he said he would, I was never happier in my whole life. But then he didn't follow through. I don't remember ever feeling worse. Bob's safe, you know? I could make a life with him."

"I just want you to be happy," Sunny said, shaking her head.

"Same here for you." Pilar grabbed the check.

"Why do you always do that? I know you aren't fixed like the queen of England. Let's split it."

"Next time," Pilar said.

"You're tipsy," Sunny said. "I'm driving you home."

〰

A FEW DAYS LATER, as VJ was leaving his office, his phone rang. The screen flashed "Pilar" and then went blank.

He called her back.

A small voice answered.

She'd been crying. "What's wrong?" he asked.

She took a deep breath. "I shouldn't have called. I just got some—well—shocking news."

"What is it? Is Grace okay?"

"Yes, she's perfectly fine. It's something else. I was seeing this guy—this . . . oh, never mind."

"No, go on," his heart pounded as he tried to sound reassuring.

"I thought we were serious and—"

"You were with him that night I called."

"Yes," she said, suddenly composed. "Do you want me to tell you why I called, or do you want to make this about you?"

"Sorry. Talk to me."

"I was seeing him . . . for a while," her voice rose. "I mean after things got serious, we saw each other a lot. We'd meet after work. After a while, he started making excuses. About two weeks ago, he told me things were going too fast, that we needed to cool it for a while. I said I understood, but I didn't. Just before I called you, I asked a friend from work to meet for a drink. She said she couldn't this evening but would like to another time. Then she asked in a very gentle voice if I'd talked to Bob lately. Then she told me that the office was celebrating Bob's engagement."

"It was so humiliating." Her voice wobbled. "My friend said she's some twenty-three- year-old bimbo who checks coats at a titty bar and enters contests on amateur night. He went there for a bachelor party for one of his buddies, got drunk, stuck a $100 bill in her G-string with his cell number written on it, and now he's telling everyone it's true love. I feel like such a chump. Why would he do that to me?"

She started sobbing again. "My friend says this girl is like some chick who made it out of East Dipshit Bayou, Louisiana, probably after she won the Miss Crawfish Sucking Pageant. I cannot believe Bob left me for some girl whose life's ambition is to win a pole dancing contest. It is beyond humiliating."

Although he knew it was totally inappropriate to mention, VJ laughed silently as he remembered overhearing his maternal grandfather talking about a woman of loose morals: "She dances on one leg. Then she dances on the other. And between the two legs she makes a living."

"I was going to church with him every Sunday, even though I hated the stupid, narrow-minded, hate-mongering preacher. I'm a lapsed Catholic. God must be punishing me," she said, her voice trialing away. "I don't even know why I called you."

"Because you're hurt."

"Maybe a little," she said. "I mean I'm embarrassed about Bob. Truth is, that's not why I'm so upset. What I'm really mad about, VJ, is I set myself up. It wasn't Bob I wanted. It was a kind of life I wanted. I'm not sure I ever even liked him. I met him right after . . . you know."

He knew.

"I kept trying and trying to convince myself."

VJ cleared his throat. "It's okay. Okay? It sounds like he did you a favor. And, know this if you know anything, no one is too good for you."

She inhaled deeply. "The moment I heard about that total sleaze, I realized that I should have fought harder for you—for us. I miss you VJ."

"I miss you too."

"Can you come see me?" she asked.

"When?"

"Now?"

He looked at his watch. "I have a dinner party. Can't get out of it this late. But I can come by after it's over."

"What about your wife?"

"Not a problem." He pictured Pilar drying her tears.

"It's been a bad day. When we hang up, I'm going to open a bottle of wine. I may even take a Xanax. If I'm asleep when you get here, come in. I'll leave the key under the doormat."

VJ ARRIVED ABOUT ELEVEN. A lamp was on by the living room window. She didn't answer his call. He let himself in and went to her bedroom. She was sleeping. He sat next to her. He touched her forehead. Her eyes opened. "Hi," she breathed, not fully focused. "Lie next to me and hold me." She moved toward the center of the bed with her back to him.

VJ took off his shoes. He decided not to take off his trousers. He lifted the sheet and blanket. She was wearing a T-shirt and thong. He had never seen someone in a thong before. He marveled at the sight. He got in next to her. She moved closer to him, pulling his arms around her. He squeezed her more tightly, wanting desperately to make love to her. Although he knew she could feel his urges, she did not respond.

At about three a.m. her daughter wandered into the room and asked for her mommy.

VJ carefully nudged Pilar to wake her. She raised her head and held her arms out. "Yes, darling, what is it?"

"I dunno. I waked up. Hi, VJ."

Pilar smiled. "Mommy had a bad day. I needed my friend to make it okay."

"I'm glad you have VJ for your friend. He's my friend, too."

"Yes, I am, Grace, you little sweetheart," VJ said, getting up, if for no other reason than to show Grace he was fully clothed. She came to him. He leaned down to receive her hug.

Pilar returned Grace to her bed and then came back, stretching.

"I think I should go now," VJ said.

"Okay. I love you," she said, still sounding half-asleep. She walked him to the door. She put her arms around his neck and pulled herself close to him. He responded, holding her tightly. She turned her face up, and he kissed her.

After their goodbye, she locked the door behind him. She wrapped her arms around herself and smiled a dreamy smile as she weaved her way back to bed.

CHAPTER 24

FAMILY LAW—IN STYLE

"FAMILY LAW—IN STYLE—SUITE," *Texas Monthly* proclaimed. "'The M&M boys will slug it out on our field just like Mantle and Maris did at Yankee Stadium,' said transplanted New Yorker Paddy Moran."

Paddy beamed as he read the quote from his new leather office chair. He also liked the color picture of himself.

"His imposing size and dress-for-success tailoring leave the impression that this is, as one of his clients said, one powerful guy."

Hot damn! That was pretty fucking good. Paddy made a note to send his salesman at Saks a copy of the article.

Muffy and Will were pictured together. She was given kudos for their Galleria-area offices that were described as "outrageous, yet tasteful. You enter a small, smart, all-white room and are greeted by a receptionist seated behind a white marble podium. If you are a woman, the receptionist directs you to a waiting area with pastel walls, Mary Cassatt prints, and white neo-French provincial furniture. A man is directed to a room with stuffed leather chairs and hunting scenes and sports memorabilia hanging on the dark-paneled walls.

"Will Marshall morphed himself from a big-firm, toxic-tort defense lawyer to a family law gladiator. 'Being a lawyer means you're supposed to help people. I was beginning to lose sight of that. Families in crisis need good lawyers. I believe our firm makes a real and positive difference to people who come to us,' Marshall said."

"Will!" Paddy yelled from his office door. "You were right. They called it neo-French. And, hey, congratulations. You're a gladiator?"

He got no response.

A temp agency receptionist toddled into his office. Will had decided to use temps until he found someone permanent who met all his requirements.

"Mr. Mar . . . Mar—"

"It's Marshall, sweetie," Paddy said.

"Thank you, sir. Mr. Marshall is seeing a client."

"Well, isn't that both fine and dandy." Paddy looked at his watch as he returned to his office. Barely nine o'clock on opening day and Will had new business. It was good, but he'd wanted to have the first client.

Mrs. Coleman's arrival at Marshall & Moran LLP had been preceded by a large Meyer lemon tree potted in an Egyptian urn. Will was showing the receptionist how to sign for it when Mrs. Coleman, who had been friends with Will's grandmother, appeared with her chauffeur, Roosevelt.

"It's from me," Mrs. Coleman said in her high-pitched, operatic tone. She was in her late eighties. She wore a black-and-white polka-dot dress with a white lace border at the neck, white gloves, a white pearl necklace, a hat with a net in front of her eyes and a brim that matched the fabric of her dress. Moving with the panache of the aging Lauren Bacall in *The Mirror Has Two Faces*, she walked past Will to his office as if she'd been there before. How she knew which door it was, Will could never have guessed.

"Mrs. Coleman, it's always a pleasure to see you," Will said.

"As promised," she said, entering his office. Roosevelt just stood there, turning his chauffeur's cap in his hands.

She handed Will an envelope. Obeying her authoritative nod, he opened it. Inside was a check for ten thousand dollars.

"This is a retainer so you will never take any matter or person adverse to me. You will get a check for twenty-five hundred every month. Make sure you always take my calls no matter what else you are doing. You will see to it that my work gets priority. Is that arrangement satisfactory, Willoughby?"

"Oh, yes, ma'am. It's too generous. I would always take your calls and put your work first, anyway."

"That's sweet. I'm sure you mean it now. But this is your first day. You'll get lots of rich clients who'll be very demanding. I want to make my deal with you now."

"Of course. It's a deal."

He extended his hand. She did not accept it. She said, "And if Roosevelt calls, then the same arrangement applies."

"Of course." Will glanced at the tall, frail man wearing a black suit. When Will was young, he sometimes accompanied his grandmother on her visits to Mrs. Coleman. Upon seeing Will, Roosevelt, wearing long pants and a T-shirt, the sleeves of which were torn off, revealing his bulging muscles, would stop his lawn work, grab two racquets and some balls and rally with Will on Mrs. Coleman's back yard tennis court while she and his grandmother chatted on the patio. Such were the days.

She rose and turned to Roosevelt. "Would you mind stepping outside?"

"Yes, ma'am. Good afternoon, Mr. Will. Nice to see you. Good luck in your new practice."

Will shook the old man's hand. "Thank you, Roosevelt. Good to know you're well and that Mrs. Coleman is still in your capable hands." He placed his other hand over the man's hand and asked, "Are you feeling okay?"

Withdrawing his hand quickly, Roosevelt straightened himself to his full height. "I'm fine."

As the chauffeur was leaving the office, Will noticed that he was trying to conceal how difficult moving was for him. Mrs. Coleman whispered, "Willoughby, he isn't fine. He isn't driving as well as he used to. I may buy a Hummer, so we will have more steel to protect us."

For a moment, Will felt privy to what he believed was the real her, to the woman behind the caricature she'd created over the years.

"Mrs. Coleman, thank you for the tree."

She gave Will a steely stare. What had he done wrong? He looked again. He realized the tree had come in an urn that was surely of considerable value. "And, especially, the magnificent antique urn," he said.

She nodded.

After Mrs. Coleman left, Paddy asked if she was getting a divorce.

"No," Will laughed. "She's not."

"I thought we were only taking family law cases."

"She's an old family friend."

"What's that got to do with it?"

"You'll learn, Mr. Moran, to take care of friends."

Paddy thought about Jed and where his divorce case had led. "Point well taken, counselor."

"Besides that," Will said, with a big grin on his face, "she gave us a ten thousand–dollar retainer to never be adverse to her, which we would never do anyway, and she's going to pay us twenty-five hundred a month so she will feel comfortable being able to call on me whenever she wants. That's not a bad start."

"Point well made, counselor," Paddy said. "God bless Mrs. Coleman. Now, if you'll excuse me, I'll go back to writing a letter to *Texas Monthly*."

The *Texas Monthly* article concluded with the following paragraph: "A board-certified family lawyer who spoke to us on the condition of anonymity said, 'They're new kids on the block, hungry and trying to make a splash in the big leagues. I haven't had experience with either of them. They're going to be up against seasoned family lawyers. They're going to be before judges who don't know them. My guess is they, and, therefore, their clients, have quite a few lumps coming.' Well, Mr. Board-Certified Lawyer, like it or lump it, Marshall and Moran are in the game."

Paddy wasn't sure that paragraph should be in the reprints.

CHAPTER 25

PILAR CINDERELLA

AFTER THE NIGHT PILAR opened her heart and her body to VJ, they could not seem to get enough of each other. Something had broken open. They both knew there was no going back.

To VJ's complete surprise, they had sex twice a day, sometimes more often. They seemed insatiable. He skipped arranging business lunches, and they made love at her house after Grace went to bed. When Georgie was out of town, he stayed the night. He'd never known such drive. He was consumed. All it took for him to get an erection was to think of her, to hear her voice, to see her, to hold her, to get close to her. Pilar was just as eager as he was.

She didn't ask about his marriage. She let go of her defenses. He gave her a generous allowance and a credit card. The financial insecurity she had experienced her entire life suddenly vanished.

At brunch on a Sunday, she said to Sunny, "Nothing he does makes me feel cheap. He's kind. He's wonderful. Grace and I want for nothing. The truth is I like caring for him. If this is all I can get, it's better than any relationship I've ever had. But, Sunny, I don't think I can live like this forever."

"Do you love him?"

Pilar nodded.

"Does he love you?"

She nodded again.

"Then I now pronounce you Lucky Man and Lucky Woman. You're already way ahead of what most people only dream about. What's marriage anymore, anyway? You've been there."

One evening, he asked, "Who are you?"

She knew what he was asking. After initially hesitating, she poured out what she had never told another person. When Pilar was eight, her mother's brother abused her. A teacher noticed the bruising. Her uncle was arrested.

It seemed to Pilar that her mother never spoke to her again. In middle school she ran with a wild crowd. A rival gang raped her. She had an abortion.

"In high school I got a job at KFC. I think it took years to get the smell of fried chicken out of my hair," she laughed. "I moved in with a friend and retreated into my studies. My school counselor urged me to go to college, but I didn't believe it was possible. I got a job as a filing clerk. I made sure I was recognized for being good at whatever I did."

He recalled her waiting while he reviewed her work.

"I always keep my antenna up for new opportunities. After a few years, networking through a friend, I got hired as an assistant office manager at Innoveismic. My ex, Ronnie, was head of security. We met in an elevator bank."

"Pilar," he said, measuring his words, "I know a respected psychoanalyst. I think it would be good for you to see her."

"I'm not crazy," she snapped.

"No, you're not, but you do have a lot of baggage. I think this woman will help you lighten your load. It wouldn't hurt."

She placed her hand behind his neck and pulled his face to hers. "For an old guy, you're very sexy."

AT THE END OF HER FIRST SESSION with Hannah Feldschtein, Pilar agreed to see her three times a week.

"She's an old Jewish woman with a European accent," Pilar laughed when she told VJ about her. Putting on her own accent, she said, "I thought no way she gonna unnerstan' a young Latina like me—never in a million years. I was soooo wrong. She's very smart and perceptive and, when she wants to be, warm and funny. She told me the physics of life is that each choice forecloses other choices. I've got a long way to go, but I'm beginning to understand why I've made so many bad choices."

"That makes me very happy," he said.

"Well, next step—learning not to make them—will be harder."

"Should I take that personally?"

Shaking her head and smiling at him, she said, "I told her about us— about you."

"What did you say to her?" His tone changed.

"Why?"

He didn't say anything.

"Why did you send me to her if you were afraid what I might say?"

"I'm not," he said, but his body stiffened. "I was just curious."

"What did she say?"

"She said if I think of myself as your mistress, we're doomed. I have to believe in my own power."

After a brief pause, she said, "There's another thing I want to say."

"What's that?"

"I don't know how I didn't run you off. I don't know why you didn't give up on me. I just thank God you didn't. I love you so much."

"So I'm not just an old schmuck smitten with a midlife crisis trophy," he said, smiling.

She placed her arms loosely around his neck. "I didn't say that. We're talking about me." She threw her head back, laughing loudly. Then her face became serious. "VJ, being your mistress isn't going to last. Do you understand? I want you and me to be partners."

"Of course we're partners," VJ replied. The way he said it made Pilar feel he was just saying what she wanted to hear.

~~~~

VJ DECIDED TO MAKE A LIFE with Pilar even without a divorce. He wanted to expand Pilar and Grace's world. He bought her a house with a yard in Southampton, a tree-lined, quiet neighborhood near Rice University. He paid for a private preschool and hired a nanny.

"This is probably dumb," Sunny said, "especially since I basically forced you into this relationship, but are you okay with him paying for everything?"

"Well, if you mean does it make me feel like a whore, no, it does not. If you mean does it make me feel like a kept woman, also no. I don't care how it looks. We're together. We belong together. He just has this impediment."

"Let me see. Oh, yes, his wife."

"Sunny, I can joke about it because I'm completely comfortable with our situation. He's even made provisions for me if something happens to him. Our relationship's really good." Then, with her voice wavering a little, she added, "At least it is for now."

<hr />

PILAR DECIDED SHE WANTED to have VJ's child, to mix their genes, and she stopped taking precautions. When she discovered she was pregnant, she felt such joy—for a moment. Then the reality that she had not discussed having a child with him hit her, and she was afraid to tell him.

That night VJ hugged her close. "I don't know what it is," he said huskily, "but you look more beautiful than ever. You're glowing." Pilar bit her lip.

She woke up the next morning wide awake. She looked in the mirror. Her pupils looked like the heads of pins. She paced. She ate yogurt to calm her stomach. She jogged after she dropped Gracie off at school. Nothing relieved the anxiety. What had she done?

That evening, when VJ came over after work and after their usual kiss and hug, she said, "There's no other way to say this. We're going to have a baby."

She held her breath. He turned bright red. She feared he was going to fly into a rage.

He took her by the arm and sat her on the end of the sofa. He sat in the chair facing her.

She waited, her lips trembling.

"I'm not good at immediately reacting emotionally to surprising news." He got up and walked out the front door. "Let me process this."

She gasped. She heaved. She pulled her feet up and wrapped her arms around her bent legs, holding them to her chest. She managed to gather enough control to suppress a scream because she didn't want to alarm Gracie.

She was still on the sofa holding her knees to her chest when he returned. He sat next to her. "I know it wasn't an accident." He pulled her close to him.

Her heart felt as if it were going to burst.

<hr />

AFTER THAT, THE ONLY RESTRICTION VJ had on where they went was Eleganté, out of deference to Georgie. Eleganté was Georgie's favorite, a welcome alternative to the stuffy clubs. It was his, too, but VJ knew Luigi wanted Georgie to feel comfortable at the restaurant. She had been an early patron. In fact, Luigi credited her with giving it respectability and making it the place to be. Luigi appreciated VJ's sensitivity and offered to cook for him and Pilar at his house.

After Raj Benjamin was born, gossips began to work overtime. Everywhere VJ went heads turned and Pilar's name was murmured. Wild rumors spread about who she was and where she was from. At a charity luncheon, two aging matrons chatted without whispering about VJ, Pilar, and the baby, not knowing Georgie was right behind them.

Georgie leaned over. "You should try following your own husbands to their pied-à-terres and see who they're fucking." She could no longer pretend Pilar did not exist.

One night VJ came into the house and found Georgie smoking on the couch, an overflowing ashtray on the coffee table in front of her. He was about to say something about the stench but thought better of it. He really didn't care anymore if the house smelled. While this was floating in his mind, the ashtray, a fine old piece from Tiffany, sailed toward him. He ducked away from Georgie's good aim and the glass crashed into the wall. This time, *she* demanded a divorce.

Georgie had started out with more money than he had, but even then he wasn't too far behind. While they were married, some of his early investments became extremely valuable, bringing his net worth to almost five billion. He had increased her separate property considerably as well. He had a fair settlement in mind before he approached Georgie the first time. An angry Georgie approached Margaret Walden, known as a ball-buster, to represent her. When she learned Walden had represented Pilar in her divorce, she was furious. She turned to her family's law firm. The divorce proceeded smoothly from that point. Really, it was more like a business deal. Georgie moved to Manhattan.

The day the divorce became final, VJ and Pilar married. Soon thereafter, Pilar discovered she was pregnant with their second child, which according to the sonogram was a girl.

Pilar felt like Cinderella. She had two beautiful children with a third on the way and a husband who adored her and the children. On their wedding night, VJ presented her with her favorite Frida Kahlo oil painting, "The Little Deer," a self-portrait with Frida's head on a doe wounded with arrows, gazing expectantly at the viewer. They hung the painting in their bedroom, the card that accompanied the painting below it read: "Because you are my little dear. Always and forever."

PART

THREE

CHAPTER 26

ANCHOR MAN

PADDY CHARGED INTO WILL'S OFFICE. "The governor just appointed Hector Elizondo to fill the family law court vacancy. You know him?"

"Do I know him?" Will replied. "In law school we called him Anchor Man because every semester he was at the bottom of the class. Somehow, he managed to graduate. I think affirmative action had something to do with it. He passed the bar, on his third attempt."

"Fuck off with your elitist bullshit. As I recall, you weren't on the *Texas Law Review*. Yet you somehow landed a job at Walker & Travis. Climbing through connections is what I call affirmative action the old-fashioned way."

Will forced a smile and nodded.

"We've been trying to figure out how we can nab at least one judge to be our guy," Paddy said. "Why not Anchor Man?" He paused. "Please tell me you never called him Anchor Man to his face."

"My mother taught me better than that. Well, to a degree she did. She never knowingly caused anyone public embarrassment, other than my father. Him, she embarrassed regularly. I'm not sure she realized blacks had feelings or that Mexicans could understand what she was saying. FYI, Hector likes me a lot."

Paddy rapped his knuckles on the desk. "Call him. Congratulate him. See if you can pick up how he can become beholden to us. It's too soon to give money to his election campaign, but we could throw a reception for his swearing in."

Later that afternoon, Will came into Paddy's office. "Right on track, partner," he said. "Not only is he delighted for us to host a swearing-in reception, but we may be able to score points with him another way. He asked if we might have work for his daughter."

"Fantastic. Hire her as our receptionist."

"Not so fast," Will said.

"Why? What does it take to be a receptionist? I managed without one before I hooked up with you."

"The first impression people get of any law firm is the receptionist."

Paddy stuffed his fists into his pockets, shaking his head. Mr. White Shoes just didn't get it.

Will said, "I'll ask him to have her call me and make an appointment and bring her resume."

"Holy cow, you'll scare her away if you ask for a resume," Paddy said, raising his voice. "Don't you understand, all the other judges are in somebody else's pocket?" He moved his thumb back and forth over his index finger. "We need one in ours."

"That's a little strong, isn't it?"

"Strong? Strong is how that asshole Judge Babson treated me when I showed up representing Mrs. Cook. You were there. At least in Elizondo's court, we'll get respect. That could spill over to the other judges."

PADDY GREETED DOLORES ELIZONDO in the reception area. Her black hair was long and pulled back. She wore a modest amount of makeup. Her clothes were appropriate for the office. His guess was that she was in her late twenties. Her presence was pleasing. He flashed his friendliest smile and introduced himself.

"It's so very nice to meet you," Dolores said. "I thought I would be meeting Mr. Will Marshall."

"You would have, but he had an appointment out of the office at this time."

"I am so sorry I am late."

"No problem. How is it for you to have a father who is a judge?"

"We are so proud of heem." Her accent was not strong, but it manifested itself from time to time. A little diversity might help business.

"As well you should be," he said. "Would you like to be our receptionist?"

"Oh, yes. It would be a wonderful job."

"Great. When can you start?" Paddy asked.

"You mean—?"

Paddy thought she was going to jump for joy. "Yes. That's what I mean.

You have the job," Paddy said, touched by her exuberance. "I tell you what. How about you start tomorrow? I'll have Mr. Marshall call you a little later. He'll give you more details."

When he learned that Paddy hired Dolores, Will asked if she had any experience as a receptionist.

"I don't know." Paddy hunched his shoulders and slumped.

Will paced angrily. "Let me see her resume."

"I don't have it," Paddy replied.

Suddenly, Will was in Paddy's face. Despite the height difference, no more than three inches separated their eyes. "Let me get this right. You hired her without finding out if she had any experience, without checking to see if she had any prior work references, and without talking to me?"

"For Chrissakes," Paddy responded, stepping back. "It's a fucking receptionist job. She's a family court judge's daughter. How can that be anything but good for us?"

"A fucking receptionist?" Will said with his voice rising. "Do you just not listen to me? The 'fucking' receptionist is the first person your clients and your prospective clients see and hear. The receptionist is our first impression."

"She's attractive and she dresses nice," Paddy said.

"Great, but there's a lot more to it than that. She has to sound professional because we are professionals."

Paddy recalled how Walker & Travis's receptionist had made him feel important and that he was in a classy place. He tried to imagine Dolores sitting behind the white marble receptionist credenza—sweet, almost attractive, and clueless. Amateur hour. His heart sank.

"The worst of it is," Will said, rubbing his forehead, "if she turns out to be a clunker, how do we get rid of her? If we fire her, then our purpose in hiring her has backfired in spades."

"You're right," Paddy said, slumping in his chair, suddenly feeling small. "She starts tomorrow. I said you would call her and give her more details."

Will inhaled and exhaled deeply several times. "Paddy," he said, "you have one of the most important attributes a lawyer can have—an uncanny instinct for knowing what you don't know and not acting when you are uninformed."

Paddy was waiting.

"Apparently that doesn't carry over to office management. Think about how a receptionist can affect the money you make."

Paddy shook Will's hand in both of his. "Partner, you said that much nicer than I would have."

Will shook his head, thinking how this man could dissuade an army with his smile. "You've made a good point, too. We need a judge. Maybe if those effete yoyos see we are tight with Elizondo, they will be more welcoming to us."

Look who's calling whom effete, Paddy thought, but he just said, "Right."

CHAPTER 27

PERDIZ BRAVA

"WELCOME," WILL SAID, ushering Randall Frazier Hetherington III, an old family acquaintance, into his office.

Hetherington was wearing L.L.Bean moccasins without socks and a light-blue linen Versace shirt that hung untucked over his white jeans. His Cartier sunglasses were pushed back casually over his longish golden hair. He plopped down on a chair.

His first words were icy. "I want a divorce. Now."

"Well, that's what we do here, Randy. Any chance of reconciliation?" Will asked.

"I'm sure she would want that, but I certainly don't."

"She would—" Will repeated.

"Right. Linda doesn't have a clue I want a divorce. She's weak. Hell, she's boring. She lives in a world that's much too small for me. I want her out."

Will noted Hetherington had said, "I want her out" not "I want out."

With his windswept hair, self-satisfied grin, and arrogant tone, Randy Hetherington did little to conceal his inner asshole. "Yeah, she's just a drag, you get me?"

"Sounds pretty simple," Will said, pulling out a legal pad.

"Not that simple. We have a daughter. I want to raise her—I'll get whatever help I need. Linda is a fucking social liberal who wants our child to go to public school. No Hetherington has ever gone to public school. You know what those public schools are like. Well, actually, you don't. Our parents knew better. And, as a parent, I know better."

"What about money?" Will asked.

"What do you mean?" Hetherington said.

"First, is there a prenup?"

"No. Keep asking questions."

"How much money do you make?"

"A lot." Hetherington was taunting Will.

"What from?" asked Will.

Hetherington spoke dismissively. "Royalties from wells on my grandfather's property. The wells allow me to follow the seasons, to shoot *perdiz brava*—that's partridge—Octobers in Spain. I hunt deer and antelope in Argentina in June. It's a beautiful life. I know what you're thinking. All that traveling—a wife I don't love, I don't know if I ever loved. What a lonely chap. But I'll tell you something interesting." Hetherington paused for effect. "Rich people from all over the world know each other. We have a community."

"Really? How's that?" Will asked.

"We go to the same places. On a hunt, or relaxing at a villa in Ocho Rios, skiing out of a chalet in Switzerland—I see the same people. People like me. Do you get my drift? If I ever feel lonely, which isn't often, I go to wherever it's in season, where I know I'll see my friends."

Will cringed. Thinking how completely out of touch Randy was, how no jury could possibly relate favorably to Hetherington, he said, "Randy, if this matter has to be tried, you may not want a jury."

"Why?" Hetherington asked.

Will shrugged. "We can cross that bridge later." He started making notes with a freshly sharpened pencil. "Let's get to the money."

Randy explained how most of his income was separate property and when the income that was community had been spent he lent separate money to the community.

"So, if I have this right, you have no salaried income. Your interest and dividends go into a joint account, royalties and capital gains go into a separate property account, and sometimes you lend separate property money to the joint account. What I'm hearing is there isn't any community property."

Hetherington leaned back and laced his fingers behind his head. "I may not be a lawyer, but I do know a few things about community property."

"Sounds like you do. In fact, the community may owe money to your separate estate," Will said, with raised eyebrows.

"Imagine that," Hetherington said. "See, I knew this day would come." Smiling devilishly, he asked, "This is all attorney-client privilege, right?"

"Of course."

Hetherington leaned in, pressing his sunglasses more firmly to his scalp. "I got married, settled down, and had a child because otherwise my dear, now-departed father would have kept me on a permanent monthly stipend with no upside but a cost-of-living adjustment. He wasn't always pleased with me, dear old dad, but I redeemed myself by marrying Linda and having a baby. That's when he let go of the purse strings, for the most part. He put her on the board of his private foundation but not me."

"Imagine that," Will said in the same flat tone Hetherington had used.

Hetherington leaned even closer. "Here's why I'm in your office. How good are you with custody cases?"

"The mother usually gets custody unless she's unfit," Will said seriously. "So far you haven't mentioned your child. Does she come along when you live the lifestyle of the rich and famous?"

"Of course not."

"Let me see if I get this right. You're an absentee father, but you want custody even though you are just fine now with leaving your daughter with her mother and you're not very involved even when you are around."

"This won't be a cookie-cutter job, Will."

"You're right about that."

"If you don't think you can get me where I want to go, I'll go elsewhere."

Will contemplated. A difficult case. A client who has yet to demonstrate that he would draw sympathy from a judge or jury determining custody. On the other hand, Randy Hetherington can afford to pay handsomely, and Muffy had been making noises about a bigger house.

"Let me talk to my partner. We'll get back to you."

⁓

WILL DESCRIBED THE CONVERSATION to Paddy over lunch at Ellie's, a restaurant that had evolved from its seventies counterculture origins in the Montrose to a tony place near their offices. Paddy always ate the chicken-fried steak, while Will usually went from table to table, visiting with people he knew. Today, however, he stayed put to explain his morning meeting.

"You say he's got lots of money," Paddy said. "We'll have an open to buy. The fees could be huge."

"There is that, and I'm for that, but he insisted he wants sole custody.

Nothing he said gave me the impression she's a bad mother or that he's a decent father."

"Sure, as of now," Paddy said, between shoveling mouthfuls of garlic mashed potatoes. "But we haven't been involved yet." His eyes were full of eager anticipation.

"What do you mean?" Will asked.

"I mean, nobody's perfect. We're creative guys. We'll figure out something. Get him back in here."

〰️

BACK IN THE OFFICE, they greeted Dolores and asked if there were messages.

Dolores looked at Paddy and then Will. Her stare was both hostile and uncertain, like a deer with one eye looking in the headlights and the other eye focused on the opposite side of the road. Will wondered how she could do that.

Dolores's cheeks were bright red. "There aren't any," she said.

"Nobody called?" Paddy said. "That's strange."

"I din say *nobody* called," she shrieked. "There were too many calls. What I said was they're no messages."

"What do you mean, 'too many calls' and 'no messages?'" Will asked as if he were cross-examining an adverse witness.

"I mean the phone. It was ringin' like crazy. Everybody, you know, they all had lots to say. I was tryin' to get it all, like you tol' me, 'keep all the messages on the computer,' and I was goin' as fass as I could and gettin' it all down and then it jus' . . . disappeared."

"It just disappeared," Paddy repeated, with sympathy.

"Yes," she said, her hands open, her eyes wide. "It jus' disappeared."

Will's hands became fists. He forced them down by his sides. "Dolores, things on a computer don't just disappear. You have to help them disappear." Will's voice was getting higher.

"Well, thas wha happened, Mr. Will. It was here, and then it was gone. Now don't get upset with me. I'm just tryin' to do my job."

Will turned red. He caught himself from screaming, "You idiot!" and stormed into his office. Paddy followed and gently closed the door.

"Settle down. Settle down. She's a sweet girl," he said.

"It was a mistake to give her a job. Get her off the goddamn phone. Have her do something where she can't make a mistake. No. No. No." He said, shaking his head. "Give her a job where her mistakes won't do us as much harm."

"Like what?"

"You tell me," Will said.

After a long silence, Will reached to his face and grabbed his chin. He smiled. "I have it. She can plan receptions for judges. The first will be her father's swearing-in reception. I'm sure he'll understand if no one comes because the invitations had the wrong date or place. We'll make his reception her test run. Besides, he doesn't need any contributors other than us. We may not even want anyone else to show up. Her job will be just to do fundraisers for him."

Paddy said nothing.

"Dolores," Will said, approaching the reception desk.

Her lower lip was trembling. While she may be clueless, Will realized she was not unscarred from prior failures.

He put his hand on her shoulder. "I think that we're the right place for you," he said. "We just gave you the wrong job for your skill set."

Her lips relaxed, and her eyes widened.

His pace picked up. "We underestimated your capabilities."

She looked up at him, her eyebrows raised.

"We have a much more important job for you. We want you to be our special events coordinator. The first event, a *very* special event, is your father's reception."

"Oh, Mr. Will," Dolores gushed, tears leaking from her eyes, "I am so happy."

CHAPTER 28

NEW FRIENDS

IT WAS ONE OF THOSE RARE DAYS in Houston when being outside before sunset was a true pleasure. Sunny and Pilar sat at a circular table that had been built around a huge oak tree in the backyard of Pilar and VJ's new home. They gazed at Grace playing hide and seek with Raj Benjamin, each darting through the finely manicured labyrinth of shrubbery that bordered the swimming pool.

"She is so sweet with him," Sunny said. "You've got a nice life."

Pilar gulped a mouthful of wine. "I hate looking at myself. I don't get it. I only gained sixteen pounds with Grace. With Raj Benjamin, I gained thirty pounds. It took me six months to get back in shape. But this time, with Moises, I gained forty-five pounds." She looked at the sleeping child in the baby carriage. "That sonogram showing a girl must have been taken at the wrong angle. He's all boy. I love him, but I don't love what he did with my body. I still have thirty of it, and now I seem to be gaining more instead of losing. It's awful. I had to call Marvin last week to tell him to increase my dress size."

"Marvin?" Sunny asked.

"Mah-vin," Pilar said, setting down her glass. "Marvin the marvelous." Then realizing Sunny had never had a Marvin to find clothes and accessories for her, she added, "Marvin is a salesman who keeps an eye out for clothes I might like." She took a deep breath. "Anyway, VJ hasn't said anything, but I know he's not pleased."

"Don't worry. You're still hot," Sunny said.

Pilar shook her head.

Sunny could see Pilar's sense of shame about her body was overwhelming her. "I'm serious, girl. You still have it. In fact, you always will. Men are drawn to you. I've seen it. You must release some chemical in the air. I wish I had it."

"I have to do something. Rich people expect thin wives."

"Thin second wives," Sunny blurted.

"My new friends are all like size two. They are all . . . perfect, and most of them are first wives."

"Your new friends?" A slight note of jealousy sounded in Sunny's voice.

"'Friends' may be too strong a word. I mean the wives of some people who are in business with VJ. They're not real friends yet, but they might be. Well, at least they've started including me sometimes."

Sunny crossed her arms and held onto her biceps.

Pilar reached for Sunny's hands and brought them together.

"You are my BFF, but you work, so I can't hang out with you all the time—and it's been hard. Many people in VJ's world haven't accepted me. These women, they seem okay. And I have to admit it's nice to have some adult company during the day."

"Do you really like these women?"

"I can't tell. They're fun and smart. They're just so, so always perfectly put together. The only parts that aren't thin are their boobs and their Angelina Jolie lips." Pilar giggled and took a swallow from her wine glass.

"One of them, Leila Esfandiary—"

"What kind of name is that?"

"Persian. Her husband has been one of VJ's investors for a long time. Anyway, she's taking me to her doctor, some genius plastic surgeon they all swear by. Leila says a tummy tuck, a little work on my thighs, and I'll look better than ever."

"I think you can do it yourself without surgery," Sunny said quietly.

"Yeah, well so far, no good."

Sunny raised her eyebrows. Pilar's words were a little slurred. "Leila also says I have to stop drinking. Apparently, it's very fattening—who knew?" Pilar started to refill Sunny's wineglass.

"No, honey." Sunny held her hand over her glass. "We've already had two. I'm driving, and I actually have a date tonight. I've got to head out."

"Really? Sal?"

"No. Joe. Remember, the guy with the sideburns? I used to see him. I liked him. But he married someone else, and now he's divorced. He called so I figured why not? Plus, he shaved his sideburns."

"What about Sal?"

"I dunno. He's gone too much. It's just a date. Something to do."

Pilar walked Sunny to the door and hugged her tightly. She whispered, "I don't know what I'd do without you."

When Sunny turned back, she caught sight of Pilar pouring herself another glass of wine.

CHAPTER 29

SMUG, ENTITLED SON OF A BITCH

RANDY HETHERINGTON SAT in Marshall & Moran's large conference room. Paddy was most proud of the room, with its plush but conservative leather chairs and its buffet table, which, for the meeting, he made certain was stocked with Eleganté's finest pastries.

Will opened. "My partner here and I have discussed your situation. We have some thoughts."

Hetherington, waving off Paddy's offer of pastries, said, "Let's hear them."

Paddy ate a Napoleon in a single bite. Wiping his hands on a cloth napkin, he switched to his most serious, polished self. "Mr. Hetherington, let's assume we could get you custody of your daughter. What would that be worth to you?"

"It's what I want."

"And you're used to paying to get what you want," Will said.

"Yes, I am," Hetherington said.

"You know the odds are greatly against you," Paddy said.

"I've been told that."

"We'll make a deal with you." Paddy said. "You engage us. You pay us our standard hourly rate plus all expenses. If you get custody of your daughter, we get a two-million-dollar bonus. You put up the two million and a half-million deposit for the hourly and expenses upfront."

"That's outrageous! Who the hell do you think you are?" Hetherington's voice skipped an octave. "You get paid your hourly rate to do your job."

Paddy stood up, towering over Hetherington. He gestured as if dusting sugar off his hands. He said in a raised but practiced, controlled voice, "What's outrageous, Mr. Hetherington, is you thinking you can get custody of your daughter. My guess is Will was not the first person you came to see."

Hetherington's face turned red. Will sat back, wide-eyed and feeling like furniture.

Paddy continued, but he relaxed his diction. "You know those guys are pussies. That's why you came here. You figured out you only have any kind of chance if we handle it."

Hetherington sat back. "What is your strategy?"

"You'll find out soon enough. I'll tell you one thing now. You will become Mr. Mom and follow a strict code of conduct until we're done. If you don't and we lose, we get our bonus anyway."

"That's . . . bullshit," Hetherington said.

"Call it what you want. Take it or leave it," Paddy said and walked out.

A few minutes later, Will came to his office.

"What did he say after I left?" Paddy asked, raising an eyebrow.

"Nada. He raced out without saying a word."

"Ah, well, can't win 'em all. Besides, I really didn't like that son of a bitch."

Will nodded, relaxing into the chair facing Paddy's desk.

The voice of their newest temp receptionist came in through the intercom. "Mr. Hetherington is back to see Mr. Marshall."

Will and Paddy looked at each other, their eyes wide open. Will stepped into the reception area.

"Just went outside to catch a smoke," Mr. Hetherington said, following Will back into the conference room. Hetherington sat for a moment, breathing loudly. "Quite a partner you have there. He's definitely not our kind of people. But that might not be all bad. I heard he cut James Cook a new asshole."

Will nodded.

"Okay. It's a deal," Hetherington said. He shook hands with Will. "Give me wiring instructions. I'll have two million five in your account tomorrow."

After Hetherington got on the elevator, Will burst into Paddy's office. "You're the greatest salesman I've ever met. That smug, entitled son of a bitch bought you hook, line, and sinker."

"*You're* calling him an SOB? I thought he was your friend."

"Not a friend. I've known him a long time, since childhood, in fact. I would not call him a friend. Now what are we going to do to earn that bonus?"

Paddy took a deep breath. He hadn't really expected Hetherington to accept. He'd acted so over-the-top to drive him away. Now he had a challenge. He liked this guy less than Grissett. Unpleasant thoughts streamed through his mind.

"Beats the shit out of me. I'll come up with something. One thing I can't figure out. Why doesn't he stay married? He does whatever he wants anyway. She'll raise their kid better than he would, and he can be with the daughter as often as he wants."

"Could be that he's getting back at his father."

"His father's dead," Paddy said.

"And your point is?"

CHAPTER 30

CAPTAIN MUFFY
TO THE RESCUE

"DOLORES, HOW'S YOUR FATHER'S reception planning going?" Will asked.

Her cheeks turned red, tears leaked out of the corners of her eyes, her lips and chin trembled.

"Relax. It'll be just fine." Will's mind ping-ponged. Letting the reception be a disaster would be an excuse to can Dolores, but a disaster would make a laughingstock out of M&M.

"I have a fun idea," he said. "My wife, Muffy, has too much time on her hands right now. Would you mind helping me out and giving her something to do?"

"What do you mean, Mr. Will?"

"Let her help you."

With obvious relief, Dolores said, "I'm sure I could do it all by myself Mr. Will, but if you think it would make Mrs. Muffy feel better to help, that would be fine."

"Great. Have the invitations been printed yet?"

"No," she said. "But we have a printer's proof." She handed him a small, flimsy card made from cheap paper.

"This is a great start, Dolores."

"Thank you, Mr. Will."

"Please call me 'Will.'"

The previous evening Will had informed Muffy of the situation. She arrived at the office thirty minutes after he called her. With a salute, she said, "Captain Muffy to the rescue."

Will introduced Muffy to Dolores. "Hello, sweetheart," Muffy said, taking Dolores's hands and looking into her eyes. "My, you're such a pretty girl. Will told me he gave you a very big and important job. He said you may let me help with some details."

Dolores nodded. Muffy looked at the invitation. "Wow, Dolores, this is outstanding. Suppose we make just a few teeny tiny changes in the wording. Let's put it on the screen." She leaned in, clicking the computer a few times. "Maybe we should use this typeface and this kind of paper? What do you think?"

"I think that would be excellent."

"Good. Now what were you planning about the food?"

"My mother and my two aunts are going to make delicious tamales."

"Well, bless your heart, I'm sure they could, but they should be with your father greeting people. They shouldn't have to be bothered with having to keep food hot and serving people."

"But they are making my father's favorite food," Dolores said.

"Wonderful. If they make the tamales the day before, I'll have my friend pick them up and serve them and a few other things. How would that be?"

"That's a good idea. That way they could go to the beauty parlor the day we're having the party."

"Exactly. What a good thinker you are, Dolores."

In Will's office, Muffy began making arrangements. She reassured Will the event would be a success, and together they brainstormed a list of people to invite, including judges, associate judges and their staff, all board-certified family lawyers, which, of course, included the members of "the club," family law mediators, client referrers, and all their past and current clients. The final list consisted of almost two hundred guests.

"Crowded is good," Muffy said, "so long as you have plenty of food and drink and an army of uniformed servers. It creates excitement. In my experience, a guest list of two hundred for a political event usually means an attendance of one hundred."

Will shook his head. "Not this time. No one will want to offend Judge Elizondo by not showing up, even if the thought of coming to our offices is abhorrent to them."

"You are so calculating." Muffy put her arms around him.

"I hope it isn't obvious," Will said.

"To none but me." She kissed his neck right below his ear.

"Let me go over this with Paddy," Will said.

Muffy moved to a chair on the other side of Will's desk. "Why?" she asked, her lips curling down.

"He's my partner. We're going to spend a lot of money on this. He'll go along with everything. It's just a good idea for partners to make big decisions together."

"Right. I'm your partner, too, but you decided to leave Walker & Travis and form a boy band with Brooklyn Paddy without discussing it with me first."

Will turned beet red, shrank a little, and gave her a look that acknowledged she was correct.

CHAPTER 31

PLAN B

RAY FOURBIRDS, A FORMER HEAD of HPD narcotics, was reputed to be the savviest private investigator in Houston. He had retired with the rank of assistant chief. After putting in twenty years, he knew nearly everyone in town and had something on most of them. While Ray's reputation was extremely good for hunting down information, his real genius was said to be in somehow finding evidence everyone else seemed to miss. With an unlimited budget and a pot of gold at the end of the rainbow, Paddy decided it was time to see how good Fourbirds was.

Fourbirds was about the same height as Paddy, but heavier. He had dark hair and ruddy skin from years of hitting the sauce—not that he ever appeared the slightest bit out of control. He strolled into Paddy's office wearing a bright Hawaiian shirt, khaki pants, and lizard boots.

Paddy explained his objective in Hetherington's case.

"Ah, young Randy Hetherington," Fourbirds said. "I *do* remember him. He liked to drive fast. He liked fast women, too. In fact, that boy would have gotten into some serious trouble if his old man hadn't used his connections wisely."

"Tell me about that," Paddy said.

"No, sir. No can do," Fourbirds said.

"That sounds like a final answer."

Fourbirds nodded. "Final answer."

"Okay, fuckhead. 'Nuff said." Paddy thought it was a good sign that Fourbirds kept even old secrets secret.

"Just get me what you can on both of them."

IN A FEW DAYS, Fourbirds visited Paddy again.

"Mrs. Hetherington is a lady. Each morning, she wakes her daughter, makes her breakfast, and sits and eats with her. She has her in a playgroup with children her age whose mothers are her friends. Her friends are a lot like her, educated, good mothers with clean livers, mostly vegan. They dress plainly, drive Priuses, buy organic foods at Saturday markets, and recycle. You know the bullshit. The lady's from Oregon. Went to some liberal college up there called Reed, then graduate school at Rice. She became an assistant professor as soon as she graduated."

"Nothing so far gives me a fucking clue as to how she met Randy and was stupid enough to marry his spoiled ass," Paddy said.

"I do know a little about that." The man waited before speaking again, clearly enjoying having an audience. Impatient, Paddy glared. "See, our boy Hetherington's family endowed an annual lecture series at Rice. Hetherington's father required him to join the rest of the family for the lecture and the reception afterwards. One year our girl Linda gave the lecture.

"My sources tell me that at the reception the old man had a come-to-Jesus meeting with his son, telling him that he'd been living a wild, aimless life long enough. He said his son needed to find a wife and that he wanted grandchildren who he hoped would grow up to be responsible members of the community. He said his instincts told him that the woman who just gave the lecture would make someone a good wife.

"Randy hadn't even listened to Linda's speech. He noticed she was pretty, even if she didn't do much about it. He tried to imagine, as he did with nearly every woman who came into his field of vision, having sex with her. She was not his type, definitely not his type. On the other hand, Randy wasn't a fool. He'd understood his father's speech to be a call to action. He approached Linda. They chatted. He asked her to dinner. She was nice enough. What she talked about was intellectual bullshit, but he knew his father approved of her. Randy decided to marry her."

Paddy got up. He laid down on his office couch like a patient seeing a shrink. Fourbirds turned his chair to face him. He said, "She was an animal rights activist. She googled our boy. One of the hits was a newspaper report that he had gotten into trouble for helicopter hunting in Africa. She confronted him about it. He knew it was a make-or-break moment. He told her he had made a terrible mistake, that he'd been cruel and inhumane. Unsportsmanlike. He said he would never consider going helicopter hunting again."

"How do you find out so many fucking details?" Paddy asked, hands folded on his chest.

Fourbirds smiled. "Randy gave up drugs and all but social drinking. You gotta give the boy credit. He can get serious when he needs to. His Daddy's come-to-Jesus talk had been some talk if you catch my drift. Anyhow, Randy set about romancing Linda. He took her on a humanitarian mission to Eritrea. He supported her causes. She was not impressed with material things, but she was impressed with how money could advance her causes. He figured out who her dream man was, and that is who he became. She bought it and fell in love. At the same time, he was also playing his father. He started going to the family office every day and wearing a suit. Randy and Linda had a small wedding—a beautiful affair—right there on the Rice campus."

Paddy interrupted. "So he married her for money. His own father's money."

Fourbirds laughed loudly. "That's a good one, Moran. I hadn't thought of it that way, but you're right on. She gave up her academic career. Their daughter was born. His father was pleased. He increased your client's allowance and gave him more authority over his own finances. Randy lived that life for about four years. Then his father died. He wasn't cold in the ground before the old Randy was back. Only this time he had lots more money with no strings attached. Before long, he was drinking heavily again, flying all over the world to hunt and screw around with old girlfriends as well as new ones. I don't know how much she cared. I'm sure she'd figured out she'd been set up, but she's a lady. She stuck to being a full-time mother and made a respectable life without him."

Paddy said, thinking out loud, "Do we have the wrong one as the client?"

Fourbirds answered instantly, "You have the one with the money. That allows for creativity."

"Let's think about that," Paddy said. "If he's gone a lot, what does she do besides take care of the daughter?"

"She goes to theater and ballet and women's seminars with her friends. She goes to meetings of her bleeding-heart organizations."

"Does she drink?"

"Wine maybe, not heavily," Fourbirds said.

"Get her credit card charges," Paddy said. "Maybe we'll come up with an idea."

"If you don't think of something, I may have an idea," Fourbirds said.

"What is it?"

"It wouldn't be Plan A. Let's see what you come up with first, counselor." Something in Fourbirds' tone made Paddy anxious.

Will watched Fourbirds leave the building and then went into Paddy's office. "Have you and that character come up with a plan to earn us our bonus from Hetherington?"

"It's a lot fucking tougher than I thought it would be. As of this moment, I don't know how we can do better than joint custody."

"That's not what you promised our boy Randy. You did a great sales job on him. How are you at managing expectations? He calls nearly every day asking what's going on."

Paddy started to say, "Asshole," but he realized his anger was misplaced. "I can imagine. Don't worry. There's gotta be something. We just have to find it."

⸝⸝⸝⸝

PADDY COULDN'T SLEEP that night. After taking the dog for a long walk, he drove, with Mick on his lap, the route where ideas seemed to come to him, down San Felipe through River Oaks, past Estelle Cook's house to downtown, and past the Bank of America building, which cast night shadows that made him think the Joker was lurking among its spires with Batman nowhere to be found. He continued past his old office with George Accurso and the Family Law Center. When he reached the Harris County Civil Courthouse, he stopped his car. He got out.

While Mick was doing his business, Paddy thought about the Grissett case. The judge's admonition stuck with him. It had been a learning experience. There were a few times he thought about crossing the line, but that moment came back, and he never violated the code. He'd come a long way since then. He'd have a lot further to fall now. Estelle Cook's divorce put him on the map as a divorce lawyer. Marshall & Moran was very successful. Still, he had yet to have a high-profile trial at the courthouse.

What drove him was getting an opportunity to wax eloquently in a courthouse drama covered by the *Chronicle*. Getting Randy Hetherington custody in a trial would be *big*. A giant payday would be nice, but he wanted something people would talk about, something that would make him a legend, something that would command respect. He was due. Fourbirds' Plan B was bound to be shady, but he couldn't come up with a plan.

He would call Margot. They'd become something like friends after he handled her case. Though he couldn't share names or details about the Hetherington case, maybe something in Margot's easy manner of talking with him would steer him in the right direction. Maybe, more importantly, away from the wrong direction.

He waited until eight o'clock in the morning. He slammed his phone into his palm when his call was directed to her voicemail.

Next, he called Fourbirds. They met at Carl's, a diner. Paddy used to hang out there with his buddies after their shifts, but he hadn't been there in a couple of years. Nothing had changed—same paneled walls and the same red vinyl booths with pock-marked wooden tables. They sat in a corner.

"Enough mousing around," Paddy said after the hostess sat them. "What the fuck is the plan?"

"You don't want to know."

"This could be my biggest victory ever. What do you mean, I don't want to know? I got the only fucking vote."

Fourbirds kept his voice low and his tone confidential, "Just let me do my job. I will give you what you need to win."

Paddy's line of sight went from Fourbirds' face to the wooden table. He studied the grooves made by knives and dark circles left by drink glasses and coffee cups.

"What's the matter?" Fourbirds asked. "Is Carl's slumming for you now?"

Paddy sighed. He sipped his very bad, now cold coffee. He called out, "Bring me a Shiner Bock, Carl!" He turned back to Fourbirds. "It's not Carl's that's bothering me. I know what to expect here. It's whatever your plan might be that's bothering me."

"Moran, this caper is in my backyard. Do you think I would take a risk?"

"I don't think you would knowingly take a risk."

"Do you think I'm a dumb ass?"

"Not that either. You haven't saddled up in this arena before."

"It's a more pussy-like arena than I've played in. What's your option?"

"If I knew of one, we wouldn't be here." Paddy shook his head, sighing.

He bit his lower lip. His stomach felt uneasy. "We're not quite ready yet. I need to get my client to have a longer track record as a faithful husband and adoring father, sober and at home."

"I think your job is harder than mine. It can't be easy making randy Randy toe the line." Fourbirds turned his head both ways, checking to see if anyone might be eavesdropping. He leaned closer to Paddy. In a tone so low Paddy could barely hear him, he said, "If it is of any comfort to you, I ain't inventing the wheel here. I did a different version of the plan when I was captain of the Narcotics Division. I nailed a guy who was running a massive drug operation. He had the best lawyers his dirty money could buy. They couldn't figure it out. We're not going to get in trouble. I'm a professional and a damned creative one."

"Linda Hetherington isn't the kingpin of a fucking cartel. For Chrissake, she won't give her kid Fruit Loops because they have genetically modified corn and refined sugar."

"And your point is?" Fourbirds asked.

Paddy looked away. *She's a good person, and he's going to destroy her*, he thought. It occurred to him how different this was from the days when he was a policeman, where the job was to get bad guys, not help them.

〰️

THE NEXT DAY Paddy called Hetherington.

"Okay, Mr. Hetherington, sir," Paddy said. "Do you think you can stay sober, quit whoring, and put off any hunting trips until this is over?"

The line was silent for a moment, and then Hetherington said, "I can't miss the opening of goose season next week."

"Where do you go to hunt geese—Nairobi?" Paddy asked.

"No, Mr. Moran," Hetherington said, clearly irritated. "Just past Katy. That's twenty miles from here."

"How long are you gone?"

"Out at three a.m. Back by noon. I got a boy to run dogs and clean birds. Been taking the same guys on opening day since I was twenty-five."

The word "boy" pissed off Paddy. He clenched his jaw. "Okay, I'll give you that one. Don't forget, pal, I've got someone watching you as closely as they're watching sweet Linda. Your incentive is Will and I get two million bucks if I win or if you break my rules. You want me to get the money the easy way or the hard way?"

"Mr. Moran, I don't like you," Hetherington whined like a spoiled twelve-year-old. "When this is over, it is not likely I'll ever see you again on purpose, but I will do what I have to do to get what I want."

"Fucking A you will."

After hanging up, Paddy called Margot.

This time she answered.

"Hello, Moran. I saw you called the other day."

Paddy wanted to tell her why he had called. Somehow he could not. Instead he asked, "Do you have plans for Thursday evening? Of course, you do. Let me rephrase that. Can you cancel your Thursday plans? We're having a reception at the office for a new judge, the Honorable Hector Elizondo."

"Sure, sweetie," she said. "Like a date?"

He hesitated. His palms began to sweat. "You'll have to meet me there. I'm a host. I was hoping we could get together afterwards."

"I'll take that as a date."

CHAPTER 32

RECEPTIONS AND DEPARTURES

MARGOT'S FIRST VISION when the elevator door opened was the tasteful Marshall & Moran wall signage hanging behind large vases of dahlias. Each vase was clad with a miniature judicial robe. She spotted Paddy's tall frame. She reached up to tap his shoulder as he was greeting other guests.

"My God, Moran, you look dashing."

Paddy leaned down to give her a hug.

"You smell good, too," she said.

That brought a satisfied smile. "Balmain," he said, instantly regretting showing off.

"And, by the way, I don't think I've ever been anyplace where 'the Honorable' was written on so many name tags," Margot said.

"It's a misnomer in more than a few cases."

"A minor detail, I'm sure," Margot said.

Muffy had not missed any detail, from her choice of flowers to food, which included ice sculptures full of jumbo shrimp, a sushi bar, and beef tender carved to order. A photographer whose pictures always made their way to the society pages snapped continuously. Margot wrapped her arm around Paddy's waist each time they were in his viewfinder.

Will was correct about the turnout. About ninety percent of those invited showed up. The judges came with their complete staff. Will prepared Paddy by telling him that if he wanted access to someone, he needed to make sure that person's secretary knew and liked him. Paddy understood. They both worked to make all judicial staff feel special. Muffy tag-teamed for them. She was especially adept at making everyone feel at ease. She loved it. It was her triumph. As they had planned, Will and Paddy gave special attention to the members of the club, working hard to convey an air of being equals without being presumptuous.

Elizondo and his family beamed.

"You have Dolores to thank for all this precision planning," Will told Elizondo.

Elizondo smiled, but he was turning his head from left to right, pulling his collar, and, as Will had always known him to, perpetually mopping perspiration from his forehead with a handkerchief.

Muffy gave Mrs. Elizondo a hug. "Your daughter's a natural. I bet she learned it all from you."

Mrs. Elizondo's face glowed with pride.

Paddy made several rounds, treating people he had never met as if they were old friends. Feeling he had completed his work, he stood with Margot in a corner, sharing small plates of beef tender and shrimp. They chatted and laughed. He felt a mounting confusion. Before her, the only women in his life he'd felt both attracted to and comfortable with were hookers. He was surprised at the feeling of heat in his loins as she stood close to him.

Shifting his attention from lust, he said, "Margot, I'm not good at thanking people, but when I think about it, I'm here today because of you."

She put her finger to his lips. "You would be here with or without me. Maybe not as quickly."

Paddy shook his head. He instinctively reached for her hands and held them gently. He was surprised to hear himself say, "You are a wonderful, beautiful person." He started to add "sexy" as he put his arm around her waist.

"You, sir, have an agenda."

He felt awkward. "I've never been able to say some things to you," he said.

"Not now. You aren't ready. I wouldn't want to divert you."

He tilted his head, looking at her.

"I'm a demanding woman, Paddy." She laughed. "You can't stop what you're doing now. It's too important to you." When he didn't speak, she said, "I can wait. Tomorrow, I'm going to France. I can start my waiting there."

"For how long?" he asked anxiously.

"Oh, for Chrissake, Moran. Don't give me the sad face emoji. I'm not going to the moon. I'll have a cell phone and email. You're a good person, Paddy. If I didn't believe that, I wouldn't be here. But you're also ambitious. This"—she gestured to the room—"is evidence of that. Sometimes those two things create a conflict. But know I'm your friend. If you ever have a problem and you can't sort it out, you can call me."

Yeah? Then why didn't she answer the phone the other night? It wasn't too late to talk to her and explain how he had approved Fourbirds' mysterious Plan B without knowing what it was. He'd definitely kill the mood if he brought it up now, and he didn't want to do that, no matter what.

When the last smiling guests had said their goodbyes, Paddy and Margot gave their compliments to Muffy. Then he escorted Margot to his red '95 Ferrari Testarossa. "I'll take you to your car and follow you home."

"Quite a car," she said.

"While I was trying to make up my mind about buying this car," he said, "the owner tells me 'Testarossa' meant 'red-head' in Italian. I was done for."

"A match made in heaven," she said.

"Like us," Paddy responded.

"Could be. You never know."

"Follow me," she said when they arrived at her car. Perhaps to let him know that fast, aggressive driving turned her on, she burned rubber as she took off, Paddy in hot pursuit.

〰〰

PADDY PARKED HIS CAR in front of her place. As he entered, he said words he had rehearsed while driving over. "You know, I was always afraid to get too close to you, for us to get beyond being friends who flirt with each other. There are lots of reasons. At first, I didn't know if a classy dame like you would be interested in me. Soon I realized you have so much confidence in yourself that what other people think of me wasn't important to you. That self-confidence was a little intimidating, too. I got past it enough for tonight to happen. I decided we should see what's there for us. Of course, you had it all doped out before I did. You're right: I am driven, and things are going well. It may not be I won't have to keep up such a furious pace much longer."

"We'll see," she said. "At this moment, just come on in. Let's find out what we have to look forward to."

"I thought you said you didn't want to divert me," he said with an impish smile.

"Oh, I think you can handle a little diversion for one night."

"Did you say *diversion* or *perversion*?" he asked, a grin overtaking his face.

"Is there a difference?" she said, lowering her voice. "Come on, Moran.

Just be the strong silent type. I don't know how long this is going to take, and I don't want to miss my plane."

"Jesus, you're leaving tonight?"

"At noon tomorrow. I'm already packed." She pulled him inside and closed the front door.

〰

THE SOCIETY PAGE of the Sunday *Chronicle* had pictures of Paddy and Will with Judge Elizondo and a write-up of the event mentioning Paddy and Margot, Will and Muffy, and many of the judges who attended.

A week later, Dolores turned in her resignation. Her family was so thrilled at her success, they decided to help her start up an event-planning business.

CHAPTER 33

PADDY'S AND PILAR'S
PATHS CONVERGE

ELEGANTÉ WAS BUZZING as Paddy wove his way through the main seating area to the wine cellar. One of Luigi's wine vendors was holding a tasting to introduce a prestigious vineyard in Bordeaux he had just landed. Across the room, Paddy saw Norma and many of The Best People, a club of which he was now a member. When he spotted VJ and Pilar, he made straight for them.

"Mr. Simon," he said, smiling, his hand extended. "And Mrs. Simon."

VJ smiled and nodded. "Pilar, this is Patrick Moran. He is a well-known divorce attorney. More importantly, he is a close friend of our good friend Margot Shear."

Paddy referred to himself as a family lawyer, but he didn't correct VJ. "Please, if you want to be friends, which I hope you do, don't call me Patrick. Call me Paddy. Mrs. Simon, we met once before, but you may not remember."

"It's Pilar. Of course, I do. You refused to take me as a client, but you gave me good advice anyway," Pilar said, smiling.

Paddy took her in. She was heavier than the first time he met her, but, wow, he could still almost inhale her.

"I hear your firm is doing very well," VJ said. "You and Will Marshall are apparently quite a team."

Paddy redirected his attention to VJ. "Thanks. We're doing fine for being new kids on the block. Some good people have come to us in their hour of need. A lot of them think we have helped."

VJ winced at the humble brag.

"That's the good news. Running a law office is another matter."

Pilar spoke up. "What's the problem?"

"The problem is I've never managed anyone or anything. I haven't even done much of a job managing myself. I'm a pretty good lawyer, but

I'm not a manager. Will is actually very good at that, but he has to practice law. We haven't found anyone who can run the office for us, and we've had some issues."

"How large is your office?" Pilar asked.

"We took the whole floor. We use about half. *Texas Monthly* did a nice article about our offices."

Moran was disappointed that instead of being impressed, she said, "I'm sorry. I meant how many people, and who does what?"

"Why do you want to know?"

"I used to be an office manager. If it's just the two of you lawyers and support staff, it shouldn't be hard to find someone to do that. My guess is it wouldn't be a full-time job."

"Well, that's something to think about."

When Paddy moved on to howdy and shake with the others in the crowd, Pilar turned to VJ. "How about that? I could probably get their office in shape and keep it that way in two days a week. You know I've been thinking about working. What do you think?"

VJ didn't answer.

Smiling as she put her arm around his waist, she said, "I know my history. I may still have a lot of work to do with the analyst, but that's one bad choice I'll never make. There will never be another man for me but you. Ever. I love you. Love you. Love you." She meant it.

VJ breathed a sigh of relief. "I'm that obvious?"

She took his arm firmly but tenderly. Marching forward, she said, "Come on. We have a job to do here. We have to taste every one of those wines."

"Easy," he said.

"You want me to skip the wine at a wine tasting?"

VJ didn't say anything.

"Fine," she snapped and grabbed a San Pellegrino.

"Do what you want," he said as the sides of his lips turned down.

After that, the glasses of wine disappeared quickly.

DURING THE DRIVE HOME, Pilar said to VJ, "You're agitated. It's about me working, isn't it?"

"No," he said quickly.

"Then, what's it?"

"You're drunk."

"I'm not!"

He turned his head slightly to her, his eyes and mind still focused on driving, "Your words are slurred. You were wobbling when we left the wine cellar and walked to the front door. I had to catch you as you got to the car. What is that if not being drunk?" He turned back to the road and added, "There's no point talking to you."

"No point in talking to me? Stop being so high and mighty. We clearly need to talk. Now."

"No. Tomorrow. You're impossible to reason with when you're drunk."

"VJ," she said. Her voice was loud.

"Pilar, I said not now." He drove home without responding to her when she spoke. When he felt the urge to reply to something she said, he gripped the steering wheel tightly. He opened her door when they got home and helped her out of the car and into the house. He went to his study, picked up a book, and began to read. He realized that similar evenings had played out too many times when he was married to Georgie. He waited until Pilar had fallen asleep before going to bed.

〰️

THE NEXT MORNING, AFTER HE was ready for work, VJ touched Pilar to wake her. She frowned and squinted and snapped, "What?"

"Listen to me. You have a drinking problem."

"I do not," she said as she sat up.

"Sweetheart," he said, using his favorite pet name for her, but his voice was not tender, "most nights when I get home you've already been drinking. Then you have wine with dinner."

"Red wine is good for you. The French are healthier than we are!"

He closed his eyes and tilted his head upward. "Pilar, don't kid yourself. You have a serious problem, and I don't want to come home to a drunk every night."

She looked at him, waiting for words to form, but before they did he spoke.

"And, besides, alcohol is sugar. It's fattening."

Her eyes flashed. "That's the real problem, isn't it VJ? I'm no longer attractive to you because you think I'm fat."

"No," he said, shaking his head. "I'm saying I don't like it when you drink."

She turned her head to the wall. "I don't believe you," she said stiffly. "I know what this is about."

"No, sweetheart," he said, this time more endearing. "I want you to get help." He kissed her on the cheek and left.

When the door closed, Pilar shouted, "You son of a bitch!" She picked up a pillow and flung it after him.

She continued throwing pillows until all were on the floor. She sat looking at them as her breathing slowed. She picked up one, held it over her stomach with both arms, and sat on the bed. There was a knock on the door. It opened, and Grace entered, dressed for school.

"Good morning, Mom." She looked around. "It looks like you and Daddy had a pillow fight."

Pilar laughed. "You're such a love." She leaped up and threw the pillow she was holding at her daughter. Grace ducked and grabbed a pillow from the floor and threw it at Pilar. She caught it, laughing, and hugged Grace. "You have a wonderful day at school."

"Thanks, I better go. The carpool should be here any second."

After Grace left, Pilar checked on the other children. The nanny had them up, dressed, and fed. She watched as the nanny read a picture book to Raj Benjamin.

"I'm afraid you're going to be in charge today," she told the woman when the story had come to an end. "I'm going to be pretty busy."

Back in the bedroom, she found Dr. MacAndrew's number, which her friend Leila Esfandiary had given her. After making an appointment, she went to her computer. She clicked through a list of law firms, until she found the one she wanted and dialed the number. "Mr. Moran, this is Pilar Simon."

"It's Paddy, remember?"

"Of course. If you're interested, I'd be happy to talk further about that office manager position we discussed last night."

WHEN VJ CAME HOME that night, Pilar greeted him warmly. "Darling, I listened to everything you said this morning. I haven't had a drink. I made an appointment with a plastic surgeon to discuss a tummy tuck."

"You don't have to do that," he said.

She saw he was embarrassed. "Don't feel guilty. I need to have it done."

"Are you absolutely sure you want to have the operation?"

"Yes. After that, I called that lawyer Moran. He said he would discuss hiring me with Will Marshall. I think they could use me."

"Why do you want to work there?"

"I feel I need to work. It's not my first choice. I'd rather work at your office. I proved I can be helpful when I worked through issues with you on that wastewater deal. I'm comfortable with helping to solve difficult problems and taking on unusual assignments and getting them done—" She stared at him. "How about it, VJ? I don't mind working for Marshall & Moran, but I'd rather have a job that really challenges me, and nothing would be better than working with you."

He shook his head.

"You *are* discounting my abilities."

"No. I'm not," he said. Pilar working in his office would surely affect morale, and he really didn't believe she would be an asset.

"I'll try taking my undiscounted abilities to Marshall & Moran." Her tone was light, but there was an edge of hurt in her voice. She recovered her good humor quickly. Earlier in the day she had decided that she would not be down on herself or angry with VJ. They needed some good times.

Holding up her index finger and smiling, she said, "Wait, there's more! I cooked. Enchiladas with *fresadilla* sauce. It's just like my *abuela* used to make. And chili con queso like Felix's used to make. Tonight, the Simon family will sit together at the table."

VJ smiled broadly, put his arm around her waist, kissed her, and said, "What's better than that?"

CHAPTER 34

PADDY'S BIG DAY IN COURT

AFTER TWO MONTHS of sending reports that Hetherington was sticking to the rules, Fourbirds asked Paddy if he was ready to move forward. Paddy hesitated. He had wracked his brain trying to conceive a viable alternative of his own to whatever evil lurked in Fourbirds' mysterious plan. He'd found none. Hetherington was raring to go.

Plan B worried Paddy, even if he didn't know what it was. From that increasingly remote place in his gut echoed the words of the judge in Grissett case: "Make good choices, Mr. Moran."

Paddy's instincts told him no. His head told him yes. He called Margot. He knew she would tell him not to unleash Fourbirds and his Plan B, even if Paddy didn't know what it was and even if without it he would surely lose. There was no answer, and her voice mailbox was full. When he called to chat about nothing in particular, she answered. When her advice was really important to him, she was MIA. He threw his phone down. Fucking bitch. She said to call when he needed her and when he does he can't reach her. He sent an email and got an away message. He sent a text and got a message that it wasn't delivered. He vaguely remembered her saying she was going to a retreat where no one could speak for a week. He poured himself a drink and called a hooker.

The next morning he tried Margot again. No answer. He took it as a sign and called Fourbirds.

"Go ahead," he told Fourbirds, "but whatever it is, do it right."

"Your timing is good," Fourbirds said. "I know just the occasion to put our little plan into action."

⁓

LINDA HETHERINGTON WAS A board member of a national organization that promoted academic freedom for university professors without tenure.

Substantial support of the organization came from the private foundation her late father-in-law had established and of which she was a board member. The annual meeting of the organization was being held in Houston. Linda was to host a reception for the most generous contributors at the Hetherington home on South Boulevard, a street with old oaks that leaned toward each other so that the esplanade was always shaded, even at high noon on the hottest days.

Fourbirds told Paddy to get Hetherington out of town. Hetherington didn't mind a quick deep-sea fishing trip in the Yucatan Peninsula.

Arianna Alexander, the assumed identity of Fourbirds' operative for the job, donated enough to be a gold table sponsor, which entitled her to an invitation to the reception. Linda found Arianna very engaging. A tall, leggy blond, Arianna claimed to be interested in women's issues on a global level, especially the right of all women to a decent education. She and Linda chatted over vegetable pâté about the organization and other topics of great interest to Linda. So lively was their conversation that they continued to talk even as the last of the guests were leaving.

The catering staff packed up and left. The valet service brought in the keys to Arianna's rented BMW convertible and left. Only Linda and Arianna remained.

"I'm enjoying talking to you so much," Arianna said. "Do you mind if we have one more glass of wine before I go?"

Linda was exhausted but agreed. While she stepped away to use the restroom, Arianna slipped some Klonopin into Linda's glass and stirred it as it dissolved.

In a matter of minutes, Linda, nearly comatose, flopped backwards on the sofa cushions. Arianna carried her to the master bedroom. She carefully removed Linda's clothes and then her own. Then, she positioned Linda on the bed so that a video camera would capture everything. Arianna said things and carefully manipulated Linda's body so that it seemed Linda was a responding, willing participant to everything Arianna did—and Arianna did a lot. In fact, Arianna appeared to be thoroughly enjoying herself. A wide-angle lens setting included video showing the daughter's bedroom door open while the sexual activity took place.

"HOLY SHIT. That video is amazing." Paddy downed the last of his drink and went to the bar to pour another round for himself and Fourbirds. "Why didn't you tell me Linda Hetherington was bi?"

"I had to surprise you with something, didn't I?"

"Damn good job." He handed Fourbirds a whiskey on the rocks. "How did you know it was going to happen?"

"Paddy, my man, you don't want to know."

"The woman with her, is she a hooker?"

"She's actually a licensed private investigator who is very enthusiastic about her work."

"To tell you the truth, she got me a little enthusiastic, too," Paddy said. "I think we've got everything we need. This is large, Ray."

~~~~

HETHERINGTON RETURNED FROM New York. On his behalf, Marshall & Moran LLP filed a petition for divorce the next day, asking for custody of his daughter. Paddy made sure he included a jury demand. In fact, even with Hetherington as a witness, he was licking his chops to get at a jury in this case. In a major break for Paddy and Will, the case was randomly assigned to Elizondo's court. Linda's attorney filed an answer and a motion for Elizondo to recuse himself. Elizondo denied it.

Paddy showed Will the video.

"How did you get this?" he asked.

"Just lucky, I guess. Randy had a secret surveillance camera."

Will nodded his head, deciding not to ask any more questions.

"We need to visit with Hector, so he won't be surprised when we introduce it," Paddy said.

Will responded, "*Ex parte* meeting with the judge?"

Paddy rolled his eyes. "You want the Pope there, too? Like we don't do it with your Anchor Man all the time?"

Will raised his eyebrows.

"It comes down to this," Paddy said. "The video gets admitted as evidence, we split a million bucks. It doesn't get in, we have a rich, spoiled brat who played by rules we set for him, and still he didn't get his way. He will be pissed. We'll lose. Your wife doesn't get a new swankienda."

He did not add, "And I won't get my big moment in the spotlight."

⁂

PADDY AND WILL carefully went over the situation with Elizondo at a steakhouse near his home in Kingwood.

Authentication wouldn't be a problem, so the only issue would be whether or not the video would be admissible as evidence. They prepped Elizondo on the rules so that he would be able to rule from the bench. They even gave him a small Rules of Evidence booklet with Post-its on the relevant pages.

⁂

LINDA'S ATTORNEY FILED a motion *in limine*, seeking to keep the video out of evidence as well as any reference to it. At the hearing, her attorney was outraged and indignant. The video wasn't what it appeared to be. His client had no recollection of the event. He didn't have access to the woman in the video because she was out of the jurisdictional limits that compel someone to be a witness at a trial and, therefore, he could not cross-examine her.

Will responded that the video had been authenticated by an expert and that it spoke for itself. The witness wasn't necessary so long as someone could identify Linda Hetherington. They would be happy to call Linda if there was any doubt whether it was her in the video.

When Elizondo denied his motion *in limine*, Linda's lawyer lost his composure, screaming that the video was highly prejudicial, and if he couldn't examine or cross-examine the woman, the trial would be a travesty.

Elizondo gaveled Linda's attorney down and threatened him with contempt. Paddy and Will could barely contain their delight.

Her attorney filed an emergency appeal. The appeals court ruled it could not hear the appeal until after trial.

With an "open to buy" on expenses, Paddy and Will left no possibilities unconsidered. The jury consultants arranged for a mock trial. The mock jury, in evaluating Hetherington as a witness, made it clear that if he was going to testify at all, which they thought he should not, he ought to be humble and respectful. A drama coach was hired for that formidable task. Paddy was admonished not to be too cute or not too full of himself. An expert was used in jury selection. An IT team produced trial exhibits.

〰〰

"SHOW TIME," PADDY SAID as he, Will, and Hetherington took their places at the counsel table for the real trial. Judge Elizondo brought in the jury panel. The courtroom was packed as Paddy began his *voir dire*. One set of consultants sat in the courtroom observing and measuring Paddy's body language and another sat outside the courtroom with tablet computers watching the trial and exchanging messages with their colleagues inside. The consultants who were not in the courtroom gave Paddy cues through a Bluetooth listening device concealed in his ear, and Paddy used the key words they fed him. Another set conducted internet searches on the jury panel members. The consultants told Paddy which jurors should be stricken using peremptory challenges. While Will made sure rules of evidence and procedure were followed, Paddy examined and cross-examined witnesses. Since the consultants couldn't sit at counsel's table, Will's job was to keep Paddy from being too full of himself.

Paddy's closing argument was short, if not sweet. "Ladies and gentlemen of the jury, the facts have been submitted to you. You have to make a decision about common decency and a proper environment for young Elizabeth Hetherington. I have no doubt you will do what is right and proper for her."

In less than an hour, both sides watched the jurors as they entered the courtroom. Not a single juror looked at Linda Hetherington. The foreman announced the decision.

Randy Hetherington was awarded custody. Linda's visitations had to be supervised by someone appointed by the court. The jury found there was no community property and did not award either side attorneys' fees. Hetherington gloated. He embraced Will and started to embrace Paddy, but Paddy shook his hand. Win or lose, Randy Hetherington was still an asshole.

Paddy strutted for days. Several times he sauntered into the Family Law courthouse, seeming even bigger and taller than usual, on the pretense of doing tasks underlings could do. He imagined other lawyers were both admiring him and jealous of him as he acknowledged them with the smile—not grin—of a victorious gladiator. He savored the victory, his new-found celebrity around the courthouse and the publicity. It was everything he had told himself he wanted. What could be better? But it wasn't. He thought about going to prizefights in Brooklyn. How good did a champ feel when his arm was raised in a fight that was fixed? Being on the wrong side of right wasn't sitting well with him.

〰〰

A DEVASTATED LINDA HETHERINGTON had neither the will nor the resources to file an appeal.

Muffy traded up to a larger house in River Oaks.

Paddy used some of his share to pay cash for a penthouse in a new, luxurious high-rise near the Galleria. Hetherington, now filled with gratitude, gave Will and Paddy each a trophy. Will's was a buck head, which Muffy insisted he could keep at the office or not at all. Paddy's was a rug made from the skin of a bear, probably an endangered species, which felt nice beneath his bare feet as he enjoyed the view from his new chrome-and-glass living room. He had to have the skin sprayed with a substance to deter Mick from peeing on it. "I guess you considered the source," Paddy said to Mick after he initiated the rug.

〰〰

AS A RESULT OF the Hetherington case media coverage, Marshall & Moran LLP became hired guns of choice whenever wedded bliss was replaced by standard issue marital anger and greed. They were going full tilt. Paddy's presence filled a room with the swagger of some of Houston's most successful trial lawyers. Will provided the requisite social status and private school access to high-end potential clients. Paddy, in his own way, nurtured his relationships with helpful judges. He entertained them, sometimes appropriately and sometimes not. He was quick to pick up on someone's needs or wants and do what he could to fulfill them. He let them be his daily guests at the Houstonian. He had floor seats for Rockets games, seats behind home plate for the Astros, and a luxury suite for the Texans. Will was happy Paddy took care of that side of the business and didn't ask many questions. Fees poured in. Busy as he was, Paddy always found time to handle the marital tragedies of the best cops. He still drove his truck to meet them weekly for a few beers and poker.

And he brooded.

CHAPTER 35

WORK AND A TUMMY TUCK

AT FIRST, WILL WAS SKEPTICAL about Pilar. He suspected Paddy wanted to hire her because of her connections—or simply because she was gorgeous—but in the interview Pilar convinced Will that he had underestimated the second Mrs. Simon. After she started work, almost immediately, Will appreciated her administrative and personnel skills. The office hummed as morale and efficiency soared. Her compensation was a pittance compared to the value she added.

Pilar contracted with a national employment services company to handle payroll and benefits. After a week of interviews, she hired a permanent receptionist who was so perfect for the job Will immediately began to worry about how to keep her. Pilar created an employee manual. She installed an accounting and purchasing system that she could manage remotely. She missed no detail to cater to the pampered clients of a family law boutique, including special, shade-grown, fair-trade coffee and organic trail mix. Everyone, including Paddy, took a training course on how to use the state-of-the-art cappuccino maker. Supply orders and other outside expenses required Pilar's okay. As good a lawyer as he was, Paddy had little control over his day-to-day practice. Pilar contacted Bernice, Paddy's former secretary, who accepted the offer of a raise, a private office, and no dress code. So what if Accurso never spoke to Paddy again?

The employees liked the certainty Pilar brought with her. Will and Paddy had different styles and Paddy, in particular, was not always consistent.

〰️

ONE EVENING AFTER PILAR had been working at Marshall & Moran for a couple of weeks, she met VJ at Eleganté for a "date."

"A cranberry spritzer," she said to Marco, Luigi's best bartender, "with a cherry and lime." She noted VJ's approving glance as the non-alcoholic drink arrived. She took a swallow and grimaced slightly. It was tart and made her long to be able to enjoy just one glass of Pinot, but VJ always looked disappointed—even disgusted—when she drank wine. She lifted her glass to him. "Cheers," she said.

"How's work coming?"

She smiled. "It's fine. Today, Paddy had a near tantrum because he couldn't find a file. He accused his secretary of misfiling, and Bernice stormed into my office ready to quit or shoot him. One person we can't afford to lose is Bernice. We found the file in his briefcase, stuck in another file. I don't pay much attention to the work they do, but they have one client—I won't say his name—who is a rich, spoiled jerk." She left out how the client stared at her like she was a piece of juicy hamburger. VJ still got jealous, which would probably never change.

"I think I know exactly who you mean."

"I probably shouldn't have said that much. Bottom line, it's interesting. And fun. Plus, I like being a boss. Not that managing that office is rocket science, but I'm filling a need. And I enjoy being around adults in a work environment, even if at least one of the adults acts like a child sometimes."

"Paddy?" VJ asked.

"Uh-huh. But now that things are running smoothly, I can take time off to have the tummy tuck. Dr. MacAndrew put me on his schedule, and Leila's promised to get me through." She'd already lost fifteen of the thirty-five pounds by herself, but Leila had assured her the operation would take care of the last twenty and get rid of the extra skin. "It's an overnight miracle. You'll see," Leila told her.

VJ grunted. "Okay, if you're absolutely certain. You know you're not doing it for me."

"It's the day after tomorrow," Pilar said happily. She squeezed VJ's hand. "Don't worry. Everything is going to be fine."

THE NEXT DAY PILAR went to a birthday luncheon for Cameron McMillan. Leila organized it. Cameron had befriended Leila and her family when they first arrived in Houston from Iran, just before the fall of the shah.

The women sat around a large round table with a pyramid of exquisite lavender and peach roses in the center. Each woman looked stunning. Unabashed, joyful, conspicuous consumers all with great taste. Even with the weight she'd lost, Pilar was definitely the heaviest woman in the room. She couldn't help admiring how beautifully put together they all looked. Intelligent women and, in Pilar's estimation, not nearly as frivolous as they often made themselves out to be. Most had advanced degrees of one kind or another. And even though they were frequently in the society pages of the paper, usually because they wrote big checks to charities, by the standards of some, they were and might always be newcomers.

Most lived in large homes in the Memorial area between the Loop and Piney Point, one of Houston's wealthiest residential areas, after River Oaks. Their children went to the best private schools, and they went to all their children's games and plays, sitting together as a group. They didn't cheat on their husbands. Plus, at some point, each of them had worked—maybe not full time, but at least a little. In addition to shopping, they all had another form of release—they gossiped. A lot. Pilar frequently worried about what they said about her when she wasn't there.

After everyone air-kissed everyone else, Pilar found her seat, directly across from Cameron, the birthday girl, who was dressed in a silk suit of the palest pink with her hair pulled into a tight glossy bun. Everyone had chipped in one hundred dollars for Cameron's present, a spectacular silver and turquoise necklace made by a local artist. Pilar glanced sideways at Cameron, trying not to stare. So thin! When Cameron excused herself to go to the ladies' room, Pilar turned to Leila. "What's wrong with her?" she whispered.

"It's not obvious?"

After they had finished their salads, Leila clapped her hands. "Cake time!" On cue, the waiter wheeled in the birthday cake, a flourless chocolate ganache with raspberry coulis. At that moment, Cameron's right eye started to droop, and she grabbed her head as if in severe pain.

"My God, she's having a stroke," shrieked Bathsheba, the wife of a neurosurgeon. She pulled a bottle from her purse, shoved an aspirin into Cameron's mouth, and instructed her to chew it. "Somebody call 911!"

The women seemed stunned. Pilar grabbed her mobile phone and dialed. The EMT came quickly, and everyone followed the ambulance to the ER.

Pilar sat next to Leila in the waiting room. "I'm not going to have the tummy tuck tomorrow. This scares the hell out of me."

"Don't overreact. The tummy tuck is a good thing. The rest of us aren't like Cameron. An anorexic taking diet pills? I'll be at your house at eight o'clock. And I'll stay with you through the whole thing. Here, take this." Leila pressed an oval blue pill into Pilar's hands.

〰〰

WITH LEILA AND VJ WAITING, Pilar's procedure went perfectly. Dr. MacAndrew told her he wanted her to be an advertisement for his work. "I want everyone who sees you to want exactly what you had," he said, flashing his perfect white teeth.

Pilar felt embarrassed. "Thanks," she said, "But I'd appreciate it if everything about my having the procedure remains confidential."

He shrugged, apparently failing to understand why anyone wouldn't want to be known for being one of his patients—for being part of his greatness.

"I want you to feel no discomfort," he said as he gave her a supply of painkillers.

CHAPTER 36

THE WINGATE CASE

WINONA WINGATE SHOWED UP fifteen minutes early for her appointment with Paddy.

"Who referred you?" he inquired as he led her into his office.

"I read your ad," she snapped.

"Our ad? I didn't know we advertised."

"I read about the Hetherington case in the newspaper. I call that an ad."

Paddy beamed.

She told him that her husband did very well as an energy investment banker, that he found out she was having an affair and didn't think their last child was his.

Paddy controlled his expression. Back home, she would be called a broad. Not particularly beautiful, but sexy and . . . *obvious*, in a whorish way that Paddy admired. Bleached blond hair, expensive clothes that revealed her voluptuous, surgically enhanced figure, way too much makeup, fuck-me heels, bee-stung lips.

"I've seen that look before, buster. This is strictly business."

Paddy reddened. "Mrs. Wingate, I am a professional." He reddened more, thinking about the many meanings of his word choice.

"My old man has a rage problem. He went crazy when he found out about the affair. He beat me pretty bad and left that night. A week later he filed for divorce."

"Hmm. He already filed? Who is his lawyer?"

"Bubba Otis. But you asked the wrong question first."

Paddy cocked his head.

Like a moll in a 1950s low-budget noir film, Winona said, "The first question shouldda been, 'Who's court is it in?'"

"Okay," Paddy said. "Whose court is—?"

"Judge Elizondo's. I understand you and your partner do real well in that court."

"Hector Elizondo is an outstanding judge. One of the finest."

"Don't need to lay it on for me, Mr. Moran. Anyway, my husband's divorce petition says he doesn't want to pay support for our last child."

"Is your husband the child's father?"

"How should I answer?"

Paddy gave her a level stare. "Always tell me the truth, the whole truth. Surprising your lawyer is not in your best interests, Mrs. Wingate. I decide how much of that whole truth to reveal."

"No."

"You'll probably be pleased to know that in Texas law there's an irrebuttable presumption that a child born during marriage is the husband's child."

"And 'irrebuttable presumption' means?"

"It's a Texas legal phrase that means whether he is or is not the real father, a Texas court will hold that he is the father for support purposes."

"That's crazy," she said with a big smile. "Okay. He isn't the father of any of them."

"Really?" It took quite a bit to shock Paddy, but he was feeling it now.

Winona shrugged.

"If this comes out in court, you are not likely to get more than half the community property."

"Mr. Moran, half will be more than enough for me for the rest of my life. Let's get it done and get it over."

"You are the first client I have had in years that wasn't greedy. How many children are there?"

"Three."

"I want DNA tests for all of the children to prove he is not the father."

"Why?" she asked.

"Because *I* want to stick it to him."

"Yeah? Well, I *don't* want to stick it to him. Get the damn thing done and over with."

"Who's the lawyer here?" Paddy asked. "You're hiring me to represent you. That's what I'm going to do."

"Read my lips, buster. I want my kids. I want my half of the community. That's it. Don't fuck up."

WINONA'S HUSBAND'S LAWYER, Gordon Otis, known as Bubba, was a long-standing member of the inner circle of family lawyers, their first black member, and one of The Best People. Paddy actually liked Bubba, who reminded him a little of himself—they were both big guys, full of confidence and bravado who enjoyed bullshitting each other. Paddy knew he'd better be ready.

At the first hearing, Bubba had to restrain his very angry client.

"Bubba," Paddy told him later that evening at a TBP gathering in the wine room of Eleganté, "you need to hire a physical trainer."

Bubba had played offensive center for SMU. Drafted in the fifth round by the Steelers, he chose to go to law school instead. No other lawyer in the club matched Paddy physically. "What do you mean, Moran? I'm in great shape. I could whip your pussy ass anytime," he said, grinning.

"You think so, lamb chop? It ain't my ass that's your problem. It's your client's. If you thought Mr. Wingate was hard to handle today, he's going to get really physical next time we're in court."

Bubba pulled his head back and said, "What's going on, motherfucker? Don't blindside me—I'm serious! I don't want to get nailed here."

"I won't blindside you. I'll give you a heads-up before I do something. I'm your buddy. I wouldn't fuck you. But we've got a good case, and I have to represent my client."

"Gimme a break, Moran. Your client is a whore."

"Easy there. I have some very dear friends who are whores."

Bubba didn't know Paddy wasn't kidding.

In discovery, Paddy obtained DNA reports for the last child and the father. He also ordered tests for the first two children. They confirmed Mr. Wingate did not father any of the children. His DNA expert told him, "More than twenty percent of children born to married mothers since 1990, their husbands are not the daddies. A whole lot of shaking going on, if you get my drift."

Paddy looked at him.

"Well, that's just the ones who get tested. The sample is probably exaggerated."

"Bubba, I told you I wouldn't blindside you. Your client has a rage problem. He's going to explode when we file our support and visitation motion."

"Okay, tell me."

"The law is with us on providing child support."

Bubba nodded. "Wait a week," Bubba said. "I need to get some more retainer from him before I tell him about this."

"Hey, no sweat, pal."

"The irrebuttable presumption was a very clever legal maneuver on the paternity issue. I appreciate your giving me the heads-up."

The following week, without his client's knowledge, Paddy filed two motions for summary judgment. One asked the court to rule that notwithstanding the results of the paternity tests, Mr. Wingate was liable for child support because of the irrebuttable presumption. The second asked the court to deny visitation since Mr. Wingate was not the father. That's when the *Houston Chronicle* began covering the case.

CHAPTER 37

CHUMPS, WHATEVER

NORMA NAMBÉ AND A HANDSOME, effeminate, slender young man rose as Paddy and Will approached her table at Eleganté.

"Darlins," Norma said, "the two richest and most ruthless divorce lawyers between here and Hollywood. You truly are two of the Best People."

Will rolled his eyes.

"Oh," she said, "This is Prentice, my CFO and number one personal assistant."

"Norma, our practice is known as family law." Paddy paused before he repeated, "*Family* law." He shot Norma a shark-like grin.

Norma grinned back at him. "That's right, darlin', family law. When there's a crisis in a family with bucks, you guys get called, am I right?"

"They don't all have bucks. Some of them have to borrow to pay us," Paddy said, deadpan.

"We aren't known for letting them get behind," Will added, then wished he hadn't said it.

"Yeah, there's a reason for that," Paddy interrupted. "If we wait, we won't collect. What we do isn't easy," he said as if he were putting down something that weighed heavily on him. "Clients call us at their darkest hour. Whether they want out or their spouse does, they're angry, hurt, and anxious or just plain vindictive. We become their new best friends. At some point, it's over, and it's like we never existed. Bye-bye, best friends. Usually, they never want to hear from us again."

Noting Prentice and Will were staring at him, Paddy recognized the possibility he had overstated his case. He put his hand on his heart. In mock agony, he said, "I want to tell you something, Norma. It hurts."

Norma laughed. "I feel your pain." She patted Paddy's arm and said in a sincere tone, "I can ease your suffering."

Prentice and Will smiled at each other, both amused to see two world-class bullshitters bullshitting each other.

"So how much are you guys making now?" Norma asked.

"Norma, God bless, we're not doing badly," Paddy responded.

Will turned his head forty-five degrees toward his shoulder. "'God bless?' Paddy said. 'God bless?'"

"How well?"

Will squeezed Paddy's elbow. "We're doing well enough," he said in a tone that made clear no specifics would be discussed.

"Fabulous, honey," Norma cooed, keeping her eyes on Paddy. "Tell me, sweetie, is this a good year or an especially good year?"

"So far, every year has been better than the year before," Will said evenly.

Norma licked her lips. "Well, good for you." She lowered her voice. "Who is your financial planner?"

"I don't have one," Paddy said. "Do you, Will?"

Will shook his head.

Norma leaned in closer. "Oh, honey," she sighed. "You need one of those to make your money grow. Little old me is getting a return of four percent a month."

Suddenly engaged, Will leaned in and said, "That's an extremely healthy return. How do you do it?"

"It is mostly secured lending that we purchase at less than face value."

Will raised one eyebrow. "And what do you charge for that?"

Norma opened the napkin in her lap and continued casually, as if describing some homemade recipe. "I don't charge a percentage of the assets under management. I just charge for results, a percentage of the profits. My clients and I have done very well that way." She threw a radiant smile in Paddy's direction. "Listen, honey, you give me a million dollars and in a year it will almost double."

"I don't have a million dollars to invest," Paddy said.

"If y'all are doing so well, why don't you?"

"I paid cash for my condo and my cars," Paddy said.

She smirked.

"You didn't grow up watching your parents' house foreclosed on," he said, "then having rent collectors bang on the door. My dad and mom never even had a car. I don't want to owe anyone any money for anything. In any event, there's not much left after taxes," Paddy said.

"You boys pay a lot in taxes?"

"We pay a fortune," Paddy said.

"Well," Norma said, "I'm sure I make more than you guys. I'm also sure I pay less taxes. If you guys pay a lot, you are chimps."

"Chumps," corrected Prentice.

"Chimps, chumps, whatever," Norma said. "Let me put it real plainly, you should only pay tax on money you spend on your lifestyle. Everything else I can shelter from tax and invest."

"How do we know it works?" Will asked.

"It's been structured by a former high official of the I, R, and S."

"Is that supposed to make it a sure thing? What's the deal?"

"Not here. Not now. We can discuss it in my office."

To signal the business conversation had come to an end, Norma nodded to the hovering waiter.

※

ABOUT 5:30 THAT EVENING, Paddy walked into Will's office. "I thought we should talk about Norma's deal."

Will sighed. "We don't know enough. It sounds risky."

"Will, we have lots of expenses we don't tell the accountant about because we know we can't deduct them."

"Right," Will responded. "Hector's freeloading and those other questionable expenses you pay. Maybe we shouldn't be paying any of them."

"If we didn't incur those expenses," Paddy said, "where would we be?"

Will reached for his pipe and tamped it. He never lit the pipe anymore, but he couldn't give up the ritual of filing it with fresh, moist tobacco and tamping it. It helped him contemplate. He could almost taste the warm tobacco flavor just by smelling it. "It can't hurt to take a look." He put the pipe down and got up from his chair.

"I'll tell her," Paddy responded. "Where ya goin'?"

"I have to take the McDougals to the club for dinner." Will feigned boredom. "They want to be seen. It's part of their campaign for membership."

The club. It wasn't Paddy's fucking club and never would be. Guys like him would never be asked to join, but those snoots hire him to get a dirty job done. At least Norma's Best People were happy to include him.

Will shrugged. "Walk out with me. We can talk."

"We have a hearing tomorrow in a custody case. And Bubba asked for a jury trial in Wingate."

"I guess he thinks a jury would help to level the playing field in Elizondo's court," Will responded.

Paddy sighed. "You think?"

Will adjusted his tie as they stepped off the elevator. "One more thing. Mrs. Coleman wants to get rid of her husband. She wants us to be aggressive."

"Aggressive? What is she, eighty-six?"

"Actually, a little more," Will said. "I guess that's why she's in a hurry."

"Let me see. She wants to dump her hired husband because he had a stroke. His *Dancing with the Stars* and John Holmes–porn star days are over." Paddy shook his head.

"That's why she married him. She loves to dance, and apparently she still likes sex."

"Then she shoulda rented him by the hour."

"That's your style, not hers," Will said. He pinched his lips, shifting gears. "I know you can construct a solution for her. She'll pay us our enormous rates with your exaggerated number of hours."

"My exaggerated number of hours? You learned how to do that at Walker & Travis. I'm a piker compared to you."

Will shrugged. "She pays the moment the invoice arrives."

"Ya know, I gotta give her credit for that."

"Credit she doesn't need," Will said.

CHAPTER 38

MRS. COLEMAN'S NONPERFORMING HUSBAND

THE NEXT MORNING PADDY bounded into Will's office. Most days, it was almost like a dance, how they moved between their offices, taking ideas, leaving ideas, responding to each other's strategy on a case. Paddy dropped into a chair. "Here's our strategy. We sue for an annulment. We say Mrs. Coleman's groom deceived her. We allege it was a marriage entered into by fraud. Annulment, no marriage. No marriage, no community property. The ballroom and bedroom bomb-out is blasted off the boulevard."

"You're so alliterative today. We have to ask her if they consummated the marriage."

"Why? He can't talk. We should explain the financial differences between an annulment and a divorce before we ask her about consummating the marriage. With an annulment, she gives up nothing. Besides, the newspapers will love it, which will be great for us."

"Yes, but not good for our client. Mrs. Coleman will feel like she's being held up to ridicule."

"Publicity is publicity, as long as they spell our name right, as my uncle used to say."

"Wrong," countered Will. "What client wants to be a laughingstock, a bathroom joke?"

"A bathroom joke," Paddy mused. He'd used that phrase with Tom Frost. It may have clinched the Cook settlement.

"Remember, this town may have millions of people, but our part of Houston is a small community. You can't forget that, Paddy. We are where we are today because of word of mouth. We could go down the same way."

"I get it."

"Good. Meanwhile, I have another idea. We should discuss Norma's proposal with Pilar."

"Why?" Paddy asked.

"If nothing else, maybe she'll ask her husband what he thinks."

Late that afternoon, Will strolled into Paddy's office. Engrossed in editing a pleading, Paddy didn't notice.

"Just as I thought," Will said to get his attention. "Mrs. Coleman doesn't want to do it."

Paddy looked up from his work. "Why the hell not?"

"She feels it would be interpreted that she was not appealing to him."

"You didn't mention that it's her money that makes her so irresistible?"

"Of course, I didn't. And besides, for an older woman she does have a certain something."

"He's only fifty-seven."

"You think those erectile dysfunction ads are only for men over eighty? Besides Mr. Bozo can't talk—he's had a stroke."

"Very true, maestro. I don't suppose the dead man's statute would be available to him to defend his honor," Will wisecracked.

"Not unless we wait to move on this until he's dead. Let me talk to her."

To Paddy's surprise, Will said, "Good idea."

The next day, a wonderful fragrance had lightly settled in Will's office. Although Paddy couldn't identify the scent, he knew he liked it. He walked into Will's office and saw Mrs. Coleman.

Paddy hadn't taken much notice of her on the opening day of Marshall & Morgan. What he saw now was a perfect replica of a bygone era: A powder blue silk suit, a pearl necklace, a hat perched coquettishly to one side, and a slight veil covering Mrs. Coleman's angular face. Paddy had only seen someone dressed that way in movies.

"Mrs. Coleman," Will said haltingly. "This is my partner, Paddy. We work together on important cases, and yours is very important to us."

"That's very nice, Willoughby. I know you're both very busy."

"We're never too busy for you," Will said. He was sincere.

"Has Will explained to you the difference between an annulment and a divorce?" Paddy asked in his most unctuous way.

"He said people could get an annulment if they haven't consummated"—she winked—"the marriage."

"That's right. Because there wasn't a prenuptial agreement when you married, if you get a divorce, you'll have to divide community property."

Will shifted anxiously when Paddy mentioned there was no prenup.

"He didn't *earn* it," Mrs. Coleman said.

"You mean he didn't work?"

"Of course, he didn't work. None of my husbands worked. I mean he didn't *earn* it." She winked again.

"That's what I'm getting to. If we allege the marriage wasn't consummated, then you can get an annulment. In that case, there'll be no issue of community property."

"I don't want people to gossip," she said, raising her nose. "They will think that I'm too old, and I'm not."

"You're not, are you?" Paddy said, with a lascivious grin.

"You can bet your sweet bippy I'm not," she retorted.

"Look," Paddy said, "we'll allege he deceived you by not telling you he couldn't perform. Erectile dysfunction."

"You're quite right about that."

"We'll handle it that way. Do you agree?"

"Yes, if there is no publicity." Mrs. Coleman pushed back her veil. Her eyes were still a girlish blue. "I like you, young man." She laid her hand on Paddy's knee. Her nails, he realized, were perhaps the only part of her that was modern—perfectly oval, painted a startling glossy red.

"Do you dance?" she asked.

CHAPTER 39

A GEO-ECONOMIC LESSON

AFTER REACHING RECORD HIGHS in the late seventies, the oil and real estate booms went bust in the eighties. Oil prices went from over a hundred dollars a barrel to the mid-twenties almost overnight, rig counts dropped about eighty percent, banks and savings and loans went under or were acquired by out-of-state national banks, and real estate occupancy plummeted.

Norma's penthouse office was located in a small but luxurious building in the Upper Kirby area just before the big bust. It was conveniently located for wealthy River Oaks residents and near good restaurants and upscale shops. The initial occupant had been the developer of the building. His next location was less luxurious—a federal minimum-security prison. Quick rise, quick fall—a sad Houston story in those years. There was a fierce debate over whether he perpetrated a fraud or was actually a victim of the savings and loan deregulation fiasco. Ultimately his conviction was reversed, but by then he was a broken man, having beaten the rap but not the ride.

The next occupant was an energy company that was forced to downsize in the Great Recession of 2008 and sublet to Norma at a very favorable rate.

As Paddy and Will exited the penthouse elevator, a twenty-something Asian woman wearing a short, clinging cerise silk dress said, "Gentlemen, welcome. Miss Norma will be with you very soon. May I get you something to drink?"

Both declined. They took seats. The furniture was in immaculate taste. A Bob "Daddy-O" Wade larger-than-life Texas Cosmic Cowboy super-realism painting dramatically dominated the space. The westward view, toward Highland Village and Memorial, was carpeted with green tree tops.

Fifteen minutes later, Paddy was pacing. Will drummed his fingers. "I am not happy," he said. "I don't like to be kept waiting. If we aren't seeing her in three minutes I'm gone."

Paddy knew Will was talking for the receptionist's ears. Sure enough, the receptionist gracefully excused herself. Almost instantly Norma appeared.

"Gentlemen, I am so sorry you had to wait," she cooed. "I do apologize. Let me show you around before we meet."

She led them through her luxuriously appointed offices. Rare Chinese tapestries obscured inlaid teak walls. Fine Italian marble floors were covered with Persian rugs.

"Wow, this is something else," said Paddy.

"Darlins', it's nothin'. What's most important is our state-of-the-art technology. We upgrade it every day. My clients' information is secure, and our knowledge of what's going on is instant."

Norma straightened to her full height. She led them into a room containing six wall monitors.

"Someone likes to watch television," Paddy cracked.

"That's Yaakov's desk. He comes in at three a.m. and leaves at about four in the afternoon. He never leaves his desk except to go to the john. He trades currency futures. He starts buying when he gets here, and he's sold out by the time he leaves. He doesn't keep inventory when he isn't awake." Opening a door, she said, "Okay, gentlemen, now the last leg of our journey."

They entered a room with no windows. The young man they met at Eleganté was sitting at a desk.

"Y'all remember Prentice," Norma said. "When I'm not here, everything goes through him."

Prentice smiled. Will gave a friendly, collegial nod.

Norma opened a heavy glass door into a very large office. In one windowed corner sat a massive antique desk. There were no papers, no clutter, only a large internet telephone. A round antique table and eight matching chairs anchored the center of the room.

A large man who appeared to be in his late fifties was sitting at the table. A furrow in his perspiring forehead looked at least an inch deep. Folds of his neck nearly obscured the sides of his shirt collar. He was breathing heavily.

"Gentlemen, this is Rance Ed Booker." Norma said his name as if it were deserving of the greatest awe. "If you were tax men, you would know that Rance Ed is the finest tax mind in this country. He used to be head of the most secret department of the CID. What he knows about saving people taxes could either break this country or force us into a new Internal Revenue Code. For now, his strategy helps a few privileged souls."

Rance Ed looked more bored than embarrassed by the effusive introduction. Will and Paddy sat facing him. Norma was seated one chair away from him.

"CID?" Will asked.

"Criminal Investigative Division of the IRS," Rance Ed said.

"The people who check out every scam you could dream of," Norma added.

"Are we here for a scam?" Will asked.

"You're here because we have something that works," Norma beamed. "When Rance Ed was with the CID, his people stumbled onto something they couldn't crack. They suspected it wasn't legal, but they couldn't figure out how it broke the law. It got all the way up to Rance Ed. It was the closest thing he had ever seen to a perfect tax shelter, but the promoters had missed something. He recommended referral to the DOJ to prosecute the promoters for tax fraud. However, the commissioner didn't want to pursue it. He said it would take too much money and time to work up a case that complicated, and if they lost, other people would try something similar. Rance Ed was so outraged they weren't going after those guys that he took early retirement. A mutual friend told me about Rance Ed and what a genius he was. I thought maybe he could help if any of my clients had tax problems.

"Up to then, I was doing great investing for people. I started five years ago with $50,000 of my own money. When I told people how well I was doing, they asked if I could do the same for them. One thing led to another, and now I'm running more than a billion. People are making at least eight percent a month. I have at least twenty million of new money coming in every month. I didn't really need to do anything else. But Rance Ed told me he had tweaked what is now the perfect tax shelter, and he could structure it for a few folks. He said if we did it for too many people, they'd just change the law."

Paddy was panting.

"But what is it?" asked Will. "I mean *really*."

"If you want to know, you've got to sign a confidentiality agreement."

"Sure, sure," Paddy said.

"Let me look at it," Will said.

Norma handed him a one-page document that she seemed to produce from midair.

"Wait a second," Will said, "if I sign this, I can't even get a second opinion on whatever you're trying to put us in because I can't disclose it to whomever I want to review it, *and* I can't even use my own CPA to do my returns."

"I don't care if you have another tax person look at it if he also signs a confidentiality agreement. Whoever it is will not admit it works."

"Why?" Will asked.

Norma sighed. "The NIH syndrome."

"NIH?" Paddy asked.

"Not invented here. If they didn't think of it, it can't be any good."

"Who do you want to have look at it?" Paddy asked.

"Elliott Foxman." Will said. "I asked the top tax guys at Walker & Travis. Each one said he's the best."

"I think he's a wuss," Paddy said.

"Yeah, that's what I heard," Norma said, wrinkling up her nose. "He's no good."

"Norma!" Will snapped. "I wasn't talking to you."

Norma pulled her shoulders back.

"Why do you say he is a wuss, Paddy?" Will said.

Norma interrupted again. "Because he's not aggressive. He may be competent, but he's not aggressive. Look, honey, if a guy who had Rance Ed's IRS position doesn't know what will work, who does? Foxman? He doesn't know shit about offshore tax planning."

"She's right," Paddy said. "He's not aggressive. He's competent but not aggressive."

Will turned so red Paddy felt he could almost see steam rising from his partner's scalp. "If I can't get a second opinion, I'm out," Will said. "Further, my family and I have been using the same CPA for decades. I'm not changing."

Did your old man a lot of good, Paddy thought.

"We hardly charge anything extra to prepare your tax returns," Norma responded.

"What do you charge?" Will asked.

"There's no point in trying to explain if you don't know what the plan is," Norma cooed. "Will, honey, I can see you won't agree unless Foxman looks at it. I'm not worried that he'll steal the idea. He's too chicken to use it anyway. Show it to him if you want. And on the tax returns, what do you think Rance Ed?"

Rance Ed sat up like a bored school child caught daydreaming. "I don't care who does his individual return," he said. "We just need to do the law firm return and all related returns."

"Okay," Norma said, "we'll write on here that you can consult with Foxman and have your own CPA do your individual return."

"What about VJ Simon?" Will said.

"Absolutely not," Norma answered.

Paddy shot Will a cool-it-will-you look.

After Norma made the changes and Will and Paddy signed, Rance Ed said, "Micronesia is made up of about two thousand small islands in the Pacific. It became militarily important to the US because of its proximity to Japan. During World War II, US troops camped there. Afterward, in the sixties, Peace Corps volunteers were sent to clean up some of the residual mess."

"Thanks for the lesson," Will said.

Rance Ed ignored Will. His voice was a perfect accompaniment to his physical presence—bored, tired, raspy, and almost gasping for air. Yet, with the timing of his pauses, he was commanding and credible. "Micronesia includes Guam, the Marshall Islands, and Kiribati, Nauru, Palau, and, most importantly for us, the Northern Mariana Islands."

Paddy was getting a little fidgety trying to understand what all this bullshit had to do with taxes.

"The United States wanted to maintain control there because of its strategic location. We also recognized a debt of gratitude to the people of the islands. The islands became part of the Trust Territory of the Pacific. In 1975, the inhabitants voted to become a US commonwealth. It remained a sovereign state, but the United States had responsibility for defense and economic assistance. The Commonwealth of the Northern Mariana Islands, we call it CNMI, has only six inhabited Islands. The total population is slightly more than fifty thousand people. Saipan is the largest island. What is important for us is that the CNMI adopted a tax code pretty much like the US Internal Revenue Code, except there is just a flat net income tax of six percent. A resident of the CNMI, even if he is a US citizen, doesn't have to pay US taxes on his income."

"Fine," Will said, "but we practice law in Houston, Texas."

"Just bear with me, hotshot," Rance Ed snapped.

Norma tilted her head and chuckled in a boys-will-be-boys tone. "Rance Ed doesn't like to stop when he's on a roll, Will."

"Until 1986, a CNMI corporation didn't have to pay US taxes, even on its US source income."

"It's not 1986 anymore," Will said. "What good does that do us?"

Rance Ed smiled, and Paddy fought the urge to say, "My, what big teeth you have."

Rance Ed said, "If a corporation was organized in the CNMI before September 12, 1986, its rights to the tax break are grandfathered."

"And people who practice law in Houston, Texas, get that break?" Will asked.

Paddy's heart thumped every time Will asked a question. Will was being an asshole, and he was going to piss them off, and then Norma wouldn't let them in.

"The short answer is yes. Now you pay taxes on all the income from the practice. Do this and you only pay taxes on the salary the CNMI corporation pays you."

Will replied, "The code of professional responsibility governs who can own stock in corporations that practice law in Texas and with whom a lawyer can share legal fees."

"We have a lawyer in Saipan who is licensed both in Texas and the CNMI. He would be an officer of the CNMI corporation."

Will kept asking questions. Rance Ed kept giving answers.

Paddy was barely holding onto the conversation. All he could do was wonder why anyone would not go for a six percent tax on profits.

"It sounds interesting," Will said, his words slow with reflection. "You're saying, we could take salaries of, let's say, five hundred thousand each and, after a six percent tax, invest the rest, a million, two million, whatever, right?"

"Exactly," Norma said.

"Where does one get a CNMI corporation?" Paddy asked. "Toys 'R' Us?"

Norma beamed. "We reviewed the CNMI corporations registry and bought every existing one formed before September 12, 1986, except the ones that were actually running a business."

"So, what will all this cost us?"

"Here's my fee schedule."

Will and Paddy said in unison, "That's high."

"We'll think about it," Will said.

"I know you will, darlin'," Norma said. "While you are, think about this: Not only do you have offshore tax planning, but you also make it very difficult for your creditors to reach these assets. I don't have to tell you, people are suing lawyers these days. Think about that."

CHAPTER 40

DUE DILIGENCE

"CALL FOXMAN TOMORROW," Will said.

"I will, but you know he'll tell us not to do it," Paddy said dismissively.

"If he does, I'd like to hear his reasons. Why are you so down on Foxman? Haven't you brought him in when clients have tax problems?"

"One, I think he looks down on me. Two, I had to quit using him with my clients because his fees made ours look too high. He's a nerd. I dunno."

"Neither of us is a tax expert, so check with Nerd Elliott. I'll have to deal with it if he undercharges us."

Paddy nodded.

"By the way," Will said, "we were going to ask Pilar to get her husband to weigh in on Norma's proposal. How can we without violating the confidentiality agreement?"

"Why bother? He'll just say Norma's scheme isn't any good. She's competition."

"Paddy, the one thing I feel confident about is that VJ Simon does *not* view Norma as competition."

⁓

"ELLIOTT," PADDY SAID, conjuring his most charming telephone personality. "I need to talk to you, ol' pal. We have this chance to save a lot of taxes. Will wants to do it, but I told him we should check with you. I thought you might give me your off-the-cuff opinion, you know, because you're my friend, and I send you business."

"It's been a while," Foxman said. "I haven't heard from you since we pulled that net operating loss fiasco out of the fire."

"Yeah, well, we haven't really had a tax issue since then."

"Okay, Paddy," Foxman sighed. "What's up?"

"Before I tell you, you have to sign a confidentiality agreement," Paddy said in a grave tone.

"Really?" Foxman responded with sarcastic amusement. "That requirement alone makes the transaction a listed transaction, meaning it has to be fully disclosed on your return. Make sure you let your accountant know."

"I don't know what a listed transaction is," Paddy said.

"A listed transaction is a tax shelter the IRS doesn't like."

"Really? Isn't that like inviting them to examine you?"

"You got that right. So, this deal begins with a bad smell, Mr. Moran. I don't play the audit lottery. I always assume the IRS will examine a deal. What more can you tell me about it?"

Paddy began to explain, in a general sort of way. He'd gotten to the part about Micronesia when Foxman interrupted.

"The Commonwealth of the Northern Mariana Islands has a special tax relationship with the US, but I don't know a lot about it. I remember a case where some businessman moved there. He made a lot of money and claimed he didn't have to pay US taxes because he was a resident there. I don't even remember who won. A key issue was being a resident there. You aren't planning on moving, are you? It would be inconvenient to get to the Harris County Family Law Center for an emergency motion."

Annoyed, Paddy said, "No, Elliott, we ain't gonna move. The corporation there would be the one that made the income."

"A corporation located in the CNMI is going to make money from a law practice here?" Foxman sounded wryly skeptical.

"Right. It contracts with me 'n Will to do the work. It pays us salaries, and we pay tax on what it pays us."

"What genius thought this up?" Foxman asked.

"Norma Nambé's consultant, Rance Ed Booker. He used to be a big shot with the IRS. He has the whole thing together."

"I've never heard that name. What part of the IRS was he with?"

"Some initials. Uh, like CIA."

"CID?" Elliott said quickly. "The Criminal Intelligence Division?"

"Yeah, that's it. He said he came across it when he was with the IRS. They couldn't nail anybody for doing it, so it must be all right. That was pretty much it, but it was a lot more technical."

"You know, Paddy, like I say, I'm not up on it, but it seems to me the US tax law changed on the Northern Mariana Islands."

"Will it work, or will it not work?" Paddy asked impatiently.

"I don't know enough to tell you. I would have to know more facts and then do a lot of research."

"How about the fact that Rance Ed Booker structured the whole thing, and he used to be a grand muckety-muck with the IRS?"

"Some of my biggest cases have been representing people who took advice from former IRS personnel. These guys try to make people believe they know things other people don't know and that they have friends with the IRS who will get things worked out if there's a problem. Most people get glassy-eyed whenever anyone talks about the tax code, even very intelligent people. Their brains shut off. They think having a former IRS guy weigh in makes a strategy bulletproof. It doesn't."

"Were you ever with the IRS?" Paddy asked.

"I always had what I considered to be better opportunities. But, you know, maybe you're right, maybe everything I'm saying is just sour grapes because I didn't work for the IRS."

"Are you being sarcastic?" Paddy asked.

Foxman chuckled softly.

"I get it," Paddy said. "Too good to work for the IRS and get your hands dirty and see how things really work, huh Foxman?" He tried to make it sound like a joke but some of his irritation came through.

"Paddy, it could be the deal of a lifetime."

"I think it *is* the deal of a lifetime."

"Then good luck with that," Foxman said.

Paddy exhaled audibly.

Foxman said, "Look, for a while, big national accounting firms and some big law firms thought they were too big and too powerful to have their tax shelters shot down. They were wrong. Some accountants and lawyers were indicted. Class action suits were filed by their clients. Small firms that weren't just aggressive, but downright fanciful in the ways they brought down their clients' taxable income, really got slammed. A big Texas firm got vaporized because their most profitable partner was brought down by the DOJ."

"What is your gut instinct about this deal?" Paddy asked.

"My gut instinct? Walk away from it."

"Why?"

"It's risky and just doesn't sound right. However, based on what I know so far, which is really nothing, I can't tell you absolutely that this isn't going to work."

"So you think it'll work?" Paddy homed in.

Foxman sighed. "Anything's possible."

꧁

WHEN THEY HUNG UP, Foxman wrote a letter to Paddy. The letter was marked, "Confidential: Attorney-Client Privilege."

> *Dear Paddy:*
>
> *You described very generally to me a plan to use a corporation incorporated in the Commonwealth of the Northern Mariana Islands to divert income from your Texas law practice that will be subject to taxes only in the Commonwealth. This is to confirm that I have given you no advice with respect to that plan. I suggest you not proceed unless you obtain a written opinion from someone who is knowledgeable in this area, not associated with the promoter, and who will not be receiving a fee or other compensation from the person promoting the plan.*
>
> *Best regards.*
> *Elliott*

He sent it certified mail and by a scanned email.

꧁

AS SOON AS PADDY HUNG UP, he walked into Will's office. "I talked to Foxman. He said it would work."

"That was fast. Did you talk to Pilar?"

"We aren't supposed to, remember?"

"Yeah, well, let's call her now."

Pilar had just gotten Moises down for the night when the phone rang. She picked it up immediately.

"We need to talk to you."

"Paddy? Will? It's 8:30. What's up?"

Speaking over each other they described Norma's tax scheme and her promised performance if she was their financial advisor.

"Whadduhya think?" Paddy asked, slipping into the thick Brooklynese accent that came out when he was excited.

Pilar looked at her notes. "Tell me again what return she's promising you. To be honest, I'm still not seeing how legal fees earned here aren't taxed here."

Paddy and Will explained again. She took more notes.

Will asked, "Do you mind asking VJ what he thinks? We can't go into the specific details, but I'd like to get his off-the-cuff opinion." He sounded nervous, and Pilar felt pretty sure that most of the enthusiasm for Norma's proposition was coming from Paddy. "He has to keep it confidential," Paddy chimed in.

"I'll ask, but I can't promise he'll give an answer."

WHEN PILAR TOLD VJ about the call, he made a face. "Hmmm," he said slowly. "You can't quote me, but I've heard about Norma's high returns. Nothing can produce those returns without being very risky. I'm skeptical of her claims. As to the tax scheme, I don't know what it is, but if it really worked, I'd be surprised if some of my large clients and, frankly, my own tax advisors wouldn't know about it. It doesn't pass the smell test. You get me?"

Pilar smiled at her husband. "I get you," she said.

"Plus, would you trust a financial advisor who dresses like Norma Nambé? Is it Marshall who wants to do the deal or Moran?"

"Moran made it sound like it was both of them, but I think it's him."

"That figures."

Pilar felt a flash of irritation. Why did VJ always have to sound so sure of himself? He didn't like Norma because she dressed over-the-top. He didn't like Paddy because he didn't have a pedigree. Well, she didn't either.

"He dresses better than Norma does," VJ added.

"Actually, she and I use the same personal shopper," Pilar shot back. "And you always say you like my clothes!" She batted her eyes at him playfully, but he didn't respond. She looked away, suddenly feeling depressed. She began to think about the blue pill waiting for her upstairs. What it would feel like to just crash down into sleep, to feel nothing but that strange floaty feeling inside. Shaking herself, she turned to her husband again.

"What should I tell them?"

"What do you think?"

Pilar shrugged. "Before they commit, they should get independent tax advice and independent financial analysis. It sounds great, but as you said, if it's so great why isn't everyone doing it?"

"Sound judgment," VJ said approvingly.

"If my judgment is so good, why can't I work with you?"

He shrugged.

She took note. "And what should I tell them the high priest of Goldfinger said?"

"Tell them I said be careful. Very careful."

Eager to get upstairs to the next pill, she stood quickly and was engulfed in dizziness. She gripped the table edge to steady herself and then sunk back into the chair.

VJ frowned. "What's going on?"

"I know what you're thinking," she said. "I haven't been drinking. Dr. MacAndrew told me to take pills to relieve pain. Sometimes they make me lightheaded."

"You still have that much pain?" he asked.

Yes? No? For a moment Pilar didn't know what to say. "Let's make a deal. You can have the pain and the pills, and I can be judgmental."

CHAPTER 41

AN INCIDENT AT
THE FAMILY LAW BUILDING

"I NEED TO LEAVE for a hearing in Winona Wingate's case," Paddy said. "Let's both go, and we can keep talking about tax evasion on the way."

"Tax avoidance, not tax evasion," Will replied. "Why do we both have to go?"

"Mr. Wingate made thirty-six million last year. His wife is going to get at least half of what is left over. She can afford for us both to go."

As he drove, Paddy began to work on Will about Norma's plan. "We pay a fortune in taxes, partly because our accountant won't let us deduct some very necessary business expenses. Contributions to the judicial campaigns—"

"Hiring prostitutes."

Paddy gave him an evil eye.

"But what if it doesn't work?" Will asked.

"Why wouldn't it work?"

"I don't know. I'm not a tax lawyer. My question is what would we do if it doesn't work?"

"It'll work." Paddy paused. "Look at it this way. We would be warehousing our money tax-free while it grows in the islands, right? If it doesn't work, the money will be there to pay any tax bill."

Will squinted. "I don't know. Pilar made it sound like VJ thought dealing with Norma was a bad idea. Not just the tax deal."

Paddy waved this away. "Muffy liked buying your new house after the Hetherington fee."

Will smiled. "There is that."

It crossed both their minds that Paddy had yet to be invited to the Marshalls' home.

Paddy parked his truck in a parking garage across the street from the courthouse. He gave a twenty to the parking attendant and said, "Keep it close, please, Juan."

"Of course, Mr. Moran."

〰️

LINDA HETHERINGTON HAD gotten up at 6:30 a.m. She'd showered and braided her waist-length hair, pinning the braid into a bun atop her head. In her daughter's bedroom, she rearranged the stuffed animals and held the soft belly of a teddy bear to her cheek.

Next she brewed green tea and prepared a bowl of organic dry cereal with almond milk and Truvia. She ate sitting on a bar stool in her kitchenette. Beside her was a place setting. Sitting on the plate was a framed photograph of her smiling, five-year-old girl, her daughter, her darling. It never failed to make her smile. Except for monthly supervised visits, their only contact now was secret phone calls. She was reading her girl *Little House on the Prairie* over the phone, Linda's favorite book when she was a child.

At precisely 7:30 a.m., Linda grabbed the phone as she heard the beginning of its first ring.

A little voice whispered, "Good morning, Mom."

"Good morning, sweetheart. I love you."

There was silence.

"Have a nice day. Do well in school."

"Thanks, Mom. I miss you." The little voice whispered.

"I miss you, too."

Linda placed the telephone back in its cradle gently as if placing a sleeping child into bed. She put on her backpack and headed to the metro stop. It was a warm day and humid—so humid that the live oaks along the streets seemed bowed over like old women bearing the burden of ancient sorrows. Linda paced the train platform restlessly. The trains usually ran pretty close to schedule. This day the train was exactly two minutes late.

At 8:42 a.m., Linda alit from the train and walked two blocks to the Family Law Center. At 8:46 a.m., she arrived and set her backpack down. She taped a poster board that had "UN" neatly printed in the same style as the Family Court sign on the building in front of "Family." Next, she put on a shoulder harness that had two places for poles to be mounted on the back. She assembled the poles and hoisted a sign that read on the front, "Impeach Elizondo," and on the back, "Disbar Paddy Moran." Then she took out a stack of broadsides. These read:

> *Through a conspiracy between Judge Hector Elizondo and Attorney Patrick "Paddy" Moran, my child was taken from me.*
>
> *I am a loving, caring mother. I took care of my daughter from birth to the horrendous moment Judge Elizondo took her from me. My ex-husband was represented by Paddy Moran. Paddy Moran gave $50,000 to Judge Elizondo's campaign in his own name. His partner, W. Marshall, gave $50,000. A contribution of $7,500 was made in the name of Erin Riordan. She works as a part-time salesperson in a lingerie store on lower Westheimer. Another $5,000 was given in the name of Jesus Ramirez, an employee of Paddy Moran. Judge Elizondo's daughter was an employee of Marshall & Moran, LLP. Mr. Moran and his stooges' contributions to Judge Elizondo are staggering, shocking, and shameful.*
>
> *Mr. Moran's record before Judge Elizondo is very, very good. It's much better than his record before other judges. Shouldn't we all wonder why?*
>
> *In my case, perjured testimony, reprehensible conduct, and an out-and-out conspiracy between Judge Elizondo and Paddy Moran got my sleazy, spoiled ex-husband, who otherwise neglected my precious daughter, custody of her and fixed it so that I could only see her once a month with a court-appointed supervisor.*
>
> *One day, I will right this injustice.*
>
> *This could happen to you unless you act.*
>
> *Work to impeach Judge Elizondo!*
>
> *Work to disbar Paddy Moran!*
>
> *Work to change the system where judges are financially dependent on the lawyers who practice before them!*

Linda handed the broadsides to people who approached the main entrance. Many refused. Many were familiar faces. She always dressed conservatively so as not to look like a kook, but with the backpack, the poles, and the sign, she figured most people would think she was a kook anyway. For the time being, this was all she could do.

As Paddy and Will approached the courthouse, Linda Hetherington saw them. "There he is!" Linda cried. "There he is! The man who stole my child! The most unethical lawyer in the history of a despicable profession!"

CHAPTER 42

PILAR IS A TEAM PLAYER

AT 9:00 A.M., Pilar was at her desk drinking her third cup of coffee. She had been trying to take prescription pills only at bedtime. That meant no diet pills, which also meant she couldn't quite wake up properly.

The receptionist buzzed her and said, "You better speak to Mr. Moran. He sounds upset."

Pilar put the phone to her ear. "Pilar, honey, big favor. I know it's not in your job description, but Bernice is out, and we're outside Elizondo's court-room, and I need the Wingate file. It's on top of my desk. I can't believe I forgot it."

"No problem," Pilar said.

"I really appreciate you helping me out," Paddy said.

His obvious sincerity touched her. It flashed through her mind that she wished VJ would—just once again—talk to her like that.

"I'll be there as soon as I can."

Fifteen minutes later, after a traffic-less, over-the-speed-limit drive, Pilar was dashing up the steps toward the Family Law Center doors, file in hand. She was so focused on her task that she didn't notice a woman approaching her until she felt her arm being touched.

"Excuse me," the woman said.

"I'm in a hurry," Pilar said apologetically, "but here." She fished twenty dollars out of her purse and held it out to the woman. As she looked up, her heart sank. You would have to be pretty unobservant to have worked at Marshall & Moran for any length of time and not know Linda Hether-ington's face.

"I don't want your money," Linda Hetherington said. "You look like a good woman. A good person. Do you have children?"

"Yes, I do," Pilar said stiffly. "But really, I'm in a hurry."

"Please take this and read it."

Pilar glanced down at the flyer. Paddy's face looked up at her. She bit her lip. Should she try to speak to the woman, explain Paddy had just been doing his job? One glance at Linda Hetherington's face told her that might not be a good idea. Her lips were trembling. She looked like she was about to cry. She also looked angry, *very* angry and desperate, like a person whose life had been stolen from her.

Pilar suddenly remembered Randy Hetherington coming on to her at the office. He'd asked her if she'd consider having a beer with him sometime, "Dos Equis," he'd said and winked. "I'm very interesting."

"And I'm very married," Pilar had replied crisply.

"Well, doesn't that make you special?" He reached out and patted her on the ass. He'd done it without the slightest tinge of fear. Rich, entitled asshole was too kind a phrase for Randy Hetherington. Pilar's sharp elbow to his ribs didn't seem to surprise him. It was sharp enough to make him bow and gasp.

Unlike her evil ex, Linda didn't look rich or entitled. She looked desperate.

"My ex-husband and Paddy Moran stole my daughter from me," Linda said. "I'm not even allowed to be alone with her."

"I'm so sorry," Pilar replied.

"I know you don't want to hear my story, but trust me, what they did to me was criminal, and it could happen to any woman. It could happen to you."

Pilar's stomach tensed. She took a copy of the flyer. "I'll read it," she said and raced to Elizondo's courtroom. Paddy and Will were waiting for her outside. Winded, she handed the file to Paddy. Only then did she realize she was still holding Linda Hetherington's broadside. Luckily, neither Paddy nor Will appeared to notice.

"Thanks—you saved us," they said almost in unison as they headed inside the courtroom.

"You're the best," Paddy added. The door closed behind them.

As Pilar walked to her car, she spotted Linda Hetherington attempting to hand out more flyers. Linda saw her and waved. Pilar hesitated a moment, then waved back. Linda Hetherington smiled and held up her right hand making a V sign with her fingers.

Pilar swallowed. Her body was trembling. *"It could happen to you."*

CHAPTER 43

GIVE HIM BACK HIS FACE

PADDY AND WILL ENTERED Judge Elizondo's courtroom. Winona Wingate was waiting there. So was a group of reporters. They rushed at Paddy.

The question from one broke through the din. "Mr. Moran, what do you have to say about today's hearing?"

Paddy moved past. Will addressed the reporters. "We'll say what we have to say after the hearing."

Paddy appraised his client. Pulling close to her, he said in her ear, "Young lady, I must say you are very good at sticking with the game plan. You didn't talk to the paparazzi gang. You dressed modestly." He gave her a thumb's up.

"*Plus*, I'm not chewing gum."

Having been forewarned by Paddy, Bubba Otis anticipated that Mr. Wingate might become violent during the trial. Seated on either side of Mr. Wingate were two young men who happened to be linemen for SMU. Each, Paddy knew, was poised to hold Mr. Wingate to his chair and restrain him from any inappropriate physical action.

When Paddy began to argue his motion for child support, Mr. Wingate jumped up and yelled, "Nobody can make me pay child support for somebody else's children!" Startled, the young men jumped up, too, and pushed Wingate back into his chair, forcibly holding him there.

Judge Elizondo banged his gavel. "Mr. Otis, control your client, or he will see the inside of a jail cell for being in contempt of this court."

Bubba whispered to his client just loud enough for the court to hear, "We know we are going to lose our motion on child support because the law, as outrageous as it is, is against us. You do have a good chance on visitation, but if you don't control your mouth, we'll lose that one, too."

Wingate was seething.

"Hear this, Mr. Wingate," the judge added, "if I rule that you have to pay child support, you will do so timely, or the attorney general of the state of Texas will throw you in jail. Do you understand?"

Wingate muttered, "Yes."

"Stand when you address the court," Elizondo said with forced authority.

"Your Honor, I would stand, but these two goons are holding me down."

Elizondo let that go. "I rule that you have to pay child support at the maximum amount for all three children. Now let's proceed to visitation."

"Your Honor, I request you postpone the hearing on visitation in light of the amended pleading we filed this morning." Bubba said.

"Mr. Moran?" Elizondo said.

Paddy's heart raced. He hadn't felt so blindsided in court since Grissett's case.

Bubba said, "Your Honor, we filed just this morning. I haven't had a chance to serve Mr. Moran."

Paddy gave him an angry glare.

"Very well, Mr. Otis," Elizondo responded. "Next case."

Mrs. Wingate grabbed Paddy's arm. "What's going on?"

"I'm not sure, Winona, but it can't be anything for you to worry about," Will said.

Mrs. Wingate ignored him. To Paddy she said, "Look, I told you I wasn't greedy. I just wanted it over. Now, what've you got me into?"

The reporters scurried to Bubba Otis. "What do you think about today's ruling?" one of them asked.

"Mr. Moran's client can't have it both ways. If Mr. Wingate is the father for purposes of child support, then he's the father for all purposes, including visitation and custody."

"Will you be seeking custody for Mr. Wingate?"

"We will."

Winona turned to Paddy. "Tell me what's going on!"

"Don't worry," Will said.

Paddy said, "We'll settle by getting you a bigger piece of the community."

"Listen up, Mr. Testosterone," Winona said. "I told you, I don't want a bigger piece of the community. *I want my kids!* He's a proud man, butthole. You've made him lose face. Give him back his fucking face, or I'll have yours ripped off."

Paddy summoned all he could so as not to reveal that he knew he had fucked up big time by disregarding his client's objectives.

The reporters turned to Paddy.

"Mr. Otis alleges your client is an unfit mother because her children have different fathers."

Had Otis not filed his motion, Paddy was going to say, "Justice was served today. A man—a rich man—who would try to deny a child's support should be denied sharing the child's life." He'd rehearsed it that morning in front of his bathroom mirror. Now, he hesitated, considering his response. Winona squeezed his arm. He could feel her fingernails through his suit coat.

Will stepped up. "We haven't read Mr. Wingate's pleadings yet. Mrs. Wingate has been an exemplary mother."

Mrs. Wingate elbowed Paddy sharply in his ribs.

"Frankly, despite his . . . despite the situation regarding child support, in many ways Mr. Wingate has been a good and generous father. That's all."

Will stuck his arm out as if parting a curtain. Paddy took Winona by her arm, walking her past Will through the reporters. "Winona, don't talk to the press," he whispered in her ear. "I'll get this worked out."

"You better."

⁙

AFTER PADDY AND WILL escorted Mrs. Wingate to her car, they saw Bubba.

"I'm sorry," Bubba said before Paddy could start in on him. "I filed an amended pleading seeking custody. Wingate got me up at six this morning to do it."

"What happened to watching each other's back?" Paddy demanded.

"My client insisted I not tell you."

"Remember this, buddy. After you're done with this client, I'll still be around. I promised not to surprise you. I kept my promise. You did nawt."

Bubba winced. "I'll make it up to you."

Breathing heavily from his nostrils like a bull preparing to charge, Paddy took a step backwards. "You better and quickly."

"It's the media coverage," Bubba said *sotto voce*. "You've told the world he's a cuckold. If you hadn't done that—"

Paddy's conversation with Will about Mrs. Coleman's pride came back to him. His mask came off. He shrugged. "Okay, I get it. I fucked up. But we have to figure out a way to fix this. This woman deserves to have her children."

"He's pretty stoked now. We're alleging a woman who has three bastards is unfit. He thinks he has a slam dunk. It *is* Texas. He might."

Paddy nodded seriously. "Yeah, well, you need to make him understand that being an unfit wife doesn't mean she's an unfit mother. I'm serious, Bubba."

"Okay, bro. I'll back-burner this until my client cools down," Bubba said.

Paddy respected and admired Bubba, but he felt betrayed. "If it was any one of those other bozos, I wouldn't be surprised, but you?"

Bubba nodded wearily.

Will intervened. "Maybe, Paddy, the way to deal with it and get your client off your . . . get her confidence back is to start by giving him some respect, restoring his dignity."

"I just did. You've made your career on appearances, Will. I've made mine on performance. Don't worry. I'll get the job done like I always do."

"I'm staying out of this," Bubba said, walking away.

"It's all about you, isn't it? We got our big case *because* of my appearance, *because* I was Hetherington's classmate at the Hill School."

"You got him in the door." Paddy nodded to Juan, the parking attendant, as they drove out of the garage. "I grant you that. But remember this: He didn't knock on our door first. Second, he only got custody because my PI brought a woman in from out of town who befriended Linda, got her drunk and doped up, took her clothes off, and had sex with her on videotape."

"Doped up? I don't remember any testimony about that."

"There wasn't any." Paddy's tone was low and cold. He kept a poker face, but his heart pounded. The flashbacks that had been haunting him returned.

Will let out a low whistle. "You never said anything about that. We could've been accused of rape or some other crime."

"Truth be told, Fourbirds never told me exactly how it came down. I'm just guessing. One thing I do know is you didn't want to know then and don't want to know now. What you did want was the giant fee I brought in. I needed you to feel just like you did—that it was right for the girl to be with the father because he could get her into the right schools and be with the right people."

"Why didn't Linda Hetherington appeal getting the video into evidence?"

"After the jury came in, she had no fight left to file an appeal. Now she's a whack job, but she does have some fight." Paddy shook his head. "She's written the Supreme Court, the State Bar, and the newspapers, sending copies to me and Elizondo. Hector's getting rattled."

"I don't like it. It's really unseemly." Will turned to Paddy. "I wished you hadn't done—well, what you did."

Paddy wouldn't let Will know how deep and constant his own regret was. "Oh, right. You and Miss Muffy sure enjoyed your share of the million-dollar bonus. Is it *unseemly* enough to move out of your new house?"

Will did not answer.

"That's what I thought," Paddy said. "You're happy to take the money. You just don't want to know how you got it."

The two partners glared at each other. Will looked away first.

Paddy pulled into one of his reserved spots when they got back to the office, got out, and slammed the door. He headed in. Will followed, nearly running to catch up. He grabbed Paddy's arm before he went inside. Paddy spun around, his hand up in a fist. Will looked at him and said, "You're right, partner. I do want the money, more than you do. I appreciate your successes." He paused a moment, then added. "The one thing I like about Norma's deal is it would give us asset protection. It would be hard to enforce a judgment against us in the CNMI."

Paddy relaxed. "That's the first positive thing you've said about Norma's deal."

"What the hell," Will said, opening the door for Paddy. "Let's do it."

〰️

UNBEKNOWNST TO WILL AND PADDY, when Linda Hetherington left the courthouse, she'd taken the train south down Main to Bell Street. From there, she walked briskly to South Texas College of Law. She did not want to be late for class.

〰️

THAT EVENING, THE OPENING story on the six o'clock news and the ten o'clock news was on Marshall and Moran: "Non-father ordered to pay child support." TMZ, which ran a story on Paddy after the Hetherington case, hired a stringer in Houston and made Paddy his only assignment. Usually Paddy liked publicity about his victories. This time his reaction was "Oh, shit!"

CHAPTER 44

PILAR'S BAD DAY
AT THE OFFICE

PADDY ASSIGNED PILAR the job of coordinating the new accounting and money transfer arrangements with Rance Ed. The excellent receptionist she had hired gave notice, explaining she was engaged to a newly divorced client. Once again Pilar was on the hunt for an ideal permanent receptionist. She drafted an ad for an online service that matched employers and prospective employees. Maybe a young, ambitious Pilar was out there, hoping to be given a chance in an upscale work environment. She might have to answer the phones if a temp didn't show up.

Pilar was the first to arrive at the office. She switched on the lights and walked into her office. Usually she liked being there early and alone. The early morning calm allowed her to collect her thoughts and organize her tasks without any distraction. This morning, though, the empty office gave her the creeps. She feared every shadow was a stalker. Dark, heavy thunderclouds blocked all sunlight. It was storming in Houston. Everything outside was wild and wet.

She had vowed to take anxiety pills only at night to help her sleep, but as she went to switch on the coffee maker, her hands were shaking so much she could hardly press the power button. She stopped, suddenly confused. How many Xanax had she taken last night? One when she went to sleep. Maybe another when she awoke in the wee hours of the morning.

The last time she had been with Leila, Leila had swallowed two Xanax right in front of her. "The secret to my success," Leila had said with a slight smile. "How many a day do you take?" Pilar had asked. Pilar detected Leila's voice slurring as she replied, "I don't count."

Pilar resolved not to take a pill. The fax machine started buzzing. It was probably spam. The noise seemed artificially loud and incredibly annoying. Loud claps of thunder seemed to shake the building. In the ladies' room, she tried to steady her hand so she could put on makeup. Staring at herself in the mirror, she felt a twinge of pride. After the operation and with hard work, she was only five pounds heavier than when she and VJ first met. She looked like her old self—maybe even better. There was something about her eyes, like she knew more now. Without thinking, she reached inside her purse and popped a pill. Then she shook another pill out from the bottle, broke it in half and swallowed one of the halves.

She walked back to her office and closed the door, not realizing she was weaving across the floor.

When she woke up, the room was bright with sunlight. The oak leaves outside the window, still wet with rain, glistened. Paddy was leaning over her.

"Look, honey, I don't know if you're drunk or stoned or what, but you need to shape up."

Pilar watched as he fetched a bottle of water from her desk, poured some into his hands, and applied it to her face with gentle pats. "Wake up. Wake up."

Her head began to clear. "Oh, my God, what happened?"

"I found you passed out on the floor."

Pilar felt totally awake now. Her eyes darted around the office. It was nearly 11 a.m. Had she been lying here this whole time? Thank God Paddy had been the first to find her like this.

"What's going on?"

She shook her head. "I'm still taking pills from the operation. This morning, I took some on an empty stomach. It was an accident, a one-time kind of thing. It will never ever happen again. I swear." She smoothed down her hair with her hands.

Paddy looked skeptical. "Fine. Can you get yourself together enough to go to the ladies' room? I'll drive you home. Will cannot see you like this. Do you understand?"

"I have work to do."

"Well, do it when you have your shit together."

"Okay, okay, okay," she said making her posture erect, breathing deeply. "I understand. You don't need to drive me, Paddy. I'll get myself home."

"You can't drive in this condition."

"I can't leave my car here. Please. VJ will wonder why I didn't drive myself."

"I'll drive you in your car and take a cab back."

"You'd do that for me?"

"Of course, I would." He shook his head, gave her a reassuring hug, patted her on the back, and held her for a moment. She felt safe, like she did with Sunny.

"Listen to me. You cannot show up at the office like this again."

"I won't."

"Good girl. I have to say something else. I think you're very special."

She squirmed away from him. "Paddy don't," she said wearily.

"For Chrissakes, I'm not hitting on you. The first time we met in my office I knew you were special. You still are, but you're doing yourself in. You've got a sweet life. You're smart. You're married to one of the biggest guys in this city, and he loves you. You have three kids. You've got it all. What the fuck are you doing?"

She processed his words without responding.

CHAPTER 45

ELEGANTÉ WILL CLOSE

LUIGI EZIO GANTÉ received a renewal lease from his landlord. New terms included doubling the base rent and a percentage of the gross receipts. The rest of the terms were also much more landlord-friendly than the expiring lease.

Luigi fumed. He sat at his desk in his windowless office adjacent to the wine cellar. He looked at photographs of himself and many of the famous people who had dined at his place. Two Presidents Bush, Nancy Pelosi, President Lyndon Johnson and Lady Bird, Ann Richards, President Clinton, every man who had ever set foot on the moon, Earl Campbell, Jaclyn Smith, Yao Ming, A. J. Foyt, Solly Hemus, Patrick Swayze, Hakeem Olajuwon, Roger Clemens, Dan Rather, Wes Anderson, Nobelist Robert "Big Bang Theory" Wilson, actor Jim "Big Bang Theory" Parsons, Beyoncé, and nearly every other famous person with a Houston connection.

He mused that his recent improvements had probably emboldened his landlord, Tom T. Del Monte, to raise the cost of occupancy. The son of a bitch thought he had Luigi over a barrel. Surely, he must have thought, Luigi wouldn't walk away from such a large investment and go someplace else.

Luigi made his way up the half-flight of stairs to the main dining room. His breathing was labored. Each table had been readied for the day's first seating—heavy linen napkins perfectly folded, crystal glasses gleaming. Fresh flowers—dahlias in festive autumn colors—had not yet been set out, but they rested in a cooler in the back. He made his way to the station at the front.

Awards covered the walls of the entryway to reassure first-timers that they had arrived at a prominent and well-recognized restaurant.

He paced into the kitchen, which gleamed with well-polished copper and steel. The gas heating the massive stockpots was never turned off. Everything was made fresh. The hand-selected produce and fish had arrived by nine, when preparations for the day began. He looked at his watch. It was almost time for him to meet with his waitstaff to go over featured items for the day and anything else important, including special reservations or events.

~~~

THAT EVENING, LUIGI TOLD VJ about the landlord's letter and his medical report.

A few days earlier Luigi's urologist told him he had a prostate problem. His cardiologist regularly harangued him about his weight and lack of exercise. "Getting too high on your own supply," he would tell him, wagging his finger. He was prediabetic. Despite his poor health, his robustness and energy abounded.

VJ said, "My friend, you have enough money to continue living as you have. I can rebalance your investments so that a very substantial portion will be risk-free. You'll have no excuses not to take care of your health. You must do that because I need you as my friend, perhaps my only true friend. Follow your instincts. I will be beside you. We will cook for each other."

"No one in the world makes *saag paneer* knishes like you do, VJ."

"That is probably because, since my mother died, no one else in the world makes *saag paneer* knishes."

The country club set had not always respected and accepted VJ, the Indian-Jewish, Israeli immigrant. Only after he married Georgie and made many of them richer was he grudgingly accepted socially. But his Mexican-American second wife, twenty-plus years his junior, would never be welcomed.

Luigi twitted her detractors by naming a dish for her that tasted so good they ordered it, a spectacular paella of saffron-scented rice and seafood with a Tex-Mex flair—subtle accents of chili, lime, and cilantro that complemented the fresh seafood perfectly.

He made certain that no dish on the menu of any of the exclusive country clubs would taste as good as it did at his place. Once, one of the country clubs brought in a chef who had been honored by James Beard. Luigi hired him away and signed him to a non-compete agreement. He knew that maneuver would not bother his most consistent carriage trade customers, The Best People. Few of them were welcome in those clubs.

Luigi hesitatingly asked, "How are things at home?"

"They've been better."

"I hope they go back to being better again," Luigi said, but he was not hopeful.

∿

THE RENEWAL LEASE had come in a letter from Tom T. Del Monte's property manager. After considering his conversation with VJ, Luigi called Del Monte. His secretary said that he would be gone for six weeks and asked if someone else could help him. Luigi told her he would wait. He wasn't in a hurry.

In ten minutes, Del Monte's first lieutenant, Conrad Parker, called Luigi.

"You called Mr. Del Monte. I'm handling things for him while he is gone," Parker said.

"You do that well, I'm sure, but I'll wait until he gets back." Luigi guessed he sounded smug. That was okay. Sometimes smug was good.

"But your lease expires next month." Parker sounded anxious.

"Goodbye, Mr. Parker."

Less than two hours later, during a very busy lunch crowd, Luigi received another call. He put it on hold until he could get to his office. On the way, he took his time personally refilling glasses and chatting with guests.

On the line, Del Monte said, "Luigi, you called?"

"Yes, Tom. Your office said you couldn't be reached for six weeks."

"Well, since it was you I wanted to call."

"I just wanted to tell you that I'm closing the store."

He waited for a response. After a while Luigi asked, "Tom, are you still there?"

"I'm here."

"You not sayin' anything," Luigi said, laying on an accent.

"Why are you closing?"

"I got a letter about renewing the lease. I decided it was time."

"Was there something about the letter?"

Luigi knew Del Monte was trying to make it seem as if he didn't know what was in the letter. That would make it possible for him to negotiate. But Parker wouldn't put that kind of increase on Luigi without Del Monte knowing.

"No, the letter was nice," Luigi said. "I'm sure you can find someone else to take the space. I mean it's a bargain, especially with all the improvements I just made." He knew it would be hard for Del Monte to rent that space. It would even be hard for him to keep the other tenants in the small, upscale center that Eleganté anchored.

"Luigi, you're an institution. Eleganté is one of a kind. Houston has nothing else like it. I have always been proud to have you as my tenant. You can't close."

"I can, and I am, Tom. When I read your letter, I was reminded of an old Italian expression my father used to say at similar times, '*Sono ferito in mio genitale.*'"

"What does that mean?"

Disingenuously, Luigi said, "To tell you the truth, I'm not sure. I wish my father was still around so I could ask him."

"It sounds like you've made up your mind," Del Monte said.

"You've probably made and lost enough deals to recognize that tone of voice," Luigi replied, cold and certain.

"I have, but for God's sake, Luigi, will you think about it some more?"

"No."

"When is the last night?"

"November twenty-first."

"I'm due back the twenty-third. I'll come back early."

"Don't bother. I don't have any tables left," Luigi said, even though VJ was the only other person who knew about the closing party. "I got a table available for lunch at eleven on the nineteenth. I'll hold it for you. Let me know." He hung up.

Del Monte was now a nonperson to him. Luigi knew that not being present on the closing night would not only be an embarrassment but also signal why Eleganté was closing. Financially, it would not mean much to Del Monte, but Luigi thought it might cause his landlord a problem with his new wife and for sure it would with his investors in the center.

Luigi immediately began making preparations for his grand finale. He wanted it to be a celebratory experience for his friends and himself with the food and atmosphere tasteful, elegant, entertaining, and memorable.

He would pay his employees generous final bonuses and make sure they all were placed in good jobs.

〰

"ISN'T THAT SOMETHING about Luigi?" Margot Shear wrote to Norma in an email from Nice, France. Margot had called VJ about her finances. He told her of Luigi's decision, but not the reason. It was the first time she had initiated a communication to Norma. Margot savored that knowing before Norma would send Norma into a tizzy.

"Oh, his health? Did his biopsy come back bad?" Norma replied in an instant message. It was two a.m. in Houston.

"No. No," Margot responded. "He's closing Eleganté. Heavens, where will you go?"

Norma called Margot on her cell phone, and instead of greeting her said, "Oh, sweetie, I knew he was closing, but I really appreciate you thinking of me."

But the truth was Norma was furious she had not heard the news from Luigi. There couldn't be anyone who spent more time or more money at the restaurant. It was, after all, home base for The Best People. He owed it to her. To hear it from Margot, of all people, made her tremble. Scumbag, motherfucker. Norma's brain seethed.

"I called him right away. I told him I would return from France to be at my regular table on closing night," Margot said. The conversation ended quickly thereafter. She'd always tried to be above petty rivalry, but sharing the information with Norma had given Margot a guilty pleasure.

Norma lost it. That was *her* table. Margot got it only when Norma didn't want it. She was devastated. She felt totally dissed. Her fingers shook as she punched numbers into her phone. "Prentice!" she screamed into it. "Call Eleganté first thing in the morning. Tell them I am coming for lunch. And get Marvin on the phone for me."

"I'm sure Marvin is asleep," responded Prentice.

"I'm waiting."

Prentice conferenced Marvin in.

"My, my, my," said Marvin. "Something has Madame in a snit."

"Don't snit me, you fucking queen," she said, but her tone was playful. She'd always gotten a kick out of Marvin.

And Marvin had to love her. Norma spent more than $350,000 a year with him. She didn't know the meaning of Last Call. She had first call of everything that came in.

"Luigi is shutting down Eleganté. I can live with that. What is bad is that Margot Shear knew before I did. I have to look amazing."

Marvin understood her to mean the center of attention.

"I accept the challenge."

"I want you in my office first thing."

〰️

MARVIN BREATHLESSLY ENTERED Norma's office just before eleven the next morning. "Oh, Hera, Queen of Women, your humble servant Marvin has arrived."

"It's about time," Norma said. "What I don't get is how Margot could have known before me."

"It isn't Luigi?" asked Marvin.

"It could be, but I doubt it. He wouldn't want to cross me."

"Why?" asked Marvin. "If he's going out of business, why should he care?"

"I would think he knows what goes around comes around."

"Lordy," Prentice thought as he entered Norma's office with stacks of papers. "If so, you have a hellacious coming around sooner or later." He placed the papers in front of Norma.

"What are these documents?" Norma asked.

"More brokerage accounts and more foreign bank accounts," responded Prentice in a bored voice.

"Am I the only authorized person on these accounts?"

"Of course. Look for yourself." He pointed to a place on the form agreement on top. Norma never read documents. She flipped through the pages, pretending to focus, quickly scribbling her name each place Prentice had flagged with a "Sign Here" Post-it tab.

"Let me look at the checks." She always looked at the checks.

"What is this one to—American Express? It is outrageous."

"It's mostly for your charges, Norma."

"Let me see all of the charges that are not mine. All of them. I pay people good money around here. I don't want them giving themselves raises."

"That's right, Norma," Prentice thought as he left the room. "You're generous to a fault. You steal more in a week than you pay me in a year. What you don't know, bitch, is I do, too."

She stood and ran a hand down the side of her body to her waist. "Okay, Marvin, what did you bring me?"

"Not yet, not yet," Marvin teased.

"Is it from Neiman's?"

"No!" he said.

"Tootsies?"

"No. Guess again."

"No more guesses," she said.

"Fine, but for this to work you have to take off your jacket."

Norma acceded.

Marvin said, "When I got your lapdog's 2 a.m. call, I realized someone was trying to take away your power. So I summoned all my resourcefulness to find the right repellent, the right potion, the right armor, and voila!" He removed the lid of a large box stamped with the signature "Eve France."

From the box he lifted a sterling silver bra held together with chain mail, hoisted it high, and then lowered it onto that part of Norma's red Chanel blouse that covered her breasts. He fastened it from behind by buckling the silver clasp of the chain mail belt. With a twinkle in his eye, he reached back into the box and retrieved silver cuffs, which he slipped onto her wrists.

Norma admired herself in the mirror. She beamed. "Oh, Marvin, honey. Don't even bother with those other bags. You did it again. I just feel so powerful." She smiled. "You and Prentice are going to join me now for lunch at Luigi's."

"WON-duh-ful, dahling. So glad you like it," Marvin said.

She pushed the speaker button on her phone. "Come on, Prentice. Today is perks day."

"Oh, and, honey, let me assure you of something," Marvin said as they left her office. "This is one of a kind. I would be surprised if the silver isn't still hot."

CHAPTER 46

THE LAST NIGHT OF ELEGANTÉ

VJ WROTE PILAR A NOTE and asked Rosa to give it to her as soon as she woke up. It read: "Tonight is the closing of Eleganté. Be ready on time, and don't be under the influence of anything."

Within hours of the news of the closing celebration, a firestorm erupted. Some of The Best People behaved badly, arguing to reserve a choice table at the most desired seating time. Luigi couldn't avoid some people feeling slighted. He considered first call, first choice, which wasn't really fair. Some people had heard about it before others. His decision was to set a deadline for all requests for specific times and specific tables. Where there was a conflict, he would put the names in a hat and draw for times and tables. Everyone would be treated fairly, equally. But many of his customers didn't believe in fairness and equality when it came to them. They were accustomed to getting what they wanted when they wanted it.

Ten people would be seated at Norma's table at nine o'clock. She kept pushing to include more, but Luigi would not relent. She did have "her table" in the center of the room where everyone could see her.

She had let him draw five thousand cash out of her hat, and, somehow, he drew her name out of his hat. The truth was it was the luck of the draw, but Luigi knew there was a part of Norma that valued paying too much.

After Paddy accepted Norma's invitation to join him, Norma called Margot at five-thirty in the afternoon in France. She pushed star eighty-six before Margot's number so the call would come from an unidentified caller.

As genuinely as she could, she cooed, "Luigi told me we have the same table but at different times. I've asked Paddy to join me at my table. I'm sure when he accepted, it didn't occur to him you'd come back from France for the closing. Would you do me the honor of joining me at my table and sitting next to Paddy?"

Margot was at once annoyed and impressed. While she didn't believe

Norma's sincerity, she had to admit that Norma had figured out the right thing to do. She felt she had no option but to accept the invitation or stay in France.

"How thoughtful of you. I accept," Margot said, doing her best to remove any edge from her tone.

"That makes me so happy. I will see you on November twenty-first at nine at Eleganté."

When Norma hung up, she was surprised that she felt relief rather than triumph. She called Luigi immediately. "Margot Shear is going to be a guest at my table."

"Thank you, Norma. That takes a load off my mind," he said.

Luigi reserved the Simon wine cellar for VJ and Pilar. Everyone's last taste at Eleganté would be a dessert named for VJ and Pilar: *tres leches* and hot *sufganiyot*. It would be Luigi's way of telling everyone how important they both were to him.

VJ called Margot and invited her to join his table. Margot explained the situation.

VJ was not frequently caught unaware. "Is there something going on between you and Moran?" he asked.

Margot didn't know how to respond. She wasn't going to say, "It's complicated." That would be too trite. She wasn't going to say yes. So she told a truth that VJ could believe. "I'm his anchor. I just need to sit with him."

VJ shrugged. "Pilar is his firm's office manager."

"I know. He thinks she's doing an amazing job."

VJ did not comment.

"I've been in France a long time. Paddy and I don't talk often—we just, we're simpatico, you know. Anyhow, I'd love to see Pilar."

"I'm sure she'll enjoy seeing you, too," VJ said, without revealing the ambivalence he felt for Margot still considering them as a couple.

〰〰

LUIGI HAD INSISTED VJ bring the entire family, the household staff, and everyone who worked at his office. Pilar suggested VJ go on ahead of her. "I'll feel less pressured to get myself and the kids ready. They've all taken naps."

"Just don't be late," he said.

"I won't, dear," Pilar said in a flat voice.

At the restaurant, Luigi was happy to take a break from table hopping when he saw VJ. They sat at the bar. Fifteen minutes later, a waiter came up to them. "Mrs. Simon and the children are here."

VJ didn't know whether he felt happiness or dread when he saw them at the entrance. The children looked adorable in their best clothes. Gracie wore a black velvet dress; the boys wore tiny white suits. Pilar, too, was dressed all in white with her hair piled high on her head. She smiled at VJ across the room.

"Hi," he said, squeezing her arm.

The children behaved perfectly, and Pilar looked beautiful. VJ felt a swell of pride. She was beautiful, so beautiful, his wife, but was she still the woman he'd been so eager to be with?

He smiled, stopping often to greet his colleagues, shaking hands with the men and graciously bowing his head to their wives. As he did, he noticed that Pilar was having a hard time walking straight.

They approached the table that included the Esfandiarys and the gang. VJ said, "Oh, look, here are the Ladies Who Lunch."

Leila leaped up. "Oh my God, Pilar. Are you the princess of the evening or what?"

Each of the men, eager to be seen with VJ, stood as he made his way around the table to shake hands and cheek-kiss the women.

Pilar stumbled slightly. Leila reached out to steady her. VJ shook his head.

Pilar stared at her husband in his perfect blue suit and green and blue tie. Why was he looking at her so judgmentally? Then again, when was the last time he didn't look at her that way? He was losing interest in her. She swallowed, fighting to gain control of her rising sense of panic. Would he stop saying hello to everyone so they could just sit down? This was the first time she had worn the eight-inch heels and they didn't fit and she had to struggle to keep her balance and they hurt. He glanced over at her again. The cold look in his eyes made her shiver. It was not the look of love. Could she blame him? She had managed to hold it together at the office since that awful day Paddy found her unconscious. But at home things had gotten worse. These days it was not unusual for her to spend half the day "napping," leaving the children with Rosa. But today she was not under the influence of anything, not that she didn't want to be.

Someone touched her shoulder. It was Leila. "Are you okay?" she whispered. With her mouth to Pilar's ear, she said, "Do you need anything? I always come prepared."

"I'm fine. But I can't walk straight in these damn heels," Pilar said. Turning to the table, she said in the most effusive way she could muster, "This has got to be the most glamorous group of people ever."

She smiled as they smiled. There was nothing like a compliment people wanted to believe about themselves to get them to stop making small talk.

VJ began making his way to the wine cellar, and Pilar gave a farewell wave to the table as she turned to follow him. Her eyes fell on Cameron McMillan. Cameron had made a recovery of sorts, but Pilar noticed that when she smiled only half her face moved. Her clothes had been carefully selected to disguise how thin she was—floating chiffon layers that wrapped around her wire-thin frame.

"Cameron, you dear, dear person," she said. "You're such a fighter. I admire how much progress you have made."

Cameron reached out and grabbed Pilar's hand and held it as if she would never let go.

VJ turned to see if Pilar was behind him and saw her hug Cameron tightly. He was pleased to see a trace of the old Pilar.

After the first course, Leila entered the wine cellar and said, "Come on, Pilar. Let's run to the little girl's room." Strong, dependable Leila must be trying to get Pilar straight, VJ thought. Why couldn't Pilar be more like her? When Pilar returned, she had a glassy look.

~~~

THE REST OF THE NIGHT was a beautiful blur. Luigi had outdone himself—cuisine that tasted like the essence of its ingredients, but which was visually transformed into something that looked almost too good to eat. VJ was astounded by pommes frites that were as translucent as an Art Deco glass brick. It was the kind of dining experience everyone should have at least once in their lives. VJ watched in dismay as Pilar toyed with her food, sipped at her wine, eating and drinking almost nothing.

He decided then that he could not go on like this. She had everything in the world she ever dreamed of and more, and she was tossing it away. He thought about all the years he had treaded water in his personal life with Georgie. How their marriage became a sham—how he had confessed to Pilar exactly how he felt, and she had replied, "We will never be like that, will we?" Yet, here they were.

~~~

LUIGI TUNED OUT EVERYTHING else as he observed VJ and Pilar. He was deeply saddened. He liked—no—he *loved* them both. He remembered cooking for them at his house early on when VJ was still married to Georgie and bringing Pilar to the restaurant was not a choice. How happy and in love they had been. He would never forget how Pilar's face had glowed.

He had done his best to create the perfect theater everyone would remember as one of the best evenings of their lives. "Do you remember that last night at Eleganté?" people would say decades later with a smile and a pang. For the Simons, however, his good friends, nothing tonight seemed to be going right. Luigi sighed. You never know how anything will turn out or what will happen next.

~~~

NORMA HAD CHOSEN her seating very carefully. Paddy was to her right. Margot was next to him. Yaakov, her currency trading "genius," was to her left, then Muffy, then Will. Margot's biggest customers occupied the rest of the table. Samantha Gray, who had won the Texas lottery, and her partner, Davida Koenig (the couple was known as "Sam and Dave"), and Jackson Monahan, the tobacco lawsuit billionaire from Orange, Texas, and his wife, Kitty Sue. Rance Ed refused to come.

She had not included Prentice.

PART

FOUR

CHAPTER 47

PRENTICE'S REVENGE

NORMA'S FATE WAS SEALED when Prentice asked if he was included for the closing dinner at Eleganté. "Oh, darlin', bless your heart," Norma had said. "There won't be room for you. I've got to take the most important clients." Prentice was outraged and heartsick. Immediately he began to put into action his plan to open his own candy store with keys she had given him.

It had taken Prentice more than a year of working with Norma to understand the underpinnings of her success. She'd grown somewhat notorious for earning astounding returns for her clients. He had always known it didn't make sense. It was only after Norma had come to rely on him to transfer the money to Swiss accounts and back again when needed did he understand. It was a classic Ponzi scheme.

Norma added an additional layer to the details Charles Ponzi hadn't thought of to attract even more money—a "legal," United States–sanctioned, tax-haven corporation so that US citizens would only pay taxes on a fraction of their income. She credited the invention of this so-called "perfect tax shelter" to tax genius and former high-ranking officer of the Internal Revenue Service, Mr. Rance Ed Booker.

Prentice was pretty sure Rance Ed was no genius. With some clever sleuthing, he discovered that while Mr. Booker had indeed been with the IRS Criminal Investigative Division, he had left under a very dark cloud.

He was also pretty sure the tax shelter wasn't legal. At one time, a CNMI corporation was a legitimate vehicle for sheltering certain income of US citizens from US taxes. Prentice had an idea it probably wasn't legitimate anymore and had never been a legitimate way to shelter income from legal fees earned in Harris County, Texas. With hard work and research, he finally figured out it was a sham.

But what was her exit strategy? Prentice couldn't figure out if she had a brilliant plan in mind or if she just hadn't thought that far in advance. With Norma either was possible.

Surely Norma knew her scheme couldn't last forever. At some point, she had to take the money and run. He didn't care what her plan was. He just had to figure out what action he could take before she took off.

And so he did. He was just waiting for the right moment. Right moment or not, Norma's failure to include him for the last night at Eleganté propelled him to spring into action.

Prentice could tie his stomach in knots by replaying Norma's dismissive voice in his head. He had been so eager to be there. The hurt and shame of just being her "boy," of not being valued, enraged him. He would never forgive her for the way she looked at him—as if he should have known better, as if he should understand that he had no reason to be at such an important event for The Best People.

Without sharing details, Prentice asked a lawyer about whistle-blower rewards for turning in people who had not reported embezzled money. The lawyer told him the IRS paid a reward for turning in tax evaders. He also said that it was never a sure thing, that the IRS liked to publicize its whistle-blower rewards to encourage people to come forward, but most whistle-blowers felt they had been deceived and cheated, and all felt they had to wait too long to collect on the rewards. "Put it this way," the lawyer said, "they have lots of rules they don't tell you about when they need you. You find out about those rules later."

Prentice left shaken. If he couldn't count on the IRS, maybe he needed to take his own reward.

While Norma and her A-list were enjoying their last night at Eleganté, Prentice was at the office having his own party of one. He used his password with building management to turn on the air conditioning and the lights. He didn't care about leaving a trail because he would be long gone by the time his late night at the office was discovered. A crew he hired from a litigation-support outfit Bates-stamped, scanned, and put on portable hard drives and in the cloud a copy of every page in every file, checks, statements of bank and financial accounts, wire transfer documentation, statements from credit card companies, mutual funds, and every other document in Norma's operation. What he did not locate because they didn't exist were portfolios of securitized, well-collateralized, high-yield, low-risk loans that she claimed produced her high returns. Even though he would no longer seek a reward from the IRS, he decided to create a diversion by providing the IRS copies of the information. They would keep Norma busy.

By the end of the night, Prentice entered the user names and passwords to access every account she had, foreign and domestic. He downloaded the most current information and wire-transferred nearly all available funds in her US accounts to her foreign accounts. Then he transferred most of those funds to an account he had established for himself at her main Swiss bank. From that account he transferred them again to an account he established in Cyprus. US agencies, he knew, could trace the trail of the funds from her US accounts to her Swiss accounts, but Swiss law should block the US government's attempts to seize the money in those accounts. Nevertheless, he liked the additional layer of protection because even the Swiss wouldn't be able to recover the money in the Cyprus accounts.

In preparation for the evening's activities, he obtained seven counterfeit passports from a former KGB operative he had learned about from hacking Yaakov's computer.

By sunrise he was gone.

CHAPTER 48

A SURPRISE FOR
WILL AND PADDY

WILL WAS PERFORMING his daily mail-opening ritual. He came across an envelope from the Internal Revenue Service addressed to the law partnership. Frowning, he put it aside. Next was a green card certified mail receipt. He put that in the pile to go to his secretary. Then an invitation to a fundraiser for Judge Elizondo with Paddy and Will among the cosponsors. Three misspellings—Dolores's fine hand at work.

He turned back to the IRS envelope. Inside was a notice that the partnership's return was going to be examined.

"Candace," he said to his secretary over the intercom, "please get Rance Ed Booker on the telephone for me."

Will waited, drumming his fingers on the desk.

Candace buzzed him. "Mr. Booker is not at that number."

"When did they say he would be in?"

"No one said anything. A recording said the number had been disconnected."

"What?" Will responded. "Call for him at Norma's office, will you?"

Several minutes passed. Candace buzzed again. "No one answers there either."

Will found an unlisted home number for Norma in his contacts. He dialed it himself and got a generic recording that the voicemail box was full.

Later, at home, Will rifled his personal mail. There were two more notices from the Internal Revenue Service, one addressed to Muffy and one to him. He opened them both and learned that their personal income tax returns were going to be audited as well.

Paddy was still at the office when Will called. "Have you gotten a notice from the Internal Revenue Service about your personal tax return?"

"I got something from the IRS yesterday, but I haven't opened it."

"I got notices that Muffy's and my returns and the partnership's are being audited. My guess is yours is too."

"Hmm. You think so?"

"This doesn't concern you?"

"Should it?"

Will's voice was steely. "I tried to reach Rance Ed Booker. No luck. Apparently he does not wish to be found. I called our friend, Norma, too. Couldn't get hold of her either."

"That doesn't sound good."

"No, Einstein, it doesn't," Will said, trying to keep a lid on his irritation. "Let me try to track down Norma. I'm sure she'll feed me bullshit, but it can't hurt."

He dialed Norma's number again. A female voice with an accent—maybe Filipino—answered.

He asked to speak with Norma, and after a short pause, he heard, "Will, darlin', how are you?"

"I'm glad to know you're in town."

"Actually, I'm not."

"Where are you?"

"Sweetie, that's too complicated to explain," she said.

Will noted caution in her voice. No cuteness or generic familiar appellations.

"We've gotten notices from the IRS that they're going to examine the firm's returns and our personal returns. I tried to reach Rance Ed, and he is nowhere to be found."

"You know, I'm not real sure where Rance Ed is myself."

"Well, do you know what this is all about?"

"I sure do. It's that vendetta the IRS has against rich people. Prentice fed them a line of BS so we'd be tied up with the IRS and wouldn't know he had embezzled money from us."

"Prentice did *what*?"

"He embezzled money, and he sent information to the IRS and the US Attorney telling lies about me. Wouldn't you know, the IRS agent assigned to the case thinks her mission is to redistribute the wealth, close the gap between rich and poor. She's half black and half, I'm ashamed to say, American Native. I'm afraid they're after you because y'all are tied in with me."

"Jesus, Norma. It would be very helpful if I could talk to Rance Ed. He set up everything. He understands everything. He has all the records. It's imperative that I find him."

"I'll see what I can do," she said.

"When do you think we can get our money?"

"I'm working on it. I'll be in touch. Ciao!"

Will poured himself a slug of an eighteen-year-old single malt. He drank it neat. It didn't burn even a little. He poured himself another.

〰〰

THE NEXT MORNING PADDY bounded into Will's office. "You were right, pal. They're examining my returns, but I'm not worried. I reported every penny. We just have to find Rance Ed. He used to be with the IRS. He knows those guys. What's to sweat?"

Will could hear a man in denial. He knew because he'd been there, but he wasn't there now. "Paddy, you're a smart man. At least you're smart about most things. Why would Rance Ed disappear into thin air if everything was fine? Plus, when I asked Norma if she could help, I got a very troubling response."

"Hey, where is Norma?"

"She *wouldn't* say."

Paddy's face fell. "That's funny," he said.

"Funny is one way to characterize it."

"Did she say when we're getting our money?"

"No," Will responded, "she did not. I fear we won't see much of that money, if any. We've lost our investment with her. Face it. Right now, we need to talk to someone about the IRS examinations."

"Let's call Pilar."

Will called on the speakerphone. When Pilar came on the line she sounded tense. "Look, guys, I keep the records. The fees go to the CNMI company, net of expenses, all per your contract. The law firm books are clean. I'll be happy to work with the IRS directly, but that's not what I do. You should find someone experienced to represent you."

"Yes, that's what we're thinking," Will said. "We'll keep you informed."

He turned off the phone. "She's absolutely right. We need an experienced tax professional. Got any ideas?"

"Let's go with Loophole Loggins," Paddy responded.

Will tilted his head and raised his eyebrows.

Paddy ignored the eyebrows. "Loggins is an old hand at this. He used to be a lawyer with the IRS. He built a big firm that does nothing but tax stuff. He's very creative."

"I guess you don't read the *Texas Bar Journal*. Your buddy Loophole was disbarred for his creativity."

"No shit."

"I'm thinking someone from one of the big firms."

"Are you crazy? You want them knowing our business? We get referrals from those guys. A hell of a lot of them become our clients, usually right after they make partner."

"How about Foxman? You had him review it for us. He said it was okay."

"Not exactly."

Will half-leapt out of his chair. "What do you mean?"

"Right after I talked to Foxman, he wrote me saying he had not advised me on it, one way or another."

"You're kidding. I would never have gone into that deal without a second opinion."

Paddy didn't respond.

Will slammed his hand on his desk. "I need you to step out of my office."

As Paddy backed his way out of Will's office, he asked, "What are the alternatives?"

"Somebody else. Showing up ourselves. Ignoring it. Leaving the country. Suicide."

Paddy arched an eyebrow and said, "Let's assume that the only alternative is somebody else. Who?"

CHAPTER 49

THE END

ALTHOUGH VJ DID NOT tell Pilar, she was so woozy on the way home from Eleganté's closing, he concluded their marriage was over. He planned to tell her the next morning, but she showed no sign of coherency. Somehow that day fell into the next and the next, and it became difficult to find a way to bring up the subject. He decided to wait for the next incident. For several weeks, life appeared almost normal—except it wasn't. He didn't speak to her. She barely spoke to him. Pilar somehow got it together for work and when they had to go out for an event but when he came home for dinner, her eyes were glassy most times and after dinner she went up to the bedroom. He stayed in his study until he was ready to sleep. It appeared to VJ that the nanny took over most of the mothering of the children.

One evening, VJ decided he had had enough. He reviewed the last few months. He believed he had tried to tell her what their problems were, but she refused to confront them. When she tried to improve, she always relapsed. She had stopped drinking, but the pills were worse. When Pilar drank she was still Pilar, although an unpleasant extension of her worst traits. On the pills, she wasn't herself. He went back to that last night at Eleganté, cursing himself for not following through with his decision to end it then and there.

He had set the price going in, and it would be easy to pay it going out. Pilar had signed a prenuptial agreement, providing her with one million dollars for every year they spent together as man and wife, plus complete financial support of the children. Not a problem. He could easily write a check, and it would be over and done. Many of his colleagues would feel nothing but relief. Many would have a hard time resisting the urge to say, "I knew from day one you were making a mistake."

He climbed the stairs and strode into their dark bedroom.

Pilar was already lying in bed with a pillow over her head. She twitched slightly.

"Pilar, Pilar!" He said firmly. "I know you aren't really sleeping. Snap to it if you aren't too doped up. Get up!"

She pulled the pillow away from her head and sat up in the dark with her feet tucked under her. "Okay, I'm up," she said. "What do you want?"

"We're through."

When he said the words, he wondered how many men had wanted to confront their wives the same way but didn't. Some didn't because they thought they were economic prisoners of their situation. Some could afford to, but they were afraid of conflict. Some could afford it and weren't afraid of the conflict, but feared change. Some feared loneliness, though any man with money knew he didn't have to be lonely unless he wanted to be lonely. He reflected on that one. There's a difference between being lonely and being alone. He snapped back to his purpose.

"Do you hear me?" Pilar stared blankly at him. He turned on his heels and walked out of their bedroom. He would sleep in his study tonight while he thought over what to do next.

CHAPTER 50

LINDA HETHERINGTON'S BIG ANNOUNCEMENT

MOMENTS AFTER LINDA HETHERINGTON learned she had passed the bar exam, she called a press conference to be held on the steps of the Harris County Family Law Center. The sun was shining. The sky was a pure blue.

She sent email invitations to TMZ, the *Chronicle*'s editorial board, all local television news departments, and all radio stations that still had news departments. The subject line was: "Corrupt Judge Elizondo Faces Challenge." She invited the editor of *The Rice Thresher*, hoping to get coverage so some students might get fired up enough to volunteer in her campaign. A group of women who had remained friends with her through her hard times attended to support her. Two were assigned to stream the event live on the website designed for her by a computer science professor at the University of Houston who had once been her student at Rice. He posted it on YouTube.

Linda wore a black pantsuit she found at the Blue Bird Circle resale shop. She had gone to a hair salon for a stylish cut. She carefully manicured her nails. It had been a while since she had spoken publicly, but she rehearsed and memorized what she had to say, hoping not to sound too professorial.

A number of curious onlookers stood around to see what was happening.

"Ladies and gentlemen, thank you for your attention. I have called this press conference to announce that I am filing for the judicial seat held by Hector Elizondo."

Her friends in attendance whooped it up. The other onlookers became more interested.

"Hector Elizondo is incompetent. You don't have to take my word for that. He got an unqualified rating by ninety-two percent of the lawyers who voted in the most recent Houston Bar Association judicial poll. Ninety-two percent! He is also corrupt.

"I'm not an experienced lawyer. In fact, just today I learned I had passed the bar exam. But I will tell you one thing I am experienced in—and I say it in quotes—'family law.' I am running because no one else should have the experience I had.

"There's an old joke: What do you call someone who finishes last in his law school class? The answer is 'Your Honor.' In fact, Hector Elizondo did finish last in his class. I might not be qualified because I finished eighth in my class.

"Defeating Elizondo—and do notice I do not call him *Judge* Elizondo—will be a victory for justice and for mercy.

"Judges are supposed to be like Caesar's wife, above suspicion." A friend who taught persuasive speaking had worked with her on the movement of her hands and arms as she spoke. At this point, as she had been coached, she began to speak in an ear-catching rhythm. "From the moment it was announced that Hector Elizondo had been appointed to the bench, he has had an improper relationship with Paddy Moran and Will Marshall. They hired his daughter. They had a reception for him at their office. They have each contributed fifty thousand dollars to his campaign fund. Friends of Mr. Moran and employees of the Marshall & Moran law firm have made contributions in amounts way beyond their means. Why would they do that? For the results they obtain in his court."

Noting the presence of media, more people stopped to listen.

"You may say it's sour grapes on my part because Elizondo awarded Marshall & Moran's client, my ex-husband, custody of my daughter. It's true, I wouldn't be here today if that hadn't happened. After being absolutely devastated by dirty tricks and the judge's complicity, I made a pledge to myself. I would do everything in my power to rid the system of those who corrupt it. Complaints by me and my attorney to the bar and the judicial commission were fruitless.

"To anyone who is watching, if you care about justice, if you care about parental rights, if you care about children, and, most importantly, if you care whether or not your neighbors might become lawless because they don't trust the system, support me, volunteer for me, vote for me."

Her friends and even some of the onlookers cheered. Linda smiled, and said, "Thank you." There was a mixture of enthusiastic and polite applause.

A reporter asked, "What sort of chance do you think you, an unknown who hasn't even been sworn into the bar yet, will have against a sitting judge?"

"That's an obvious question. What's your name, ma'am?"

"Freda Grazier with KUHF, Houston Public Radio."

"Wonderful, I am a regular listener and a long-time member. Ms. Grazier, my belief is once the facts have been submitted to the people, they will elect me. I will work as hard as I possibly can to inform the voters. I will knock on doors until my knuckles bleed. I hope others will support me. I can't do it alone."

The TMZ stringer put a microphone in front of her face while his cameraman had an angle that captured them both.

"Aren't you the same lady that demonstrates in front of this courthouse and shoots Paddy Moran with Silly String?"

She was prepared for the question. There were numerous videos of her on the internet. "That's me, I'm proud to say. But peaceful demonstrations and acting outrageously to attract attention to a deplorable situation haven't worked. The bar and the judiciary have turned a blind eye to the misdeeds of their own. Thank goodness the great state of Texas allows the people to elect their judges. I am confident that they will turn out Hector Elizondo and elect me."

This time, people who had gathered at the press conference roared with an approval that surprised Linda and the media.

⁂

NO TELEVISION STATION bothered to cover Linda's press conference, but with the KUHF coverage and the video getting more than a thousand hits by eight o'clock that night, the CBS, NBC, ABC, and Fox affiliates scrambled to get coverage for the ten o'clock news. Hetherington's friends sent the stations videos of her announcement. Each sent a reporter to interview her.

Channel Eleven led its newscast with "Breaking news! A newly licensed lawyer announces her campaign for judge on the day she passes the bar examination." The voice was over videos of Linda running to shoot Silly String at Paddy. Without saying so, they treated her as if she were a kook.

However, the next morning a *Chronicle* columnist picked up on Linda's campaign. The newspaper's headline read, "Is No Experience and No Record Better than Bad Experience and a Highly Questionable Record?" The columnist then went into the Hetherington case and Linda's background. "She has a PhD, she taught at Rice, and she graduated near the top of her class in law school." The reporter compared Paddy's and Will's results in Elizondo's courtroom to their results in other courts. She cited Elizondo's poor showing in the bar polls. She ended her column with, "I am not ready to dismiss Linda Hetherington as a viable alternative to Hector Elizondo. Let's see, Dear Readers, how this campaign develops."

The TMZ stringer had called Paddy before the ten o'clock news. "Thanks for the head's up, buddy. I won't talk to any media before I talk to you." Paddy then called Will. "We have another problem." He explained the situation.

"You're kidding," Will said. "She isn't even a lawyer, is she?"

"As I understand it, no, but she will have been sworn in in time to qualify."

They conference called Elizondo. "Hector, make yourself scarce until we have vetted you on this," Paddy said. "If the media does find you, just say 'No comment' until we tell you what to say."

They prepared Elizondo's press release. It read: "I have been informed that Linda Hetherington has filed to run against me for the seat I now hold. That is her right. Ms. Hetherington's situation is a sad one. She was devastated when she lost custody of her daughter, but the facts were such that a jury of twelve good citizens of Harris County found awarding custody to the father was in the best interests of the child. Ms. Hetherington's subsequent antics at the courthouse certainly do not demonstrate a judicial temperament. I believe fervently in the First Amendment, but exercising one's constitutional right of free speech and being qualified to act as a judge are two different matters."

TMZ got Paddy for the record. "It's a travesty," he told them. "The woman lost it after she lost custody of her child. Judge Elizondo is a fine judge. He worked his way through law school. He is an example of the opportunities minorities have in America—to attain the lofty and most honored places in our society. He dispenses justice and mercy in a fair and impartial way."

"Are you saying you see no merit in her being a judicial candidate?"

"On the contrary, I think that while the campaign is going on she won't be charging at me on the courthouse steps like Don Quixote with Silly String. In my book, that has a lot of merit."

"Thanks, Paddy," the stringer said when the camera was not rolling. "I can always count on you."

CHAPTER 51

HOUSTON, WE HAVE A PROBLEM

WILL WAS IN THE pastel conference room with Anne Arden, the married daughter of the oldest sister of Billy Caldwell. Will's father had been friends with Billy's father from kindergarten at River Oaks Elementary School until Will's father died. Back then, the only children who went to the school lived in the immediate neighborhood. Deed restrictions and segregation had the desired result of there being no Jews, no Asians, only a few Hispanics, and, of course, no blacks, even if they lived in the servants' quarters. Times had changed for the school, but not for the Caldwells.

The Caldwells were rich, and they were numerous, but not so numerous that there was not enough money for several more dysfunctional generations to live without financial concern. They were so difficult, Will wondered on occasion if there had perhaps been some inbreeding. But their countless problems provided a remunerative and steady flow of work for him.

He nodded sympathetically, playing the fatherly, consoling counselor as Anne told him about her problems with her husband. His pastoral moment was destroyed by the boom of Paddy's voice coming from the direction of Pilar's office.

"What do you mean there isn't any fucking money in the bank?" Paddy shouted. "You motherfucker! I put lots of money in the bank, and I fucking want some back now. *Now!* You are in charge of the money so where the fuck is it? Have you been fucking stealing from us?"

Anne gave Will a disapproving look. Although it was her most frequent expression, this time Will was clearly embarrassed.

"Uh, excuse me, Anne. It sounds as if my partner is upset about something. That's very unlike him. Let me see what is going on."

"I must say I never understood why you would have that wretched, crude man as your partner. He's beneath you." Her voice dripped with condescension. Her prune-like lips were pursed and tightly drawn above her curveless chin. Her eyes narrowed as she glared at him. In that moment he saw how truly unattractive she was.

"He's a fine lawyer, Anne. Very effective. We each make our contributions here. I'll be back in a few minutes."

Will found Paddy in Pilar's office. "I'm with Anne Arden," he said. "Your screaming is so loud it sounds like you're in the room with us. What's going on?"

"We have no money in the bank. That's what is going on," Paddy said.

"Pilar," Will said. He was both intense and calm. "Is that true?"

"It is." There were dark circles beneath her puffy eyes. She looked as if she had spent a long, sleepless night crying.

"Are you okay?" Will asked.

"I'm fine," she said too quickly. She put her right hand to her face. "Thank you for asking. I—uh—was up with one of the kids last night. But things here seem pretty serious. Paddy's right. You really don't have any money in the bank." She looked at Will, as if pleading for him to intercede. "As I was trying to explain to Paddy, the Internal Revenue Service has levied the firm's bank accounts."

"Levied our bank accounts? We don't even owe them any money!"

"They must think you do or they wouldn't have done that," she said. "Let me get the bank officer on the phone. He can explain it to you."

Over the speakerphone, the bank officer explained that the IRS had levied the firm's account and their personal accounts as well.

"Our personal accounts?" Will finally asked.

"Yes, gentlemen. They levied your personal accounts as well."

"We don't even know what this is all about. Look, we're going to need money. Don't we have a line of credit?"

"Actually, you do. You haven't used it in a while, but you do. I don't know if it will be affected by this IRS action, however."

"Look, here!" Paddy yelled. "We need money to pay our staff, keep our door open, and put food on the table!"

"Sir, I—"

"That's alright," Will said quickly. "We'll ring off now. Please get back to us on the line of credit ASAP. Thank you."

"So why would the IRS levy our accounts?" Paddy asked.

"I don't know. I don't know," Will said, distracted. "I need to get back to Anne Arden. No, wait." He felt his shoulders hunching over, his feet shuffling, his head drooping. "I'll bet there's no hope of getting our money from Norma."

Pilar interrupted. "I quit sending money to the CNMI corporation the moment I learned about the IRS examinations."

"Thank you, Pilar. We should have thought of that ourselves." Will turned to Paddy and said in a flat and hopeless tone, "We're broke, aren't we? It's happening to me. Just like my father."

As the initial shock passed, Paddy seemed to strengthen again. Maybe it was just his anger, but that alone was a powerful force. He stood to his full height, tightened his tie, put his hand on Will's shoulder, and said, "Partner, we are temporarily without cash. We aren't broke. Unlike your father, we will come back."

Will nodded, unconvinced. "I have to tell Muffy." He forced himself back to his office to resume his meeting with Anne.

Paddy turned to Pilar. "I'm sorry. I was completely out of line—I shouldn't be here shouting—or swearing or, for Chrissake, accusing you of anything." He slumped, "There is no one in this world—"

Pilar patted him on the back, and then squeezed his arm. He looked like a sad puppy. "Accepted," she said. "It was a shock. Don't worry. I'll help you guys get through this."

He nodded with gratitude. "You doing okay, honey? You look a little—" he drew a frown in the air.

She shrugged. "Let's see what we can do for you guys."

CHAPTER 52

NORMA IS ACCUSED

THE STORY BROKE at four o'clock. US Attorney Chappy Chapman and IRS official Dan Martinez called a joint press conference at the Federal Courthouse. Chapman said, "In a forty-six-count indictment, Norma Nambé was charged with crimes including mail fraud, money laundering, RICO violations, and tax evasion. Also indicted was Rance Ed Booker, a former special agent with the Internal Revenue Service who left the IRS in disgrace. This is one of the largest Ponzi schemes since Madoff. It is bigger than Stanford. Bigger than Teresa Rodriguez. Some of Houston's most prominent people not only put their money in Norma Nambé's phantom investments but also went along with her plans to evade income taxes."

On *News at Five*, after video of the press conference and multiple shots of Norma accepting best-dressed awards, the reporter summed up the situation: "Norma Nambé, the flashy, big-bling, high-profile financial advisor and café society figure whose name has been prominently associated with charity balls and who received accolades as one of the nation's top female minority entrepreneurs, has had a quick and dramatic fall. Ms. Nambé is currently being sought by the FBI and the IRS as the mastermind of a Ponzi scheme and tax scam. Her whereabouts are not known. Today both the FBI and IRS raided her luxurious offices. We'll be bringing you more on this late-breaking story. This is Nichole Randolph, *'News at Five.'*"

Will heard the news on his car radio coming back from the courthouse. His hands were shaking so much he couldn't use his cell phone to call Paddy. When he got back to the office, he told Paddy what he had heard.

"Well, that brings it all together," Paddy said. "I really got us into a doozy, didn't I?"

Will looked away from Paddy, then down and nodded his head.

"What are you thinking?" Paddy asked.

"I was thinking about how we got into this."

Paddy nodded his head. "We can't fuck around anymore. We need a tax lawyer."

Will stared at him.

"Whoever you want is okay with me," Paddy said.

"I asked Pilar to make inquiries. More specifically, I asked her to get a recommendation from her husband. I also called someone at my old firm. Just like last time, the same name kept coming up first. Foxman."

Will wanted to cleanse his mind of the phrase that reverberated in his head—"smart Jewish tax lawyer"—but he couldn't.

Paddy sat down heavily, his legs spread wide, his hands holding his head. "Okay, Will, but you call him."

Foxman was clearly surprised to receive a call from Will. He made room in his schedule to meet with them in his office at seven that evening and told them to bring any documentation they thought might be helpful or necessary. Anticipating the request, Pilar had already put a file together. They were as prepared as they were going to get.

NO ONE WAS AT the receptionist's desk when they arrived, but Foxman immediately came out to greet them. He led them into a conference room. A laptop sat open on the conference table.

"What brings you calling on me?" he asked.

Will looked at Paddy, who looked as if he were trying to make himself invisible. "Elliott, the IRS levied our law firm and personal bank accounts," Will said. "They took everything but what was in the trust account."

"They didn't take that because of my victory in the *Rainwater* case," Foxman said.

"I remember that," Will said. "Rainwater deposited large amounts of cash he got in deposits for legal fees, probably from drug dealers, and the DOJ tried to get the money and make him identify the clients and Rainwater wouldn't. That was a fine win for you."

"Thanks. Why did they levy your other accounts?"

Paddy could not resist cutting in. "We don't know for sure, but we suspect it has something to do with Norma Nambé."

"You went into that deal?" Foxman blurted out.

"Yes," Will said. "We did, and we need our money now. We don't know where it is, and we don't know where Norma is."

"Something about Norma popped up on my computer," Foxman said.

"She's been indicted for fraud, conspiracy, money laundering, RICO, and tax evasion," Will said.

"So why does her indictment end up with your bank accounts being levied?"

Will and Paddy explained to Foxman everything they knew about Norma, Rance Ed Booker, and the CNMI corporation.

When they finished, Foxman said, "Gentlemen, you do have a problem."

"Duh," Paddy mumbled.

"What can you do for us?" Will asked.

"I'd like to think about it. First I would try to get them to lay off taking any more drastic action until the facts are sorted out and it's determined if you really owe any taxes. There's a chance I can get them to do that."

Paddy perked up. "What else can you do for us?"

"I didn't say I *could* do that. I said there's a chance. That would be a start. Then I'll see where we can go from there. We need to find out what is going on in a more deliberate fashion. It's going to take a lot of time, a lot of hard work. I am going to have to bring in a contract paralegal and maybe even a contract lawyer. If not, I will associate with one of the large firms to work with me on this."

Before he could continue, Will and Paddy both started to speak. Paddy stopped and nodded at Will. "Don't contact any of the large firms without discussing it with us first. We have sensitive relationships with some of them," Will said.

"Got it. Initially, I'll have to immerse myself in this thing. Every document must be reviewed. I'll access a software program that can actually read PDF copies of documents and look for key words and phrases as well as, believe it or not, concepts. That'll speed things up. Plus, I'll have to conduct a thorough investigation of Rance Ed Booker."

Paddy raised his hand. "I'm sure you have great sources, but I have a private investigator, Ray Fourbirds, a former assistant chief in the HPD. He has lots of contacts."

"Thanks. I'll be happy to use him. I need to ferret out everything there is to know about Booker."

Paddy said, "I called Fourbirds earlier. He got back to me and said Booker had been booted out of the IRS."

"That was in the news report I heard," Will added.

"That's good. That's very good," Foxman said. "Bottom line objective is to find a way to reduce your liability to as little as possible." He looked at Will and then at Paddy. "On the one hand, for me, it's an interesting challenge. On the other hand, for you, you face a huge possible tax liability. *Huge.* And let me tell you, I am not trying to frighten you, but those people don't have the same limitations other creditors do. There's no such thing as an exempt asset to them. No homestead exemption. No retirement plan exemption. They can take your socks, your underwear, and your wife's wedding ring. They can take everything. And, they have unlimited resources."

Will nearly blacked out. The house. Oh, no. Not the house. Muffy would die. He looked at the floor and tuned out.

"So what do we do?" Paddy asked, sounding earnest but not anxious.

"If you want me to help you, sign an engagement letter and give me a retainer and a deposit."

"How much do you want?"

"Take a deep breath. It's a lot."

"How much?"

Foxman wrote on the top sheet of a legal pad, tore it off, and handed it to Will and Paddy.

"Damn," Will said, suddenly back in the moment.

"Why do we have to put up such a large amount?" Will asked.

"The nonrefundable part is because everything else I'm handling is going to have to take a back seat to this, for the most part, and I am going to have to turn down other new matters that come to me for the time being because of my commitment to you. The other part is a deposit for fees and expenses."

"Isn't it academic? We have no money," Will said.

"Well, they got what was in your accounts on that day. It isn't a constant sweep. The money will come from your future collections. I'll tell you what I'll do. If you sign the engagement letter and give me a power of attorney to represent you before the IRS, and if I can't get them to agree not to levy your bank accounts again, at least for a specified period of time, then I withdraw and you don't owe me a thing. If I can get their agreement, I want the money immediately and each month when I send you a bill I expect it will be paid immediately so that the deposit stays up until we are through."

"And if we don't want to spend that much?" Will said.

Foxman rose, picked up a copy of the *Houston Bar Association Pictorial Roster*, handed it to Will, and said, "I'm sure you could find someone else."

"Elliott, would you let us talk privately for a few minutes?" Will asked.

"Sure. My office is right next to the conference room. Oh," Foxman added, "there is something else. Nothing goes without saying, so I better say it. The IRS could pursue this on a criminal level—criminal tax evasion. I will tell you now, I hope and think that is not likely, but they might."

"How could they?" Will practically screamed. "We could lose our law licenses! We relied on Norma and their own Rance Ed!"

"Well, Norma isn't a tax expert on whose advice you could rely. But Rance Ed is a different matter. Not a slam dunk, because he wasn't *your* advisor, but a very good fact. If they raise the possibility of criminal action, we will work that angle."

"What if you can't find Rance Ed?"

"I'll deal with that. Frankly, not finding him could be to your advantage," he said. "For me to do my job right, I'll need your help."

"Of course," Will said.

"Good. Start by constructing a timeline, beginning with how you got into the deal, who you talked to, et cetera, up until this evening when you came here. I don't run a morals show. You can't embarrass yourselves by telling me anything. What I don't want is surprises. I don't want the government knowing something I don't know."

"I make that speech to every client," Paddy said.

"Then shame on you if you don't follow your own rule."

Will and Paddy said they understood, and Foxman got up and left, softly closing the door behind him.

"Whoa, whoa, whoa!" Will said. "I thought you said this guy was a nerd."

"Actually, I said wuss."

"Okay, a wuss. He certainly didn't sound like a wuss asking for a very sizable nonrefundable retainer and a large deposit. He wasn't rude about it, but he was close to it."

"He sounded confident."

Will reached for the right words as he continued, "Very assertive."

"I wonder if we might have been better off if you had come alone," Paddy said.

"I did some checking on Elliott. His clients are referrals from other lawyers and accountants. His track record is excellent. Most of the time his clients don't have to go to court and don't get embarrassing publicity, at least about their taxes. If they do go to court, he wins a lot more often than he loses. He is the go-to guy the white-collar crime lawyers call when clients have tax issues associated with their financial crimes. Maybe he's just had more successes than he had when you last worked with him. Was he putting on a show for you, taking advantage of our situation? Maybe."

"I hope not," said Paddy. "But he's sure a lot cockier than he used to be."

Will said, "I'm going to use Elliott."

Paddy looked up. "With or without me?"

Will nodded.

Paddy wondered if Will was just learning to be more assertive or this was the first step in Will breaking away from him. "Okay," Paddy said. "We'll both go with Foxman."

Will opened the door of the conference room and called out, "Elliott." When Foxman returned, Will said, "We'd like to hire you."

"I'm honored to represent two lawyers with your reputation and standing in the family law bar. It's high praise."

Paddy rolled his eyes. The fucker sure had come a long way.

Will said, "Keeping our reputation and our money is why we're engaging you."

"Then we need to get started."

Will noticed the "we." He took that to mean Foxman was now as one with them.

"Just make sure no more money is sent to the CNMI."

"That dumb we're not," Paddy said.

"Actually, our office manager stopped that immediately after we got the IRS notices," Will added.

"That was smart. As soon as I have the engagement letter signed by everyone and the IRS authorizations forms I attached, we'll be off."

"Thanks," both Will and Paddy said.

"Guys, I'm sorry you have this problem." Foxman's tone changed. There was less hubris and more compassion. He walked them to the elevator.

Paddy swallowed as they rode down. "I take it back about Foxman," he said. "He seemed professional, competent, and appreciative that we came to him when our asses were on the line."

Will sighed. "Now I have to explain all this to Muffy."

"Just blame it on me." Paddy said. "She will anyway."

CHAPTER 53

MAKING CHICKEN SALAD

AFTER THE ELEVATOR DOORS CLOSED, Elliott Foxman jumped, landed in a Heisman pose, and said, "Yessssss!"

He returned to his office and sank into the most comfortable chair. If he were a cigar smoker, now would be the time to light up Red Auerbach-style. "That son of a bitch Paddy Moran crawled to me, and *he* has to pay *me* a big retainer."

But he had to give Paddy some credit. He'd taught Elliott something, maybe a lot of things. Sell yourself, which sometimes was more important than how you performed. The more some clients pay you, the more they respect you. Never, never, never make the task ahead look too easy.

But Paddy had humiliated him. He'd told people he thought Elliott was a chump. Paddy's disdain wasn't because he didn't get a great result for Paddy's client in a divorce settlement; it was because Elliott figured out how to fix Paddy's screw up very quickly and charged by the hour, so he made a very small fee. In Paddy's mind, that made Elliott a chump. Paddy discounted him. If *The Wall Street Journal* hadn't made his win in the *Rainwater* case a front-page story, he may have never recovered.

Elliott rose from the chair and paced. On reflection, Paddy had done him a favor, really. He had left the firm he had been working for because his colleagues saw him the way Paddy had—a reliable producer but never a rainmaker. He saw his choices as going with another law firm or going solo. He concluded he wanted to be a host instead of a guest, so he took the entrepreneurial leap of opening his own shop. The eyes of attorneys who don't practice tax law usually glaze over when they hear the "t" word. They want someone they are comfortable with to send clients to with tax problems. The referrals began coming in. His successes led to more referrals and bigger cases. He was doing well. So why did he still feel anger at Paddy? He owed him for where he was today. But his dismissiveness and disrespect still smarted.

Elliott picked up the phone and imagined a conversation with Paddy:

"Paddy, it's Elliott."

"You called to crow because I'm such a dumb schmuck."

"No, I'm didn't. That's not to say you weren't a dumb schmuck."

"Will and I are really relying on you, Elliott."

"I know. I know. I wanted to thank you."

"You're kidding. For what?"

"I know what you said about me after I turned a malpractice situation for you in Malowitz into a premium fee for yourself."

"How do you know?"

One of the lessons Elliott learned: never mention names. It leaves people hanging and that's a good thing. He imagined did not respond to Paddy.

Instead, after a pause Paddy said, "And you aren't pissed at me?"

"I was."

Then Paddy said, "I was worried about it."

"That's why I called, to let you know I'm not carrying a grudge. Some tough times are ahead of us. There are no guarantees. You have enough to worry about. I wanted to take that one off the table," Elliott imagined himself saying.

In reality, he sat at his desk, his fingers poised to dial Paddy. Paddy had gotten them into the deal with Norma, so from this point Elliott guessed Will would be calling the shots. Should he let Paddy off the hook?

He hung up the phone without dialing. "Let the fucker stew."

CHAPTER 54

PADDY HAS A BRAINSTORM

PADDY WAS SITTING ON THE COMMODE, thinking about his current circumstances. Mick took his usual position at Paddy's feet. He knew he would never be poor again, but broke was looking like a distinct possibility. He did not like the thought of being broke. Trying to figure out which creditors would wait and which ones wouldn't, he had hoped, would remain a thing of the past. He liked living in a fancy high-rise and having a Ferrari and a Mercedes sedan at his sole disposal. He liked people sucking up to him. He was more than pleased with his status quo. He had made it by finding a niche, a place where rich people would spend money and not count it. Now everything could change. Like the rich crow in *Fritz the Cat* who still kept a jar of peanut butter stashed away, Paddy still had his truck. Everyone knew he and Will had invested with Norma. Big deal. They weren't the only ones who were suckers. The publicity about the IRS levies? Everybody hates the IRS. It might even make some people want to help him. The trappings he wouldn't miss so much. But the respect. Losing the respect would be hard. Grissett's crack, "Paddy Moron," came back to him.

He knew he couldn't count on quick riches from some unexpected source. He wasn't going to win the lottery like Norma's victim Sam. He didn't have a rich relative to leave him money. Hell, he *was* the rich relative. Will's situation was different. His wife would inherit plenty eventually. The one thing that was certain was Paddy's determination to find a way to bounce back.

Margot had warned him about Norma. He had no idea how she would react when she found out what happened.

Until that night at her house after the Elizondo reception, he never really imagined it was possible they might get together. He had seen so much of marriage in his practice and before that as a cop, he had long ago decided to pass it up. That's why, no matter how desperate he was, marrying a rich woman wasn't on Paddy's list of possible solutions. Margot, on the other hand, he did think about. She liked him. He knew that, but he didn't think she liked him enough to really settle into a relationship with him. Wouldn't he have heard more from her? Paddy sighed. He was no prize potato, as his mother used to say. With Margot not being an option, he was just fine with his casual arrangements with women. He paid for them when he wanted them, and he didn't have to put up with them otherwise. Cold but efficient. As for love, Mick gave him unconditional love; that was enough for him. Still, he thought about Margot.

Paddy realized he only had one option to make enough money to get ahead of the IRS and then some. Just do what he'd been doing, only more so. He needed some big hits. Or, better, one really big one to get them caught up so they could start building a cushion. Where would it come from? How long would it take? Will was in the same boat—probably worse. To save himself and his partner, Paddy needed the kind of divorce that kept on giving. Something along the lines of Elizabeth Taylor and Richard Burton. The Donald and Ivana. Lots of heat. Lots of emotion. Lots of anger. And lots of money. And lots of publicity.

He got up quickly, his movement so abrupt Mick cowered.

"Easy, boy. Easy," he assured him. He needed a list of the richest people in Houston. *Texas Monthly* had a list. So did *Forbes*—America's billionaires and multimillionaires, who was who, and who was rising up through the ranks. It would be easy to find the Houstonians on the lists. The *Chronicle* had just published a list of the hundred highest-paid executives and highest net-worth individuals in Houston. There were more than ten billionaires. Paddy set to compiling his list and handicapping it as if he were going to the racetrack. He made some general assumptions. 1) People with old money are less likely to divorce. They may screw around and make each other's lives miserable, but they are more likely to stay married. 2) Highly paid executives dump their wives and marry younger women. The stories that came out about those Enron guys and their baby brides. 3) Apply the right pressure and a sharp lawyer can make any divorce more heated, but he has to have a pretty good idea where to apply the pressure and that meant research.

When he had finished, Paddy scanned his list. He was surprised to see so many unfamiliar names. A lot of dot-com guys were among the new blood, but most were in energy-related businesses. Many lived outside the tollway. He counted twenty-one who'd made more than ten million dollars last year. Holy Christ. He needed more information. He left a voicemail for Ray Fourbirds.

The next question was would he want to represent the husband or the wife. He quickly decided on the wife. Wives never worried about how much they spent on a lawyer because at the end of the day the husband would pay for the fees. A lot of them liked taking their future ex to the cleaners; hell, most of them loved it.

Then a thought struck him right in the stomach. Things were not going well with the Wingate case. A highly publicized loss could cripple him. Take care of business, he urged himself.

RAY HAD GAINED WEIGHT since Paddy had last seen him. He was easily over three hundred pounds, but he still carried himself with the authority of the Native American chief he claimed was an ancestor. He was conspicuous, but Paddy didn't use Fourbirds to shadow people. He'd proven that he had more strengths uncommon to most private investigators. When Paddy wanted to know who was doing what and with whom or to whom, Fourbirds delivered.

First on Fourbirds' to-do list was determining which ones on Paddy's list were married. Then whether or not they were on their first marriage. Then whatever information he could gather.

Two days later, Fourbirds reported. Houston's top ten in compensation were all men. Eight were married. Only four were married to a first wife, three to number two, and one to the fourth.

"The highest-paid guy made over one hundred million. Not bad for a working stiff," Fourbirds said.

Of those with the highest net worth, two were women and eight were men, including VJ Simon. Three were not married. Three were married to their first spouse, two to their second, one to her third, and one to his sixth. That was Mal Malowitz who he had already represented twice. No. Real estate was in the dumps anyway. He could rev up that old warhorse another time. This case had to involve mega-money.

Paddy decided to scratch those still married to their first spouse. He figured they were the least likely to come undone in time for his schedule. The first one is usually the hardest to leave. It gets easier after that. That left seven, four of whom made the big bucks and three who were the richest. Including the spouses, that made fourteen possibilities. He realized that even after he got past the current crisis, this process might be a pretty good way to find clients going forward.

Paddy instructed Fourbirds to use creativity to learn everything about the fourteen that might be helpful to him in his quest to realize his biggest payday ever.

FOXMAN DOES HIS THING

ELLIOTT FOXMAN HAD LEARNED long ago not to rely on a "kinder, gentler IRS," but rather on his own careful reading of the Internal Revenue Code, the Treasury Regulations, and the *Internal Revenue Manual*; observing Treasury's process; and his uncanny ability to find a solution by connecting seemingly unrelated information. Also, as the years passed, his reputation and relationships with IRS personnel was a help. He never left district counsel, appeals officers, revenue agents, or revenue officers with the feeling he didn't respect them for the job they did and the sacrifices each had made to be career IRS public servants. His feelings were genuine, but he still pulled out all his creative stops when he was pursuing a case. As long as he was dealing with IRS people who were listening to him, he never raised his voice or pointed a finger. His style was not to be hostile or adversarial unless his opponent either gave him no choice or played a dirty trick. Elliott realized how much discretion IRS personnel had, so why be antagonistic without good reason?

Some—very few actually—who worked at the levels Foxman dealt with had that "just putting in my time" attitude commonly believed to be characteristic of civil servants. Those few were referred to by tax practitioners as "T & E and home at three," meaning the kind of revenue agent who would examine the easy targets of travel and entertainment deductions in an audit, propose a few changes, and skip everything else unless there were obvious red flags. Even fewer abused the power and resources of the IRS. For those that did, with self-righteous contempt, Foxman would use every means he had to get justice for his client while teaching his adversaries a lesson they would never forget. Most auditors, however, whatever John Q. Public might think, were bright, hardworking, responsible, and reasonable. Inexperienced auditors were usually the most difficult, combining as they did a lack of real-world experience with a limited comprehension of the Internal Revenue Code.

Elliott had developed his method of dealing with the IRS. His first step was to figure out how to get them to exercise their discretion in favor of his client. He did this through using polite, careful advocacy and credibility. Selling rich lawyers who participated in a tax evasion scheme would be a challenge.

He called area counsel, and the next day he met with a relatively new attorney in the counsel's office who had been assigned the case. Foxman didn't know her, but she knew who he was. The revenue officer from collections also attended. He had taken the precipitate action against Paddy and Will. His boss was also present. To Elliott's surprise, an attorney from the Criminal Tax Division of the Department of Justice was there as well.

He hoped this first meeting for Paddy and Will would not be hostile. His general rule was not to allow clients to meet with the IRS, but they had specifically requested that Will and Paddy attend. Since he was seeking discretion, Foxman agreed. He had instructed Will and Paddy not to speak unless he told them to. If they were asked a question, they were to wait until Foxman asked them either the same question or a different version of the question. He warned them to follow his instructions. "Don't go lawyer on me," he said sternly.

They met in a conference room on the third floor of the George Thomas "Mickey" Leland Federal Building, on the south edge of downtown Houston. It had become a federal building as a result of the savings and loan collapse of the early 1990s. It was named for Houston Congressman Mickey Leland, a larger-than-life character who died in a plane crash in Ethiopia while on a humanitarian mission to rescue starving Falasha and bring them to Israel as members of a lost tribe under the Law of Return. The conference room was scantily furnished with blue industrial carpeting—pure, unmemorable, reduced budget General Services Administration.

After introductions, followed by a few minutes of the government people and Elliott exaggerating prior encounters to the level of close friendships and updates about their colleagues, current and retired, Foxman turned to business.

"Norma Nambé is a swindler and a promoter of a bogus tax shelter. She could not have conceived of or executed the tax fraud without the assistance and imprimatur of one Rance Ed Booker. Like it or not, Mr. Booker was a bad apple who came out of your barrel. His credentials carried the patina of legitimacy. If pictures of sex offenders can be put on the internet as a warning, surely the IRS can do something similar when one of their own goes bad. Why should the IRS do that? Because many people think that someone with IRS experience has expertise and integrity. And, for the most part, that is correct. Not this time."

Foxman paused, making eye contact with each government person.

"Norma and Rance Ed used that patina to trick my clients and others into paying a lot of money to follow a scheme that Rance Ed assured them was in accordance with the law and okay with the IRS. Yes, Paddy and Will diverted their income through a maze. Yes, Paddy and Will may owe taxes. They probably don't owe much, as I see it, because the fraud loss would offset their income that flowed through the cockamamie scheme. Furthermore, my clients had no intent to commit tax fraud because they believed what they were doing was perfectly lawful. Norma Nambé used her charm, promoting Rance Ed's IRS experience to convince my clients that they were doing something legal and risk-free. It would be counterproductive to shut down their law practice by continuing to sweep their bank accounts. Even without the money that went through the CNMI company, my clients are in the maximum tax bracket. The government needs that money. Their law practice is not a criminal enterprise. Their employees would go from being taxpayers to being on welfare. There's no benefit to shutting them down."

At that point, the arms of each member of Foxman's audience moved to a folded position.

"My clients can't afford to wait very long. After I reviewed their choices with my clients, they insisted I take every avenue I could to let them conduct their business without government interference."

Foxman stopped speaking. There was silence. The area director looked at IRS area counsel. He turned to the Department of Justice lawyer who nodded.

"Gentlemen, please wait outside while we discuss this," district counsel said.

Foxman picked up his briefcase and led his clients out to the hallway.

As soon as the door closed, Paddy asked, "What's going on?"

"What's going to happen?" Will asked.

"Worst case, they tell us you should have known. If it's too good to be true, it's too good to be true. And you were—their term would be—willfully blind."

Will turned ashen.

Paddy's nostrils flared as he said, "You gotta be shitting me." His entire face turned beet red.

"I don't think that will happen," Foxman said. "The DOJ lawyer wouldn't be here if he wasn't involved in the prosecution of Norma and Booker. My guess is his objective is to make you cooperate. Sometimes they indict people just to get them to cooperate."

"This is unbelievable," Will said as he put his hands in his pants pockets and began walking in circles.

Foxman said, "I'll make sure they understand that if they back off, let you guys collect your receivables and conduct your business, these civil servants will not risk being embarrassed by having their decision reversed in a very high-profile case. That's huge for them. Stay calm. Let's see what happens."

Will and Paddy nodded. Foxman sat down and began typing notes on his laptop. After another fifteen minutes, district counsel stepped out, her arms still folded. "Elliott, you and I need to talk." Her voice was tense.

Foxman looked away from her. He winked at his clients, then followed her into an office. Will and Paddy could hear both of them raising their voices. Then it got quiet. A few minutes later, Elliott and the IRS attorney returned.

Foxman said, "Gentlemen, I need to meet with those folks without you."

Will asked, "Could you please explain what is going on?"

"I could," Foxman responded, "but I think it's best if I go directly in."

Paddy gave Foxman a menacing look. Enough for showmanship.

"I tell you what, I do need to talk to you both for a moment."

Turning to counsel he said, "Gabrielle, I'll be right in after I have a brief, privileged conversation."

"Keep it brief," Gabrielle said, going back into the room. "Knock when you're ready."

Elliott glanced at the closed door. He said in a very low voice, "Gentlemen, is there anything that could possibly relate to the IRS investigation that you haven't told me?"

Will said, "I can't think of what that might be. Paddy, what about you?"

Paddy shrugged, shaking his head. He wondered what Fourbirds had done to capture Linda Hetherington in the video.

"You're sure?" Elliott asked.

"I am," Will said.

"I'm sure," Paddy said, revealing no concern.

Will's hands were clasped behind him and he rocked back and forth, from his heels to his toes.

"With cable and internet news going 24-7, time has to be filled and anything about Norma is hot," Foxman said.

Paddy hoped a congressman would get caught doing another congressman and divert attention from Norma.

Foxman continued, "Washington has directed both IRS and Justice to look good in this case. They missed Norma's massive fraud until her assistant blew the whistle to divert attention from his own embezzlement. They need to show progress. Coming into this meeting, they weren't very happy. A quick fix would be to throw you guys into the pit."

"Well, guess what," Paddy said. "We aren't happy about it either. We're victims! Fucking victims! Do they understand that? Do they understand we are broke?"

"That's exactly how I pitch it. Now let me do a little selling." Elliott returned to the conference room.

"Paddy, I don't like this. You got us into it. I should have been more diligent, but I relied on you. I'm thinking the worst mistake I made was getting involved with you."

Paddy's blue eyes flashed. He pointed at Will. "Your fucking star had fallen out of Walker & Travis's sky. You checked out your options. You got together with me because you thought it was your best choice, and it fucking was. I'm thinking the worst mistake I made was thinking you weren't such a pussy. Before I got together with your candy ass, I had a million in the bank and a rep as someone to be reckoned with."

Elliott came out. He sensed his clients' tension.

"Relax, guys. I think we're good. Will you both cooperate in all their investigations of Norma and Booker?"

"Sure," Paddy said. "Why wouldn't we?"

"You'll have to waive your Fifth Amendment privilege."

"I ain't got nothin' to hide here," Brooklyn Paddy said, but still the Hetherington case gnawed at him.

"Neither do I," Will said.

"I hope not. That's a big deal to the DOJ. I let them think it was a big deal to you."

"What else?"

"You drop your collection due process appeal and release any claims you might have."

"Will it be a mutual release?" Paddy shot back. Professor Bingo didn't raise no dummy.

"That would be nice, but it doesn't work that way with the government," Elliott laughed. "They will agree not to pursue any criminal or civil fraud penalties against you if nothing new comes up."

"Is that a big deal?" Paddy asked.

"What do you think?" Foxman snapped.

"What else?" Will asked.

"They take fifteen percent of your gross as a deposit on any tax liability you have. You get back eighty-five percent of what they grabbed, and we keep on working on the tax issues."

"The liens?" Will asked.

"Agree to their terms. They're off tomorrow."

Paddy and Will looked at each other.

"Sounds good to me," Will said.

"Amen," Paddy said.

"Fine. Let me go back in there."

About a half hour later, Foxman walked out. He was smiling. "It's a deal."

"That was good, Elliott," Will said.

"Yeah," Paddy chimed in, "those guys listen to you."

"Well, I think they wanted to do the right thing." Foxman's tone had a blend of sarcasm and false humility.

Paddy didn't say what he was thinking, that Foxman was very good at his job and that he made it look easy by controlling the room, the agenda, and the atmosphere without people even realizing what he was doing. He also deferred his ego, at least when he was dealing with the government. It was also Paddy's style to control the room and the agenda, but he did it with a sledgehammer, and his ego was always out front.

Foxman was smooth. Very smooth. He focused on the objective. Paddy would remember that.

"Okay, we have some breathing room," Paddy said.

"You now have the opportunity to catch up with me. You'll have your funds back tomorrow, so you can put up what you agreed plus another fifty thousand."

"What's the fifty thousand for?" Will asked.

"I get success bonuses. It's in the engagement letter. Just remember, guys, you wouldn't have anything to put in your accounts if it wasn't for me." Then, in a firm voice, slightly louder than before, Elliott said "Tomorrow!"

"Look who's got the authoritative voice now," Paddy marveled to himself. "Deal," he said, as much in tribute to Elliott's performance as anything else.

"Keep in mind this only gets you out of the trap. It only allows you to work for them, in a sense. My job is to work on making what you will have to pay them a manageable amount."

Will looked like he was about to burst into tears of relief. For a moment Paddy felt the same way. Maybe Marshall & Moran could leave the bad times behind. But as he drove back to the office, Paddy's stomach clinched tightly. His old man had once told him, "When shit happens, it just keeps happening." He had a sense more shit would happen.

***

SURE ENOUGH, BACK at the office, Winona Wingate was waiting for him without an appointment. She was chewing her gum ferociously and swinging her handbag.

"Hi, darlin'," said Paddy. "How's it going?"

"Don't darlin' me, you dumb fuckup. Get my divorce and custody issues over soon and in my favor or I'm going after your ass."

Paddy sighed. "For what exactly?"

"For trying to show you had the biggest dick instead of doing what I hired you to do."

"Now hold on there, Winona."

"No. I've done everything I can do to calm my husband down. I even gave him a blow job last night. Now do your fucking job."

"I'll do the best I can."

"Don't do the best you can. That's what screwed this up in the first place. Do what I tell you to do."

He put both of his hands up in an "I surrender" pose. "Okay, okay."

"Get back to me by tomorrow." She stalked out, leaving a trail of her overpowering perfume.

Paddy was shaken. He did not need a high-profile bad result.

CHAPTER 56

THINGS ARE NOT GOING WELL WITH PILAR AND VJ

MARSHALL & MORAN'S BANK ACCOUNT crisis occurred one day after VJ told Pilar they were through. The night of the law office crisis, VJ had come home for dinner. He seemed concerned about her. He laughed at her imitation of Paddy. But after the children had been put to bed, he said she was slurring her words. She denied it. Soon, they were fighting again. He called her a drug addict. She called him a judgmental asshole. Things went downhill from there. Pilar popped two more pills. She fell asleep.

The next morning, before she felt fully awake, Pilar studied herself in a mirror. She was thin again. "You'd think that would make him happy," she said aloud. Opening her vanity, she reached toward the back, behind the rows of neatly folded silk underwear. Finding her pill bottles, she grabbed an upper.

She popped it into her mouth and drank some water to wash it down. With closed eyes, she waited for the relief she knew would come. But it didn't. She just kept replaying her fights with VJ.

"We're through," she repeated, staring into the mirror, trying to collect her thoughts. The words VJ had said to her were just beginning to register. The finality in his tone convinced her he knew exactly what he was saying. Pilar felt sadder than she had felt in a very long time.

"I want you to listen to me very closely," he had said last night. "Don't think I didn't really mean it. I do. Repeat after me, 'We're through.'"

"If we're through, what are you doing here?" she'd asked.

"To see for myself, one more time, what you have become. To see for myself that we don't belong together."

She knew no matter how hard she tried, she would never forget his reply.

"What I've become? What I've become? Am I some creature of your creation that escaped? I am what I am. What have *you* become?" She heard herself saying the words, trying to look as if she were putting up a fight. But inside it wasn't like that. She accepted the finality of what he was saying. She knew VJ. She knew challenging him wouldn't work. She had witnessed him making major decisions, seemingly on a whim, and she knew that once he decided something, really decided, he was done. Everything after that was clean-up. He wasn't someone who spent a lot of time looking back.

In that moment, she had become enraged and began screaming and throwing things.

"Thank you, my darling," he said, smugly, "for yet another confirmation." He ducked a Manolo Blahnik pump she hurled at him and left. "Say it. We're through," he said as he closed the door. Remembering, she collapsed on the bed. She fell back asleep almost instantly, as if it had all just been a bad dream.

〰

PILAR STRUGGLED TO HER feet. What was she doing? It was past noon. She needed to get dressed. She glanced about, feeling exhausted and disoriented. Pulling on her robe, she dashed to the children's wing. They weren't there. Her heart started pounding. "Rosa!" she yelled for the housekeeper.

"Si, señora," Rosa appeared.

"*Dondé estan los niños?*"

"*En el campamento.*"

Pilar looked at her watch. At camp, Rosa had said.

"Who took them?"

"Señor."

Her mouth went dry. VJ was already beginning to draw battle lines. He never took the children to camp or to school.

She realized that she could lose them. He could take her children from her. Linda Hetherington's admonition came back to her: "It could happen to you."

Her head was pounding. She managed to locate her cell phone. She speed-dialed Sunny. "Listen," she said when Sunny answered. Her voice breaking, Pilar told her best friend exactly what was going on.

"What do you want to do?" Sunny asked.

"What I want is outside of my control. All I can do is make the best of it being over." She began to sob.

"Shh, shh," Sunny said. "Are you sure it's over? Listen, when I was with you two at the beginning, I never saw a man so obviously in love. My ex never looked at me like that."

"Sure, he did," Pilar said, trying to sound genuine but having flashbacks to how Sunny's ex would hit on her whenever Sunny wasn't around. "Anyway, Sal does. I've seen it."

"Sal—well, maybe. But I know VJ really loved you. If it's over, I guess it's over. What are you going to do about the kids? I mean if he wants the kids? He's rich. Super rich. Super rich people make the rules."

Pilar grew anxious. "You're scaring me."

"Don't panic," Sunny said. "Just be a model mom. You were a great mom before. Be one now."

Pilar hung up, and her body heaved.

TWO HOURS LATER, she was dressed. She had washed her face and combed her hair. She had taken a quarter of a pill. Not enough to knock her out or make her feel like she was floating but enough to keep her from climbing the walls.

When she had signed the prenup, she thought she and VJ would live happily ever after. Her lawyer had told her she hoped so, too, but the agreement was just in case they didn't. If she and VJ turned out not to be part of the Happily-Ever-After Club, Pilar would receive a million dollars for every year they were married. At the time, that was more money than Pilar could even imagine.

That was then. This was now. It was a joke that she was worried about how she was going to live on only four million dollars. She knew she wouldn't have enough to live the lifestyle to which, thanks to VJ, she had become accustomed. She could manage that. It was his dismissal of her with the writing of a check—a check that represented a small fraction of VJ's total fortune—that aroused her to action.

"If I'm going down, it will not be without a fight," she said to herself. She vowed to get off all meds, be a good mom again, and find a good—no, a *great*—lawyer.

At first, she thought of the lawyers who represented VJ's first wife,

Georgie. If she persuaded one of them to represent her, it would drive VJ nuts. But those lawyers were business lawyers, not divorce lawyers. If there was one thing she had learned working at Marshall & Moran, it was that divorce law was a unique area that sometimes required expertise in areas they didn't teach in law school. She thought about calling Margaret Walden, who represented her when she signed the prenup and who had handled her first divorce, the one Paddy had recommended. She was competent. She would certainly look after Pilar's best interests. Margaret Walden was a heavyweight when she kayoed Ronnie's featherweight lawyer. However, taking on VJ wasn't just the big leagues, it was the World Series. Margaret Walden would never make it there. She needed a shark who would stop at nothing, take no prisoners, who wouldn't rest until she had gotten her due and then some. She wanted a lawyer who wouldn't make it just about money, but about respect and fairness. Pilar knew right then who she was going to call. There was no one else.

CHAPTER 57

PADDY INTO THE FRAY

PADDY ANSWERED THE PHONE on the third ring. He was pleased to hear Pilar's voice on the other line. He could tell she was trying to sound casual, which piqued his interest. "I'm planning to come in tomorrow," she said. "Will you have some time to see me on a private matter?"

"Sure thing. Just come straight to my office when you get here."

Although he tried to sound as if he had no idea what Pilar might wish to discuss, the moment she said "personal," Paddy knew exactly why she called. He had to restrain himself from dancing around the room when he hung up. Fate was smiling on him again. This was the dream case that could rescue him. And yet, he felt strangely conflicted.

Pilar was divorcing Mr. Money Bags. Or was he divorcing her? It didn't matter as long as the divorce itself turned into a real battle, and Paddy was willing to bet it would.

On the other hand, he truly cared about Pilar. He knew the pain she must be experiencing now and what was likely to come. That was sad, but he wasn't responsible for her predicament. If she was going to go through it, it would be great for both of them that he represent her. This could be the mother lode but so much would depend on who was the lawyer on the other side.

He considered who might represent VJ. Terry Lyons was a lightweight. VJ might like Bubba Otis, whom Paddy no longer trusted. Magnolia Goldstein was a distinct possibility. He could see how VJ might choose her. The good part of that is she hated Marshall & Moran. The bad part is she might be too restrained. She hated Paddy but not enough to let things get out of hand. She sure wouldn't want to give him a chance to rack up lots of billable hours. Sooner, rather than later, she would be sure to shut everything down.

For the case to be all that he envisioned, everything would have to be choreographed. All morning, Paddy mulled over this problem, laying out scenarios, considering other various possible legal opponents, rejecting them, and moving on.

Then the perfect solution came to him. Perfectly dangerous. Perfectly effective. Perfectly nasty. Guaranteed to succeed if everything fell into place. Will would have to be his opponent.

Will was working from home that day. Paddy called him and said they needed to talk face to face.

Half an hour later, his partner walked into Paddy's office. "What's up?"

Paddy leapt to his feet. Closing the door, he put his finger to his lips. "I have the dream case," he whispered. "Listen carefully. Pilar asked to speak to me about a personal matter first thing tomorrow morning. My guess? She and VJ are splitsville. I am going to represent her."

"When did she engage you?"

"She hasn't, but she will."

"Let's assume you're right. I remember it got around that she signed a prenup, a generous one, but it was supposed to be as tight as a drum."

"Maybe. I haven't seen it yet, but that won't matter because I'll be representing her, and you'll be representing him."

Will's eyes widened. "That's craziness. We're partners. How can we represent both sides in a divorce?"

"We can't now. We're going to split up."

Will mulled this over a moment. He had been thinking of splitting up the firm. Muffy had been urging him for weeks, but he hadn't expected Paddy to be the first to suggest the split. "Why?"

"Why? How about so that we can get all the fees in the biggest divorce-fee case ever? There's no other way to control both sides."

"Seems like a long shot to me. How do you plan to make this work?"

"I'll tell her I would very much like to represent her, but perhaps she should interview some of the other usual suspects. If she does, that will disqualify them to represent him. She'll pick me."

"You sound awfully confident."

"I am. For her, I'm the best possible choice. When she hires me, you and I will immediately have a big blowup and break up our partnership."

"This is going along pretty fast. What's going to keep me from being disqualified, and, more to the point, how do we know VJ will engage me? That's a pretty big leap. He didn't use either one of us before."

"We weren't even in the picture then. Anyway, that was a white shoes divorce."

Will laughed. "You're right," he said. "For all practical purposes, they didn't use lawyers. They used investment bankers. The joke was Goldman Sachs wanted to put a tombstone in *The Wall Street Journal* when the sealed decree of divorce was entered."

"But this one," Paddy said, "is going to be bare knuckles."

"It's really that bitter?"

"I have no idea, but if it's between you and me, we'll make it the bitterest ever."

"So our split up, what'll the animus be?"

Annoyed by Will's unnecessary use of a twenty-five-dollar word, Paddy said in a mocking tone, "The animus will be that we are pissed off at each other over the Norma thing. That will be the animus, asshole."

"Don't be so touchy. After all, we aren't really splitting up."

"Well no one is going to know that other than you and me."

"When it's over, what will happen?"

"We'll kiss and make up. What else?"

At that moment, they were both thinking the same thing. All the negatives of their partnership suddenly filled the front row seats. This breakup, even though feigned, brought a startling feeling of relief.

"If nothing else," Will said, "we've been a bloody great winning team."

There was that British shit again. Geez, where did Will even come up with that stuff? "Yes, we have, Will. It's been good for me. It'll be good again. But this will be our finest hour. It's a shame no one will know about it."

He thought Will would appreciate the "finest hour" shit. He was right.

Will grinned and shook Paddy's hand. "Our finest hour," he repeated.

CHAPTER 58

VJ AND PILAR CHOOSE GLADIATORS

THE MORNING VJ LEFT THE BEDROOM, dodging a shoe, he was filled with a sense of challenge. One thing he knew about was winning. And he needed to position himself for a win.

His first maneuver was to sit down for a rare breakfast with his children—pancakes and oatmeal—which he cooked himself. Then he took them to day camp, an experience so new for him he had to learn the name of the camp and find out where it was. He knew Pilar would come undone when she saw he had taken the children. Using them in this way made him feel like a heel, but shouldn't he have been spending more time with his children all along? Wasn't that what good fathers did? He watched Gracie and Raj Benjamin bound from the car, skipping down the path to camp. He tooted his horn. They both turned. Grace blew him a kiss. He loved them. Suddenly, he recalled the days when he and Pilar first began having telephone conversations. Sometimes she would ask him to wait while she talked to Grace. He had never heard anyone else talk so lovingly to a child. Then, an image flashed through his mind of Pilar pushing Grace through the park in a battered old stroller.

VJ was growing disconcerted. These thoughts were inconsistent with his current plan of action. He focused on Pilar as she was now. She was pathetic. She would be no match for him in a legal battle.

꧁꧂

THE MINUTE HE GOT to his office, he called his lawyer.

"Read the prenup. Tell me if there's any way to break it."

He got a call back. "It's iron-clad."

"Are you telling me that because your firm prepared it?"

"I'm telling you that because it's true," the lawyer replied.

"So there's no way it can be broken?"

"Iron-clad documents have been broken. In fact, it happens too often. What I'm telling you is that this prenup is as well drafted as a prenup can be."

"You are telling me a court might not enforce it, right?"

Ben Trost emitted an audible sigh, the sigh of someone who feared that his most important client, his most prestigious client, the client who paid him the most fees, the client who resulted in the most referrals, was going to be unhappy with him.

"Ben, tell me, am I right?" VJ repeated.

Trost said with resignation, "VJ, everything was done to make this airtight. She had her own lawyer. Pilar and her attorney both signed it and ratified it. The agreement provides your wife a million dollars for every year of marriage, an amount we figured a jury in Harris County, Texas, would surely think was generous. There are no flies on this document. But that doesn't mean that something can't happen in the courthouse."

"How do we keep something from happening?"

Again, the words were a question, but the voice was a statement. "We get the best family lawyer to represent you."

"And that's not you?"

"No, I'm a corporate lawyer. But it also isn't anyone in my firm. I wouldn't want to be in the position of having to defend an agreement we had prepared. I think that's a definite conflict of interest."

VJ considered what Trost had said. He felt his years of trust and confidence in Trost had been validated by that remark. However, he decided now was not the time for compliments.

"Who do you recommend?"

"I have my initial thoughts, but let me make sure."

"When?"

"Later today or tomorrow."

VJ paused. He considered giving Trost some assurances about their relationship. Then he decided it was too soon. "This is a priority," he said.

Trost's shoulders slumped. He had lost more clients by referring them to divorce lawyers they ended up hating than by not pleasing clients with his own work. He wouldn't want to blow this one.

PILAR FILLED SUNNY'S MUG with green tea and then her own and set the teapot on an owl-shaped trivet between them.

"You don't want to stay with him then?" asked Sunny.

Pilar replied in a voice so low Sunny had to strain to hear her. "To be honest, I'd like to get myself together again, go back to being who I was, and try to see if he and I could be like we were before. He hasn't changed. Well, maybe a little, but the problem is me." She thought about confessing to Sunny about the pills. Knowing Sunny, she probably had it figured out anyway.

"Why don't you just see if you can get him back? You're owning up to your problems. Won't he give you a chance?"

"Trust me—that's not an option. I need to make the best deal I can and go on with my life." Pilar's voice wobbled slightly. "I need a lawyer to try to get me more than I get under that stupid prenup. There's really just one I would trust to help me: Paddy Moran."

"Your boss?" Sunny asked. "Well, I did some research when you started working for him. I think you're right. Paddy Moran, if you can get his attention and keep it, would be the best."

"He has a terrible reputation, but that's what makes him so good."

"What do you mean terrible?"

"I mean," Sunny said, "people say he stoops to anything to win."

Pilar remembered her encounter with Linda Hetherington. "VJ is very competitive. He doesn't like to appear so, but he always is. If he feels challenged, he responds in spades. I don't think it would be good if Paddy stirs him up."

"Just remember, the lawyer works for you. Keep him reined in. And," Sunny added in a stern tone, "start getting your act together, girl."

Pilar gulped. "I'm trying."

PILAR TOOK A HOT SHOWER. Then she dressed carefully in business attire. She applied her makeup sparingly but enough to accentuate her dark brown eyes.

When she walked into Paddy's office, she could tell her appearance impressed him.

"Pilar, wow, you look . . . what's up?"

"Paddy, I'm seeing you in a professional capacity. VJ and I are having serious problems. We may be getting a divorce. I want you to be my lawyer, but only if we get a few things straight."

He decided to skip his usual speech about trying to work it out.

"Sure. Sure."

"First, you have to get my approval before you take *any* action. I know my husband well."

"What do you mean?" Paddy asked.

"I have a line in mind. I'll know when you're about to cross it. You have to check with me about everything you're planning. No surprises."

Paddy narrowed his eyes. He didn't like what he was hearing, especially in this case when having control was everything, but winning her as a client was more important.

"Well, sometimes I have to act quickly."

"I'll make myself available anytime."

"Pilar, you came to me, I am guessing, because you wanted the best. Is that right?"

"Yes, that's right."

"You have to trust my judgment."

Pilar decided not to mention how Paddy's going overboard had backfired on Winona Wingate. "Suppose you were the world's greatest person at defusing land mines."

"Yeah, okay."

"And suppose I hired you to defuse land mines on my property."

"Yeah?" Paddy said, wondering to himself where she was going with this.

"If I know where the land mines are, you should know what I know before you start walking around."

She smiled at him. He had never seen that exact smile before. It was close to the one she'd given him when he first met her, in his old office, with her baby and her black eye. The smile widened. Paddy suddenly felt dizzy. He understood how VJ had fallen for her. He took a deep breath to calm himself. "Don't shit where you eat," his father had said, when Paddy talked about how good looking a new lady cop was. His father's advice was given seldom or with that much tenderness.

"I understand. You know your husband. I'll check with you. You made your point very well. I'm impressed."

She smiled again. This time it was a different smile. "Now, about the fee. VJ pays it, right?"

"That's the way it usually works, but I've been told you have a prenup, and I haven't read it yet."

"I do have a prenup."

"You also have three kids."

"Grace, the oldest, VJ adopted after he paid Ronnie to give up his parental rights. Raj Benjamin and Moises are his with me. I want more than the prenuptial says I am supposed to get, and I want full custody of my children."

"I'll dissect the prenup word by word. If I get you more, I want to be paid for the result. I want a percentage of the excess over and above my hourly fee."

"If you can't get me more, why should you get anything?"

She was one sharp cookie. Her comment reminded him of a similar conversation with Estelle Cook.

"There is plenty of work to be done. Plenty. How did you select the lawyer who represented you when you signed the prenup?"

"Her? I used Margaret Walden. You sent me to her."

"So I did. She's pretty damn good. What did Margaret say about the prenup?"

"Basically, she said that on the one hand it was pretty generous for someone in my present circumstances, and that there was no other hand because they had made it absolutely clear that they would not change one word."

"And your response was?"

"I didn't care. I loved him so much. He was so good to me. I would have signed anything because he had already given me what no other man had, what no other person had, certainly not my parents. He made me feel good about myself. He made me feel like I was a good person, a smart person, a good mother, a person worthy of someone like him. Until I met him, I was worried about making my two-hundred-dollar car payment, about making it from one month to the next."

"And now?"

Pilar realized Paddy would never understand it really wasn't about the money. She shifted her position in the chair. "Are you kidding? He spends more than a million for a work of art all the time. Do you know what it costs to run our house for a month?"

"No. How much?" Paddy asked.

"I have no idea. A lady in his office writes the checks. There's no mortgage payment. He paid cash for the house."

"You run our office, but you don't run your own house?"

"Do you have any complaints about how the office is run?" Her tone was suddenly icy and professional.

"No," he said, pulling back.

"It's like I was saying, before I met VJ, there was rent, groceries, car payments, phone, electric, clothes, cable. If there was anything left over, maybe pizza and a movie and happy hour with my friend Sunny. Now, if I buy a dress, even on sale, it costs more than I used to make in a month." She waited for Paddy to absorb what she had told him.

"He knew that would happen," he said. "He knew that in no time at all you would be used to a lifestyle where a million dollars was nothing."

Paddy studied her. She could have been anything from being on a building maintenance night crew to the bride of the president of Mexico or a movie star or in C-level management of a big company. She was here by her will, hard work, looks, and as he saw it, one opportunity she made the most of. It would be a mistake to underestimate her. It would be a mistake not to listen to her.

They were not so different. Both had come up from nothing. Both were playing in a league no one expected them to be in, including themselves.

"Let's break it down," Paddy said. "You're telling me that based on your background and previous life experience, you thought that the prenuptial agreement was not only fair but generous."

"Yes," she said.

"But you were about to change to a lifestyle you hadn't dreamed of and that you could not come close to maintaining if all you had was what was coming to you under the provisions in the prenup."

"Yes. I do think his advisors had thought it out the way you describe. But I don't think VJ was focused on that. I think he was just like me. He thought we would be together forever."

"Come on, Pilar. His advisors work for him. You're not telling me you really believe that horseshit!"

Pilar glared at Paddy. She looked like she was about to cry. It was clear she still loved the guy.

"Do you remember if you signed another document affirming the prenup after you married?"

"I signed it the day we got back from our wedding trip, our honeymoon."

"At that time, nothing had really changed. You hadn't begun to live the life of being Mrs. VJ Simon."

"*Correcto.*"

"I have an idea." Paddy furrowed his brow as he talked to her, looking directly into her eyes. "I think that I have a fighting chance, a good one, to break the prenup on the legal theory that he misled you by causing you to enter into the agreement by putting in an amount of money that would appear to you to be not just adequate, but generous, even though he knew it would be totally inadequate to maintain your new lifestyle."

She could see the pride in his face. He didn't realize she had steered him so that he thought that was his idea. She waited to see if anything else occurred to him, but he was silent. "Right," Pilar said. "Totally." She got up. As she was leaving, she turned and said, "You might also consider that it would not be in the best interests of the children to have to go from one lifestyle to another when VJ has his visitation rights."

"Right."

CHAPTER 59

CHOICES

PADDY'S BREAKUP WITH WILL was reported on the front page of the *Chronicle* under Gloria Goforth's byline. At Paddy's urging, Will gave it to her so she could scoop TMZ. Paddy wanted the attention of the larger readership of the *Houston Chronicle*, but he didn't want TMZ to blame him for getting scooped. Norma had been a front-page story readers couldn't get enough of, so the connection to Norma, as well as their high-profile legal practice, made page one news: "Divorce Kings Go Splitsville" was the headline.

"The partners who wrote the book on the high cost of leaving your spouse have broken up themselves. Will Marshall and Paddy Moran's law partnership is over. Confidential sources say the relationship got rocky when they discovered they were victims of Norma Nambé's Ponzi scheme and then became irreconcilable when that spilled over to their well-publicized problems with the IRS.

"They are also at the center of the bitter election campaign between sitting judge Hector Elizondo and Linda Hetherington. Will Marshall would not comment on that. He would only tell this reporter that he and Moran had personal differences. Moran was not available before press time. A confidential source said problems between the two had been building up and that the recent difficulties with the IRS were the last straw. The breakup appears to be bitter. It will certainly be interesting to see them battle each other. I bet it won't be long."

Except for mentioning the Elizondo-Hetherington campaign, the article was just what Paddy and Will wanted.

THE NEXT MORNING, Paddy got a telephone call from Margot, who was still in France.

"Hi, sweetheart," he said. "You heard about Norma swindling me, and you're calling to say 'I told you so'?"

"No. That's not my style."

"I didn't think so. You heard Will and I broke up?"

"No, I didn't," she said.

Puzzled at her unfriendly tone, he asked, "Why did you call?"

"Tell me about the Hetherington case," Margot said, sounding like his first-grade teacher when she caught him doing something wrong.

"She's a nut."

"If she's a nut, you made her a nut," Margot snapped. He had not heard her use that tone since she challenged him the day they first met, except this time it was nasty, too. His stomach tightened.

"What do you mean?"

"I read about her announcement, so I called and talked to her. You did it, didn't you? You had someone get her doped up and made it look like she was having sex with a woman next to her daughter's bedroom so that your client could win custody of her child."

"Do you really believe I would do that, Margot?"

"I would like not to, but my gut tells me it's very possible you did just that. Will you level with me? Is what she is saying true?" Margot asked.

Paddy pursed his lips, squinted, and said, "The honest to gawd truth is, I don't know for sure."

There was silence.

"My guess is she pretty much has it right."

"Paddy, I hired you to take my case because you were hungry, you were smart, and you were resourceful. I loved the way you relished the challenge of the little guy taking on the big guy."

He thought back to that time. It hadn't hurt that he had nothing interesting going on then, had little to lose and, of course, she was beautiful and higher in social strata than anyone else he knew. Doing a good job for her could launch his career into a higher orbit and, in fact, it did. That's how he got the Cook case. By the time Hetherington came in, he was playing on a very different field.

"Actually, it's because you were such a sexy babe."

"Not the right time to say that," she said. "What you did to that Hetherington woman was wrong. It was just plain wrong."

"Her husband hired me to accomplish an objective, and I did, just like I did for you. Case closed."

"You don't get it, do you?"

"Get what?"

"You crossed the line," she said.

He knew he had. He could not count the times he relived his reaction to her not answering the phone that night and how it spurred him to make a decision he knew was wrong. He wanted to say, "Why didn't you answer your fucking phone? I had a chance to make a really big splash and I needed your filter. I got what I thought I wanted—a giant win on a huge platform and respect—and nothing's been the same since, for better and for worse."

Aloud he said to Margot, "I did it because I owed a duty to my client."

"I'm surprised you didn't gag on that one," Margot snapped. "If you had a duty, it was to refuse that spoiled, arrogant no-good as a client. What you pulled on Linda Hetherington and what you did with the judge—you really think I would believe you did those things in furtherance of your duty to your client? You heard the siren song of a higher calling for Randy Hetherington? Paddy, Paddy, Paddy. Shame on you. Nobody sins for somebody else."

The way she said "sins" evoked a sense of dread he had not felt since he was a child. "If you were the client, what would you have done?"

"I would have stopped you."

He felt a chill. He remembered his concern the night Fourbirds told him he had a plan. How he and Mick had driven around nearly all night. He had been just thinking, sometimes speaking out loud to Mick as if he might answer.

"I'm getting off the phone," Margot said. "I'm going to get back with Linda Hetherington and make a generous contribution to her campaign."

He said nothing. He felt like shit, but he would not apologize or ask anything of her.

"And, there's something else. Remove me from all your contact lists. And in those dark moments, when you don't know who else to call, don't call me." After a pause, she said, "We're finished."

He knew it before she said it, and he felt more internal pain than he could recall in his entire adult life.

"Margot—"

Paddy heard the click on the other end of the line. "Crazy bitch," he said out loud, but he couldn't really think of Margot as crazy or a bitch, and she wasn't wrong. There was no way he would have won the Hetherington case fair and square. The fix was in. Knowing his big show trial was a fraud haunted him. Now it had cost him Margot. Needing to obliterate his sense of loss and guilt, he grabbed a bottle of Irish whiskey from the liquor cabinet. He didn't bother with a glass. He sat in his recliner, called the dog over, turned on a *Riverdance* video with the volume all the way up, opened the bottle and drank.

BEN TROST STEWED. He hated having to recommend an attorney for VJ. He had gone through the same process for himself. He had chosen Will Marshall because of his big-firm pedigree and because he had managed to reach the top echelon of the divorce lawyers. He thought it was a plus that Will brought in Paddy to brainstorm. While it was going on, he experienced an almost prurient pleasure turning the screws on his ex-wife and her lawyer. It was as if he was someone else. Now, thinking back, he felt shame. He had won. It wasn't a fair fight. Her lawyer was a family friend, competent but outmatched, and his ex didn't deserve the treatment she received.

Will was a gladiator. His social demeanor was different than his practice demeanor. Yet, in Ben's mind, in a sense, despite their surface differences, Will and Paddy were a matched pair. Trost did see a difference. He thought what Paddy got from his practice was all about ego. He didn't know enough about Paddy to guess what in his past drove him, but he felt pretty sure he was right. Paddy didn't mind being recognized for who and what he was—he accepted it as part of the territory. The way Trost saw it, Paddy was committed. On the other hand, Trost believed Will was all about the money, and that made him a complete cynic in his practice. It occurred to him that Paddy may have more humanity. Will checked it at the office, and Paddy took it home with him. From what Trost could tell, Will had convinced himself that he was not the person who ramped up cases to justify padded hours and used his connections to curry favor with judges, opponents, and referrers. Instead, Will always saw himself as the person he believed he was meant to be, and his practice was just a temporary sideshow to unwind from the anomalous circumstance of having inherited a social position without the money to sustain it. Will's partnership with Paddy allowed him to enjoy a lifestyle to which both he and Muffy believed they were entitled.

Despite Will's attitude of being above it all, Trost had no doubt he had probably learned every trick in Paddy Moran's playbook. If VJ really wanted to win—at all costs—Will would be the right man for him. Still, he thought he should sleep on it, which was a practice he had learned from VJ. And if Pilar hired Paddy, he would find someone else. He had heard Magnolia Goldstein was effective and perhaps even principled. He wasn't sure if that was a plus or a minus.

〰

TROST CALLED VJ the next morning.

"I'll give you two choices," he said. "Magnolia Goldstein and Will Marshall. I lean toward Marshall."

"It is very interesting that you would mention Marshall. My wife is the office manager of Marshall's law firm. Second, the front page of the *Chronicle* reported his law partnership was breaking up. What do you suppose the dissolution of their partnership means?"

"Frankly, I'm not entirely sure. It's a little too quick for me to handicap. Paddy and Will were pretty formidable together. But I think Will would be the very best for you. He may act like an effete social butterfly, but he plays very brutally in his practice. It's true he was born with a silver spoon in his mouth, but the spoon tarnished when his father lost all the family money. He's had to work hard for everything he has."

"I read in the paper that not only did he lose everything with Norma, but he may have a big IRS debt."

"Well, his being hungry is a double-edged sword. He'll probably get to you on his fees, but I'm sure he'd be trying very hard to prove he doesn't need Moran to win for his clients, especially if the split with Moran is bitter."

VJ drummed his fingers on his desk. "Why don't I want Moran? My friend Margot Shear thinks he is a great lawyer."

"That's a fair question." Trost paused.

"Are you there?" VJ asked.

"I was thinking about your question. Here is my answer. One, Will Marshall is a known quantity to me. He was my lawyer in my divorce, although Moran pitched in. Two, I think you'll be able to relate to him better. That's just a guess, because you relate to everyone well."

VJ knew Trost well enough to know he wasn't fawning.

"The other reason is that Moran has an absolutely terrible reputation when it comes to legal ethics."

"Let me understand this. You recommend Marshall, who until maybe yesterday was Moran's partner, but Moran is unethical and Marshall is not. That's a conundrum, is it not?"

"Indeed it is," Trost responded. "I suppose it gets down to perception and appearances."

"To me it gets down to who will do the best job for me."

"You say that, but I know how important your reputation is to you. I say go with Will."

"And Magnolia Goldstein?"

"She would be an interesting choice."

"Why is her name familiar to me?"

"Probably because you wrote a check to her. We brought her in to review your divorce decree and settlement with Georgie to make sure we didn't miss anything in the Family Law Code."

"You don't seem inclined to recommend her."

"She's different. She works hard. She's smart and shrewd."

"I'm waiting for the downside."

"The judges don't like her. She makes them work too hard. She's diligent. She demands a record of every objection she makes that is not sustained."

"And?"

"And she appeals when she loses and frequently wins her appeals."

"And?"

"She doesn't settle easily so when a case goes to trial, the judges have long memories of being reversed, so they don't exercise much non-appealable discretion in her favor."

"You're saying she's not a good ol' boy?"

"I'm saying that."

"Sounds like a match made in heaven. I want to interview her."

CHAPTER 60

VJ HAS TO MAKE A CHOICE

HOUSTON WAS AGOG to see what would become of the famous Marshall & Moran offices. Neither Will nor Paddy moved out. Pilar coordinated the transition. Paddy took the ladies' reception area and conference room and Will took the men's. The reception area out front was the DMZ, serving both of them. If one called the old phone number, the receptionist answered with the telephone number. If someone asked for Will, she said, "His new telephone number is 713-DIVORCE, but I will connect you." If someone asked for Paddy, she said, "His new telephone number is 832-DIVORCE, but I will connect you."

There had been some contention about who got which area code. Will thought he was entitled to 713 because Houston's first area code was part of his legacy. Typical Will. Neither wanted 281. Paddy gave on that one.

Nearly every day both TMZ and Gloria Goforth in the *Chronicle* had an item about one or the other of them. In their split they were even more media-fascinating than they had been as partners.

Will and Paddy were never seen speaking to each other. They communicated business matters by letter or memo. Their secretaries acted as intermediaries to handle administrative issues and other aspects of their having been partners, such as making sure only one remained as attorney of record in any pending cases. Houston watched. Surely one day it would boil over.

VJ's secretary called Will for an appointment and requested the appointment be at VJ's office. Will realized this was an early test of who was going to control the relationship. He believed the issue was critical. VJ was powerful, used to giving orders. For Paddy's and Will's plan to succeed, VJ pretty much had to give Will free rein. But if VJ didn't hire him in the first place, then the plan meant nothing. Will capitulated.

Will arrived at the top floor of the Simon Capital Building. He had been to offices of many wealthy people before. Never before, however, had he seen offices like these. Nothing was overstated. Everything appeared to be exactly where it was supposed to be. The effect wasn't ostentatious, but it was breathtaking.

He announced himself to the receptionist who sat behind an elegant curved wood banquette. She appeared to be Indian. Her accent was English.

"I'll tell Mr. Simon you are here."

Moments later a young Asian man entered the reception area and walked toward Will.

"Mr. Marshall, come with me, please."

Will entered a room dominated by high-definition screens. The first one he noticed was a Bloomberg political terminal. The war room at Norma's office came to mind. However, he knew this one was for real. Whatever was going on in the world that might be at the cutting edge of business was beamed into this room at dizzying speeds. Seated at a half-moon desk, positioned so that by wheeling his chair he could see each monitor, was VJ Simon. He had on a Polo shirt that had been washed more than a few times. His hair was a bit askew, revealing some thinning. Facing Will, he motioned to one of two armchairs in front of him. Will sat down. The chair proved less comfortable than it looked. The young Asian man sat in the other armchair. Will had taken the seat before he realized that Simon had not extended his hand.

"Mr. Simon—" Will realized it was pointless to introduce himself. He felt uncomfortable. He began sorting things in his mind. Since he and Paddy weren't supposed to be speaking to each other, he couldn't know that Pilar had engaged Paddy. Since it was not otherwise known Simon and Pilar were having problems, Will could not let on he knew why the appointment had been made. He told himself to relax. "Mr. Simon," he repeated, "you called this meeting."

"Yes, I have a document I want you to read." He handed Will the prenuptial agreement.

"I want you to tell me if a court will enforce it as it is written."

Will knew this was a test. Despite Simon's unprepossessing appearance, his presence exuded power and magnetism. Will would have to avoid falling under his spell. "You understand that Pilar has been our office manager."

"Mr. Marshall, please answer my question."

"My guess is I will probably give you the same answer after reviewing it that I can give you before reading it."

VJ didn't respond.

"Mr. Simon, are you planning to engage me?"

"I am certainly considering it."

"I'm sure you are aware of attorney-client privilege."

"I'm aware of that concept."

"It can be lost if someone who is not within the privilege is privy to the communications."

"You mean Ross, here?"

"Yes."

"Ross doesn't practice law, but he is a licensed attorney. I value his judgment. He'll probably participate in any meetings we have."

Will nodded. He felt challenged. He needed to come out of this with VJ and Ross having confidence in him. "Would you like me to look at this agreement now?"

"If you would be comfortable with that."

"Certainly," Will said. "I may want to do some research, but I don't have a problem looking at it now to see what my initial reaction is."

"Very well. Ross, please show Mr. Marshall to the small conference room."

VJ recalled he had first seen Pilar in that conference room. He called to Will as he was leaving.

"Mr. Marshall, anything you hear or see about my business doesn't leave these offices. If it does, you could be violating securities laws, confidentiality agreements, and more. Do you understand that?"

"That goes without saying."

"I have found that things that go without saying often need to be said."

Smarting from VJ's jab, Will got comfortable in the conference room and studied the document. It was drafted well. No surprise there. The language was plain. He admired that. It was signed by Pilar and her lawyer, Margaret Walden. It included Pilar's acknowledgement that her attorney had explained the document to her and she understood it.

It looked enforceable. Will knew he was about to reach the first of what might be one of many make-or-break tests of his relationship with VJ.

Will returned to VJ's office and said, "Mr. Simon."

VJ turned to face Will, "Mr. Marshall—"

"Will," Will interjected.

"Will." VJ Simon did not invite Will to call him "VJ."

"I've taken an initial look at the agreement."

VJ didn't respond.

Will looked straight into VJ's eyes. "I'm going to give you a lawyer's answer."

No response.

"This is a well-written agreement. The language is not ambiguous. Your lawyer did a fine job. I believe we both know, however, what happens in court or even a settlement negotiation cannot be predicted with certainty."

"Are you telling me that she can get more than it says she can get in that agreement?"

"I am telling you that's a possibility." Will let that percolate for a few seconds. "Ask the lawyers who prepared it. They would probably say the same thing." Will straightened his back as he buttoned his suit coat.

VJ wondered if Trost had prepared him for that question.

"You will probably find a lawyer who'll assure you he can make it stick. If it turns out he's wrong, he'll have a valid rationalization for the result. He might be right. It might stick. I'm telling you it might stick. I am also telling you, it might not."

"Tell me about you and Mr. Moran."

"What do you want to know?"

"Why aren't you together?"

"There's no one reason. It has been brewing."

"Suppose I engage you and my wife engages him—won't there be a conflict?"

Will's heart raced even though he had anticipated the question. "Technically, there's no conflict. We're no longer partners." He changed his posture so that he was even more erect from his tailbone to the top of his head.

"You said 'technically,'" Ross interjected.

Will hoped to portray more self-confidence than he really had. "We're not partners. We divided our offices. We try to avoid seeing or talking to each other. But it hasn't been very long. I can see why you would be concerned, Mr. Simon."

"What if you kiss and make up?" VJ asked.

"That's not going to happen," Will said. His response was quick. His tone was resolute.

"You sound sure," VJ said.

"I'm sure." Will said. "Has your wife hired Moran?"

"I don't even know if she's talked to a lawyer. I told her it was over, so, if she has, I wouldn't be surprised. Moran knows your tricks, doesn't he?"

"I know his better than he knows mine."

"How can that be?" VJ asked.

Will found himself saying out loud things he had long held inside. "It's in the difference between our natures. Paddy likes to brag. To me, he's transparent. It's his ego. I am rarely surprised by him."

"He was just as close to you as you were to him. Can't he read you?"

"He probably could if he set his mind to it, but he didn't while we were partners. Frankly, I think he discounted my abilities."

VJ nodded.

Ross nodded.

Will noted the nods. He could tell that his response must have been consistent with their scouting reports and conclusions.

"Why did you stay partners?" VJ asked.

"It worked for both of us. We both brought important qualities to the table."

"Will we have an edge?"

Easy. Easy. Don't overplay it, Will said to himself. Aloud he said, "People like me always think they're the best. Moran's the same. That's a trait in the best of breed. The fact is, he and I are both going to try to outdo the other, to get the best of the other. The difference is, I think I know how to beat him at his game."

VJ frowned. Ross crossed and uncrossed his legs. VJ said, "I don't want to have to pay while the two of you are trying to prove whose dick is bigger."

Will noted VJ was intentionally using a profanity outside his usually proper vocabulary.

"This will not be about you and him. Do you understand that?"

Will stiffened. Assuming his best righteous indignation posture, he said, "Mr. Simon, I'm a professional. I would like to think that I wouldn't let my differences with Mr. Moran interfere with my duty to you or any other client. If you ever think that's happening, tell me. But please understand every engagement is a contest. If Moran represents Pilar, he'll have to create confusion and diversion to distract from the plain meaning of the prenup. If I'm representing you, he'll have something to prove in addition to winning."

"Aren't you saying it will cost me more money to engage you?"

"It may, but you'll benefit because I'll try even harder than I normally do."

"You mean you don't always give your best?" VJ was taunting him.

Will's stride was not broken. "Not every case merits pulling out all the stops. I don't play those cards unless it's necessary. When it is, I have to take actions that fan emotions and cost more money. My guess is your divorce is going to be one of those, no matter who the lawyers are. It's human nature to get even more up for the big game. You're famous and wealthy. Your divorce will be news. If Moran represents your wife and I represent you, it will be a very high-profile matter."

"Doesn't that suggest that if she hires him, I shouldn't hire you, because this thing will just escalate?"

"That's your call," Will said, proud of himself for not being too eager. He let the silence linger before he spoke. "But," he continued, "I would say no, because he's going to turn it up anyway. He has to override the prenup. I don't think he's going to do that by just writing briefs. If in fact she does engage him, no one would be better for you than me." Will focused on his breathing. "The difference is, maybe he's going to underestimate me. He thinks his street smarts make him more effective than I am. I'm not going to underestimate him. But you need to understand that he's very good."

"That's my understanding."

"It's going to go back and forth. She was a gold digger. You took advantage of her. She's an awful mother. You're an awful father. Et cetera. Et cetera. Et cetera. Plus, there's something else." Will paused. Again, VJ did not fill the silence with words. Will realized this time his own silence tactic that worked on nearly everyone else didn't work on either VJ or Ross.

Will broke the silence. "On the surface, it seems simple. Either the agreement is enforced or it isn't. If it's enforced, what's left is custody and child support. If it's not enforced, then it's about how much more she gets. That could be as much as half of what you've made since you were married."

VJ breathed deeply. He had made a lot in the relatively short time they were married.

"The legal costs in this case are either going to be very expensive, or very, very expensive. Paddy and I would each do what we can to make the other's client look bad."

"That's necessary because?" Ross asked.

Will turned to Ross. "Positioning. Putting Mr. Simon in the best position to accomplish his objectives. We're either going to react to Moran or we're going to make him react to us."

"Moran or whomever she uses," Will added.

"You haven't even asked me what my objectives are," VJ said.

"You've told me you want to enforce the prenup."

"Yes. In my world, a deal's a deal. She and I made a deal."

"Okay. What about the children?"

"I want what's best for them."

"What's that?"

The Hetherington case crossed VJ's mind. After a long silence, he said, "We'll talk about that if I engage you."

"What if while you are deciding your wife comes to see me?" Will asked.

"She may come to see you, Mr. Marshall, but she won't hire you."

"You seem awfully sure about that."

"I have mastered dealing with the well-born, their affectations, and their condescending airs. I had to do that for a long time because I needed people like that to invest with me. Pilar would not put her trust in you, not like your carriage-trade clients do."

"Why would she trust Moran?"

"I know that you believe you've had to work for everything you have, and, by the way, I respect how you accepted responsibility for yourself after your family's money was gone and how you assessed your situation when your mentor, James Cook, imploded and with him your chances for success at Walker & Travis. I really do."

"The man does his homework," Will thought.

"But Moran came from a poor, Irish family. He grew up in a seedy tenement in Brooklyn. He clawed his way to where he is now. That's something Pilar can relate to. He won't be able to fool her. But she'll have a certain comfort with him that she'd never have with you because his roots aren't so different from hers."

As Will absorbed this, he better understood what made VJ so successful. Compilation of data followed by thoughtful analysis. Impressive. "Understood," Will said.

"So how would you proceed with the case?"

"Obviously, I certainly haven't worked out an entire game plan. We have to assume they will attack the prenup. My thought is we go for an early knockout by filing for a summary judgment on the basis that the prenup is clear and unambiguous and should be enforced as written. They have to get past that. Texas courts are pretty good about enforcing prenups that satisfy the statutory requirements. Your wife's attorney is going to have an uphill battle. If the judge doesn't grant our motion for summary judgment, he or she will still need to convince a jury that it should go beyond the plain, clear language of the prenup."

"Can that happen?"

"It could. If it does we would appeal. Assuming it gets all the way to an appeal, the odds are definitely with us. Her attorney will have to make new law. Paddy and I have made new law before. There are no guarantees it won't happen here. Chances are it would be over way before an appeal would be final."

"Why?"

"Because you probably won't want to wait that long. She won't want to wait that long. No one will want to wait that long."

"And me. Why won't I wait?"

"With you, it will depend on what is at stake."

"I'm impressed so far, Mr. Marshall. You make a lot of sense. With me, it will not be the time. I have time. It will not be, I don't think, an issue of me having to defeat her. Although there must be some of that. Foolish, huh? But I think what may concern me most is a risk. Not the risk of costing me money. The risk of losing and having my name synonymous with her victory—the "Simon case," like Miranda. That's not how I wish to be remembered. My name is on a concert hall. There's a business school named for me and a hospital wing in the medical center. I don't want the Simon case to be part of my legacy, win or lose."

Will hadn't expected him to be so candid. It opened the door for a settlement—and it wouldn't be a small one. Paddy had a contingency and . . . well. That'll be good for all.

"Mr. Marshall. I know who you are. I know about your practice methods. You've said you are a professional, so I'm sure we both hope that I will respect you for the job you will do for me. That will be even better for you than for me."

Will had a feeling VJ was playing him again. This client was not going to be easy. To get through it, Will, and Paddy, in turn, would have to play it perfectly. If Will lost VJ's trust, it could be very serious. He needed to close the sale.

"Mr. Simon," he piped up, "I'm truly honored that you're considering engaging me. I work for people in one of their most unhappy circumstances. It's hard on them and, whether or not you believe it, it's hard on me, as well. I'll try to help you get through this as best I can, with as much of your money and your pride and your peace of mind intact as possible."

"Spare me that, please, Mr. Marshall. I have children. There's no question that they'll be well provided for. I'd like them not to be scarred by this process. As for my wife, the money that she has coming to her under that agreement is more than she dreamed we would ever have before we married."

"I'll do my best," Will said. "I'll start off with a more careful review of the prenup."

"Why don't you start by calling Ben Trost? He made a careful legal analysis at the time the agreement was prepared and has done so again, recently."

"Excellent. He's a brilliant lawyer," Will responded.

"Yes, he is, and he recommended you. You may send me an engagement letter. Send a copy to Mr. Trost, too. How much of a retainer are you going to ask for?"

Will named a very large amount to be paid up front.

"If I engage you, I'll pay you half of what you asked for your retainer. And if I'm pleased with your services when it is over, twice that amount at the end."

"Your reputation precedes you. I trust you, and I accept the challenge, Mr. Simon."

Will was used to wealthy clients. He usually created a relationship balanced in his favor from the outset because the playing field was his and not theirs. This time his client would be a man with an air that made him the captain of any field. Ego drove James Cook to manage his own divorce. That wasn't what was going on here. It was VJ's ability to listen, to gather information, process, and with a taller, wider view than everyone else, make intelligent, informed decisions.

"Fine."

Considering the tone of VJ's voice, Will knew he would be working hard for every dollar he earned. "Well, then. Done," Will said.

VJ was amused by Will's British affectation.

"Where are we in terms of your relationship with your wife?"

"I'm still living at the house. I told her I wanted a divorce. I'm not sure she really believes me. If nothing else, she's alert to the possibility."

Will nodded, a concerned look on his face. By not saying anything, he would let VJ conjure up his own assessment of any damage he had done.

"I want the cards stacked in my favor to have a better chance to have the agreement enforced and better positioned regarding my children."

"It would've been better if you hadn't tipped her off."

VJ didn't miss a beat. "Pilar is not dumb. She knows our relationship has deteriorated. She has enough lucid moments to know she needs to anticipate something."

"Lucid moments?"

"Pilar has a substance abuse problem. She went from alcohol to prescription drugs."

"I wasn't aware of that. I never saw any evidence of that at the office."

"Apparently she can hold it together when she has to, but she has certainly been a mess at home."

"I suggest you move out."

"Why?"

"Why do you want to keep living with someone you want to divorce?"

"For the children."

"If you have a problem seeing the children, let me know. If you are concerned about how the children are being cared for, let me know. Move out."

"Well," VJ said, "she and I are from different generations."

Not quite sure what VJ meant by this, Will seized on the remark as an opportunity to solidify his relationship with him by showing he understood how different the man was from his soon-to-be ex-wife.

"It isn't the age difference or the eras you have experienced differently. She isn't in the same class as you." The moment the words left his mouth, Will realized he had made a giant gaff. VJ's face changed. He glared at Will, who felt he had been pierced with hatred.

"Sir?" Will asked, his anxiety visible.

"I'll be in touch," VJ said as he turned his head to a monitor. The meeting was over. Will got up and left shaken.

WHEN THE DOOR SHUT behind Will, VJ slammed his fist on his desk. Ross jerked to attention. VJ could feel himself literally burning up with rage. "Snot-nosed, blue-blood, blood-sucking divorce lawyer," he steamed to himself. VJ boiled as he remembered the stuffy look on Will's face. *What does he know about class?* VJ thought. *Pilar, with all her faults, and at her worst, has more class than Marshall will ever understand. And I almost hired this prig purveyor of unrest to represent me against her.*

Half an hour later, VJ Simon was staring across a spectacularly messy desk at Magnolia Goldstein. Not only was her desk piled high with papers, her whole office was full of stacks of files and books. Among the piles of paper were potted plants, various African sculptures, and several balls of yarn, along with a variety of what looked to be in-progress sweaters. Magnolia chuckled as VJ picked up a ball of yarn from the arm of the chair he was sitting in. "What can I say?" she said. "I like to knit when there's a slow day or I just need to distance myself from people's miseries." Her face was like her office—well used, a bit of a mess, but somehow surprisingly attractive.

"Okay, Mr. Simon, what's this about?"

"I would think it's obvious. I want a divorce."

"Does your wife want a divorce?"

"She hasn't said so. She isn't happy, but probably not."

"You've discussed it?"

"I've told her I'm done. I have a prenuptial agreement that was confirmed by a post-nuptial agreement. Here's a copy."

He extended his hand with a copy of the agreement, but Magnolia didn't take it.

"If it's so iron-clad, why do you need me?"

"I'm also told that courts can be unpredictable."

"That would be true." She slid her glasses down to the tip of her nose. Peering at him over the rim, she said, "Tell me about you and your wife."

VJ gave his version of their life and personal histories.

"That's interesting, Mr. Simon. Why do you want the divorce again?"

"I don't like what she's become."

"And you've tried to work this out?"

"I believe so, but her dependencies make it impossible."

"You have children?"

"Three."

"Is she a good mother?"

"She has been, but lately the nanny has taken over."

"Have you had couples counseling?"

"No."

"Why not?"

"It hasn't been discussed. She sees a therapist, but not often enough, and she doesn't follow through."

Magnolia Goldstein rocked back and forth in her chair. VJ studied her.

"Let me think about this, Mr. Simon. I'll get back to you."

VJ was first puzzled, then amazed. "You mean—you mean you're going to think about whether or not you want me for a client?"

"Yes sir."

VJ gripped the seat of the chair again for a moment. A flash of anger passed through him. Then he relaxed. There was something about this odd-looking, frizzy-haired woman that he found appealing. He smiled. "That's not usually the way it works when I interview someone."

She sighed. "I'm sure that's right. Thank you for coming, Mr. Simon." She got up, wended her way around stacks of papers, took his arm, patted his forearm, and led him through the door.

CHAPTER 61

THE FIRST TO FILE

LATER THAT EVENING, Paddy called Pilar. "I'm done with the petition. It's ready to file."

"Don't file it," she said.

Paddy's heart raced. "Did you change your mind?"

"It isn't my decision to get a divorce. It's his. Let him file."

"That's bad strategy. In lawsuits, just like in the western movies, the first to draw has the best chance of winning."

"That would be shortsighted. When my children ask me, I can tell them that their father wanted a divorce. He filed it.'"

"I disagree."

"Great. Disagree. Just don't file first."

Paddy was bursting with things to say. "But—"

"Before you say a word," she said fiercely, "remember our discussion. We do what I want. *Comprende?*"

⁂

PADDY MET WILL in the men's room. After making sure they were alone, he spoke in a hushed voice.

"Pilar is hard to control. She won't let me file a petition first."

"Did you know she has a substance abuse problem?"

Paddy pursed his lips and furrowed his brow. "Did Simon tell you that?" His tone was noncommittal.

"Yes."

"Interesting . . ."

"What's more important is that Simon hasn't engaged me. I think I blew it."

"Is there something you're not telling me?" Will shook his head. He didn't want to tell Paddy that Simon had turned his back to him after he made his class comment and how awkward he felt as he left the room.

"Who else do you think he might be talking to?"

"My guess is Magnolia Goldstein."

"Magnolia might appeal to him. Is there anything you can do to make sure it's you he picks?"

Will swallowed. "Maybe."

"Then do it." Paddy turned on his heels and walked out of the men's room.

"Do it," Will repeated. "Do what?"

〰

VJ CALLED MAGNOLIA Goldstein's office twice. No answer. He asked Ben Trost to call and leave a message. Finally, the next morning, Magnolia Goldstein returned his call.

"Ms. Goldstein," he said, feeling ill at ease. "I'm glad you called. I would like to engage you."

"Mr. Simon, I'm honored and I'm flattered, but I'm going to pass."

"Pass? You mean you won't represent me? Why?"

"You haven't tried hard enough."

VJ gritted his teeth. "Don't you think I should be the judge of that? You haven't seen my wife when she's passed out or when she's throwing things at me."

She sighed. Then in a tone that reminded him of a favored grade school teacher denying his request to take a make-up exam because he attended a soccer match, she said "I'm sure you've had some terrible times, VJ." She said his name with great comfort and compassion. "And I'm sure you'll find someone who will be very eager to represent such a rich and well-known, and, I must say, well-respected person. You can probably find a flotilla of lawyers who would sell their grandmothers for a chance at you. But—and, let me assure you, I *do* have great respect for you and all you've done for the community—I'm just not feeling it. You get my drift?"

After taking several deep breaths, VJ asked, "Would you represent my wife?"

"I don't know. If you go through with this, she would need me. Frankly, if you go through with it, you would need me, too."

"I would need you! How would *I need you*?" She had pressed a button. He was seething.

"You're a smart man, Mr. Simon, an intuitive one as well. My guess is at some point if you can step back, you will get past the emotions that brought you to me. You will figure that out, and if you do, then you probably won't need me. One thing I will tell you. In your case, it isn't about money. I am asking myself, why are you trying to make it into a fight? I'll tell you what my gut tells me. You aren't over the marriage, and you aren't over her. If you were, you'd give her ten times what she would get in the prenup and move on without looking back, because I don't think you are the kind of man who would withhold what would be fair as a matter of control or spite. In my opinion, I don't think you're ready for a divorce, and you may never be."

"Ms. Goldstein, I would remind you that you are a lawyer, not a therapist. Whether or not I am ready, as you put it, is outside your field of expertise."

In a calm and measured tone, she replied, "I understand your thinking that, VJ, but I've been doing this work a long time. Knowing who is ready and who is not may be my *greatest* expertise. Try to fix things up with your wife. If you can't stop loving her, divorcing her isn't going to do you any good. Good luck."

She waited for him to respond or hang up. He hung up.

He called Trost. "Ben, you won't believe this." He recounted his conversations with both Marshall and Goldstein and his impressions of both.

"I told you she was different. Plus, there is a rumor she's not well and that could have influenced her."

"Maybe, but what nerve. She said she couldn't take me as a client because I don't really want a divorce!"

"Do you?"

"Yes, of course I do!"

"And Marshall?"

"That one thing he said about Pilar and class really bothered me."

"My guess is he thought he was selling."

"It cost him the sale."

"I'll give you some more names."

WHILE HE HAD BEEN stewing for two days after his men's room chat with Paddy, Will formed a plan and called VJ. As soon as he was put through, he cleared his throat.

"Mr. Simon—"

"What?" VJ snapped.

"There's something I need to say. That comment I made about your wife and class. I shouldn't have said it."

"You're right about that, but you did, and if you did you must have meant it."

Will picked his words with care. "I'm going to be candid. In the world I grew up in, people thought like that. In the world I have experienced since . . . since my family had its troubles, I have learned how wrong-headed that thinking is. Someone—someone known for being rich and obnoxious—once said something like that to me about my former partner, and I felt rage. In part, of course, it was because I felt it was a comment about me. Even though I do have a great deal of animosity toward Moran, I still admire what he has accomplished after starting with no more than a lot of ambition and brains and a willingness to do whatever it took to get where he wanted to go. I think I would feel rage if someone said that about Moran even today. I called you because when I thought about how I must have sounded, I was embarrassed. I said something I didn't really mean, because I thought it was something you wanted to hear. I was wrong."

After a long moment, VJ said, "Mr. Marshall, you have yourself a client."

Will filed the petition with a motion for summary judgment to have the prenup declared valid. Since cases are assigned to judges randomly, there is no shopping for judges in Harris County. If someone doesn't like the judge assigned, withdrawing the lawsuit and refiling isn't an option. The case goes to the judge to whom the case was originally assigned. Late the same evening Will and Paddy met again in the men's room to discuss their lucky break—that Hector had been assigned the case.

"The gods are with us," Paddy said.

"We need to get Hector in the program," Will said. "He was very nervous when we split."

"He's always nervous. He needs to wear dress shirts made of the same material workout shirts are made from, the kind that wick away perspiration. I should probably have some tailor-made for him."

"Put that on your to-do list. In the meantime, calm him down. Let him know we're working together."

"He can't make any quick rulings. Everything has to be drawn out."

"Very drawn out," Will agreed, already calculating the paychecks he would be drawing.

"I need to tell Pilar she's out of a job now that you're representing VJ."

⌇⌇⌇

THE PAPER WAR BEGAN. Paddy filed an answer to the petition and an opposition to the motion. Deposition notices were sent to everyone who could possibly have had any knowledge of any facts: Leila and the girls, Rosa and all the servants, VJ's Mexican investors, VJ's Persian investors, VJ's Waspy investors, Sunny. But Pilar balked when Paddy told her he was going to take the deposition of her first husband, the awful Ronnie.

"Why do you want to take *his* deposition?" she asked.

"I want to show that VJ buys whatever he wants, including people. He offered that asshole a very big payday to sell his parental rights."

"I wanted him to do it. It was the best thing for Grace."

"That," said Paddy, "is not what this is about."

Pilar shrugged. She really didn't mind Paddy making Ronnie squirm.

⌇⌇⌇

"EXPLAIN TO ME AGAIN— why does Moran want to take *his* deposition," VJ asked after Will told him Paddy had noticed her ex. "He signed a confidentiality agreement. He isn't supposed to disclose the terms of our agreement."

"Why did you do it?"

"Because he was a terrible father. They separated when she was barely six months old. He never exercised visitation. Grace never knew him. What kind of person would sell his parental rights anyway? Pilar was a wonderful mother, and I wanted to be the child's father just like I am with the other children."

"Great. Just don't mention the part where she was a wonderful mother."

"But she was."

"But she isn't now."

"I never said that."

"Mr. Simon, please keep your eyes on the prize."

※

AT SUNNY'S DEPOSITION, Will grilled her about Pilar's consumption of alcohol and pills. Her answers were deemed vague and confusing. Dr. McAdams, the wonder doctor who performed Pilar's tummy tuck, was grilled about prescribing narcotics. He assured everyone within listening range that all Mrs. Simon's pain prescriptions were appropriate for her pain level and perfectly safe.

Ben Trost was deposed. He was grilled about his conversations with VJ, who successfully invoked attorney-client privilege. Margaret Walden, Pilar's lawyer for the agreement and for her divorce, was deposed. Pilar waived the privilege. Walden's responses were that Pilar was without guile and completely trusting of VJ. VJ and Pilar both drew the line at deposing Luigi. "That's okay," Paddy said. "He's been a good friend to both of you and to me, too. I don't want to get him involved either." They probably would have agreed not to call Margot, but unbeknownst to them, Paddy told Will she was off limits.

It went on. Depositions. Document production. Forensic accountants. Procedural motions. Hearings. Full-court press. Every month the invoices got larger and larger.

To VJ, it seemed as though their lawyers were the equivalent of chess grand masters. Two experts fighting toward checkmate. He convinced himself the issue was the sanctity of the contract, a principle that should prevail over any other sanctities that might be invoked.

To Pilar, Will and Paddy were both being scumbags, but Paddy was *her* scumbag. She admired his cleverness. Besides, she believed everything he did was, in his mind, in her best interests.

CHAPTER 62

#LINDA4JUSTICE

LINDA HETHERINGTON'S CAMPAIGN was gathering momentum. Women's groups were early supporters. A men's group of fathers without visitation held a fundraiser for her, as did a group of family law attorneys who had not done well in Elizondo's court. Volunteers began a door-to-door campaign.

Judges are elected county-wide in Texas. Judicial elections are down ballot. Most people will just pull the lever for a straight party ticket because they don't know any of the judges. Linda Hetherington's campaign strategy was to educate the potential voters to find her on the ballot, identify and target the ones who were likely to vote for her, and get each one to vote. Harris County had nearly four million people, but voter turnout was usually low. It would not be easy. All emails, print, and internet material contained reproductions of the ballot. Margot Shear's contribution was used to fund a poll a week before early voting began. Her polls revealed Hetherington's direct-contact campaign was effective. On the eve of early voting, Linda's strategists planned a social media and text message campaign to remind people to vote. A large-print mailing directed to older voters was timed to arrive the same day mail-in ballots arrived.

Hetherington ran endorsement ads in all Houston's many ethnic newspapers. She got support from the Women's Campaign Fund. Contributions from people on its email list started pouring in.

Her team held another lawyer fundraiser. More movers and shakers came than before. Some lawyers who contributed to Elizondo gave to her campaign as well, hoping to hedge their bets. "I appreciate the contributions and will put them to good use," she said in a short speech, "but don't think it will buy you anything in my court, except maybe a bathroom recess." The crowd loved her.

AS ELECTION DAY DREW CLOSER, Will and Paddy met frequently in the men's room to plot their strategy in the increasingly profitable Simon divorce.

One evening Paddy appeared preoccupied. "Will, there's something else we need to talk about," he said. "I'm reading in the paper and hearing that Hetherington's campaign is picking up steam."

"I know. Muffy said she was hearing that, too. Mostly from Rice people. What do you think?"

"I think we ought not to stick our heads in the sand. We need to get Elizondo some money and some support," Paddy said.

"We can't do it together," Will responded.

"What do you suggest?"

"I'll call Bubba Otis and Lyons," Will said, "and see if they and some others will sponsor something. I'm sure Bubba will call you."

"I'll tell Bubba I will donate but not to put me on the sponsor list. Our Wingate trial is next week. He wants to stay in Hector's good graces. Why don't you get your asshole buddy Randy Hetherington to get some money into the campaign?"

"Good thought, but it needs to be after the last pre-election reporting period. Hector's campaign needs to get the Hispanic community in line— get them to express their outrage that a distinguished judge from their community is being attacked by an Anglo woman. Do you think Hector could arrange that?" Will asked.

"I can only suggest," Paddy said.

◦◦◦

OTIS AND LYONS PUT TOGETHER a group from the club and some who aspired to be members to sponsor a fundraiser. Elizondo insisted Dolores plan it. She, of course, fouled up. Nevertheless, through an aggressive, follow-up telephone campaign, the members of the club and the lawyers who wished they were members gave generously. They also gave generously to other family law court incumbents running, even those running unopposed. What remained of The Best People seemed to side with Hetherington.

While trying to stir up support for Hector, Paddy was also putting out fires. He met with Bubba several times trying to negotiate a quiet settlement of the Wingate matter. Bubba said his client wanted custody and child support from her, with a 45-55 split of the community in favor of Mr. Wingate. Winona was outraged. Paddy convinced her to agree to mediation. He was not optimistic. He had fucked up badly on that one. He knew Pilar knew why he had fucked up, and that could be the reason she was keeping him on a short string.

〰

AS THE ELECTION GOT CLOSER, Linda Hetherington's yard signs began sprouting throughout the whole of Harris County like roadside bluebonnets at Easter time. As signs were pulled up or defaced, they were replaced almost instantly by Linda's growing group of passionate volunteers.

Linda challenged Elizondo to a debate, and he refused. In a twist on the empty-chair tactic, she debated videos compiled of an inarticulate, perspiring, ineffective Elizondo appearing to respond to embarrassing questions. Her video pastiche soon went viral on YouTube and Facebook.

For a lowly judicial contest, the campaign got an unusual amount of media coverage. A *New York Times* article highlighted the campaign as part of a larger story on judicial campaign contributions by Texas lawyers. Linda's Facebook and Twitter followers doubled, then quadrupled, then skyrocketed. Soon she received contributions from all over the United States. Many came with comments not just from women but men and even from children who felt they had not been treated fairly on custody issues. She had become a national icon—the wronged woman, the avenger of all child custody injustice everywhere. TED Talks contacted her.

Elizondo's political consultant, chosen by Paddy and Will, organized a Hispanic group that tried to brand Linda as a kook and her campaign as racist. Elizondo's ads portrayed him as a child of immigrants who had succeeded through hard work and determination. Every picture showed him in judicial robes. The bumper stickers said, "*Sí Se Puede!* Vote for Judge Elizondo!"

〰

AT THE WINGATE MEDIATION, after everyone made choices from the lunch menu, the mediator made his speech and then Paddy and Bubba made theirs. Then the parties went into separate rooms.

The mediator began his process. He went to the room with Paddy and Mrs. Wingate and then met with Mr. Wingate and Bubba. He tried to get an idea of how firm they were on their positions. This process repeated itself throughout the day—the mediator talking to each party in turn, making notes, carrying compromises back and forth, and urging resolution. After returning from yet another meeting with Mr. Wingate and Bubba, the mediator returned to Winona and Paddy's room. "I want to meet with my husband, alone," Winona said. "No lawyers. Not you."

"I thought one of your issues with Mr. Wingate is that he has a serious rage problem," the mediator said. "I don't think that's a good idea."

"I don't either!" Paddy said.

"Mr. Moran, I have no respect for what you think is a good idea. Mr. Mediator, I can deal with my husband. If you are afraid of his rage problem, I'll sign a release."

The mediator shrugged, raised his eyebrows, and said, "I'll present that."

This time, he came back quickly. "Mr. Wingate is in favor of a one-on-one."

The Wingates went into a conference room. At Mrs. Wingate's urging, Mr. Wingate kept his voice down, and Paddy, who was hanging around the door, couldn't make out a single word. An hour later they came out.

"We've decided to reconcile."

Paddy and Bubba were stunned.

"You're sure?" Bubba asked.

"We're sure. Dismiss the divorce. And, by the way, we're thinking about suing both of you. Instead of sending more bills, consult with your malpractice carriers."

Paddy looked at Bubba. They both raised their eyebrows, then turned to the Wingates and nodded in unison.

"Here's to true love. Ain't it grand," Paddy said to no one in particular.

⁂

THE *HOUSTON CHRONICLE* ENDORSED Linda Hetherington. Early on election day, her supporters planted numerous signs at each voting location. During voting hours, Linda had at least one supporter handing out literature at every voting precinct in Harris County. Some met with hostility in the Hispanic precincts, but most were welcomed. People who felt victimized in custody battles appeared to exist in every neighborhood in Houston. The polls closed at seven. By eight fifty-nine, Elizondo had conceded by email.

Linda's campaign manager read the email to the crowd at campaign headquarters, which was jammed with supporters, lawyers who wanted her to see them there, and ladies and gentlemen of the press. The election party was loud and joyous. When Linda took the podium, the crowd was so large it spilled out into the street. Those gathered applauded, cheered, whistled, shouted, and stomped their feet. The noise was deafening.

A smiling Linda Hetherington removed her reading glasses, releasing them so that they hung like a necklace. She held her hands high in a V, then brought her palms down in an attempt to quiet the crowd. An air horn blasted.

She laughed and raised her hands again. She motioned again for quiet and began to speak.

"It's traditional for the winner in an election to be gracious toward her opponent," she said, sounding like a seasoned campaigner. She paused. The room was completely silent. "But then I wasn't a traditional candidate, was I?"

The crowd broke into a roar of laughter, clapping and stomping for more than a minute. She raised her hands to shush them again.

"I won't start being traditional now. Initially, I ran to unseat Hector Elizondo. With the help of you people here and, it's hard for me to believe, thousands more who I've never met, we unseated a corrupt and incompetent judge."

More clapping, yelling, and stomping.

"As I campaigned, I realized that if I succeeded, I was going to have to sit in his seat. The last few weeks, when victory appeared possible, I began to appreciate the awesome responsibility of being a judge. I want you to know that I am honored and humbled to have that responsibility. You have my solemn oath that I will respect at all times the bench you have elected me to, and I will never, never, abuse the power that will be invested in me."

She turned her head to the side to clear her throat and regain her composure. Blinded by cameras flashing, she raised her right hand and, as loudly as she could speak, said, "So help me, God!"

There was complete silence for a brief moment. Someone began to sing "Amen, amen, amen." Soon the entire crowd joined in, swaying together.

Linda Hetherington was shaking, fighting to hold herself together. When the singing stopped, she managed to say, "Good night. I love you all. Thank you! Thank you! Thank you!" She managed to remain composed until she disappeared into the small office behind the makeshift podium.

Her campaign manager told the media that if they would respect her private moment, she would be available to them in time for the ten o'clock news. To their own surprise, they did.

CHAPTER 63

ANGEL OF THE BARRIO

WHILE LINDA HETHERINGTON was sprinting to victory, Pilar, about-to-be-the-ex-Mrs. Simon, was working hard to get her house in order. She had finally gotten herself off pills by easing away her use. Day one, she cut each pill in half. Day two, she took a half of a half. In a few days, each pill was an infinitesimal grain of powder, too little to have any physical effect. Knowing she had that little piece made it easier. She also spent as much time as she could with her children, looking back with great guilt for the times with them when she was altered. And she committed to daily physical exercise and drinking more water. Lots of water.

Monday, Wednesday, and Friday began with some brutal Pilates. Who knew, she marveled, that moving just a little bit could hurt so damn much? She had to admit, the workout was working. She had hired Craig Rich, who Leila swore was Houston's best fitness trainer. But then Leila always swore whoever she used or whatever she bought was the best. Craig developed a strict regime for her. Pilar didn't mind working out nearly every day; it helped clear her still-shaky mind.

Still, she often felt a longing so intense she could almost see it—a blue light buzzing around her eyes, calling on her to swallow a pill and know a single moment of perfect calm. But then she always shook herself back to reality. Exercise. The kids. Lunch with Leila and the gang.

Pilar had not expected Leila to stay by her side. Since her husband did business with VJ, Pilar figured Leila and the gang would drop her. She was wrong. After she and VJ split, Leila and the other wives invited her to join them more often than before. She did fear being too close to Leila and her pills, but both her willpower and her gratitude prevailed. She was so pleased their acceptance of her was not contingent on her connection to VJ.

"I don't get it," Pilar said to Sunny one day on the phone. "VJ and I are not together, yet they still want to be seen with me."

"It probably never occurred to you that they like you."

Pilar realized it had not. "That's good to know. But the truth is, it's all just so meaningless," she said.

"What do you want?"

"I don't know," she said, "but I'm going to think about it."

After she hung up the phone, she told Rosa to watch the children. "I am going out for a drive." At first, she had no idea where she was going, but she soon found herself pointing the car toward her childhood neighborhood—el barrio. She hadn't been back in a long time. She cruised down familiar potholed streets, past small houses, many in disrepair, and a park sprayed with graffiti. She passed a building with a short line outside it—a low, dusty building. The sign above the door read, "Navigation Free Clinic."

Feeling as if she were on autopilot, Pilar parked her new Lexus SUV just up the street under the shade of a magnolia tree. She walked in. The entry room, well-lit with fluorescent lights, but worn and dingy, was packed with people. The chairs and couch were stained and torn. The woman behind the counter had a kind face, but she looked harassed and incapable of managing the long line of people waiting to be seen, Pilar noted. After noticing Pilar staring at her, she said, "Can I help you?" Making her annoyance obvious, she added, "Are you lost?"

"No," Pilar replied. "I just—"

"If you don't have an appointment, the waiting time is three hours," the woman said.

"Thank you." Pilar turned on her heels. As she left, she thought, *You just watch out. This girl is coming back.*

〰

BACK HOME, Pilar found the website for Navigation Free Clinic. It was a United Way agency, but clearly it was woefully underfunded. United Way rated its service and managerial and financial controls as low, but the need it attempted to fill was great. Pilar clicked on the board list. She did not recognize a single name.

Her research revealed the clinic was the only place people in her old neighborhood could go for medical services outside of an emergency room. "Only affordable provider of basic medical services," read one article from the *Houston Chronicle*. A few volunteer doctors donated a day a week to see patients. Two paid nurse practitioners were full-time.

She called the chairwoman of the board of directors, a professor of public health at the University of Houston, who told her that the clinic was a mainstay for many families in the area who had no health insurance. The clinic gave free flu shots and vaccinations. It provided postnatal care to mothers and infants. The clinic couldn't handle major emergencies. The chairwoman confessed there were troubling management issues, but she was so busy teaching that she didn't have time to do much more than she was doing. "I feel responsible," the chairwoman said. "I'm from that neighborhood."

"So am I," Pilar said. "I'll make a deal with you. I will contribute twenty-five thousand dollars if you will let me be the unpaid CEO and COB for six months."

"Are you sure, Mrs. Simon? I'm—I'm overwhelmed. We would be delighted!"

"I also want to expand the board," Pilar paused a beat. "Significantly."

Less enthusiastically, the woman gave her assent. "I do know the clinic won't survive if we don't do something," she said. "We're having problems with the United Way review."

The next day Pilar worked the phones from morning until night. She roped in Leila and the gang and got them to make calls. At the end of the day, she had learned something important about herself. When she really wanted something, people found it hard to say no to her. Leila gave ten thousand and so did Cameron McMillan.

By the end of the first week, Pilar had raised seventy-five thousand. She identified a medical records and accounting system that met federal grant guidelines and purchased the necessary hardware and software. She hired a grant writer, who began applying for funds from foundations whose mission statements fit the cause. Pilar knew this was just a start. She needed to build an endowment so the clinic would have long-term operating capital and the capacity to make improvements. She called Leila and made her biggest pitch yet.

She wanted the gang to adopt the clinic as their cause, to work to change lives together. They would have to commit for the long haul.

When Pilar finished talking there was silence on the other end. For a moment, she panicked and wondered if she had gone too far.

"I'll do it," Leila said. "We'll all do it." Leila pledged another twenty thousand. She also started volunteering one day a week at the intake desk. At first, Leila's Spanish—which she claimed to speak fluently after a couple of years in Madrid post-college—was nearly impossible for anyone to follow, but within a month, she got along just fine. "This is the most fun I've had in years," she confessed to Pilar. The rest of the women volunteered a day as well, even Cameron.

Pilar gave them all meaningful assignments. Leila convinced a designer to make uniforms for her crew of volunteers. After that, Pilar could hardly keep up with the number of socialites who suddenly wanted to volunteer at "Pilar's clinic," as they called it. Pilar was always quick to say, "It's the neighborhood's clinic. It belongs to the people who live there."

Pilar took a hands-on approach to management, volunteers, and paid staff. She didn't hesitate to use tough love. None took easily to it. The employees weren't used to having a real boss and being held accountable. At first, there were complaints, but she firmly yet kindly let them know that they had a sacred duty to the people of the neighborhood and to the people and organizations that invested in the clinic. The volunteers needed and wanted guidance. Seeing her friends fully engaged in the mission of the clinic revealed to her a competence and sense of purpose and commitment she had not seen before.

Some of the volunteers didn't last. A few long-term employees—including the receptionist Pilar had observed on the first day—left, but within three months she had an able, energized group.

She made sure everyone understood that every patient who walked through the doors was treated like a treasured customer. "People deserve respect, understanding, service, and a smile," she insisted. "We can't heal everyone, and we can't always get them what they need immediately, but we can always let them know we care, even the difficult ones. Don't treat them like they're charity cases." She established ways of evaluating the clinic's services. Every single patient filled out bilingual satisfaction surveys. The data was used to make improvements. Security guards were employed. The clinic opened earlier and stayed open until eight o'clock in the evening.

Usage increased dramatically. Wait times were lowered. Neighborhood volunteers landscaped the grounds. A nursery donated rose bushes. Local artists painted a mural on a once-dingy side wall. One national foundation offered a hundred thousand dollars if that amount could be matched by local donations. Pilar hit the phones again. Private family foundations in Houston stepped up to the challenge and soon Pilar had her match—two hundred thousand—which would keep the clinic operating through year-end. Buzz about the changes reached numerous corners of the city, including the newsroom of the *Houston Chronicle*. A reporter, who had also grown up in the barrio, drove by the clinic. Impressed by what he saw, after some investigation, he learned the guiding force of the success and growth of the clinic was Mrs. VJ Simon, the same Mrs. Simon who was currently embroiled in a public, messy, expensive divorce. He called Pilar. "How did you become 'the angel of the barrio?'"

"That's very nice but embarrassing. I'm not sure this is a good time for me to get publicity."

The reporter was very insistent. He convinced her that it would call positive attention to the needs of the neighborhood. She agreed so long as the divorce was not mentioned. A long story that began on the bottom fold of page one ran on a Sunday with the headline "The Angel of the Barrio: To River Oaks and Back Again."

The front page included a close-up of Pilar looking focused and intent beside a snapshot of Leila and the girls in their uniforms, posing as if they were in a Rockettes kick line.

VJ read the article from beginning to end. When he was finished, he put the paper down on the table in front of him and sat staring at the photograph of his soon-to-be-ex-wife. He dialed her number, hung up, then dialed again. In that instant, he recalled she had done the same thing when Bob dumped her.

She picked up, and he cleared his throat. "Pilar, I read about what you're doing in the paper today. I didn't know. I'm impressed."

"You didn't miss that twenty-five thousand, huh?" she said dryly, referring to her initial donation.

"I noticed," VJ replied stiffly. "I didn't know you were running the place. I'm proud of you. I mean it."

"I'd rather you admire me than be proud of me."

She was thinking that VJ had always been condescending in just this way, but back when they were together, she had never said anything or when she had he had never understood, not that this mattered now.

"Pilar, I do admire you," he said quickly.

Then why is your lawyer always filing, filing, and filing again things that make me out to be such a piece of shit? Pilar thought. She said, "Thanks. That means a lot coming from you now."

Before he could say more, she hung up the phone.

CHAPTER 64

AN OVERHEARD CONVERSATION

THE MORNING AFTER THE ELECTION, Paddy called Pilar and asked her to meet at his office that afternoon. She agreed. In the lobby, she juggled her purse and a large bottle of smartwater and hit the elevator button. Suddenly she squirmed with discomfort. She had to pee. She glared at the bottle of water. The door opened, and she stepped into the empty elevator. She began to dance from one foot to the other, wondering why the elevators that go the least number of floors always take the longest. Finally, the door opened. She hurried to the restroom, raced to the nearest stall, slammed the door, and hung her purse on the hook.

Just as she was about to flush she heard the restroom door open followed by a man clearing his throat. Puzzled, she became perfectly still. At first, she thought the sound came through a vent or some other way that sounds carried over from the men's restroom. The door opened again and someone else entered. Suddenly her mind played back what her eyes had seen but had not registered as she made her mad dash to the stall—urinals. She was mortified. She lifted her legs so that no one would see them beneath the stall door.

She heard Paddy say, "The election was a killer." The voice that responded was Will's. She was surprised. *These two guys don't speak to each other*, she thought.

"Are you sure no one's in here?" Paddy asked. Pilar's heart was beating so strongly that she thought it might be audible.

"It's clear," Will said.

"The election was a killer. I've been up all night," he said. "We need to ramp this thing up into high gear and get it over in a hurry. Hector only has about two more months on the bench. Lord knows what will happen if that crazy bitch Hetherington inherits this case."

"My fees are good but not nearly up to what we'd hoped," Will responded.

"I'm doing okay but the big enchilada is the contingency. We need to get that baby out of Dodge in a hurry," Paddy said as he was leaving.

"Until that time, partner," Will said. She could almost hear in his voice the smirk on his face.

Rage began to replace Pilar's panic and shock. She heard Will leaving. Another man entered, did his business, rinsed his hands, and left. A few seconds later, she flushed. She waited a moment more before cautiously and quickly exiting the men's restroom. As she did, Linda Hetherington's face flashed in front of her eyes, not the triumphant woman on the front page this morning, but the desperate woman who had approached her at the courthouse. Paddy had told her the only reason he was urging her to take aggressive positions in the divorce was so she could continue to lead the kind of life she had learned to enjoy and deserved, so the children wouldn't have to go from one standard of living to another every time it was VJ's turn to have them. "You're a good person," he had said. "You deserve the best." Because of their history, she had trusted his advice. Now, she realized he meant *he* deserved the best. She wanted to kill him. She started to march right into his office and fire him then and there, but her instincts told her to wait.

She went to the receptionist. Flushed, nearly out of breath, she asked her to tell Paddy she wasn't feeling well, and she was going home. She would call to reschedule.

As soon as she got into her car she called Sunny, the one person in the world she realized she could trust. "That's crazy," Sunny said. "Call VJ immediately."

VJ agreed to see her, and they arranged to meet at a local coffee shop on lower Westheimer.

She was waiting for him, sipping an almond milk latte. He joined her without ordering anything.

"It must be important. What's going on?"

She looked directly into his eyes. "Paddy and Will are in cahoots. They didn't really split up. They have a coordinated plan to get us mad at each other and run up the fees. Now that Elizondo has lost, they see they have to make what they can and run."

VJ blinked and stared at her. He wondered if she could have ever been more beautiful than she was at that moment. "The Angel of the Barrio"— well she certainly looked the part now—healthy, focused, impassioned.

She also looked deadly serious. He managed to lower his eyebrows and say in a firm tone, "How do you know this?"

"You won't believe me."

"Try me. I will."

Pilar groaned. "Actually, if you think about it, it's funny. By accident I went into the Lou instead of the Louise," she said and told him about overhearing their lawyers. "We were played," VJ whispered.

Pilar reached across the table and covered the back of his hands with her palms, her eyes intently on his. "VJ, I have never stopped loving you. The divorce was your idea. When you said it was over, I knew you well enough to know you didn't mean maybe. I gave up. I had no alternative but to make the best of it, and, to be honest, the prenup wasn't fair. So I hired Moran. When you started firing cannons, I let that son of a bitch manipulate me, and I fired back."

"You had become another person—one I didn't want to come home to."

"You're right. I had," Pilar said in a firm voice. She squeezed his hands.

VJ returned her grasp. "You look like the Pilar I knew. You sound like her. You're acting like her." He kissed her hand.

Pilar's eyes began to tear.

"So you're coming back?" she said.

"Pilar, I'm not as quick as you are emotionally. We need to take this slowly, okay? I'll see you when I get the children tonight. We'll talk then."

Looking down, she nodded.

"In the meantime, try to think about how we can get those bastards." There was no unbridled anger in his voice. It was the tone of a brilliant tactician faced with a challenge.

"VJ," she said smiling, "some parts of you don't change. So, if the game is on, I don't think we should be seen out together. What about this? You pick up the kids and take them to dinner. I'll tell the help to take the night off. After you bring the kids back tonight, we'll put them to bed. Then, we'll talk."

Just then, her cell phone rang. She showed VJ the caller ID. It was Paddy. Motioning to him to be quiet, she answered the phone.

"Pilar, darling, are you all right?"

His unctuousness made her sick. "Thanks for your concern. I really appreciate it. Something suddenly upset my stomach, so I left."

"I hope you feel better soon. Let's talk in the morning. If you feel well enough, come in tomorrow. You have a good rest tonight."

"Sure thing. I'll call you tomorrow." Pilar hung up. "Son of a bitch," she said to VJ.

When Pilar got home, Rosa told her that the cable guy had come and fixed the wiring. "What cable guy?" Pilar asked. Rosa shrugged. "From Mr. Simon's office," she answered. It was time to go pick up the children. Pilar waved off Rosa. "I'll get them," she said. At the thought that tonight VJ would be coming over, she felt a thrill.

※

AT ABOUT 4:30 P.M., one of Houston's dense rainstorms, called a "gulleywhumper" by long-time natives, descended. It was still pouring when VJ arrived an hour later. He entered through the garage, carrying several plastic bags of groceries. "Forgive me for not being green today, but the paper bags would have fallen apart in the rain," he told Pilar. He was a sight—completely drenched from the knees down. As he was removing his shoes and socks and rolling up his pant legs, the children greeted him in the kitchen.

"Daddy, you look funny," Raj Benjamin said.

"You're soaked," Grace said.

"Not true. I'm dry from the knees up."

Pilar entered. "What are the groceries for?"

"I felt like cooking," he said.

Pilar bit her lip. "Kids," she said, "would you excuse your father and me for a moment?"

Grace looked down sadly. Pilar led VJ into another room.

"I heard what you said earlier," Pilar said slowly. "You said you weren't sure what would happen with us."

VJ broke in. "We aren't one big family yet. Maybe that will happen, but I can't forget everything that went wrong between us."

"I understand," she said evenly. "And since we aren't one big happy family yet, that means we might not become one. It has been hard enough to keep the children from being too distressed. Why do you want to risk raising their hopes if they may be dashed again? I'm just sayin', the one-big-happy-family cook-off might not be such a great idea."

"I didn't want to take the kids out in a storm like this, so I decided to cook. That's all. Pilar, relax. Trust me."

She nodded. "Not a problem. I'll leave."

"No. That's ridiculous. The streets are flooding. I barely made it here. Don't go out."

"My SUV is high off the ground. I'll be fine."

"Please."

She shrugged.

"There's something else," he said. "I had suspected this house was bugged by my attorney, Mr. Marshall. I had it swept this afternoon by the *cable* guy. I left the bug. It's in the master bedroom."

"Good thing I don't have any lovers."

"I disabled the GPS on my phone and in the car, so your attorney can't track me."

"Isn't the outside of the house being watched as well?"

"Spy cams, the ones you have at the gates and in the back for security."

He pulled a cell phone out of his pocket and handed it to her.

"It's prepaid and not traceable. I have one, also. Here are the numbers. We only talk on these phones on matters regarding Marshall and Moran."

"Okay. Is that all?"

He hesitated and then said, "Yes."

They went back to the kitchen.

"Hey, kids. Your dad wants to cook for you tonight. Isn't that a great idea?"

"Will it be as good as McDonald's?" asked five-year-old Raj Benjamin.

Grace interjected, "It will be better. Lots better."

"Really?" Raj Benjamin sounded doubtful.

"Really," Grace said, glaring at her brother. Both Pilar and VJ heard in the sound of her voice and her look of desperate hope that indeed they would again be one big happy family. A day ago, Grace's response would have broken their hearts. Now they both felt a stirring of hope. Nevertheless, Pilar gave VJ a stern look and started to leave the room.

"Where are you going?" Grace asked.

"I have some errands," Pilar said.

"It's too rainy to do errands. Besides, you'll miss dinner." Grace was pleading.

Pilar glanced at VJ. He nodded.

Pilar shrugged. "Okay."

VJ's main dish was a combination of samosas and kreplach with ground beef and mashed potatoes. Raj Benjamin was not disappointed, especially with the dessert—the old standby—vanilla ice cream with hot fudge sauce. They each read to the children at bedtime. After the children were asleep, they went to the study to talk.

"Can you believe those money-grubbing bastards? I'm sure that judge is in on it as well," VJ sighed. "How did we get to this place?"

"I accept responsibility," Pilar said. "I had never been loved by anyone the way you loved me and not just as a sex object, but for my whole being, and I had never loved anyone, really loved anyone, before you. It scared me. Maybe I thought I was undeserving or maybe I thought if I loved you too much then losing you would be unbearable. Then everything got totally messed up when I started listening to Leila."

"Leila? What's she got to do with it?"

"Leila got me started on pills. She and that creepy Dr. Dreamy. She takes them like candy." She looked into his eyes. "Don't tell me you didn't know?"

"I didn't," VJ confessed. "The night of the closing—at Eleganté—I thought Leila was the one who was trying to keep you straight."

"Boy, did you get that wrong. She's the one who got me high that night," Pilar said.

"You were wobbling when you came in."

"Right, and if you were wearing the ill-fitting stiletto heels I was wearing, you would have fallen flat on your face. She got me high when she came down to take me to the lady's room. But it's okay. I don't blame Leila. She's just who she is. And you know, she's so much better since she started volunteering at the clinic. I think maybe she needed something worthwhile to focus on. Anyway, the real problem was me. I didn't have any sense of myself. I felt so dependent on you and so scared of everything. What your friends thought. What your associates thought. I even worried that you would die because you're older and that life without you would be unbearable."

VJ processed that. *It was me she wanted. It wasn't my money. It really was me*, he thought.

"So I became self-destructive and drove you away."

"I never understood what you were doing or why," VJ said. "I couldn't get through to you. After a while I gave up. I figured I could find someone else, find what you and I had again. But I don't think anyone else could replace you. I missed the Pilar I used to know."

Pilar smiled. "We might have been okay if I hadn't started taking the pills. But after the surgery, I believed having a prescription gave me permission. I had a pill for every moment. If I had the slightest ache I took a pain pill. If I felt woozy from a pain pill, I took an upper. And so on. Soon that was my whole life. After you dropped the D bomb on me, Sunny came over. What a friend she is! She helped me realize what I was doing to myself and that I had better shape up. I had already lost you. If I didn't change I could lose my children, too. That's when I began to get control of myself again. It didn't happen overnight. Your lawyer—Will— probably thought I was doing that to position myself for a custody fight and, to some extent, he was right. You have to know, VJ, there is no way I would give up the kids without a fight—make that a nuclear war. The final piece was the clinic. My work there provided a sense of accomplishment. For the first time in my whole life, I believed in myself. No part of me needed affirmation from you or anyone else. I didn't have to look to anyone but myself for validation. I fully acknowledged responsibility for the loss of our relationship. I accepted the finality of that loss. I never once thought about finding someone else."

VJ took a deep breath.

"As I got better, I began to realize Paddy was manipulating me even though I thought I was in control."

"There were some very mean-spirited tactics," VJ said.

"I did go along with them," Pilar said. "He didn't do a thing without my approval in advance."

VJ marveled that she could be so without guile.

"And you, Mr. Nice Guy? I expected to be trashed as a mother. But who claimed all the art was his, including 'The Little Deer?'"

He shook his head, unsmiling. "Guilty. Will told me to do it because it was so valuable. He did surprise me with his brilliant maneuvering and responses to Paddy's tactics. I didn't think he was that clever. As it turns out, he probably wasn't. It's now clear that it was a giant sting with the two of them and that idiot judge." VJ took a breath. "The question is, how do we get back at them?"

"Why don't you and I get back together?" Pilar said mischievously. "That'll give our *family* lawyers a big shock."

"I said I need to get used to the idea. In the meantime, those guys have to be stopped. It isn't revenge, Pilar. I'm outraged. The judge is history, but they're evil."

Pilar reflected on his words. "I'm not taking up for Paddy or making excuses for him, but I don't think he's evil. I met him when he first started out. He was kind and caring. He never hit on me. You didn't know this, but I passed out at the office. He was very concerned when he found me. He never told anyone. At some point, probably during the Hetherington case, he crossed the line. After that, he was different. Damaged. I can't help it, VJ, I'll always like Paddy at least a little bit. That's why I am so mad he did this to *me*."

VJ rolled his eyes.

"This may piss you off, VJ, but give me a break on you needing time. Don't deceive yourself into thinking you're blameless. You were dismissive. You should have let me work with you. Then, you gave up on me without making any effort. Who knows if it would have made a difference? At this point, who cares? I couldn't be any better than I am now. As for Paddy, I'm in shock. I knew he liked winning. I knew he liked the trappings of success. I knew he liked the power. He liked being feared. He liked being sucked up to. Maybe most of all he liked people needing him. When I worked for them, I didn't see any shady stuff. The Hetherington trial was already over. All I saw was the rough and tumble of the kind of law they practice. I didn't see anything unethical—not like this."

"Wait a minute," VJ said. "You just gave me an idea. What do you think about us contacting the Hetherington woman? Perhaps she can help us come up with a plan. I bet she's done her homework on those guys."

"Do you really think that's a good idea?"

"I don't know. Let's think about it."

"While you are thinking about it, how about I help you remember what you've been missing."

Pilar closed the door to the study securely. She approached him, went to her knees and tugged at his belt. He did not resist, not in the slightest.

Afterwards, VJ said, "Hmmm," smiling broadly. "That's hitting below the belt."

She threw her head back and laughed the laugh he loved.

VJ left, feeling as if he had just stepped off a roller coaster. He thought about how much his life had changed in the space of just a few hours. He didn't recall ever feeling happier. He was also excited with the challenge of getting Marshall and Moran their due. He and Pilar as a team would be unbeatable, as Hakeem Olajuwon described the Houston Rockets after their first NBA championship.

He called Pilar on the burner phone, reminding her not to talk to him if she was in the bedroom. He admonished her to limit their conversations to the cell phone, in person, or by an encrypted email system that VJ had created for confidential transactions.

"I'll set you up with a safe computer so that we'll be able to communicate by instant messaging. It'll be completely private. Maybe the NSA or the Russians could crack it, but we aren't on their radar. Well, maybe I am, but they won't share with Marshall or Moran."

"You never know," she said snickering.

Later, VJ lay in bed trying to visualize a plan. What was the objective? Expose and discredit Marshall and Moran. Get them disbarred? That would destroy them financially, but maybe they owe the IRS so much money they're already destroyed. Send them to jail? Was bringing Hetherington in a good idea or a bad one? What would she want other than just nailing them? *She wants her daughter back*, he thought. Then he mulled some more.

〰

EARLY THE NEXT MORNING, VJ and Pilar met near Linda Hetherington's campaign headquarters. Campaign posters were still on the windows. More posters and other paraphernalia were strewn about inside. The floor was covered with confetti and paper horns. It looked like the day after a New Year's Eve party.

"Hello?" a voice called from inside the storefront. "Can I help you?" It was Linda Hetherington.

"Ms. Hetherington? Or should I say Your Honor?" Pilar asked.

"Not yet," she said, casting a curious glance in Pilar's direction. "Don't I know you?"

"My name is Pilar Simon. We met once on the steps of the courthouse." Pilar stepped inside.

"If you don't mind, I'd like my husband to join us."

"Of course," Hetherington said, but she looked confused.

VJ stepped in and looked around. "Is there anywhere we can talk?" he asked. "In private. As long as you don't mind meeting with us."

"Frankly, Mr. Simon, who *wouldn't* meet with you? And you, Mrs. Simon, as well," she added, nodding at Pilar and smiling. "I am intrigued as to why the two of you would be coming together to see me. I'm not a business lawyer and," nodding at VJ, "I know Mr. Marshall represents you in the divorce—and," nodding to Pilar, "Mr. Moran represents you, which troubles me. One, because my feelings about them are quite well known, and, two, I'm about to be the judge in your case, so this meeting might mean I have to recuse myself. Is that what you're after? Trying to get me out of the case?"

VJ pulled back. "No. That never occurred to me."

"Or me," said Pilar. She smiled at Linda. "If you'll hear us out, I think you'll see that. But first, we must have absolute assurances that this conversation is completely confidential."

Linda looked startled.

"Well, of course, unless you tell me you're planning to commit a crime," she said, recovering.

VJ told Linda their story and their objective. When he finished, Linda Hetherington smiled. "Delicious!" She smacked her lips. "But why are you trusting me with all this information? Can't you bring them down without me?" VJ nodded toward Pilar. "Maybe we can and maybe we can't," Pilar said. "It's our guess that you have meticulously collected information about Moran and maybe Marshall as well. If you share that information with us, it is bound to be helpful. Second, it doesn't take someone of uncommon intelligence to figure out no one would be more interested than you in having that information put to its highest and best use, and, working together, we are more likely to deal a devastating blow to Messrs. Moran and Marshall."

"And," Linda added, "Elizondo as well."

VJ looked at her and grinned, "Sure. I guess that's dessert."

"As I said, delicious, but the main course for me is getting my daughter back. At a minimum, after we go public, this will certainly allow the case to be reopened."

"Of course," VJ said.

"Do you two want to engage me as a lawyer?"

"You tell me," VJ said.

"Will I be providing legal services?"

"You will certainly be counseling us."

She looked at him, hoping he would continue because she didn't know how to respond.

"And, of course, I—I mean we—will pay."

Linda straightened up. "Pay me?" She laughed.

"Why are you laughing?" he asked.

"First, you have delivered a package to me that I have dreamed for years to get. Second, I've never had a client before. You two are my first."

VJ looked at her incredulously.

She said, "I started campaigning the moment I learned I passed the bar. I never even thought about practicing. I just wanted to knock Elizondo off the bench and find a way to get Moran. I don't even know what to charge."

"I can help with that," Pilar said. "Don't forget I was office manager for Marshall & Moran." She glanced at VJ. "How about eight hundred an hour?"

"What?" Linda asked.

"Eight hundred an hour," Pilar repeated. "Why should we pay you less than Marshall and Moran charge us?"

"Quite right." VJ reached to take Pilar's hand. "In fact, make it eight fifty."

"Mr.—Mrs. Simon—there have been many months where I haven't had that much in my bank account."

"Do you accept the engagement?" VJ said.

"Yes, so long as my engagement is completed before I am sworn in."

"The sooner the better," said Pilar.

Linda first looked stunned, then she beamed. "Mr. and Mrs. Simon, I'm not sure you both really need me, but I accept the engagement because I don't want to miss a moment of this."

VJ handed her an untraceable cell phone with his and Pilar's numbers as the only contacts. He instructed her to it use only for telephone conversations relating to the engagement.

"There'll be expenses," he said. "You may want to hire private investigators. I recommend two. I recommend a former FBI agent who I have used and respect."

Pilar interjected, "Another is a former colleague of Ray Fourbirds—Moran's PI. He knows Fourbirds and, my guess is, he knows what was done in your case. Don't let him know much. Certainly, he is not to know who your clients are. Just get information from him. Hint that your clients are rough customers, and if he lets Fourbirds know anything is up, you can't be responsible for what your clients may do."

"What else do you want me to do?"

"Think about what we have discussed and come up with a plan. Anyone who can execute the long-term plan you did—going to law school, running against Elizondo—knows how to create a plan for this. The question is can you create a short-term plan that can be executed and completed before you are sworn in?"

"I believe I can."

CHAPTER 65

A SIMPLER PLAN

THE PLAN LINDA HETHERINGTON came up with was simple. "Audio equipment may lawfully be placed in the men's room," she told VJ when she followed up with him. "It's a public place. While there might be an expectation of privacy when one is doing his business, there's no expectation of privacy for conversations," she said, as if she were delivering a lecture in constitutional law. "However, a video inside the men's room is more than dicey. A video outside the men's room to catch them entering and leaving is not. Put that with audio of their conversations, properly authenticated and time-stamped, and you've got your proof."

"I'll take care of arranging the mechanics," VJ said. "By the way, Pilar and I have a present for you. You knew Pilar was the part-time office manager for Marshall & Moran until the divorce proceedings started?"

"Yes, she said that."

"During an office visit with Moran," VJ continued, "she told him she knew she wasn't working for him anymore, but she thought of something she may have missed. She asked if she could review the accounting records. He agreed. She got documentation, including receipts for payment to the woman in the video and her itemized time entries, proving how you were framed. It will help put together your case for reopening custody of your daughter."

Linda gasped. "Oh, thank you! You can't know what this means. And to think you're paying *me*."

LATER, VJ DISCUSSED with Pilar the next stages of the plan. He told her he'd arranged to have the equipment installed after-hours. It was calibrated to turn on when it recognized Paddy's or Will's voice. VJ had Elizondo followed. His PI noted when he went to places such as Paddy's health club, which he did on a regular basis. Pilar's review of Marshall & Moran's financial records established that Elizondo didn't reimburse Paddy.

VJ met with Trost. He told him the facts and the plan they were following. After Trost reviewed the evidence, he said, "First, I'm happy to hear you aren't getting a divorce."

"So your law firm may have dodged a malpractice bullet on the pre-nup," VJ said laughing.

"I guess there's always that. However, while I might have worried about losing you as a friend and a client, I don't think I worried about being sued. The real thing is—if you will excuse me for sounding schmaltzy—you seemed very happy with Pilar," he said in a tone that may have had a note of ruefulness. He raised his eyebrows. "Second, I'm impressed with the work you, Pilar, and Hetherington have done."

"I want to take it to the DA," VJ said.

"I think it's a federal case, so it should go to the US attorney. But whichever way you go, state or federal, it won't be easy. I'm not saying the US attorney would protect those guys. In fact, I'm sure he would see it as a notch on his gun to knock off a judge, much less high-profile lawyers. My concern is they may not be geared up to develop a case like this, and, for sure, not on your timetable."

VJ started tapping the toe of his right shoe on the parquet floor in Trost's office.

"So nothing happens?"

"I didn't say that. We have to help them."

"How?"

"There's a lawyer who used to be a top federal prosecutor. He's in private practice now. We hire him to put together the case. I mean work it up as if he were going to try the case for the government and then bring it to the US attorney. That way, all the US attorney has to do is present it to a judge to get authority for electronic surveillance. Assuming Moran, Marshall, and the judge incriminate themselves in what they believe are private conversations, the US attorney will take it to a grand jury, which will—almost as the day follows night—give the US attorney the indictment he asks for."

"Let's do whatever we have to do," VJ said.

With the work product of the former prosecutor in hand, Trost went to Chappy Chapman, the US attorney, who immediately saw an opportunity to advance his career. He obtained legal search warrants for taps and bugs that included Elizondo's chambers.

Pilar and VJ kept up their posture of being intent on divorce. Paddy and Will continued to milk the media circus by feeding reporters tips from "sources who chose to remain anonymous."

In early December, when Elizondo had less than a month left on the bench, the hearing on Will's motion for summary judgment to have the prenuptial agreement declared enforceable was held.

At the hearing, Paddy sat at his table with Pilar, and Will sat at his table with VJ. Judge Elizondo came out. The bailiff announced, "All rise." Everyone rose. Elizondo said, "Be seated." As he was about to speak, he saw Paddy motioning with his head in the direction of Elizondo's chambers.

Elizondo said, "Before I begin the hearing on this motion, I would like to speak to counsel in my chambers."

Paddy and Will followed Elizondo, not looking at each other and not speaking before the door closed.

"What's going on?" Elizondo asked.

Paddy bore down. "I just want to go over what we discussed before. After oral argument, you're gonna rule the prenup is unenforceable. That will jump-start a settlement and soon it will be done."

Elizondo began to perspire profusely. He loosened his collar.

"You owe us, Hector," Paddy said.

"I haven't been on the bench long enough to qualify for a pension. I don't know how I'll make a living when I get off the bench. This Hetherington woman has ruined my reputation."

Paddy nodded. He and Will knew this would be coming. Up to now, what they had given to Elizondo for his personal use was not significant to them. They knew this was different.

"I'll tell you what," Paddy said. "When the Simon case is settled, Will and I will get back together. We'll bring you in as counsel. We will give you a signing bonus that doubles your judicial salary."

Will silently looked at the ceiling.

"That sounds very fair, Paddy. You're all right with that, Will?"

Will nodded.

"Then we're good," Paddy said.

Elizondo mopped his neck, fastened his collar button, and pulled up his tie. Paddy and Will left first and returned to their respective counsel tables. Moments later, Elizondo entered. He called the court to order. Paddy and Will made statements supporting their positions. Then Elizondo said, "I deny the motion for summary judgment. I find there are fact issues as to whether or not the premarital agreement is enforceable."

VJ gave no visible emotional reaction. Will jumped up and shouted, "That's outrageous! We intend to file an interlocutory appeal immediately!" Then, to Paddy, in a stage whisper, "We better have settlement discussions immediately."

"Of course," Paddy said, beaming. He squeezed Pilar's arm. She gave him a sharp elbow to his ribs. He looked at her quizzically. "Pilar," he whispered, "we just got what you want. Ding dong! The prenup is dead. Now we can settle for a lot more than what you were going to get."

THE NEXT DAY, with a former judge acting as mediator, VJ and Pilar agreed to a settlement in which she got thirty million dollars. Paddy was ecstatic. When the money was paid, his share would be twenty-five percent. Part of it he would have to give to Will, but there would be more than enough for him to be back in style and earn the grudging admiration of his peers.

Linda Hetherington was sworn in. The following Monday, Will and Paddy announced they had reconciled their differences and Hector Elizondo was joining the firm as of counsel.

The next day, one assistant US attorney and two FBI agents charged in to Paddy's office, showed him an arrest warrant and cuffed him before he could say a word.

When he finally found his voice, he said, "What's going on here, guys?"

"You ought to know better than we do," responded the assistant US attorney. He gave Paddy the Miranda warning as he led him out of the office. As they entered the reception area, Anne Arden marched out of Will's office, saying, "Well, I never."

Will's face was a deep red. He was crying. "You can't do this," he sobbed.

The assistant US attorney leading Will out of his office said, "Keep walking."

Will looked up to see Paddy.

"Man up, asshole," Paddy called to Will as he and his captors took the first elevator to arrive.

Outside, a hand pressed the top of Paddy's head down as he eased into the back seat of a black Suburban. "Maybe I can't beat the rap, but I sure as hell couldn't beat the ride," he mused, wryly muttering an old criminal defendant's lament, as the vehicle proceeded to the federal courthouse, "and it has been a helluva ride."

The US attorney himself arrested Elizondo in his chambers.

The local media had been alerted by the US attorney's office that something big was about to happen. Stationed at the front door of the US courthouse, they caught the moment when Paddy, Will, and Elizondo made the perp walk in handcuffs into the federal building. A magistrate ordered them held until a hearing to set bail the next morning. They turned over civilian clothes and possessions and began the intake process.

〰

EVEN IF DONE in the gentlest manner, a body cavity search could not be anything other than demeaning and uncomfortable for all but the perverted. As a former policeman, Paddy knew the procedure was routine, but he was not fully prepared for the actual experience. He could hear from an adjacent room that Will was not at all prepared for the search of his bodily cavities either. He assumed the same was true for Judge Elizondo. It was a procedure not completely dissimilar to a prostate examination, which itself was a rude invasion, but at least it was performed by a physician who had a duty of care. The intrusion caused Paddy to produce a spontaneous bowel movement, much to the disgust of the tech performing the procedure. At first Paddy was embarrassed, but then he found humor when he decided he should characterize the incident as having made a statement. A statement without waiving his rights against self-incrimination.

After being allowed to shower, he donned his new wardrobe, an orange jump suit. "Not an Armani," he wryly mused to himself. He was taken to a holding cell.

US Attorney Chappy Chapman issued a statement: "Justice should be blind, but not blind with greed. The people must have faith in the fundamental fairness and impartiality of our system of justice if we are to have order in our society. Those who make a mockery of it must not go unpunished."

Paddy and Will were charged with bribery of a public official and a RICO conspiracy. Elizondo's charges were accepting bribes, money laundering, and tax fraud.

Paddy sat in the cell. He knew he was supposed to hire an attorney. Instead, he used his call to ask the condo concierge to walk Mick twice a day and make sure he had food and water until he made bail. He really didn't think it mattered what attorney he used. He had that figured out when they appeared before the magistrate. They were all guilty, but if Paddy had doped it right, he was going to take the biggest fall. Elizondo would be portrayed as dumb, hapless, too trusting, and over his head as a judge. Will would be the fine young man who had been corrupted by Paddy. And Paddy would be the New York guy, the smart guy who figured the angles, a giant, corrupt version of *My Cousin Vinny*. The only thing he didn't understand was why he felt nothing. He wasn't angry. He wasn't frightened. He thought back to the judge's admonition in the Grissett case and to Margot not answering her phone before he decided to go with Fourbirds' plan, whatever it was. "Shame on me," he mumbled to himself. "Shame on me."

\~\~\~

HE MADE BAIL by putting his condo up as security. It didn't have a mortgage.

Soon after his arrest, Elizondo was diagnosed with early onset Alzheimer's disease. The disease was advancing rapidly. He was declared incompetent to participate in his defense, thus, would not be tried. Dolores moved back home to care for him.

Paddy knew he had to have a lawyer. He finally interviewed several white-collar criminal lawyers. He chose one he had represented in his divorce. "This will give you a chance to get even," Paddy said.

The lawyer shook his head. "Sorry about this."

"I had a good run. I made some bad decisions. I got caught. End of story. I'm gonna need whatever cash I have to keep the condo."

"I get it. It's exempt from your creditors."

"Right. Why don't you take the Testarossa for your fee? I'm sure I won't be using it for a while, anyway," Paddy said, without intonation.

"Look, usually I take as much as I can get up front because that's the only shot I get with most clients."

"For sure that would be true with me."

"I know. But I also know I can't do much for you. Not too many juries would give you much sympathy. We're going to have to do the best we can on a plea bargain, because I can guarantee you since Chapman has been deprived of his show trial against a judge, he won't be coming to you to get a plea deal for your cooperation. The Testarossa is too much." He laughed. "I've never said that before."

"Sooner or later I'll get out. I may need a favor."

"You got it."

"I know you'll enjoy your ride more than I'm going to enjoy mine."

"Paddy, this is an odd thing to say, but you're a stand-up guy."

Paddy nodded and shook his hand. "There's pretty good evidence that's not a universally held opinion." Paddy looked at his lawyer. "I'll tell you, buddy, it's a lot like poker. To win, or at least minimize your losses, you have to be patient. When you're dealt a bad hand, fold. The way I was going, sooner or later, I would have been fine. There's always another hand coming. My fuckups have been when I was too anxious to win. That's what took me down. Well, that and my ego."

He was not surprised that Will agreed to be a cooperating witness against him and entered into a plea agreement with the Department of Justice that the court approved. Will blamed the inappropriate conduct with Judge Elizondo on Paddy. He acknowledged his guilt by admitting he had been willfully blind. The judge, a Bush 43 appointee, received letters from many prominent people well known to the judge attesting that Will was a fine person who had made a mistake and requesting he be treated with leniency. Many of them attended the sentencing hearing. It seemed like a country club reception in the lobby outside the courtroom. The judge sentenced Will to three months at the Federal Detention Center in downtown Houston and seven years' probation. He was required to perform ten hours of community service a week for the entire seven years.

Paddy was sentenced to seventy-two months in prison.

LINDA HETHERINGTON SUED WILL, Paddy, Judge Elizondo, and her ex-husband. She got a fifty million dollar judgment, including punitive damages, and was awarded sole custody of her daughter. All the defendants were jointly and severally liable. Elizondo had no assets that were not exempt. Whatever money Paddy had made after Norma wiped him out was insignificant. The same was true of Will. Muffy's property could not be touched. Will and Paddy did have insurance. Their carrier initially denied coverage but settled for half of the maximum amount of the policy—five million dollars. Randy, her ex, wrote Linda a check for forty-five million dollars. He rarely exercised visitation rights with his daughter. The President of the United States offered to nominate Linda to a special cabinet-level position to promote equal rights for women. She declined, saying she wanted to remain a family law judge for as long as the voters would re-elect her.

THE DENOUEMENT

WILL

Because he had a felony conviction, Will could no longer practice law.

Mortified by the scandal, Muffy nevertheless stood by Will throughout his sentencing. A few months later, they had a quiet divorce that became final while he was in the Federal Detention Center. There was no community property left to split. His plea bargain prohibited him from selling a story about his life.

Before Will's fall, he feared he would become his father. Now, in addition to being poor, he was shamed in an even worse way.

On Will's last day at the detention center, Mrs. Coleman and Roosevelt were waiting as he was being processed for release. The three of them walked outside together. It was a beautiful April day, the temperature in the seventies.

She put a cigarette in her FDR-style cigarette holder, lit it, and said, "Willoughby, isn't it so good to be outside?" She was not referring to his release or the weather. Her white-gloved hands trembled as she struggled to bring the cigarette holder to her mouth. Having succeeded, she shifted the gaze of her steely blue eyes to Will. She exhaled, rasped a cough, and said, "The time has come for us to buy a Hummer."

Will smiled, shaking his head.

"I suppose an armor-plated Lincoln sedan might do. The car keeps bumping into things. I just don't think it's safe for us to be in a regular car anymore."

She paused.

"Hummers have all that steel," she said. "It's like being in a tank. We'd be very safe." She had said that before. Perhaps she had forgotten.

"Well, perhaps you would be," Will said. "But what about the other people?"

"What other people, Willoughby?"

"The ones who might be struck by the Hummer," he said.

"Oh." Mrs. Coleman took another drag, throwing her head back, then exhaling so the exhaust was directed to the sky and not at Will.

"Well, you know, truth be told, Roosevelt had another little stroke. I didn't mention it when I last visited you. He stays in the main house in my daughter's old room. The housekeeper and I have been taking care of him. He's made great improvement, but I told him to stay there. I've been doing the driving. He sits in the front seat with me."

Will was bemused. He thought about how much not only the times but also the circumstances had changed. A lifetime of service begat being served by one's mistress.

"How's your driving?" Will asked.

"I'm a great driver. Where are you going to be living?" she said.

"For now, with my mother."

"Oh, good. She'll like having you around."

Will did not respond. He envisioned his mother treating him as she had his father after he had lost his money.

"You'll have some extra time on your hands now. I could use someone to take charge of my affairs. You won't need a law license to do that. I trust you completely. I even have an office at the house for you to use, and," she paused, took a deep drag from her cigarette, blew it out, and said, ever so considerately, "come to think of it, perhaps you could take us places and pick us up."

ELEGANTÉ

Luigi Ezio Ganté eagerly and lithely made his final inspection of his new Eleganté before the first seatings. A grateful Search Homeless Services had told him some homeless men would proudly be wearing the exquisite Italian suits, shirts, and belts he donated, having pledged to himself never to wear large-size clothes again. Now sixty pounds lighter, with a clean bill of health from his doctors, he felt a *tarantella* rhythm in his step, a rhythm that had been missing the last time he dragged himself to perform this ritual.

Eleganté's doors were just about to reopen. An icon was returning to Houston. In moments, its glitterati would be assembling there. Though he'd had other restaurants through the years, Eleganté was his signature, his legacy. He had won the war with his landlord. The new Eleganté was at the old location, but Del Monte was charging the original rent, and he paid Luigi a generous amount for new tenant improvements. Luigi spent it and then some to create a look that was both timeless and twenty-first century. *Architectural Digest* did a pre-opening feature. Pilar and VJ Simon lent some important pieces from their art collection to hang, which alone commanded attention from an entirely different national audience. Only the dining room at the Hotel du Pont in Wilmington when it had its amazing collection of Wyeths could compare. Having such fine art necessitated a security system and was just one more element that distinguished the new Eleganté from all other possible competitors. There was even talk of making it the location for yet another remake of *The Thomas Crown Affair*.

For the first six months after the closing, he hadn't missed his restaurant universe. Then, he began to think about reopening. His thoughts were not of returning to something old but of creating something new that would propel Eleganté into the forefront not as a nostalgic blast from the past but as a creative, post-millennial example of a new elegance. Had it been a long time? Had it been a short time? It depended on who was counting.

He reflected on what he thought at the time would be the last night of Eleganté. When he planned that night, he had no idea that his decision to close would be the catalyst in a saga that—how to put it? —had rather changed the pecking order of some of the tables for the opening night of his new creation.

As he looked across the room at those tables, he mused, "There'll be some new faces. New stars mixing with long-time friends." He nodded as countless images went through his head. *There'll be some who won't be here. Some of The Best People*, he thought with a wry smile.

LINDA HETHERINGTON

Linda Hetherington became a distinguished jurist. She remained on the bench for many years. She refused appointments to appellate courts, even the Texas Supreme Court, because she felt she could do more good just where she was. After a few years, she also began teaching a sociology class at Rice University on how families are affected by custody disputes. Using some of the money she collected from her lawsuit, she established an institute at Rice to do research in the area. She fell in love with a fellow faculty member. They married in Vermont. Her daughter was the happy maid of honor.

SUNNY

Sunny married Sal, and they had two children. She joined him in Buffalo, New York, where he started his own business. VJ invested in the business, which did very well. The two couples take a vacation trip to Hawaii nearly every winter.

PILAR AND VJ

Pilar and VJ reconciled. To the extent two people can, given the vicissitudes of life and the inevitable disagreements when both are strong, intelligent people, they lived happily ever after, as business partners in the renamed Simons' Company, as cotrustees of the Pilar and VJ Simon Foundation, and as husband and wife, until death did them part.

PADDY

At Paddy's sentencing hearing, one person, Jed, who had risen to assistant chief in the HPD, spoke up for Paddy. Bernice sat in the courtroom, as did Professor Bingo. Pilar attended, urged by the Department of Justice to speak in opposition to leniency. Before the hearing was set to begin, Paddy saw her looking at him. He told his lawyer he wanted to have a private word with her. She raised her eyebrows. With pursed lips, she nodded assent.

They sat face-to-face in a small room off the main courtroom. When Paddy said hello, Pilar made a face as if she were tasting something sour.

Although Paddy's intention had been to say something short and dignified, his feelings got the best of him. He burst out, "Let me see if I got this right. You're mad at me. Jesus. So tell me, sweetheart, tell me one thing I did that wasn't in your best interest. You bet I was going to benefit from the sting, but you were going to be the big winner. You would've gotten twenty?—no—nearly thirty times more than your prenup pittance? I may have been feathering my own nest, but news flash, baby, you were the one who was going to get the whole golden goose. Then I got busted, and what happened to the indignant Mrs. Simon? She's back with the king rooster. Sweet, huh? I hope that all works out for you—this time."

"That's not true. You didn't do it for me. What you don't know is I went into the men's room by mistake and heard you and Will conspiring against VJ and me."

So that's what happened, he thought to himself. It took Paddy a moment to absorb it, but he was unbowed. "Do you think I would have taken the other side?"

"I don't know. I really don't know."

"Yeah? Well, I'm not saying what I did was okay. But ask yourself this, since the first moment we met, what have I ever done to fucking hurt you? I looked out for you, Pilar. When you were a fucking mess, who had your back? Don't look down your fucking nose at me. I was always fucking there for you."

"'There for me.' I'm so tired of that phrase. Where is 'there?'" Pilar's hands were shaking. She bit her lip hard. "Paddy, you didn't do this *for* me. You've been a good pal to me, but this? I—I can't forgive you—at least not now. I know there's good in you. Find it again and lose what you know you need to lose."

He pursed his lips and nodded. "Basically, I'm good people. Hey! I'm one of The Best People."

Pilar swallowed.

"Get your sweet ass out of here," Paddy said. "We're done talking."

He looked away from her. He took a moment to compose himself before tapping on the window. The guard escorted him back to the courtroom.

Pilar did not testify against him.

Paddy got a break because his six-year sentence would be served in Bastrop, Texas, at a low-security federal correctional facility primarily for people convicted of white-collar crimes. He figured he might get out in four years, eleven months, and two days.

Paddy received no letters and no packages. During the first six months, Luigi, Bernice, and Jed were his only visitors. Luigi had inherited Mick, Paddy's dog. He brought pictures. Finally, Paddy had a fourth visitor, Elliott Foxman.

"Why'd you come?" he asked.

"I was going to Austin for the Memorial Day weekend. Bastrop is on the way, so I thought I'd come by to see how you're doing."

Paddy nodded.

"What's it like here?" Foxman asked.

"What can I say? I can't leave. Other than that, it's tolerable."

"What are your fellow inmates like?"

"Most of them are okay. I'm friendliest with two guys. Get this, one's a former federal judge. The other is an ex-congressman."

Foxman's eyebrows raised.

"You meet some high-class folks in this joint," Paddy said, followed by a "heh-heh."

After a long silence, Foxman said, "At least they didn't get you for tax fraud."

"Yes," Paddy said, annoyed with Elliott for having patted himself on the back. "You did take care of that. It's a shame I can't send you any referrals. I'm sure you don't want any endorsements from me."

Foxman laughed. "You never know."

He nodded to Paddy and left.

That night, Paddy asked if he could make a phone call. He was allowed to dial out on a special inmate pay phone. The party he was calling was not available. He left a voice message: "Margot. This is your least favorite inmate. You can't call me back. We don't have cell phones in the cells. Ha. Ha." He left instructions how to email him at corrlinks.com. After he hung up, he sighed heavily and thumped his heart with his closed fist. He checked his email every day after that. Nothing from Margot.

Three days later, on May 25, 2015, the Memorial Day flood came to Houston and the Hill Country. The drought was over in Central Texas, in a big way.

A few months passed.

One night, in the recreation room, Paddy was watching television with his two pals. As was their custom, they tuned to the channels with infomercial shows. None of them could make a living doing what they had done before their respective falls. Looking at infomercials was a way to possibly come up with a plan to make money when they got out.

They took turns as to who got to hold the remote. Tonight, it was the former judge. He gave each program about three seconds before he moved on. With prestige and honor gone, his primary mission was a slam-dunk, return-to-being-rich scheme.

After a channel change, Paddy heard a familiar voice. The judge changed the channel again.

"Whoa, Your Honor," he said. "Go back!" As a courtesy, the inmates referred to each other by the title from his former life.

"What is it, counselor?" the judge asked.

"Uh, flip back to that last one, please," Paddy said.

The judge hit the "last" button on the remote.

A radiantly smiling Norma Nambé filled the screen. She was dressed like a queen, with a jeweled tiara and a robe of velvet with gold lapels, cuffs, and hems. A yacht gleamed in the ocean behind her set against a clear, blue sky.

A large, heavy-jowled man, dressed like a naval commodore, sat in a throne-like deck chair. He had dark puffy circles under his eyes and a bored but confident look on his face. It was Rance Ed Booker.

"They got to be fucking kidding!" Paddy yelled, standing up from his chair. His heart was racing. He could feel a pulse throbbing in his temple.

After a quick, dismissive glance at Paddy, the judge and the congressman returned their attention to the queen-like woman and the commodore.

"Ladies and gentlemen," Norma said, in an exaggerated Texas drawl, as if to emphasize the anomaly of her voice and her outfit.

"You have probably heard if it sounds too good to be true, it's too good to be true." Her pace quickened. "Thinking that way is for suckers and losers. Winners know a golden opportunity when they see one. They know how to make what's too good to be true come true," she said, looking directly into the camera, her body challenging anyone who dared to take issue with her.

"We will show you," she said and used both hands to seductively open the robe. She straightened slightly, put her left foot forward and turned her hips toward the camera to allow the viewers to absorb the full effect of her outfit—the chain mail vest with the external steel bra that Marvin had procured for her and a white, gold-trimmed gown that clung to her body revealing a now slightly ample, but fetchingly well-curved body.

"We will show you," she repeated, "how you, too, can become rich and have a yacht and follow the sun, or do whatever you darn well please."

"We showed many, many people how to make a fortune in foreclosures," she continued. "In fact, that's how we bought this yacht. You can charter it from us for fifty thousand for a week's cruise—lots of folks do—but we also have a hotel, resort, and golf club in Saipan, in the Commonwealth of the Northern Mariana Islands. We let Harrah's run our casino for us. Come and see us!"

Paddy shook his head back and forth in disbelief. His two friends were fixated to the TV screen.

"But that is not what I'm talkin' about," Norma said. "In fact, you can have our materials on how to be a millionaire in foreclosures for free. Just go to the website you see on the screen now—4closeuniversity.com—we'll let you download it for free.

"Here's what I'm talkin' about. This will make you rich, just like it made us richer. It's how to make a fortune with what some folks call social networking. I call it money networking."

Pointing her finger at her television audience, Norma said, "We'll mentor you, and you will make lots of money. You'll have your own personal website and learn how to generate leads that put money in your pocket. Just go to the website on your screen now—themakeyoumoneyuniversity. com—watch the video and then, with a few clicks, you will be in business."

Placing her hands on her hips, putting her right foot forward and turning her torso slightly to the left, she said, "This is pretty important: because you will be using our servers, which are not located in the United States, all the money you make will be tax-free."

The camera panned to Rance Ed. At the bottom of the screen were the words "Former High Official with the Internal Revenue Service." He nodded with calm confidence.

The judge and the congressman turned to Paddy, expecting a response.

Paddy shut his gaping mouth, smiled, and shook his head. He mused to himself. "No get-rich-quick schemes for me. You know what would be crazy? Working for Linda Hetherington at her institute. Who would know how to foil the bad guys better than me?"

At that moment, a guard entered to say, "Mr. Moran. You have a visitor. A Ms. Margot Shear."

It took a moment for Paddy to absorb the words. Then, his heart raced. His mind reeled. His hands trembled. His pace quickened, almost overtaking the guard. He felt the pain in his face of a broad smile.

THE END

ACKNOWLEDGMENTS

WHEN I WAS IN MY TEENS, three people encouraged my writing. Sadly, two of those people—Sue Davidson, my cousin and a wonderful writer and social activist, and David Westheimer, my sort-of uncle who wrote great novels—are no longer alive. The third—my friend Barbara Robins Friedman—who I am pleased to say is still my friend—survived all these decades to see I finally have a novel out.

Over the course of writing this book, I had a number of readers, the first of whom was Gretchen Bohnert, who read a draft in 2004 and marched into my home one day in early 2009, tossed the manuscript to the floor, and said, "If you don't finish writing this book, someone else will write it." So far, no one else has. Other readers include Bobbie Newman, who was dogged and helped with nuancing the title, Julia Paust, Mark Yudoff, my sister, Cyvia Wolff, Phyllis Lefkowitz, Andrea White, Al Reinert (now of blessed memory), and Jenny Karotkin. Their comments and encouragement helped me keep going.

I engaged a number of editors along the way. Some were more helpful than others. The ones whom I appreciate the most are Mary Jane Taegel and Jay Hodges.

Thanks to Letitia McHatton, my former assistant, for her editing and formatting. A shout-out as well to my assistant, Sonia Vasquez.

My daughter and fellow writer, Lee Ann Grossberg, MD, has given me lots of pep talks and suggestions of programs and books to improve my writing skills. Veronica Matovich helped with the many things that had to be done after the writing was completed.

I am certain I would not have written the book if it were not for the thirty-plus years of stimulation provided by Inprint, the amazing Houston organization that celebrates readers and writers. A special thanks to Rich Levy and Marilyn Jones.

ABOUT THE AUTHOR

MARC GROSSBERG is an observer and a listener. He has a passion for his family, friends, and clients, and for books that entertain and provoke him. He has practiced law in his native Houston for over fifty years. He has somehow overcome being a Board-Certified tax lawyer and one of the Best Lawyers in America to write *The Best People*. Marc is a proud product of the Houston public schools, The University of Houston, and The University of Texas School of Law. He lives in the NOW and goes wherever his "green light" tells him the intersection might be interesting.